# Chestnut Cove:

# Poseurs and Portraits

## B. A. Howell

BA Howell, Publisher

Published by B. A. Howell

ISBN 978-1-7342536-0-3

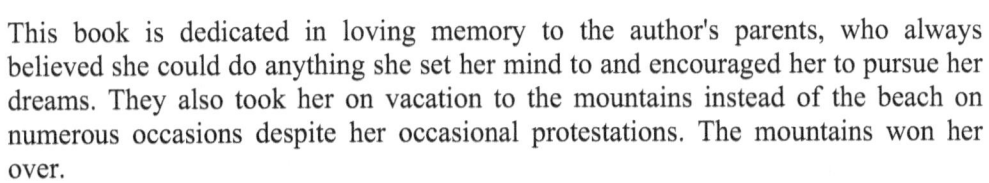
This book is dedicated in loving memory to the author's parents, who always believed she could do anything she set her mind to and encouraged her to pursue her dreams. They also took her on vacation to the mountains instead of the beach on numerous occasions despite her occasional protestations. The mountains won her over.

# Acknowledgements

The author would like to thank those who provided encouragement, support, suggestions, and assistance along the way, with special recognition to Allen, Dianne, Jeri, Annie, June, Carol, Teddy, Kristen, and the Auburn Writers Circle and Auburn University Novel Writing class, especially Larry, Cindy, Crystal, Robin, Jennifer, Pete, Julia, Kathy, Sherri, Erick, and Kelly.

Editing by Annie Wiegel, AnneElizabethco.com

Cover design by Kristen Ingebretson, penmeetpaper.com

Cover photo by the author

# Chestnut Cove Books

Chestnut Cove: Poseurs and Portraits, set in Spring 1979

Chestnut Cove: Love and Lessons, set in 1955-1956

Chestnut Cove: Belles and Balls, set in Summer/Fall 1979

Chestnut Cove: Devils and Daughters, set in 1958 (coming in September 2021)

Chestnut Cove: Odds and Inns, short stories set in the 1950s through 1960s
(coming in the future)

Chestnut Cove: Inns and Outs, short stories set in the 1960s through 1970s
(coming in the future)

Chestnut Cove: Revenge and Rapprochement, set in Fall 1979
(coming in the future)

Keep up with what's next with the characters of Chestnut Cove at bahowell.com

# The Stuart Family

John Stuart: President of Chestnut Cove Inns

Sandra Duncan Stuart: John's wife and CCI board secretary

Jeanette Stevenson Stuart Hathaway: John's mother

Carlisle Stuart: John's late father; Jeanette's 1st husband

Winston Hathaway: Jeanette's 2nd husband; John's stepfather

Matt Hunter: John's 2nd cousin; CCI VP of Operations

Kathryn Stuart: John and Sandra's eldest child

Doug Stuart: John and Sandra's 2nd child

Maggie Stuart: John and Sandra's 3rd child

Chris Stuart: John and Sandra's youngest child

Claudine: Winston's daughter

Harold: Claudine's 3rd husband

Rainier Smythe: Claudine's son

Giselle Smythe: Claudine's daughter

# Chestnut Cove Inns Headquarters
# Department Heads

Jonah Jones: Head of construction and maintenance

Hoyt Dalton: Head of accounting

Craig Fielder: Head of finance

Griffin Krebs: Head of personnel

Andrew Stein: Head of marketing

Sam Lawrence: Head of legal


# Chestnut Cove Inns- Elkford Lead Personnel

Pam Grant: Senior assistant manager

Janelle Humphries: Head of housekeeping

Gabriel Wilson: Head doorman

Boyd Temples: Deputy head of security

Fleur Girard: Head chef and restaurant manager

# Chapter 1

*Wednesday, April 11, 1979*

The driver exited his beloved sports car and looked around for any sign of the person he expected to meet. No other vehicle occupied the mountain bald surrounding the remote shack, but he knew the absence meant nothing. He walked under the shed half of the structure to a door lacking any kind of lock. Anyone who got this far either didn't need permission to enter or deserved whatever greeted him on the other side. He opened it and stepped inside the tiny cabin.

Red coals burning in the wood stove provided barely enough light to navigate the interior and just enough heat to knock off the chill descending in the late evening and the dampness from the earlier rain. A soft voice spoke from the darkness across the room. "You're late. Did you get lost?"

The man smiled at the sound. "No, not too likely considering how many times I've been up here, even if it's been about two years since my last visit. I got held up leaving work. One of my assistants assisted me by delaying my departure. I need some more good help."

"I'll keep your plight in mind. Pull up a chair and take a seat."

"Mind if we get a little extra light in here first? It's almost pitch-black. If I didn't know your voice so well, I couldn't swear I'm talking to the person I'm supposed to meet tonight." Though too dark to see his face, his light and cheery mood shone through in his tone and matched his broad smile.

The other person giggled, the sound of a young woman enjoying herself. "If it is light you desire, it is light you shall have." She rose from her chair and walked to a shelf where a lantern and matches rested, navigating with ease in the darkness. She struck a match against the wall of the cabin and lit the lantern. As she moved back to the card table with her burden, its light reflected off the heart-shaped, silver locket he knew so well.

"Better?" she asked as she set the lantern on the table.

She started to retake her seat, but the man reached out and pulled her into his arms. "I think I deserve a hug before we get down to business, kid." In a softer, more serious tone, he added, "I've missed you, and I'm not the only one. This needs to end."

The young woman returned the embrace and laid her head on his shoulder for a moment before whispering, "I know. Soon." She pushed away from him enough to raise up on her toes to kiss his cheek. Then she stepped back, returned to her chair, and waved for him to take the seat next to her. "First we need to finalize our plans."

~~~

*Monday, April 16, 1979*

"Miss Hogencamp, please make sure you take a couple of photos of this area. I particularly like the old timbers overhead. It shows how well they built this mill years ago." Elliott Starnes pointed up at the beams overhead, and his assistant set her notepad and pencil aside while she raised the thirty-five-millimeter camera around her neck to snap some photographs of the area indicated.

Miss Hogencamp was a severe looking young woman who kept her hair pulled back in a tight bun and wore horn-rimmed glasses not at all befitting her youthful face. As fastidious as Mr. Starnes, she suited him well as an assistant.

When she completed photographing the timbers in question, she pointed ahead. "Mr. Starnes, there is some kind of tar or oil on that doorway."

Elliott turned his attention from the old beams to the spot indicated by his assistant, wary of getting anything on his expensive suit. As usual, he was dressed impeccably, though not at all properly for touring an ancient building with a real estate agent, but he never varied his style and quality of dress, regardless of circumstances.

"I see it. Thank you for the warning, Miss Hogencamp." Elliott took care to avoid the oily doorjamb when he passed by it. He stepped to a window, careful not to let his sleeve touch the dirty sill when he leaned forward to look out. "Mr. Dean, you said the property reaches to the river. Do you know what governmental agencies would need to grant approval if my client wanted to construct something along or in the river?"

Mr. Dean, the real estate agent, scratched his chin. "I'm not sure, but at least the city would expect some say if your client were to use it in conjunction with a business. Also, this is a dammed, navigable river under control of the federal government. I believe they would need to approve anything built out in the water. Do you think your client wants to open a marina? We have one of those up river about half a mile. Not sure there's a need for another one."

Elliott sniffed in disdain. "I never discuss detailed information regarding my clients' interests in a piece of property. I am tasked with asking questions of all possibilities in order to ensure I cover any area of interest to my clients each time I research and view a property. They pay me quite well for both my thoroughness and my discretion."

Mr. Dean took a self-conscious, backward half-step. "Er, yes, certainly. I didn't mean to overstep into your client's business." Message received: Mr. Starnes would ask the questions; Mr. Dean's job entailed supplying answers, preferably correct and complete answers.

Elliott gave a curt nod but said nothing more. He knew Mr. Dean had tried to unload the old mill for his own client for some time. The last thing the man would want to do was offend Elliott and risk tainting his report to his potential buyer.

Mr. Dean broke an uncomfortable silence. "Is there anything else you'd like to see? We've viewed most everything as we made our way up here to the top floor. We can stop on the way back down if you want to look at something a second time."

Elliott turned to his assistant. "I believe we've covered everything, have we not, Miss Hogencamp?"

"We haven't yet inspected the roof from on top of the building, Mr. Starnes. We only viewed the exterior of it from a block away and from here underneath. I believe your client would want at least a cursory check of it from atop the roof itself." She pointed to a hatch with a ladder attached to the wall beneath. "I would be happy to climb the ladder over there–I believe it leads to an access point on the roof–and take some photos for you." The young woman cocked her head ever so slightly to the right and held his gaze, waiting for Mr. Starnes to concur.

"Yes, you are correct, of course. If you wouldn't mind carrying the camera up there and taking a series of photographs, I believe my client would be most appreciative." Elliott turned back to Mr. Dean. "Would you be so kind as to go up ahead of Miss Hogencamp and open the access cover? I assume your client will not object to our inspection of the roof?"

Mr. Dean cringed, but after a momentary delay he put a foot up on the ladder. It creaked as one of the anchor bolts holding it to the wall shifted. He put another foot up, took a quick look back at Mr. Starnes, hoping he might change his mind, and then ascended to the hatch.

Twenty minutes later, Mr. Starnes pulled his car onto the highway for the long drive back to his office in Coughton. 'Miss Hogencamp', her horn-rimmed glasses tucked into her bag and her hair loose, sat in the passenger seat poring over the notes she took and the building and property specifications they received from Mr. Dean. A silver locket, previously tucked out of view inside her blouse, dangled from her neck. When they reached Elliott's office, the young woman took the collection of papers and the camera and film rolls and put them in her own car, leaving Elliott four crisp hundred-dollar bills.

~~~

*Friday, May 4, 1979*

"OK, Herb, I'll get it." Laura hurried to the rear of the small diner to get more coffee. Before she could retrieve it from the storeroom, Herb called, "Get number four cleared off. I don't want a bunch of dirty tables when we get a wave of customers."

Laura closed her eyes and shook her head. Patrons occupied two of the dozen tables since the man from four departed, so Herb's concern made little sense. However, she did as bid with a smile. She refused to let Herb's constant yelling, short temper, and rudeness get to her. At nineteen, she lacked experience to apply for better positions, so she needed to keep this one for now. Her previous work involved running errands for a couple of elderly neighbors who insisted on paying her and a summer waitressing before her senior year in high school. Neither provided significant justification for a better place to hire her. She would pay the small price of putting up with Herb for now to help her get something better in the future. She also needed to stay on Herb's good side because one day she would need him for a reference, though she doubted he would say anything good about her if he knew she planned to quit. He never had anything good to say about her or anyone else for anything.

Laura set the new tin on the counter behind Herb. At least she didn't need to make the coffee; Herb thought no one but him could make it right. She hurried to table four to clear it.

The young woman in the back, corner booth signaled to Laura. Setting her burden of plates and cups next to the sink, she hurried to booth twelve. The lady had become something of a regular over the last few weeks, stopping in around midafternoon several times when the diner was almost empty. She also tipped decently, a rarity among their usual clientele; definitely someone Laura wanted to attend to well because she needed all the money she could earn. Her grandmother, with whom she lived, received a small fixed income from a pension and suffered from some health problems. Laura's earnings ensured they could make ends meet, she could afford to take one class a quarter at the local business school, and they could splurge once a month by going to a matinee at the movie theater a few blocks away.

"What can I get for you, ma'am?" Laura asked, making sure she smiled at her customer.

"Hey, this thing's leaking. Get a mop and clean it up before I slip and fall," Herb yelled.

Ignoring him for the moment, Laura asked her customer again, "What can I get you?"

"Just a glass of tea for now," the young woman said. "I'm debating between the apple pie and the peach cobbler. Are either of them made from scratch?"

"Laura," Herb bellowed. "Did you hear me? Get the mop and get this water up. What if the health inspector came in right now? They'd shut me down, and you'd be out of a job."

Laura sighed in frustration. "I'm sorry. I'll be right back with your tea. Oh, and no, neither is made from scratch." She wanted to add what a good thing that was considering Herb's actual abilities as a chef but thought better of it.

"Go ahead and take care of your boss's little spill. I'm not in a hurry. I'll debate the merits of the pie and cobbler for a couple of minutes." The young woman gave Laura an encouraging smile and waved her away.

"Thank you. I'll get your tea." Laura hurried back behind the counter. "Let me get number twelve's tea, and then I'll get the mop while she's deciding what else she wants."

"Fine," Herb grumbled. "Just get this puddle up."

Laura delivered the tea to her customer, hurried to the storeroom to get the mop, and managed to soak up the water in a couple of minutes. The only other customer in the diner, at table two, waved to Laura when she came back from returning the mop to the storeroom, and Laura glanced toward booth twelve to see if the young woman appeared ready to order. However, the woman was busy making notes in the margins of a sheaf of papers–something Laura saw her do on previous occasions–so Laura hurried to table two.

"What else can I get you, Mr. Larson?" Mr. Larson was a longtime regular who stopped in almost every afternoon for a doughnut and a cup of coffee, complained about the quality of both, argued with Herb about whatever sport was in season, and tipped Laura a quarter. Not a bad tip for less than a two-dollar tab in Fred's Diner.

"Just the check, Laura. I think the doughnut was a little staler than usual today. Probably left over from two days ago instead of yesterday. Coffee was pretty bitter, too."

"I'll be sure to let Herb know. Maybe tomorrow it will be better," Laura said, trying to sound hopeful about something she knew wasn't probable. She pulled out his check from the pocket of her uniform and handed it to him.

"It won't. Never is." He handed her the correct change to cover the charge and a quarter for the tip. "I'll see you tomorrow, Laura. Hold back a fresh doughnut for me if you ever spot one around here."

"I will, Mr. Larson." She waved as the old man shambled out of the diner and then hurried back to booth twelve. "Have you decided between the apple pie and peach cobbler yet, ma'am?"

"I think I'll pass on both and just finish my tea." The woman seemed intent on her work, so Laura nodded in acknowledgement and left the customer to her papers.

Ten minutes and three Herb outbursts later, Laura returned to check on booth twelve as Herb disappeared into the back and the diner became blessedly quiet. "May I get you a refill on your tea? Would you like to change your mind about the pie or cobbler?"

The young woman shook her head, still somewhat distracted, but the sheaf of papers was no longer in sight. She pulled out her wallet and set a couple of dollar bills on the table–far more than required to cover the tea and a tip. Laura reached for the bills, but as she did so, the woman startled her by reaching out and putting her hand over them to prevent the waitress from picking them up. With her other hand, the woman held out a folded paper napkin. She flipped it open just long enough to ensure Laura realized a note was inked inside, closed it, and passed it across along with the dollar bills.

The young woman slid out of the booth and walked to the door without further acknowledgment of Laura other than a small nod. She disappeared out the door before the stunned waitress thought to open the napkin and read the note. Just as Laura began to do so, Herb bellowed from the back room, so she stuck the napkin into the pocket of her uniform and hurried to see what he wanted.

Not until she was walking home two hours later did she remember the napkin stuffed into her pocket. She pulled it out as she walked and unfolded it. She stopped cold when she read it. "Take this to Chestnut Cove Inn. Ask for Matt and give it to him." A line was drawn below the first note, and a succinct second note followed. "Matty, hire her." Laura reread the words several times, trying to grasp their meaning. She knew a little about Chestnut Cove Inn, a small, high-end hotel chain based in Elkford, but never considered applying for a job there. She had too little experience for somewhere that fancy. A former waitress at Fred's who worked at the upscale hotel as an intern in high school told her about it, but the girl hadn't been hired back as a permanent employee after she graduated. Considering Herb encouraged the girl to find other employment after three weeks at Fred's, Laura wasn't surprised CCI, as it was known to the locals, didn't want the girl as a full-time employee.

Laura stuffed the napkin back into her pocket and began walking toward home again, though this time at a much slower pace than usual. She tried to decide if there was some kind of joke or hoax involved, but she couldn't see any reason why the young woman would perpetrate such a thing. She seemed kind and understanding as Herb made his incessant and sometimes conflicting demands. She never seemed to pay much attention to anything except the paperwork she brought with her. Laura wondered once or twice who the woman was and what she did but never spent a great deal of time considering the matter.

Now she wondered who the young woman was to send Laura to someone at Chestnut Cove Inn and tell the person to hire her. Hire her for what? As Laura considered that thought, she realized whatever job might be open at the hotel would almost certainly pay better than what Herb paid her. Assuming this was legitimate. After all, it was unorthodox. Why would the young woman even think Laura would want another job? Laura realized the ridiculousness of that thought. The woman had been in the diner several times; she knew the food was bad, business was slow, and Herb was a royal pain. Who wouldn't want a better job?

The sudden feel of raindrops brought Laura back to the moment, and she hastened her steps, pushing the thought of the napkin to the back of her mind. She reached the small corner grocery near her grandmother's apartment and ducked inside to pick up a couple of items for dinner.

# Chapter 2

*Monday, May 7, 1979*

John Stuart, President and Chairman of Chestnut Cove Inns, rapped on the boardroom table with his knuckles to bring some semblance of order back to the group of managers assembled for their weekly staff meeting. "Let's settle down so we can finish." The voices quieted, and John continued. "I have one more item on the agenda to discuss. We put together a package on a potential new property I want us to consider for development into a new hotel. Mrs. Pierce will pass out a copy to each of you. I want everyone to go through it and be prepared to discuss the pros and cons from the perspective of your department next week.

"Let me remind each of you this information is confidential. We do not want anyone outside the management team at CCI to know we are interested in this property, so you are not to share it, not even your staff. Review it yourselves and do your own due diligence. We need to come to a quick conclusion about whether we want to acquire and develop it. We'll discuss it next Monday in detail and reach a decision before the end of the week." John slid his chair back to stand before he added as an afterthought, "Does anyone need to discuss anything else?"

Craig Fielder raised his hand. "Mr. Stuart, will you be available to answer questions about this property before we meet again next Monday?"

"Yes, of course, Craig. Ask your secretary to call Mrs. Pierce to set up a time once you read through the package and do some preliminary investigating, and it's John," he reminded his newest manager. Craig began his tenure at CCI only the previous week, taking on the new position of manager of finance. "OK, if there's nothing else, let's get back to work." John stood and strode from the boardroom while his secretary passed out the packages to the trailing managers.

When John reached his office, he was surprised to see his wife waiting for him. "Hey, honey, what brings you here this afternoon?" He leaned down for a quick kiss.

Sandra Duncan Stuart smiled up at her husband. "I wanted to see if I left a sweater up here. I can't find it anywhere at home, and it isn't one either Maggie or Chris would borrow." Sandra no longer involved herself in most day-to-day operations of CCI, but she still maintained her office on the top floor of the headquarters building for the occasions when her husband wanted her opinion or advice on a project.

"No, I can't imagine either wanting to wear something their mother wears. Did you find it?"

Sandra shook her head. "I'll look again at home. It must be mislaid somewhere." She took a seat on the sofa, and John joined her. "Was there anything of interest in your staff meeting this afternoon?"

With a sigh, he said, "We handed out the packages on the Pearl site. I gave them until next week's meeting to study it and told them I want us to decide whether to pursue it by sometime next week. They know I don't want to let somebody beat us to the punch again. Can you be here next Monday? I'd love for you to listen in and get your opinion afterward."

Sandra nodded. "OK, I'll put it on my calendar, but remember if it runs long, I'll need to leave to pick up the girls from school."

He picked up his copy of the property data package and handed it to her. "You already know most of what's in there, but you need the whole thing." John looked at his watch. "It's almost time for the girls to get out of school now, isn't it?"

"Normally, but Maggie is in detention today, remember?" She sighed as John made a face at the reminder. "I made arrangements for Chris to walk across to the high school and sit and read or work on her homework in their library until I pick them up an hour later than usual."

"That means we'll suffer through another unpleasant dinner conversation tonight. We should consider sending her to her room without supper if she won't accept that she did something wrong and received proper punishment for it. We never had problems like this with KD and Doug. What did we do different with Maggie?" John shook his head in bewilderment.

"Each of our children possesses a different personality, John. You know that. All have had their moments, too, though in different ways. I admit Maggie is a challenge in a way the first two weren't at this age. Some of her friends are a bad influence on her, starting with Giselle. Because they're cousins of a sort, we're limited in our ability to restrict their interaction."

Sandra frowned at the thought, though she was used to dealing with John's stepfather's family by now. The conflicts with Winston Hathaway's family were long-standing, but John tried to maintain the relationship for his mother's sake. Jeanette Stevenson Stuart Hathaway was a whole separate challenge. She never accepted Sandra's place in John's life and opposed John and Sandra's marriage more than twenty years earlier. She made it clear in the intervening years her opinion of Sandra had not changed. Jeanette still made quiet comments to her friends and others about how Sandra trapped John into marriage when they were in high school by getting pregnant.

Jeanette also cast doubt about whether John was the father of their firstborn child and referred to the child as a bastard regardless of the fact John and Sandra married months before KD's birth. Sandra regretted not fighting harder against those attacks. She and John once thought if they ignored them Jeanette would finally give up making them, but she did not.

Jeanette hadn't limited her attacks to just Sandra and KD either. She also had little use for second child Doug and intimated on occasion that perhaps he wasn't John's son. Both Doug and youngest child Chris were blond and blue-eyed, taking most of their looks from Sandra's side of the family, something Jeanette didn't fail to point out. In Jeanette's mind, failing to look like John made for good support for her claim Doug could be someone else's child. On the other hand, Jeanette readily embraced Maggie, who looked like a good mix of Stuart and Stevenson genes with little resemblance to Sandra. That made Jeanette happy to claim her third grandchild despite the girl's maternity.

Most humorous to Sandra was the resemblance between KD and Maggie though KD took even more of her looks from the Stuart side of the family. Both girls inherited the auburn hair and hazel eyes of their great-grandmother, Kathryn McDougal Stuart, for whom KD had been named. Sandra looked up and saw the portraits of her two oldest children hanging on the wall, painted in the spring before each graduated from high school. She smiled at the likeness of her eldest child. There could be no real doubt in the minds of anyone who had known John's grandmother; he was KD's father. That included Jeanette despite her vindictive, hurtful comments made for more than twenty years.

~~~

Craig sat down and opened the property data folder. Before he read even one line, he heard a firm knock on his office door. Without waiting for Craig to bid him to enter, accounting department head Hoyt Dalton barged in and began speaking. "We need to set a time to go over the information on this new property and put together some cost estimates. Of course, they won't be too good, but we'll do the best we can. My schedule is full tomorrow, so let's plan on meeting in my office Wednesday. Say ten o'clock? I'll direct my people to put together some preliminary numbers for what I think this thing will cost us."

While Hoyt spoke, Craig had stood and walked to his office door and pushed it closed. He turned back and took a couple of steps toward Hoyt before responding to the decree. "I appreciate your offer to assist me, but I'm sure I can provide the financial estimates Mr. Stuart desires as soon as I receive the necessary input from you and the other departments. After all, he hired me to make his financial projections. Also, Mr. Stuart was very specific about not utilizing our staff or even letting them know about this property."

As he continued, Craig watched Hoyt's complexion darken and a vein on the side of his neck begin to pulse. "As soon as you get me the data on previous acquisition and conversion projects, I'll extrapolate some estimates taking into consideration similarities and differences, inflation, and any specifics available from Jonah Jones on the construction end. Staffing will vary based on what we include in the project. I'll speak to Matt Hunter about that. I'm sure he already has an idea about that since I've learned he's pretty much in on all major projects with Mr. Stuart before anybody else hears about them."

Craig gestured toward the door, leaving little doubt the conversation Hoyt rudely began was at an end. "I'll be sure to let you know if I have any questions about your raw data. Just make sure I get it by first thing Wednesday morning."

A silent, seething Hoyt turned on his heel, jerked open Craig's door, and stalked out of the office without comment. Craig watched his counterpart storm past the finance department secretary's desk and out into the hall. Once he heard Hoyt's door slam far down the hall, Craig returned to his desk. He sat down and turned to the computer terminal to his left, entered the information to log onto the system, and waited for the computer to grant him access to the financial database.

Leaning back in his chair, he wondered if Hoyt realized much of the data required was already accessible on the system. At least it was supposed to be. One of Craig's tasks would be to verify whether hard data he received from accounting correlated with what Hoyt's team entered into the CCI computer system.

Another task involved speeding the conversion from the cumbersome Limmer computer system to IO, the new system the company began to implement months earlier. After more than a year of discussions, tests, and bitter arguments among John, Matt, and senior staff, Matt finally won the day to switch to IO the previous summer. His surreptitious implementation of the revolutionary computer system at the CCI flagship hotel in late 1977 proved Matt's championing of it justified. One of the highlights of Craig's resume happened to be proficiency in both systems, making him an ideal candidate to finalize the conversion of the financial system over Hoyt's continued resistance.

~~~

The door to his office slammed behind him, and Hoyt stormed to his desk and sat down to stew. Craig Fielder's very presence galled him. From the creation of the corporation when the adjacent hotel was built, one CCI department handled everything related to money. Hoyt had reigned as its manager for nine years, but in February John called Hoyt into his office and informed him the accounting and finance functions would be separated. Hoyt would remain head of accounting; a search would be conducted for someone new to become head of finance.

Once he got over the initial shock, Hoyt argued against the plan. He tried to find out who convinced John to follow such a course of action. It caught Hoyt off guard when the president took offense at the suggestion someone else pushed the plan and he just went along with the idea. When Hoyt accepted that his boss would not be swayed in separating the departments, he pushed to insert himself into the process of hiring the new finance manager, but John declined to include anyone except Matt and Sandra.

In the end, Hoyt could only convince Griffin Krebs, head of personnel, to allow him to sort through the applications for the position before John saw them, giving the accounting manager the opportunity to eliminate any candidates he might not be able to control. Despite all his efforts, somehow Craig Fielder bypassed personnel and won the job of finance department head. In less than a week on the job, Craig had thus far proven himself impervious to Hoyt's interference. Hoyt slammed his fist down on his desk and picked up the phone to call an old friend.

~~~

Matt Hunter, John Stuart's second cousin and best friend, walked across the lobby of Chestnut Cove Inn's flagship hotel toward the hallway leading to the back offices. Matt had worked with John and Sandra to establish the original inn and performed a variety of jobs there. With a much more outgoing and flamboyant personality than either of the Stuarts, Matt had served as the manager of CCI Elkford since it opened. He also held the title of Executive Vice President for Hotel Operations with responsibility for overseeing all their properties. Most of the managers at their other hotels had been brought to Elkford for a short time to be trained in the company's way of doing things before assuming management of another site. Then Matt monitored their work as they assumed their new job to ensure his training took hold.

He was also suspected of keeping a close eye on the operations of their other hotels by sending people to stay in each to test the staff's efficiency and attention to detail. While Matt never admitted to these secret spy missions, the rumors of them were rampant, and almost everyone stayed on guard, determined not to be caught short by Matt's spies.

Pam Grant, the assistant manager on duty at the Elkford Chestnut Cove Inn, looked up when Matt entered the office behind the reception desk. "Hey, Matt, was there anything interesting from the staff meeting this afternoon?"

Matt smiled, but the smile didn't quite reach his eyes. "No, it was as boring as usual. How are things here?"

"They're fine. Housekeeping finished cleaning all the rooms, and the empty ones are ready for new guests. We have two reservations for guests expected to arrive by four o'clock. One is for the couple who requested a mini-fridge in their suite stocked with a selection of juices. They'll be in 504, and it's been taken care of. We had a pretty good crowd for lunch. Fleur hasn't sent the totals over yet, but they were busy." She looked down at her notes. "I think that covers what you missed while you were over in the headquarters for the last couple of hours. Do you need me to handle anything for you?"

Matt shoved the staff meeting out of his mind to focus on Pam's question. "No, just checking in," he said before he flashed a half-smile at his long-time assistant. "It sounds like you have everything under control here. I'll be in my office if you need me, Pam." He disappeared out the door and down the hallway as quickly as he had appeared.

Matt entered his private office and tossed the new location packet onto his desk. He poured himself a glass of water and sat down to open the folder. Dumping the papers within it onto his desk, he spent about five minutes shuffling through them before stuffing them back into their folder and placing it on the corner of his desk.

Picking up his phone, he dialed a number from memory. When a voice on the other end answered, he began speaking without preamble. "The package for the proposed new location went out today. John told them he wants a decision on whether to move forward on acquiring it by the end of next week. It's time to move on our own plan." He listened, nodding in silence, before concluding, "Yes, I remember the protocol we agreed on: couriers only from this point forward."

# Chapter 3

*Friday, May 11, 1979*

The list of questions he needed answered was tucked away in the inner pocket of Elliott's suit coat when he climbed the steps of the realty office. A small instamatic camera rested in his right pocket. He had read through his list of questions several times in his motel room the previous night and again during breakfast. His client wanted him to gather as many details as possible about the property, and Elliott would not disappoint. He adjusted his tie, brushed a spec of lint off his jacket, and pushed open the door of the agency.

"Good morning, sir," greeted the receptionist. "How may we help you today?"

"I'm Elliott Starnes. I have an appointment with Mr. Hodges this morning."

The receptionist looked over at her phone where an illuminated button indicated a telephone line was in use. She gestured to the chairs along the opposite wall. "Please take a seat for a moment. Mr. Hodges is on the phone. I'll let him know you're here as soon as he gets off, Mr. Starnes."

"Thank you." Elliott sat down to wait and take stock of the small office. He glanced around the reception area, pleased to note it was neat and clean.

After about five minutes, the receptionist picked up her phone and punched a couple of buttons. "Mr. Hodges? Your ten o'clock appointment is here. Yes, sir." When she hung up and turned to him, Elliott leaned forward in anticipation. "Mr. Hodges will be right out."

Mr. Hodges, in scuffed shoes and ill-fitting jacket, appeared almost before she finished speaking. He strode across the small anteroom, a folder tucked under his arm, and extended his hand. "Good morning, Mr. Starnes. I'm sorry to keep you waiting, but I had a call from another important client who needed a few minutes of my time. I have the information on the property right here." He patted the folder he carried. Papers peeked out of it in three directions. "Why don't we drive out to the site? I can tell you what I know about it on the way."

Elliott stood and shook Mr. Hodges' hand. "That would be fine. I appreciate you showing me the property."

Ten minutes later, the two men neared the old warehouse in question. "Would you mind driving around the perimeter before we stop to go inside?" Elliott asked. "I'd like to get a good look at the property from the road on all sides first."

"Sure, I'd be glad to. Why don't we stop back here for a minute so you can see it from this vantage point first? Then we'll drive down the hill and around the building," Mr. Hodges said.

Elliott nodded, too busy staring down the last two blocks at the old warehouse to speak further. He ticked off his list of questions. Several had been asked and answered during the drive to the site, but he wanted to be sure he didn't forget anything. He noted the condition of the old warehouse's exterior, the subject of one of his questions. It wasn't terribly run down and appeared to be structurally intact, but a more rigorous inspection would determine that. Some of the red brick was stained in places, but those could be cleaned or the whole exterior painted. From this vantage point on a rise two blocks away, he could see a bit of the roof but not enough to make any determination about it.

Elliott remembered the camera and pulled it out of his pocket. He leaned out the window and snapped a couple of photographs.

"Quite an impressive old building, isn't it?" Mr. Hodges said. "She's in mighty good shape, too, for her age. Ready to drive down to her?"

"Yes, I've seen enough from here."

They eased down the hill and came to a stop at the traffic light at the southeast corner of the building. When it changed to green, Mr. Hodges turned left and drove along the south side of the property.

"The structure runs almost to the road on this side and on the east, which leaves little room for parking. I hope there's more elsewhere." Elliott knew it wouldn't pay to let Mr. Hodges think he was excited about the property. He raised the camera and snapped another photograph.

"There's plenty of parking for the trucks on the back–the west–side. We'll see that in a minute. How much truck traffic do you expect through here daily if I may ask? Maybe we can get the city to help you out with some little allowances along the street. You know, holding the trucks outside until you can move them up to the warehouse." Elliott noticed Mr. Hodges glance over at him, hoping for some clue about what kind of use he intended for the building. So far, he had been quite reticent with answers.

"I'm not certain." It was the same answer Elliott Starnes gave twice before. He was here to gain information, not give it away.

Mr. Hodges turned right and slowed to allow Elliott to get a good look at the rear of the building with the loading docks and available parking for trucks. "You can get several trucks in there at once. It's not like it's a tiny space to maneuver in back here."

"Yes, it could prove adequate for our purposes."

Mr. Hodges held his breath, waiting for further elucidation, but none came. He reached the corner and turned right again, traveling along the north side of the structure. At the midway point, they turned into a smaller parking lot. "As you can tell, this is the parking lot for the administrative staff with the office right here out this end." Mr. Hodges waved toward the low addition to the building, which thrust out from the much taller main warehouse. He pulled into the spot nearest the door and stopped. "Ready to go inside and take a look around or do you want to walk around out here a little first?"

"Inside now would be fine, though I would like to walk the perimeter before we finish and take more exterior photographs." Elliott stepped from the car and stared up at the streaks of rust along the sheet metal siding on the office. The siding needed to be replaced.

Mr. Hodges unlocked the door and stood waiting. "Ready to go in?"

Nodding, Elliott followed his counterpart inside.

~~~

Laura stood across the street and stared at the hotel's imposing edifice. She had circled the block twice so far, each time stopping to study the front of the old, converted mill. She passed it a hundred times before but never considered entering it. As a local, she had no reason to stay there and as a nineteen-year-old of very modest means couldn't even afford to eat lunch in its restaurant. The thought of working there never crossed her mind. Surely the employees possessed some level of polish she lacked and no doubt a great deal more work experience.

It had taken her several days to decide to act on the napkin note's instructions. More time passed before she got an opportunity to leave the diner early enough to walk to the hotel and arrive at what she thought would be an acceptable time.

Again, she wondered about the identity of the woman who scribbled the note and her reason for doing such an extraordinary thing. Laura dismissed the idea the whole thing might be a hoax. She thought herself a good judge of people and felt sure the lady had been very serious. Nothing about her struck Laura as frivolous or flighty. She thought the young woman to be in her early to mid-twenties, but she carried herself far differently from college students and workers of a similar age. Maybe a graduate student? However, that didn't explain the note.

Laura sighed in frustration and began yet another circuit around the block. This time she stopped across from the hotel entrance, took a deep breath, and marched across the street. She walked up to the large double doors where a liveried doorman waited. After a quick look down at her waitress uniform, Laura almost laughed at the disparity. She would have worn something more suitable but owned little that qualified. Besides, she came straight from work at the diner, only taking time to tidy her hair and freshen the little makeup she wore. She did her best to look as professional as possible, and it would have to do.

"Good afternoon, ma'am," the doorman greeted. He opened the door for her, a complete novelty to Laura other than the acts of a couple of boyfriends. She'd never entered any kind of business with someone standing by to open the door for her.

"Good afternoon," Laura responded with a smile when she stopped to speak to the cheery gentleman. "I'm supposed to ask for someone named Matt. Do you know where I might find him? My instructions were a little cryptic."

"Sure, go right to the reception desk. Tell the people there you're supposed to see him. They'll take care of you. He's a nice guy. You'll like him. Everybody does."

The doorman's assurance bolstered Laura's confidence. While she didn't clarify to him those cryptic directions came scribbled on a paper napkin from Fred's Diner, his proclamation that everybody liked Matt gave her a warm feeling.

"Thank you for your help." She smiled at him and stepped across the threshold to follow his directions.

A few feet inside, Laura stopped and looked around the vast lobby in awe. The butterflies she tamped down a moment earlier came back in full force. She hadn't known what to expect, and it pleased her the lobby wasn't some gilt monstrosity. It exhibited an understated elegance. Navy, green, and lavender décor offset the dark stain of furniture and paneling with signs here and there of the original beams of the old mill. Pots with live gardenias and rhododendrons added color as well as a soft, fragrant undertone. She noted the restaurant entrance to the left with a lounge farther down the same side. A bank of elevators stood across the lobby where a handful of people waited to ascend to their rooms.

She steeled herself and moved closer to the reception desk. One young man staffed it, and he was busy checking in a guest, so Laura stood to the side to wait. She became more self-conscious of her uniform's deficiencies when she admired the navy-blue blazer worn by the young man. Though similar to the livery the doorman wore, it lacked the gold braid of the doorman's uniform, which seemed to fit the position he held at the entrance of the hotel.

At last the young man waved to a bellhop attired in similar fashion to the doorman, though with less gold braid. The bellhop, burdened with two large suitcases, led the guest toward the elevators. Laura stepped forward and waited for the young man to finish punching something into the computer terminal in front of him.

He looked up and stared at her for a moment like he seemed unsure of any reason for her presence. "May I help you with something?" His voice displayed a lack of enthusiasm at best.

Taking a deep breath, Laura repeated the words she practiced earlier. "I was told to come here and ask to see Matt. The doorman said to ask for him here?"

"This area is for guests and staff," the young man snapped. "What do you want to see Matt about? Where did you even hear his name? Do you know who he is? Who sent you here to see him?"

The young man's rudeness compared to the affable doorman stunned Laura. Taking a shaky breath, she tried to explain. "A lady said to come here and ask for Matt. I'm supposed to talk to him."

"About what? What lady sent you? Are you selling something?" His voice echoed across the lobby. "We don't allow solicitors in here."

Laura flushed in embarrassment. "I am not a solicitor. She told me to come here and ask for Matt. She wanted him to hire me."

"If you knew anything at all worth knowing, you'd know people applying for jobs at this hotel do not march in the front door, walk up to the reception desk, and demand to see the manager. Matt doesn't hire the maids or waitresses or whatever it is you think you're qualified to do. He has department heads to handle such things." He pointed toward the door, hand shaking in anger. "Get out of here before I have you thrown out."

Laura pulled the napkin from her pocket and held it out for the young man to see.

"I'm sorry. I didn't mean to come to the wrong place, but she gave me clear instructions to come to Chestnut Cove Inn and ask for Matt. I didn't ask for a job. She wrote it on here and handed it to me at the diner."

The young man laughed. "How stupid are you?" He reached across and snatched the napkin from her. "You must be an idiot to think this is anything but a bad joke." He crumpled the flimsy note and threw it into the trashcan behind him. "Now get out of here and don't come back."

Laura turned and fled. Tears streamed down her face as she dashed out past the doorman. When she bumped him in her haste, she mumbled, "I'm sorry," but continued to rush down the sidewalk as he called after her.

~~~

Martha Colquitt heard the end of the ruckus in the lobby as she returned from checking with the housekeeping staff on the fourth floor. By the time she reached the desk, only Jared was there, but she could tell something had him out of sorts. "What was all the yelling I heard? Did you have a problem with a guest?"

"Nothing for you to concern yourself about," Jared snapped. "Did you ensure housekeeping prepared those rooms on four? The Malperns should arrive to check in soon. Their rooms need to be spotless." He kicked the trashcan up under the counter.

"Yes, they're fine." She wanted to pursue the issue, but assistant manager Jared outranked mere clerk Martha.

Jared kept his head down reading information on the computer terminal, but Martha noticed his harder than normal breathing and red face. She watched him fidget at the terminal for several more minutes before he abruptly left the reception area for the staff office behind them. She listened but heard nothing from the back. She still had the commotion on her mind when the Malperns arrived with a procession of luggage carts being wrangled by two of the Chestnut Cove Inn bellhops. She began calling up the needed information on the computer to check in the new arrivals and pushed the earlier ruckus to the back of her mind.

~~~

Martha's shift ended, and after collecting her purse from her locker, she returned to the AM's office behind the front desk. She was checking the work schedule for the following week when Gabriel, the longtime doorman, entered the room.

"Hi, Gabe, are you done for the day, too?"

"Almost. I need to take care of one thing before I leave. Have you seen Matt? He said he'd return late this afternoon, but I haven't seen him yet," Gabriel said.

"No, he probably got hung up somewhere. Anything I can help with?"

Gabriel looked around the office, concerned someone would overhear him. Paul and Donald now staffed the reception desk with Donald taking over as the assistant manager on duty, but Gabriel hadn't seen Jared leave. Though the young AM held no sway over his position at Chestnut Cove Inns, Gabriel respected the decorum of the hotel. He didn't want to end up in a squabble with the hot-tempered assistant manager at all, much less so near an area where guests might overhear them. "Did Jared leave for the day?"

With a shrug, Martha said, "I think so. He sure was in a snit today. Did you hear the dustup this afternoon?"

He took a step closer to her and lowered his voice further. "Yeah, that's what I want to talk to Matt about. Did you see what happened? I heard it, and I saw the young lady run out of here. I'm not sure what else went on, but a disturbance occurred in the lobby, and as far as I could tell the assistant manager caused it. Neither Matt nor Mr. Stuart would be happy about that, and I think they need to know about it."

Martha's brow furrowed. "I heard the end of it, but I had gone up to four to check on the accommodations for the Malperns, so I don't know what happened. I heard Jared shouting when I got off the elevator. I didn't see anyone else when I reached the desk. You say a young lady was involved? Did you know her?"

"No, I've never seen her before. She was young, wearing a waitress uniform, very pretty, neat, well-spoken. She walked up from across the street a few minutes earlier. She told me she was supposed to ask for Matt and wanted to know where to find him. She acted a little nervous–not guilty nervous, maybe a little unsure of herself, out of her element. I saw her walking earlier. I think she circled the block before she crossed the street to the hotel. Like maybe she needed to get up the nerve to come in. I told her to go to the reception desk and ask for Matt. I forgot he was out, or I'd have told her, but Jared should have been able to tell her when she could come back to catch Matt, or he should have asked her to wait for him to return. Instead, a few minutes later she came hurrying back to the door. I opened it for her and saw her crying. She bumped into me and apologized but kept running."

Gabriel looked Martha in the eye before he continued. "Matt needs to know about something like that no matter what. The fact she came here asking for him in particular makes it even more important he hears about her. Oh, she said something else. She mentioned the message to come here to see Matt was cryptic." He nodded his head slowly. "He definitely needs to know that."

Martha leaned back on the desk. "You don't know anything more about the cryptic message? I wonder what..." She stopped speaking, stood, and hurried out to the reception desk. She returned a moment later with the trashcan she saw Jared kick under the desk earlier. She poured the contents onto the floor, and Gabriel knelt beside her to shuffle through the pile of papers.

Neither knew what they were looking for until Gabriel found part of a torn napkin. "We need to find the rest of this." He held up the piece in his hand for her to see. On it were written a few letters: "tty, hir". Within minutes, they found and pieced together most of the napkin, though some bits proved too damaged to recognize. Regardless, they managed to salvage enough of it to determine it must be the cryptic instructions to which the young woman referred.

"We need to tape the pieces onto something," Martha said. She stood and retrieved a sheet of notepaper and a roll of tape from the desk. They secured the fragments in place as best they could and put other bits too damaged to do anything with into a manila envelope along with the reconstructed part of the napkin. "Let me take the trashcan back out front and ask Donald if he's heard anything from Matt. Surely he's checked in if he isn't back by now."

She hurried out to hold a quick consultation with Donald and returned. "He said Matt should be back any minute. Do you want to wait and talk to him?"

Gabriel nodded. "Yeah, I want to make sure he knows exactly what I saw and heard. He'll want to ask me some questions about it. He always thinks of things other people don't, and I need to be here to provide any answers I can."

~~~

Matt studied the reconstructed note while he listened to Martha and Gabriel tell their story. He interspersed their narrative with a few questions about the events each witnessed and about the girl herself. Only Gabriel and Jared had seen her, and Donald had confirmed to Martha that the young AM left the hotel as soon as his shift ended. However, the fact the longtime doorman saw and interacted with the girl would prove invaluable.

Gabriel's history with CCI dated back to the original inn. He started as a combination bellhop, doorman, and security guard. Eventually, he became one of Matt's most trusted pairs of eyes at the flagship hotel. Chestnut Cove Inns wanted to maintain the highest level of service and hospitality possible. To do so meant Matt needed to know about anything amiss, and he couldn't be everywhere. Therefore, he needed people he trusted to know what to watch for and what information to pass along to him. Gabriel was one of his best.

Matt set aside the napkin at last and focused his full attention on the two people seated across his desk. "Gabe, did you notice if her waitress uniform had any kind of name on it?"

Shrugging, Gabriel replied, "Nothing. It was a standard, off-the-shelf uniform: light blue with white trim on the pockets and collar, but no name, neither hers nor the name of the place she works."

"What about the girl herself? Anything stand out?"

Gabriel closed his eyes as he thought about what he saw of the girl, trying to pick any tiny detail from his memory to help Matt's quest to learn about her. At last he shook his head. "Not that I can remember. She was neat. She didn't wear much makeup, and her hair wasn't done fancy. She wore it pinned back with little barrettes on each side."

Matt nodded. "Something easily repaired. Did she carry a purse or any kind of bag with her?"

Gabriel thought for a minute. "No, nothing. She could have put a small wallet, lipstick, maybe a comb in the pocket of her uniform though. The pockets were big enough."

"Again, enough to repair what she needed since she didn't wear much makeup and wore a simple hairstyle."

"Yes," Gabriel said. "Oh, there's one other thing. She didn't smell of any kind of perfume, but I remember a faint food odor." He considered a moment, nodded, and said, "Yeah, like she'd been at work at a little restaurant beforehand."

Matt allowed a slight smile. "Like a greasy spoon?"

Gabriel nodded again as he thought back to his short interaction with the girl. "Not a fancy place. Burgers, grilled cheese, breakfast, that kind of place. You think she was at work there until just before I spotted her circling the block this afternoon?"

"That's my guess. You said she arrived about four-thirty, which would fit getting off work about four o'clock if she works nearby." Matt leaned back in his chair. "There can't be too many small diners within walking distance of here even if she's a good walker. Gabe, describe her to me one more time." He picked up a pen to write down every detail Gabriel could remember.

~~~

Shifting the phone to better hold it between his shoulder and ear, Elliott replied to his client's latest question. "No, it isn't too bad, though I can't yet see your vision for it. The structure limits you to a couple of stories regardless of how you build out the interior, but it might still be large enough to do what you want with it. I can make some rough calculations on how the interior might divide, though you're better versed in those details than I am."

Elliott looked down at the notes he made when he returned to his motel room after inspecting the warehouse. The tour took a full three hours, wandering through the dark, dank, leaky warehouse itself and the somewhat cleaner office which still had electricity powering a few functioning lights. He checked the parking lot and walked the whole perimeter while searching for some semblance of his client's vision for the wretched derelict. His patron wanted a thorough examination of the building, and Elliott would provide one.

He glanced across the room at his abandoned Oxfords. The cost to replace them would cut into his commission for today's venture; so would the cost of the doctor's appointment he would need to get a prescription for more hay fever medicine. At least he managed to avoid getting anything unpleasant on his suit. He inspected it in detail when he returned to his motel in case it needed to go to the local cleaner. Perhaps Mr. Hodges had the right idea as to the proper attire for inspecting the old warehouse. He needn't worry about his scuffed shoes and plaid jacket tonight.

"Yes, I intend to spend the evening working on a more detailed report. Both reports will be ready tomorrow." He listened for a minute. "Yes, I think it's possible. I think the asking price is a little high for the area. With the right plan, you might recoup your investment within a couple of years." He listened once more. "No, I don't think it's probable the owner will come down much on the price. Mr. Hodges made sure to let me know others are interested in the property. He even told me someone wants it for something other than a warehouse. I was careful not to let on we already knew that, of course. I'll include all his comments in the warehouse report tomorrow. I will arrive at your office promptly at eight o'clock in the evening if that time still suits you." He stopped once more. "Yes, I remember. Back door. I'll see you then."

# Chapter 4

*Saturday, May 12, 1979*

Jared glared at Martha. Though rare, such summons weren't unprecedented, but this one came too soon after the incident the previous afternoon to be coincidental. He admitted he might have been a little overzealous, but he knew he took the right action. Matt would agree once he heard the real facts.

"I'll be back in a few minutes," Jared said. "Try not to screw up anything while you're alone at the desk."

He marched into and through the office behind the reception desk and down the hall toward the back of the hotel. When he reached Matt's closed door, he raised his hand to knock but stopped. He needed to ensure he got his temper under control first. His probationary period as an assistant manager would last two more months. It wouldn't do to get bounced back to desk clerk, and an angry confrontation with the boss could hardly end better than a return to clerk-hood. It might end much worse. He closed his eyes and took several deep breaths before he raised his hand and tapped on the door.

"Come in," a voice said. Not Matt's voice, a woman's.

Jared opened the door and took a couple of tentative steps into the room. A young woman held some sort of paper studying it, but she stood with her back to the door, so Jared couldn't be sure of her identity. He cleared his throat and said, "Matt wanted to see me. Is he here?"

The young woman slid the sheet of paper into a manila envelope and laid it on the desk before turning to Jared. "Yes, he's in the back. He'll be here in a minute. Have a seat." Jared recognized her as Matt's assistant from his other office, the Executive Vice President's office in the nearby headquarters of the hotel chain. Vicky something, he thought.

A door on the other side of the room opened, and Matt entered. Jared knew it led to a back hallway and Matt's private quarters. The confirmed bachelor had lived in a suite built for him since the hotel opened. It was convenient for him, but it made some of the staff nervous. A semi-private entrance down the secluded rear hallway allowed him to come and go at will, so often the staff didn't know if he was in the hotel or not.

Matt looked at the young woman as if awaiting an answer to an unasked question, and she nodded. "If I learn anything, I'll let you know," she said.

"Thanks, Vicky," Matt said. "I'll do the same." The young woman nodded again, walked to the rear exit, and left the room. When the door closed behind her, Matt turned his attention to Jared, who stood in front of the desk. "Take a seat, Jared. We need to chat a little about yesterday." Matt pulled out his desk chair and sat down.

"Sir, I don't know what you've heard, but–" Jared began, but Matt cut him off.

"Sit down, Jared. I'm about to tell you what I heard." Jared did as directed and took a seat. "First, I heard you shouted at someone in the lobby of this hotel. There aren't many instances when that's acceptable behavior for either staff or guests, and I haven't heard of any of those circumstances occurring yesterday afternoon." Jared started to speak again, but Matt held up his hand. "You'll get your chance to explain. Second, I understand the person at whom you shouted was a young lady who asked to see me, and yet I received no message from you informing me of her visit. Now, would you care to explain how either of those makes you a good assistant manager of this hotel?"

Jared swallowed hard, caught between worrying about his job security and his indignation someone distorted his actions and took them out of context. "Sir, I admit I raised my voice above what is proper decorum. I apologize and assure you it will not happen again, but I don't think I spoke as loud as you heard." He tried to read Matt's face, but it betrayed no hint of whether he accepted Jared's assurance.

In hindsight, he wondered who heard him yelling. Probably Martha. She acted tense earlier. Did she rat him out to Matt? And the nosy doorman Matt seemed to hold in such high regard compared to people in more important positions like assistant managers. Who else? Maybe the hostess stationed at the front of the restaurant? At least no guests were present in the lobby at the time.

When Jared forced himself to continue, his tone shifted toward the pedantic. "As for the girl who came in yesterday asking about you, I realized she heard your name somewhere and thought she could walk in the front door of the hotel and ask you for a job and bypass the normal application process. She obviously knows nothing about working for a large, prestigious place like this. I told her she needed to go through personnel, not you, and she pulled out a cheap paper napkin with a note written on it saying to come here and ask you for a job."

He stopped his narrative to interject, "Can you believe it? A napkin? She expected me to believe somebody wrote such a thing on a napkin and sent her in the front door of an exclusive hotel to ask the manager to give her a job. Who would believe such a thing?"

While Jared was on his tear, Matt picked up the manila envelope the young woman laid on the desk. He pulled out a sheet of paper and held it up for Jared to see.

"This napkin?"

The color drained from Jared's face when he saw the flimsy note he snatched from the waitress the previous afternoon, crumpled, threw away, and later retrieved and tore into pieces. Only now, someone had taped the remnants onto a sheet of notepaper.

Matt asked again, "This napkin with a note written on it addressed to me? One pulled from the trashcan behind the reception desk yesterday afternoon?"

"Sir, you can't believe that is anything but a ruse by somebody trying to–"

Matt interrupted him with a brisk wave. "It is not for you to decide whether or not a note addressed to me which comes to this hotel in whatever form or fashion should be ignored or acted upon. I don't care if it's brought in here by a vagrant and written on a gum wrapper. If it is addressed to me, it will be delivered to me. Furthermore, the deliverer will be treated hospitably and encouraged to remain until I am available, if possible. Considering in this case the deliverer was the subject of the note, it is even more egregious you didn't ask her to wait or make an appointment for her to return to see me. Not only that, the assistant manager on duty, whose job is to act on my behalf, treated her with rudeness and anger and sent her away in tears."

Jared refused to believe he acted improperly, but he knew he must accept Matt's judgment, so he bowed his head. "I'm sorry, sir. It won't happen again."

Matt stared at Jared in silence before he continued. "I hope not. If it does, it will be the last time, and this matter will be discussed again at a later date." Matt leaned forward and put his elbows on his desk. "I need you to tell me what you can about this young lady. We still need to straighten out the problem you created."

Jared's eyes went wide, and he started to argue until he remembered his precarious position. He slumped down in his chair, eyes focused on the floor. "What do you need to know?"

"I need to know anything she told you about herself or you noticed about her: where she works, what she wore, anything which will help me locate her. I don't suppose you bothered to ask her name?" Matt picked up a pen and sat poised to write down anything Jared could tell him.

Jared's face flushed when he remembered one of the first instructions he received when hired to work at the front desk at CCI: get people's names and contact information. "No sir, I didn't ask her name or anything else."

"OK, tell me what she looked like. What was she wearing? Did you see anything to indicate where she currently works? I understand she wore some sort of uniform?"

"Yes, like a waitress would wear. Not a nice one like our restaurant staff wears. I think it was either blue or green. Maybe striped." Jared accepted his fate and tried to remember as much as he could, reciting details and answering Matt's questions as he probed for any tidbit to help the search.

~~~

"Hey, Doug." A petite blonde waved from across the room as soon as the young man stepped into the fraternity house. He gave her a quick nod and turned in the opposite direction. It wouldn't deter her, but at least he might manage a few minutes to speak to some of his friends at tonight's party before she caught up to him. A handsome and pleasant young man from a well-to-do family, Doug Stuart never lacked for attention from the fairer sex whether he wanted it quite so often or not.

He managed almost a whole minute speaking to a couple of friends before the blonde arrived at his side and slipped her arm through his. "I was beginning to think you wouldn't make it tonight, Doug." She poked out her bottom lip. "I almost settled for leaving a few minutes ago with Dylan." She hugged his arm tighter and purred.

"I'm glad I didn't."

Managing not to roll his eyes, Doug said, "Hi, Sheila, how are you?"

"I'm great now that you're here. Let's dance." She tugged on his arm in the direction of the stairs to the basement from which a distinct disco beat emanated.

He tried to extricate his arm from her grasp with a gentle tug, but she held firm. "Maybe later. I need to grab something to eat first. I haven't eaten dinner yet, and it's ten o'clock. I'm starved. I'll catch up with you later maybe."

"Oh, I'll go with you." This time, she tugged in a different direction to lead him to the buffet laid out in the dining room. "Why were you too busy to eat dinner until now? Did you do something fun today? You could have called me. I would have been happy to go along."

"No," a resigned Doug responded, allowing her to lead him along. "I worked all day." Thankfully, when they reached the buffet Sheila eased her hold on his arm enough for him to pick up a plate and begin filling it with food.

"Work? Why would you need to work? Your family owns Chestnut Cove Inns. You're rich. You don't need to work, Doug. Just tell your dad to send you some more money." Sheila picked up a plate and dropped some chips onto it.

Doug realized she wanted anyone else with an eye on him to know she was eating with him. It wouldn't make her his official date for the evening, but he knew that wouldn't matter to the determined girl. "My parents don't just give me money, Sheila. I work at the hotel every summer, and during the school year I work most Saturdays at a small company near Tech. Not enough to cover all my school expenses, but enough to cover extra things like my car insurance and gas. Besides, it's good work experience for me." Doug made it to the end of the buffet and grabbed a can of soda from the cooler on the floor. He tried hard not to get annoyed, but this was not the first time he held a similar conversation with Sheila as well as with numerous other people over the course of his first year at Coughton Tech.

"That doesn't seem very fair. You work more than some boys who don't come from rich families. Why do you need work experience? Won't you go to work for Chestnut Cove when you graduate?" Sheila's pout returned as she followed close on Doug's heels when he headed through the house to find a place to sit and eat.

He spotted Joseph Jones, his childhood friend and fellow Tech freshman, and ignored Sheila's ongoing diatribe about his time management and future employment while he maneuvered through the crowd to claim a seat across from Joseph. Sadly for Sheila, there were no empty places next to Doug, but she seated herself on the stuffed arm of his chair with her chips and dip and continued their one-sided conversation.

Joseph smirked at his friend. Both were well used to the attraction Doug and his parents' money held for young women, and Joseph always enjoyed watching various expressions flit across the Stuart heir's face during an unwanted pursuit. Both young men were between girlfriends at the moment, a situation with which each was happy, though Doug began to rethink the matter while he chewed on a slice of pizza. A steady girlfriend could help fend off at least some of the unwanted attention he received.

When Sheila paused her monologue to eat a chip, Joseph broke into the conversation. "Did you finish with your project at CasCav tonight or do you need to go back to work on it tomorrow afternoon? I can go in to help if you need me to." Like Doug, Joseph worked part-time at the small company.

"Yeah, I'm done with it." Doug noticed Sheila perk up at the notion he might be free Sunday afternoon or evening, and he hurried to clarify his plans for the day. "It's a good thing I finished today because I need to study for a big Monday morning exam and finish homework for two other classes. I'll be busy most of tomorrow studying."

A young woman he dated for a few weeks during the fall walked into the room, and he cringed at the determined expression on Sheila's face even before she plowed forward with the expected but unwanted invitation. "Omicron is having a party next Saturday, Doug. It will be better than this one. You should come." Glancing over at Joseph, she added, "You can bring your friend. It starts at nine o'clock at the chapter house. Say you'll come, please?" She leaned close and put her arm around his neck and gave him a wet, sloppy kiss on his cheek.

"Uh, I need to find out how much work my boss wants me to do next weekend, but we'll try to make it, won't we, Joseph?" Doug looked over at Joseph to warn him to either help with an escape from Sheila's grasp or get dragged to the Omicron party, too.

On cue, Joseph dived into the fray. "Oh, wow, didn't we promise our families we'd go home to Elkford next weekend? Some big shindig at the hotel, right?"

Doug wondered what kind of fictitious shindig they could invent should they need to elaborate. "Oh, yeah, and Mom will kill me if I don't go home for it." He turned back to Sheila, who was already pouting. "I'm sorry, Sheila, but it's one of the downsides of my family owning a business. Sometimes my parents require me to attend events at the hotel. Joseph's father sits on the board, so he needs to go home to attend, too."

Sheila abandoned one line of inquiry for another. "I've never been to the hotel in Elkford. It's the biggest one you own, isn't it? We stayed in one of the Chestnut Cove Inns somewhere else on a vacation in the mountains a few years ago, but not that one. It's probably the nicest one, too."

Sheila's hint did not go unnoticed, but Doug's familial pride kicked in, and he began to give her a little history of the family business. "They're all about the same as far as how nice they are, but they feature different décor and so forth depending on where they're located and what the building used to be and what the area is known for. The flagship hotel in Elkford is on the Wolf River in a valley in the foothills of the Appalachians. It's in an old mill, which belonged to my dad's grandparents. The mill had been closed a few years, and it was converted into a hotel about ten years ago when demand for rooms became too high for the old inn farther up in the mountains."

Doug hit on something of particular interest to Sheila. "The old inn was in the family mansion, wasn't it?"

"Well, I don't know if I'd call it a mansion, but it's a big, old house. My dad's grandparents lived there, but we never lived in it. Mom and Dad and Uncle Matt turned it into a country inn after my great-grandmother died. Chestnut Cove was the name of the mountain cove where it's located, and that's what my great-grandparents called their home, and my parents used the name for the original inn. The name stuck when they converted the mill into a bigger hotel. When they built more hotels, they made the name of the whole chain Chestnut Cove Inns." Doug stopped, feeling he had rambled on too much about the family business and would bore everyone around him.

"Does your family live in the mansion now? It must be huge to get turned into a hotel." Sheila's eyes glowed with visions of an enormous manor house. "Will you inherit it and live in it one day?"

Doug couldn't prevent a look of disgust from crossing his face. "No, it doesn't belong to my parents, so I won't inherit it. Besides, I have sisters who will receive part of whatever we're fortunate enough to be left by our parents one day. It's not like I'll get everything they own, and I hope they live for a very long time. I'd rather keep my parents around than receive anything of theirs." He stood, his plate still half full. "I'm beat. Are you ready to go, Joseph?"

Always sympathetic to his best friend's plight, Joseph rose from his seat. "Yeah, let's get out of here. See you around, Sheila." The two young men exited without further words from Doug.

# Chapter 5

John covered the more mundane issues at the beginning of the staff meeting to get them out of the way before the management team delved into the subject of primary interest. The meeting start had been delayed a couple of minutes while some of the managers greeted Sandra. He also introduced her to Craig Fielder. Per her policy with new CCI executives, Sandra invited Craig to dinner at the Stuart home, and they established the upcoming Saturday for his visit.

John pushed the sheet of paper with his agenda on it aside and flipped open a folder containing information about the proposed hotel site passed out the previous week. "I've spoken to a couple of you about this property we're considering for a new hotel. I'd like to go around the table and hear everyone's take on it so we can learn the pros and cons from each department's perspective. As I told you at our last meeting, we want to make a decision as soon as possible so we can move on this within the week if we choose to pursue it. As most of you know, we lost out on a piece of property we were very high on last year. I don't want that to happen again if we can prevent it.

"Jonah, you want to start us off? You've done some preliminary investigation of the structure and the shape you think it's in based on the data you got from your tour of it a couple of weeks ago. Obviously, we won't know enough about what kind of shape it's in until we make an offer the owners accept and can do a more detailed inspection during due diligence but go over what you have for us so far."

Jonah Jones stood and walked to the far end of the table and turned on the overhead projector. He placed a transparency showing a list of major components of the structure on the glass stage and checked the focus on the screen behind him before he began.

"Based on what we observed, the foundation looks good. It's only a few feet down to solid rock, and I didn't see anything to cause concern. The walls of the older part of the building look sturdy, so I don't anticipate any significant work there. Of course, we may want to do something aesthetically, but we'll decide what that is down the line. The metal siding on the office is stained with rust, but I expect we'll want to brick it up to match the older part as best we can." He looked toward Sandra, who still played a significant part in deciding the look of their hotels.

Sandra nodded in agreement. "We can work out those details if we acquire it, but

I agree we want a consistent façade. The old brick is much more attuned to what we would want. Would there be any problem matching it?"

"We might not find a perfect match, but we can get mighty close." Sandra nodded again, and Jonah continued. "The roof isn't too bad, but I expect we would replace it regardless. It's old, and it's easier to do that as part of the conversion to a hotel instead of going back in a few years when we're operating. That's what we've done before with these metal roofs.

"As for the interior, there's only enough height for two stories no matter what, which will be different for us. I've spoken to Matt at length about potential arrangements of guest rooms, restaurant, lobby, and hotel operations areas, and I've made some preliminary sketches of the ideas we've come up with. I don't see much variation in overall cost among the options so far, at least not enough to ask Craig to make multiple pro forma estimates. It's all too preliminary at this point, so the estimates can't be very accurate yet.

"Finally, the exterior has a fence around the old loading dock area we would take down, which isn't a significant cost, but parking is limited, so we need to either acquire access to parking nearby or build a deck as part of our construction. A small one—two stories—would get us the parking we would need, but there's an empty lot across from this property that's about half an acre. I expect we could buy and pave it a lot cheaper. The valets could park and retrieve cars from there in a couple of minutes. I did a little checking, and I'm pretty sure we could get it for about four-thousand dollars. It will take another couple to pave and stripe it. I've given Craig the information on it to include in his estimates." Jonah stopped and glanced around the table. "Any questions?"

Hoyt cleared his throat but said nothing. Jonah resumed his seat, and at a nod from John, Matt stood to discuss the operational side of the proposed hotel.

When the meeting broke up over an hour later, the managers filed out of the room to return to their offices. Sandra hurried to catch Matt, who had arrived a few minutes late and thus not been available for her to buttonhole beforehand. When he turned in her direction, she waved to him, and he stopped and backtracked toward her, and they exchanged a warm hug. "Matt, I've asked Craig to dinner at our house Saturday evening. Will you be able to eat with us that night?"

"Sure, Sandra. Shall I bring the wine?" Matt pulled out his pen and scribbled a reminder on his notepad.

"That would be great. I think I'll get John to grill steaks, so bring something red. Are you sure you won't get hung up and run late? You know how often that's happened lately. I can get the wine if I need to." Both were aware Matt's schedule had suffered the last few months while he broke in a couple of new assistant managers.

"No, no, it won't be a problem. Pam is working Saturday, so I won't have any difficulty getting out of here." He looked down at his watch. "I need to run. I have an errand to take care of. Kiss the girls for me and tell them I'll see them Saturday."

"OK, Matt, we'll see you then."

Matt started toward the door but stopped and turned back to Sandra and to John, who walked up to join her. "Hey, will Doug be home this weekend?"

"I'm not sure. It's getting close to the end of term, and he wants to study hard these last few weeks to keep his grades up. He wants to come home one weekend before finals, but I'm not sure he'll get to. Do you need to talk to him?"

"I might need a little help on something soon. I know John wants him to work in the headquarters this summer, but I'd like to borrow him a couple of times if he's interested."

John piped up at last. "You're not trying to corrupt another of our children, are you?"

"Never," Matt said with a flash of his trademark grin. "I'll see you Saturday, Sandra. I need to do some corrupting elsewhere this afternoon." He waved and hurried to the elevator, leaving Sandra and John shaking their heads and wondering what Matt could be up to this time.

~~~

An hour later, Matt leaned back in a booth in the third diner on the list he composed Saturday evening. He checked out two on Sunday in his search for the girl who had been sent to the hotel to see him, but neither proved to be the right place.

This afternoon, he thought maybe he found the right diner, though not the right girl. There was one waitress on duty. She wore a uniform like the one Gabe described but looked far older than the girl he sought. He waved to get her attention for the third time to request a refill of the weak coffee, to no avail. He was positive this woman would never be sent to him for a job. He gave up, tossed enough money on the table to cover the cost of his coffee and coffeecake, and stood to leave. At the last minute, he reached back to the napkin dispenser, pulled out a napkin, and stuck it into his jeans pocket. He walked out the door of the diner wondering about the odds both the waitress's uniform and the type of napkins used would match those he sought. Then he shrugged. He'd know soon enough if the napkin in his pocket happened to match the pattern and texture of the one Martha and Gabe rescued. If they matched, he'd be back tomorrow.

When he returned to the hotel, he pulled the napkin from his pocket and laid it out on his desk. Then he retrieved the manila envelope from his desk drawer, pulled the reconstructed napkin out of it, and laid it next to the one he brought from the diner. Once he compared them for a couple of minutes, he tossed the new napkin into the trashcan, put the reconstructed one back in the envelope, and returned it to the drawer. Picking up the phone, he dialed an extension in the headquarters building. His call was answered on the second ring.

"Chestnut Cove Inns, Executive Vice President's office. May I help you?"

"I think I found it. Place called Fred's Diner. It's about seven blocks north and west of here. Mean anything to you?"

"No, but I'll check to see if I can find any reference to it or anywhere near and let you know," said Vicky Jones. "Give me the exact address." Matt gave her the information and hung up to consider his next step.

The following morning, Matt once again sat in Fred's Diner. The same waitress who had been on duty the previous afternoon waited on him, but a second girl covered the far end of the diner. Matt watched the newer one as he sipped his tepid coffee. From what he saw, she worked much more efficiently and seemed far more pleasant than his waitress, who if anything made an even worse impression on him than the day before. The new girl also matched Gabe's description.

By the time he left the diner, Matt knew two things: the second waitress's name was Laura, and she was almost certainly the young woman who had been sent to see him at the hotel. If by some chance she wasn't, he'd try to hire her anyway. Now he needed to decide how to approach her. After the way Jared treated her at the hotel, Matt wouldn't blame her for calling the police on him if he approached her the wrong way.

~~~

*Thursday, May 17, 1979*

Matt skipped a day of appearing in the diner to avoid arousing notice. Neither the first waitress nor Herb, the owner, seemed likely to take much note of anything, but Laura might. He dressed casually on his previous diner visits, eschewing the expensive suits and ties he wore when working at the inn for jeans and a pullover. For his third visit to Fred's Diner, he resumed his normal style, dressed to look the part of manager of Elkford's crown jewel. This time, he waited until late afternoon to arrive at the diner, hoping only Laura would be on duty with Herb. He wanted a chance to engage her in casual conversation and get a closer look at her to assure himself she was the girl in question and to judge the best way to approach her about the clash with Jared at the hotel.

He was disappointed to find a third waitress, Meredith, on duty at the diner. However, because she was quite chatty, he realized he could use her to his advantage. He ordered a cheeseburger and was blessed with some good fortune when Herb went to the back room as soon as he finished making Matt's burger, content to let the diner's lone waitress take care of its sole patron.

Matt flashed his most charming smile when she brought his cheeseburger. "Thank you. It smells great. You must love working every day in a place that smells so good."

The girl's eyes lit up, and she practically bounced in place as she chatted at Matt. "Oh, it's great here. I love it, but I don't get to work every day. I'm the weekend waitress, but I also fill in for Helen and Laura when they need to miss work. That's why I'm here today. Laura was supposed to work, and she did for half a day, but she needed to take her grandma to the doctor. She's really old and has a couple of things wrong with her I think." Meredith's eyebrows contracted with the exertion of recalling the ailments. "Like maybe her heart or her foot? Anyway, Laura took her to the doctor today. Just a regular appointment, not any emergency, but she needed to be off. Herb wasn't too happy, but he agreed because I could fill in." She stopped and drew a breath.

"That's too bad about her grandmother. Nice of–what did you say her name was? Laura?–to take care of her grandmother so well. Many people wouldn't want to bother." Matt's comment was enough to set the girl off on another excited verbal ramble.

"Maybe, but Laura and her grandma are really close. In fact, Laura lives with her. Right around the corner. Well, about a block down. Or two blocks maybe. She likes it because she can walk to work and not use her grandma's old car. It still runs, but she's afraid of wearing it out if she uses it too much. Working here, she can walk to work instead of driving, and she can even walk home on her lunch break if she needs to check on her grandma. Of course, then Herb won't give her extra time to eat lunch, but she doesn't eat much anyway, and she carries an apple or a banana with her so she can eat it while she's walking." Meredith paused for another breath.

"It's convenient to live so close to work she can walk, especially to get back home during lunch to see about her grandmother. I hope they don't live in a building where she needs to climb stairs with a heart condition or a bad foot." Matt put as much sympathy into his words as possible.

"I think they live on the second floor, so she's got a few stairs to climb, but not too many. It's like a four-story building, so it could be a lot worse." Meredith paused as a thought bounced around in her head for a moment. When she latched onto it, she continued. "Oh, but it's got an elevator. I forgot about that, so she doesn't have to walk upstairs. I think they added it a few years back when some new owner bought the building. They made some nice improvements. I think that's when Mrs. Phillips moved in there. Laura didn't live with her then. She moved here after she finished high school last year. Her family lives out in the country somewhere. She moved here to get a job 'cause there wasn't anything much where she grew up and to go to school part time–she takes one class a couple of nights a week–bookkeeping I think–and her grandma needed somebody to help her." Meredith's face flushed from her exertions, and she stopped for another breath.

"Things worked out well for both Laura and Mrs. Phillips, didn't they? She found a good job here and can take some classes, and Mrs. Phillips has someone to help her. Good when things work out well for everyone, isn't it?" Matt said with a wide smile.

"Well, everyone but me. Herb can't afford but two full-time waitresses and one part-time. That's me. Helen's never going to leave here, and Herb would never get rid of anyone as good as Laura, so the only way I'll ever get to be a full-time waitress here is if Laura leaves, but she can't leave because she needs the money to take her class and help out her grandma. She doesn't get much pension money." Meredith looked a bit sad for the first time, but Matt wasn't sure if it was because of her empathy for Mrs. Phillips or if she didn't think Laura likely to clear a path for Meredith to ascend to the second full-time waitress position at Fred's Diner.

Certain he had amassed all the useful information he could expect from the waitress, Matt made a production of looking at his watch. He exclaimed, "I didn't realize how late it is. I have an appointment I must get to." He stood and pulled out his wallet.

"But you haven't even taken a bite of your burger." Meredith pointed at his plate, positive her customer was unaware he hadn't eaten anything.

Matt stifled a smile as he pulled out a ten-dollar bill and handed it to her. "Gosh, no wonder I still feel hungry."

"Do you want me to wrap it up so you can take it with you? It won't take but a minute," she offered as she walked toward the cash register to get his change.

"No, no. I'll have to pass." Matt hurried to the door and pushed it open.

"Wait, you haven't gotten your change," Meredith called after him.

Matt turned back to her and flashed another winning smile. "Keep it for your tip. Thanks for the conversation, Meredith, and don't get discouraged about your job. Maybe something will happen to cause Laura to quit Fred's soon, and you'll get the full-time job you want."

Meredith's face had lit up with the large tip, and she became downright giddy at Matt's suggestion Laura might leave so Meredith could get her desired promotion. "Think so?" she asked Matt's departing back. "I wouldn't want anything to happen to Laura though. She's really nice, and I like her a lot. I wouldn't want to get her job at her expense."

Matt turned and stepped back through the doorway. "You have a good heart, Meredith. Hang in there, and things will look up for you." He ducked out again and hastened down the street toward his Lotus.

Meredith smiled at his encouraging words and the crinkling of all the dollar bills in her pocket. She suddenly wondered how he knew her name since she didn't remember telling him. When she turned and saw her reflection in the decorative mirror hung on the wall behind the counter, she realized she was wearing her necklace with the gold script "Meredith."

# Chapter 6

*Friday, May 18, 1979*

Matt studied the familiar apartment building. The new owner a few years back happened to be John Stuart, who wanted to invest in local property to help raise the quality of some of the older commercial sites in Elkford. As John's closest friend, cousin, and sometimes business partner, Matt toured the building with John before he bought it and a couple of times during renovation. Finding where Mrs. Phillips lived based on the information Meredith provided wouldn't have been difficult given the resources available to Matt, but it had been child's play once he realized his cousin owned the building. One phone call after his last visit to the diner provided him with the apartment number, phone number, and full names of Mrs. Phillips and her waitress-granddaughter-roommate.

Matt adjusted the lapels of his impeccable suitcoat and entered the building, taking the steps to the second-floor two at a time. He turned left at the top of the stairs and walked down the brightly lit hallway to apartment 205. He raised his hand, rapped on the door, and stepped back a couple of feet to wait. After a full minute, he heard the bolt draw, and the door opened a few inches.

"Mrs. Phillips? I'm Mr. Hunter. Someone from the building's management company called you earlier to say I'd like to stop in and speak to you?" Matt tried to sound reassuring to the elderly lady.

"Yes, hold on a moment, Mr. Hunter." She pushed the door almost closed, and Matt heard her remove the chain. She opened it wider, and he got his first glimpse of Mrs. Phillips and the inside of the apartment. "I'm a bit confused still about what you want to discuss, but please come in, and I'll try to listen closer and understand. My granddaughter should be home soon. She'll help me understand better." She toddled back into the apartment after beckoning Matt to follow her. "I'm sorry I'm a little slow nowadays to grasp things. I used to be quite sharp in my day, but I'm afraid my mind isn't what it used to be."

"I think we all slow down a little as we age, Mrs. Phillips. I'm sure you deserve to take your time now. I'm in no hurry. We can talk as long as we need to if you're up to visiting a little while." Matt wanted to be as reassuring as possible after learning Mrs. Phillips' actual health issue was the beginning of some form of dementia, not the heart or foot problems Meredith guessed.

"Please sit down, Mr. Hunter. May I get you anything to drink? A glass of tea or a soft drink or a cup of coffee? I don't have any coffee made, but I can make some in just a few minutes." Mrs. Phillips took a couple of steps toward what Matt thought was her kitchen.

"No, thank you, Mrs. Phillips. I don't need anything at all. Please don't feel you need to wait on me. I'm imposing enough on you this evening as it is." Matt hated he misled her about the reason for his visit, or rather had her misled by Vicky who placed the earlier call for him. The idea that Mrs. Phillips felt confused by what was meant to be a somewhat muddled reason for the management company sending someone to speak with her this evening didn't help him feel any better. He hoped he would receive forgiveness in the end for the means he used to finagle a private conversation with her granddaughter.

Mrs. Phillips sat down in her chair across from the one Matt took. "Now, please explain to me the problem with my apartment. Are we behind on the rent? I'm sure Laura mails it on time every month. Perhaps a check got lost in the mail?"

"No, ma'am, there's no problem with your rent payment or anything else. You and your granddaughter are model tenants." Matt's guilt level rose another notch. "Mrs. Phillips, will your granddaughter be home soon?"

"Laura? Yes, she should be. She doesn't have class tonight. She worked at the diner today. She's a waitress there, just a few blocks away. Let me see, I have a note somewhere." Mrs. Phillips fumbled through a couple of magazines on the table next to her chair. "Laura always leaves me a note which says where she will be and when. Ah, here it is. She worked until four o'clock then planned to go to the library. Laura likes to read, so she goes there almost every week. She had two books due today. She'll get at least one new one to read while she's there. Then she will stop at the grocer's near here to get a few things. We go on Sunday afternoon in the car to get groceries and other things, but Laura stops a couple of times a week at the local grocer to pick up fresh fruit and vegetables. Oh, but you asked if she would be home soon. Let me see."

Mrs. Phillips read the note through again and looked up at the clock on the wall. "Laura should be here in a quarter hour. Perhaps a little later if it takes her longer than expected to choose a book. Is that too long for you to wait to speak to her? Did she do something wrong?"

"No, ma'am, I've heard nothing but good things about her. That's why I wanted to speak to her. A friend of mine met her and recommended I talk to her. You see, I don't actually work for the company that owns your building." Mrs. Phillips looked alarmed, and Matt hurried to allay her fears that he was some sort of conman. "I work for a company with a close connection to the one that owns your building." The older woman looked less anxious but still unsettled, and Matt decided he must come clean with her. "Mrs. Phillips, my name is Matt Hunter. Your granddaughter came to see me about a week ago, but I never got to meet her because someone who works for me didn't do his job and pass along that information to me. Instead, she was treated poorly and left the hotel upset, quite understandably."

"Oh my, you work at that hotel?" Mrs. Phillips' hand flew to cover her mouth. "Laura didn't tell me what happened, but she was very excited about the chance to interview at such a prestigious place. Then she came home upset and wouldn't tell me anything except she didn't get the job."

"She has every right to be upset at the way she was treated. I've spent the last week trying to find out who she is and where to find her. You see, there's no question about her being hired. It's a question of whether or not she's willing to work for Chestnut Cove Inns. I came here to apologize for the way she was treated and to convince her to give us another chance to hire her."

"Oh, that's very kind of you. I'm sure your hotel would be a better place to work than the diner, but I would hate for her to work somewhere she isn't treated well no matter how nice it is otherwise." Mrs. Phillips gave Matt a hard look, causing him to doubt whether her dementia was too severe in spite of the bit of dithering he observed so far.

"No, ma'am, there won't be any ill treatment of her tolerated. I already spoke to the young man responsible for that, and he is aware he must be on his best behavior from now on." Matt thought Mrs. Phillips' features relaxed a bit with his reassurance.

"I'm still a little confused about how my apartment is involved in all this?"

"It isn't, Mrs. Phillips. I'm afraid I used it as a bit of subterfuge to invent a reason to come see you and your Laura. The connection is that when I finally learned her name and where she lived, I realized her apartment was in a building owned by JSS Holdings. John and Sandra Stuart own JSS Holdings. John Stuart is also president of the Chestnut Cove Inns hotel chain, and I'm the manager of the CCI hotel here in Elkford and Executive Vice President for Hotel Operations for the chain." He reached into his coat pocket and pulled out an embossed business card and handed it to her. "John and Sandra are also my closest friends. I used those connections to find out how to contact you and your granddaughter and to gain an audience with you this afternoon. As I've said, I wasn't trying to deceive you. I just needed a way to convince you to meet with me here and give me the chance to speak to her in private to apologize and try to convince her to come to work at the hotel."

"It seems to me you tried very hard to deceive me, though not with any malice."

Matt grinned at her. "I can't argue with your reasoning."

"I suspect this was hardly the first time you've deliberately deceived someone, Mr. Hunter. You do it very well. I hope it's usually done with such altruistic intent." Mrs. Phillips' penetrating stare almost made Matt uncomfortable. Almost.

"I try my best, Mrs. Phillips." He tried to look contrite but was saved from the unusual effort when the rattling of a key in the door distracted both. It opened, and the young woman Matt saw three days earlier at the diner walked into the small living room.

"Who are you?" Laura demanded.

Matt could see her mind working as if searching for some missing detail. He stood and reached into his coat from which he drew out a manila envelope. "Hello, Miss Maddox. I'm Matt Hunter." She looked confused at the name, not quite making the connection yet. Matt realized she had no idea what his last name was, having heard him referred to only as Matt. He opened the envelope and extracted the notepaper with the napkin taped to it. When he held it up for her to see, her mouth fell open. "Miss Maddox, I'm sorry about your treatment last week when you came to the hotel. I'd like to speak to you now if that's acceptable to you and your grandmother."

When Laura found her voice again, she asked, "You're the Matt the note referred to?"

"Yes, I am, and I'd like to fulfill the direction I was given in this note. I was instructed to hire you, and I'm here to do so if you're still interested. I'm offering you a job at Chestnut Cove Inn starting as soon as you can give your notice at Fred's Diner."

Laura waved for Matt to sit back down, and she took a seat on the small sofa near her grandmother. "Um, exactly what kind of job would it be? I have some constraints with hours I can work. I need to be able to do some things for my grandmother. Also, I'm taking a class a couple of nights a week. I'd like to continue that."

Matt resumed his seat and breathed a sigh of relief, his posture more relaxed than before. If Laura's primary concerns were adjusting her hours around her grandmother's needs and continuing her education, he could accommodate those to bring her aboard. "First, let me assure you we'll work with you on your schedule both when you need to be off to do something for your grandmother and when you need to attend class. We encourage our employees to get as much education as they want and try to work with them to ensure they can attend their classes.

"As for what your job would be, I'd like for you to work the reception desk as a clerk, but we want to figure out where you feel you fit best. I understand you're taking a bookkeeping class right now, so I assume you have an interest in some sort of business career down the road, and we can give you that. We'll also work you into a short rotation of other jobs so you can learn a little about all the operations of the hotel. You already know about being a waitress, but we'd have you spend part of a day working in our restaurant as a waitress, maybe fill in for an hour or two as hostess, and also spend a little time shadowing the head chef. We'd do something similar with housekeeping, maintenance, security, the event planners, and the concierge.

"Once you've learned a little about all the hotel's parts, we'll sit down and talk about where you fit best. We'll decide together. We won't try to put you in a job we think you do well but isn't something you enjoy. If you don't like what you're doing, it will show eventually, which isn't good for either you or the hotel. However, I think you'd be great up front at the desk as soon as you have a chance to learn the basics of the hotel. Based on what I know of you so far, I think you'd make an outstanding assistant manager in a couple of years."

Laura's eyes widened. "Assistant manager? I don't know anything about managing a hotel. I'd never even set foot in your hotel until last week. I've only stayed in a hotel–no, not a hotel, a motel–a few times in my life. I've never stayed in anything like Chestnut Cove Inn. How could I become an assistant manager in a couple of years? What does an assistant manager even do?"

Matt flashed a devilish grin. "They run the hotel for me. I teach them how to run it, and then I wander out to visit nice older ladies and con them into letting me stay to chat and make job offers to their granddaughters."

Laura laughed. Then her eyes widened, and she gasped, "I saw you in the diner."

"Yes," Matt said with a chuckle. "I've visited it three times, though only once when you were there. It took me a few days to run down the right diner and find you. Not so long once I discovered your friend Meredith could be so helpfully chatty. She saved me a good day's work at least."

"She talks constantly about things she shouldn't, but she means well," Laura said, her affection for her friend obvious. At last, she approached the one question Matt wouldn't answer. "The napkin...the lady who wrote the note on it. Do you know who she is? She didn't sign it. Well, you must know her because you took it pretty seriously to spend so much time and effort to find me. Getting a note about hiring someone written on a paper napkin is unorthodox. I haven't seen her in the diner since she gave me the note. I was worried about what I'd say to her if she came in after...after I went to the hotel and things didn't go well."

A smile flitted across Matt's face. "Yes, I know her, and unorthodox is a perfect description."

~~~

Later in the evening in a more upscale part of Elkford, Jeanette and Winston Hathaway arrived home from yet another dinner at the country club. John Stuart's mother lived to socialize with her perceived peers. Tonight, she had suffered through an unexpected warm snap in order to show off her latest acquisition. A recent trip to Woodbury's mall netted her a mink wrap courtesy of her husband's generosity, though he hadn't been aware of his largess until just before they departed for the club.

Jeanette allowed Tanya to remove the new wrap and start down the hall with it before calling after the retreating maid-cum-cook, "Tanya, please bring coffee into the sitting room."

"Yes, ma'am. Just let me put this away." Tanya continued down the hall toward Jeanette's bedroom with the fur wrap.

By the time Jeanette caught up with Winston, he already occupied his usual chair in the sitting room, which formerly served as a bedroom for one of his grandchildren. For now, Jeanette had converted it into a sitting room to allow them to maintain a separate room to, well, sit, other than the more formal living room. "Winston, do you want the newspaper?"

Tanya's footsteps hustled past the door headed toward the kitchen as the man answered his wife's inquiry without lowering his golf magazine. "No, I read it this afternoon at the office. There was nothing of interest in it. You may read it if you like."

Jeanette lowered herself onto her usual chair across from him, shifted herself to her perceived correct angle, crossed her legs, and assumed a stately posture. When settled upon her throne, she looked around for their daily correspondence. "Tanya, bring me today's newspaper and mail."

A few seconds later, Tanya's footsteps could be heard echoing down the hall before her head popped into the sitting room. "You called, Mrs. Hathaway?"

"Yes, where is our coffee?"

"I was just getting it, ma'am."

"Well hurry up about it. Mr. Hathaway is ready for it, aren't you, Winston?"

Winston looked up from his perusal of his magazine. "Hmm? Oh, yes, coffee."

"I'll be right back with it, ma'am." Tanya took two steps down the hall toward the kitchen before Jeanette called her back.

"Tanya, bring me the mail and the newspaper while you're here." Jeanette leaned back and picked up her reading glasses case she kept tucked between the cushion and stuffed arm of her chair.

Tanya reappeared and walked to the small table at the end of the room where she had been instructed to deposit each day's correspondence. Picking up the small stack, she brought it to Jeanette.

"Oh, just put it all on the coffee table for now, Tanya, and do hurry with the coffee."

The maid set the newspaper and few pieces of mail on the coffee table within easy reach of her mistress. "I'll be right back with it, Mrs. Hathaway." Tanya hurried out again.

When the coffee was finally delivered and served, Jeanette allowed Tanya to retreat for a time and sat back in her chair to sip the fancy imported blend she discovered a couple of weeks earlier. "Winston, your coffee is getting cold."

"Hmm, oh, yes." Winston tossed aside his magazine and leaned forward to take his cup from the tray. When he took a sip, he grimaced. "Are we still drinking this awful swill?"

Jeanette stared hard at him. "It is not awful. It is the very thing they are drinking on the continent now." She continued sipping her own in silence. Winston set his full cup back on the tray and picked up his magazine again.

When she finished her coffee, Jeanette placed her cup back on the tray and picked up the newspaper. She laid aside the sports, business, and classified sections and spent the next twenty minutes perusing the local news, obituaries, and any social articles she could find. Sadly for Jeanette, nothing in the way of true society pages existed any longer.

She laid the sections she had been reading on the tray next to the coffee for Tanya to take away later and picked up the mail. There were two bills, which she laid back on the table. Winston would take care of those.

Jeanette turned her attention to the one civilized letter in the day's mail. She didn't recognize the return address, which listed no name, but it bore a French address and postmark. A cold gnawing began in the pit of her stomach. She almost tossed the letter onto the tray unopened, but it was possible it came from some old friend who happened to be in France.

Jeanette loved France. Actually, she loved Europe in general but Paris most of all. Her love for it had been one reason she and her mother set about attracting a suitable husband who could indulge her love of travel to places like Paris, and they succeeded marvelously the first time. She and her first husband, Carlisle Stuart, traveled there several times before the war. They took John once when he was a baby.

Then the war broke out. Carlisle had been adamant to sign up and do his part. His parents supported his decision, so Jeanette and little John were left to live in the old family home, Chestnut Cove, with Carlisle's parents, Alistair and Kathryn Stuart, while Carlisle went off to war. That wasn't too bad in many regards, for Jeanette's love for the Stuart estate had been almost as much a reason for her to capture Carlisle as his ability to take her to Europe each year until the war broke out on the continent. Only Kathryn McDougal Stuart's disapproval of Jeanette's every action cast a shadow on her enjoyment of those years when Carlisle was away at war.

When the war ended, Carlisle came home both physically and mentally injured, suffering from the effects of a terrible airplane crash followed by capture behind enemy lines and imprisonment for almost a year. There had been no more trips to Europe for Jeanette; both Alistair and Carlisle would be dead within five years of the war's end.

A little over a year after Carlisle's death, Jeanette married Winston Hathaway, scion of another prominent family. Two major disappointments followed soon after her remarriage. First, Jeanette learned Winston's family had lived beyond their means for some time, with her new husband among the worst offenders. There would be no Hathaway money coming to him in the future. He also lost his position at his former father-in-law's bank in Woodbury when he unceremoniously dumped Hortense, his first wife, to pursue the newly-widowed Jeanette.

Jeanette's second major disappointment would be an even bigger blow. She had expected she and her new husband and John would live together in the Stuart's grand old mansion with John's grandmother, Kathryn Stuart, but the old dragon had been of a different mind. The newlyweds returned from their honeymoon to find Jeanette's things removed to a small cottage on the Stuart estate far from the main house. The old woman decreed it was Winston's duty, not hers, to provide for his new wife as well as for his daughter, Claudine, from his previous marriage and to pay the cost of the alimony he owed Hortense. While Mrs. Stuart would allow them to live on the estate, Winston would need to find a job to otherwise provide for his family.

It was only because of John they were even allowed to live in a cottage on the Stuart estate. Thirteen-year-old John retained a room in his grandmother's home in addition to one in the cottage with his mother and stepfather. His grandmother decreed he could come and go between the two houses at his own discretion, for his grandmother doted on him as much as she disliked his mother. Jeanette resented how the older woman made such a decision regarding John without consulting his surviving parent.

On the other hand, it had left her with a glimmer of hope she would regain favor and one day return to live in the larger house. John had been Kathryn and Alistair's sole living descendent at the time. At the least, Jeanette had been positive her son would inherit the home and choose to live in it full-time after his grandmother died. Then Jeanette had planned to return to it and reign as its mistress.

Unfortunately, the old woman thwarted that plan also. When Kathryn McDougal Stuart died eight years later, her will stipulated that the Stuart estate be divided in half after a few bequests to faithful staff, close friends, and favorite charities. She left John half of the residual. The other half was left in trust for his three-year-old daughter. Her half included the Chestnut Cove estate and much of the Stuart property.

Moreover, control of the child's trust went not to John Stuart, whom Jeanette was sure would have allowed her to move into the mansion even though he hadn't wanted it himself. Neither did control go to the evil woman who tricked John into marriage when he was barely eighteen by claiming to be pregnant with his baby. Instead, the dragon left stewardship of the little girl's trust to John's second cousin, grandson of Kathryn's sister and John's closest friend. He was also the child's godfather. Jeanette hated Matt Hunter almost as much as she had hated her former mother-in-law.

She threw the unopened letter onto the table. "Winston, we need to eat dinner at the club soon with Hoyt. Have you seen him lately?"

Winston, roused from an almost nap, sat up. "Hoyt? No, not recently. I spoke to him on the phone a couple of weeks ago. He's been busy with work. I can phone him Monday to see if he's available for dinner sometime next week."

"Please do. We've been remiss in keeping in touch with him since Paula left to spend time at her sister's." When her husband made no further reply, Jeanette plowed onward toward her current objective. "Winston, I believe it's time to broach the subject of you being placed on the board of directors of the hotel again. Hoyt would be an excellent ally to discuss the matter with John and ensure he knows how much value your insight would bring to the management of the company. After all, you are John's stepfather and the only father figure he has known for nearly thirty years."

"If you think that's wise, Jeanette, by all means discuss it with Hoyt. You know how much I think of the boy and how much I am always willing to provide him with any guidance he might need."

For more than twenty years, Jeanette felt she had been forced to beg her son for funds for the least little thing. He reminded her he provided them with a home and Winston with a job and that should be enough. John had grudgingly hired his stepfather to work at JSS Holdings a number of years ago after the man lost yet another bank job. However, since John expanded his hotel business and created a board of directors to help oversee it, he had evaded her attempts to get him to put his stepfather on the board. It was insulting John didn't see how useful Winston's advice would be in advancing the hotel. Moreover, it was degrading for John to consider him only worthy of being a paid employee at his smaller business instead of a valued voice of sage advice for the company which supported John's family along with many others and was considered the jewel of Elkford.

"Yes, unfortunately he has been averse to listen to your advice in most cases and unwilling to heed it on the rare occasions he's listened." Jeanette's mien took on the look of someone who had bitten into a particularly bitter persimmon. "The only people he ever listens to are that woman he married and his cousin."

"Those two and the other one." Winston knew better than to name the third.

Jeanette snatched up the unopened letter from the table and ripped it open. She was disappointed but unsurprised when only one small item fluttered into her lap from the destroyed envelope; in spite of herself, she picked up and unfolded the newspaper clipping. She tried to ignore the photo at the top and simply scan the article, which appeared to have been clipped from the society page in some French tabloid.

Her French wasn't very good, but it was sufficient to determine the article described some exclusive party held the previous month in Paris. It was very much in keeping with several similar clippings she received anonymously in the last few years from Paris, Rome, Milan, London, and Monte Carlo. They were always about some exclusive event attended by wealthy and connected young men and women with one particular young woman featured prominently. The same young woman who sent the clipping. The same young woman who knew Jeanette adored Europe and had been denied the funds by John to return there for more than twenty years.

Jeanette wadded up the clipping and threw it across the room. Her son and the vile woman he married insisted on naming their first-born child after his paternal grandmother, and the younger Kathryn Stuart did all she could to live up to the old dragon's name including tormenting Jeanette in a style which would have made the elder Kathryn proud.

# Chapter 7

*Saturday, May 19, 1979*

Laura tried to stifle a yawn as she made the rounds of the diner refilling the coffee cups of the early-morning patrons. Although she managed to get minimal sleep the night before, she was glad it was her turn to work the Saturday morning shift with Meredith. The work provided a welcome distraction from her thoughts.

She lay awake in bed until late the previous night processing the events of the evening. She smiled when she recalled her grandmother's forwardness in pointing out to Matt Hunter that while he had offered Laura a job, he hadn't told her how much he would pay her. Matt apologized for being remiss and pulled out one of his business cards, turned it over, and wrote an amount on the back before passing the card to Laura. It was almost thirty percent more than she made at Fred's in wages and tips, and Matt explained she would receive annual raises based both on the cost of living and on her performance, something that would not happen at Fred's. She would also get an increase when–if–she received a promotion to assistant manager or some other position with more responsibility.

Despite the improvements in salary, job security, and potential for advancement Matt offered her, she had asked for the opportunity to think it over and discuss it with her grandmother. He agreed she should take time to consider things and told her to call him with any questions.

He also gave her the name and phone number of someone in the corporate office to contact if she had any questions and couldn't reach him at the hotel. He looked a little chagrined when her grandmother asked if she was the same lady who called earlier to set up Matt's visit, thus participating in his little charade. He admitted as much with a slight blush but hastened to insist Vicky only followed his instructions and among her multiplicity of talents was dealing with the personnel department when Matt circumvented their process to hire someone. That caused yet another small amount of concern on Laura's part, but Matt insisted he held full authority to hire and fire at his hotel with only a top corporate officer capable of overruling him, which had never happened.

Matt left, and Laura confessed the details of her visit to the hotel to her grandmother. Over dinner, they discussed the merits of accepting Matt's job offer and tried to think of any negatives involved in it. So far, neither could think of any issues other than the few blocks farther for Laura to walk to CCI, but the increased pay would allow them to buy a better car she could drive every day before too long. She would mull over the offer for the rest of the weekend before making a final decision.

"Hey, you working this morning, or are you gonna let Meredith cover the whole place?" Herb snapped. He gestured at a couple who had entered and seated themselves at booth nine.

"I'm sorry, Herb." Laura hurried to greet them and take their order. "Good morning. What can I get you? Coffee to start with?"

"Yes, please," the woman said. Laura, still holding the coffeepot, filled the woman's cup.

"For me, too," her husband said. "We'll need a couple of minutes to decide what we want to eat."

Laura filled his cup also. "OK, I'll be back to check on you in a few minutes." She offered them a bright smile before she hurried back behind the counter. "We need more coffee, Herb. Do you want me to make some?"

"No, you know I always make it. Just check on the rest of the customers," Herb grumbled. "Try to stay awake this morning. I expect today to be busy, and I need a waitress who's alert."

As Laura ducked back out from behind the counter to check on her customers, she remembered what the doorman said about everybody liking Matt. So far, she sure liked him better than Herb, and she was one step closer to being sure she would accept Matt's job offer.

~~~

A speeding car pulled out from behind and passed Craig's slower vehicle. He admired the navy-blue Dino until it roared out of sight around a curve. Then he spotted a safe place to pull off the road ahead and eased his car off the pavement. He picked up the paper with directions to the Stuart home from the seat beside him to check the distance against the odometer reading from his last turn: four-and-a-half miles to go. He had found little time to explore Elkford and the surrounding area during his first three weeks in town. Today he made some time. He left his new apartment an hour early so he could investigate areas off the main highway leading into the mountains while he made his way to the Stuart home, which lay in that direction.

However, now it was time to quit his sightseeing and drive to his new boss's house. While only an informal dinner with Mr. and Mrs. Stuart and Matt Hunter, Craig didn't want to leave a bad impression by showing up ten or fifteen minutes late. He checked the flowers which lay on the front passenger seat, a gift for Mrs. Stuart. He wanted them to arrive in good shape.

Pulling back onto the highway, Craig continued onward until he reached his turn. A long driveway meandered through a stand of pines, and he drove along it slowly for a few hundred feet until he came into a clearing of about an acre. In the center of the open area stood a nice, well-kept, two-story brick home. It wasn't overly large but sufficient to comfortably hold a family with four children. A light-blue Lotus Elan was parked on the curved driveway in front of the house. Craig had seen the

Lotus before in the parking deck at CCI. He stopped beside it and picked up the flowers from the seat of his car.

Before he reached the top of the front steps, the door opened, and Matt Hunter waved him inside. "Hey, Craig. Did you have any problem finding this place?"

Craig stopped in the doorway to look at the view of the mountains. "No, none at all. I left a little early to explore out this way. It's beautiful. I can see why the Stuarts live out here."

"Yes, it's always beautiful no matter the season. During some parts of the year, it's breathtaking."

Sandra entered the hallway behind Matt. "Hi, Craig, come on in."

"Thank you, Mrs. Stuart." Craig nodded his head at her and held out the flowers. "These are for you. Thank you for inviting me tonight."

"Oh, those are lovely, Craig. Thank you, and it's Sandra, please. John is on the patio manning the grill if you two want to go on out there to chat while I finish getting my part ready in here. Matt, would you show him through to the back?"

"Of course, Sandra. Come on, Craig. We'll go supervise the boss while he grills our steaks. He still thinks he can grill better than I can even though I've been proving him wrong for at least twenty years. Right, Sandra?" Matt called to her retreating form.

"Still not getting into the middle of that argument, Matt," she replied before disappearing in the direction of the kitchen. Matt grinned and gestured for Craig to follow him.

~~~

An hour later, Sandra had just taken the last two dessert plates into the kitchen when she heard the front door open and close. "Girls, come in here a minute," she called, and daughters Maggie and Chris appeared at the kitchen door.

"Hi, Mom. Is there dessert?" Maggie asked.

"Yes, there's strawberry shortcake. I'll get you some once the men move into the study. Go into the dining room and meet Mr. Fielder. Then you can go upstairs but remember to be quiet tonight while we have a guest."

"Yes, ma'am. Do you want us to help clean up in the kitchen?" twelve-year-old Chris asked. Maggie shot her younger sister a withering look.

"No, I'm just putting things in the dishwasher, and I'm almost done with that, but thank you for offering." Sandra waved the girls toward the door. "Go on in there."

The girls did as directed and walked through into the adjacent dining room. Chris went straight to Matt and wrapped her arms around his neck. "Hi, Uncle Matt."

"Hi, Chrissie," he said as he returned the hug. "Did you go riding today?"

"No, but I hope to go tomorrow." She stepped back when an impatient Maggie nudged her.

"Hi, Uncle Matt," Maggie said as she gave him a more subdued greeting.

"Hey, Maggie, how are you?"

"I'm OK. I'll be glad when school is out. Maybe then Mom and Dad will start looking for a car for me." She shot her father, seated on the other side of Matt, a quick look before adding, "You remember my birthday is less than a month away, don't you?"

Matt managed to suppress a laugh. "I'm glad you reminded me of that. I wouldn't want to forget your sixteenth birthday."

Aware of where the current discussion would lead if left unchecked, John interrupted before there could be any further mention of cars and Maggie's birthday. "Girls, this is Craig Fielder. He started working at the headquarters a couple of weeks ago. Craig, these are our two youngest children, Maggie and Chris," John said, pointing at each girl in turn.

Craig smiled and said, "Hello, girls, it's nice to meet you."

"It's nice to meet you, too, Mr. Fielder," Maggie said with muted enthusiasm. She had not failed to notice her attempt to bring up the subject of her sixteenth birthday and her corresponding need for a new car had been aborted by her father.

Chris added, "Yes, it's nice to meet you. Are you the new finance manager?"

"Why, yes, I am," Craig said. "You must keep up with the business."

"I try, but it's hard with schoolwork and chores and riding. Do you like horses?"

"I have ridden some, though it's been a few years. I heard there is quite a nice riding stable out this way the CCI concierge recommends to hotel guests looking for a way to enjoy the mountains other than by hiking or driving."

Before Chris could begin an expository monologue on the recommended stables, which not coincidentally happened to be where her horse was kept and where she usually rode, John intervened. "Chris, maybe we can arrange for Mr. Fielder to go riding with us before long, and you can fill him in on all the best trails. Run along upstairs and do a little studying. You both have final exams coming up."

"Yes, sir," Chris said. Maggie, who had remained sulking in the background once her car conversation with Matt had been curtailed, rolled her eyes at the idea of studying on a Saturday night. She exited the dining room without further acknowledgement of anyone. Chris bid Craig and Matt goodnight and followed her older sister out of the room.

A loving smile graced John's lips as he watched the girls depart. "If Chris got started talking about horses, we wouldn't get to talk about anything else tonight. She loves to ride, and she's learned a good bit about taking care of her horse."

Craig turned back to John and said, "They must be bright girls." John nodded in acknowledgement. "Your son attends Coughton Tech?"

"Yes, he's finishing his freshman year. He's majoring in business, but I'm not sure his heart is in it. I think it's more a matter of what he thinks he should major in since he expects to work in the hotel headquarters when he graduates."

Matt added, "He's worked at the hotel every summer since he was old enough, and he's a smart, hardworking kid. He's learned a good bit working as a bellhop and lifeguard and observing how we do things."

"I believe I saw his portrait hanging in your office?" Craig asked.

"Yes," John said. "We had both Doug and KD sit for portraits when they graduated from high school. He's home from college this weekend, but he's out this evening with his friends. You'll meet him this summer when he's working in the office."

Sandra reentered the dining room with the coffeepot. "Does anyone need more?"

Once cups were refilled, John suggested they retire to his study to discuss in more detail the financial data on which Craig had been working. The three men settled comfortably with Matt and Craig each seated on one of the leather armchairs and John on the small sofa for a few minutes of pleasantries before they got down to business. Craig realized Matt and John were waiting for Sandra to join them. He had learned quickly that Sandra still knew a great deal about the inner workings of the hotel and, along with Matt, was among John's closest advisors.

An avid car enthusiast, Craig seized the opportunity to shift the conversation in that direction. Turning to Matt, he asked, "Is that your Lotus out front? I've seen it in the parking deck at the hotel."

"Yes, she's mine. One of my many vices." Matt grinned at John who rolled his eyes at his cousin.

"Maybe your worst vice besides corrupting my children," John said with a laugh. "Speaking of which, do not think about buying Maggie a car for her birthday. She wasn't even a little subtle earlier."

Sandra entered the study in time to hear John's admonishment. She took a seat next to her husband and gave Matt a hard stare. "Seriously, Matt. No car for her. You know as well as we do she is not ready to handle any kind of sports car. She isn't even ready to handle my Town Car. She needs something small and underpowered, assuming she can pass her driving test."

"I promise. It isn't like I have a habit of buying expensive sports cars for your children when they turn sixteen." Matt tried to look offended when John and Sandra burst out laughing.

"No, you're only two for two so far," John reminded him. "At least KD and Doug are good drivers."

"Oh no, now let's be fair. I bought KD's car with her own trust fund money in consultation with her. KD bought Doug his car from her trust fund. I simply provided advice and helped facilitate the purchase." Matt shifted to trying to look innocent but failed at that, too.

"You had control of the trust fund when she turned sixteen, not KD. You could have said no. I admit you couldn't have done much by the time Doug turned sixteen, but you could have discouraged her from buying him a Corvette." John tried to look cross with his cousin, but the twitch at the corner of his mouth belied his attempt.

Matt leaned back in his chair, hands behind his head and a smug look on his face. "The last I checked, neither car had a scratch on it and neither of the kids has ever received a ticket."

John chuckled, giving up trying to cause Matt to feel any guilt for circumventing the will of the children's parents. "Neither of them may ever get a speeding ticket. They can outrun the police cruisers without breathing hard. I'm more worried about them wrapping one around a tree. At least they both have other more reasonable vehicles to drive so they aren't always driving around in those high-powered sports cars."

Matt's chest puffed out in pride. "Don't worry, John. They're both great drivers. I taught them to handle those cars as a condition of buying them."

John saw his opening and took his turn to flash a smug grin. "Ah, so you admit you had some control over their purchase."

All four adults laughed as Matt sought a way to backpedal out of his corner.

~~~

*Sunday, May 20, 1979*

The stables remained almost pitch-black inside as the skies to the east began to lighten. The horses breathing softly in their stalls and the wind rustling the leaves of the oaks and hickories, which provided a thick canopy for the small compound, made the only sounds. The small stable, a rustic cabin, a couple of other outbuildings, and nearby a modified boathouse were so secluded that few people knew they existed; even fewer gained admittance. Only a trusted caretaker and a handful of close friends and family were ever granted access, and those on a limited basis. This provided a retreat from the madness of the rest of the world for the owner. Here, one could sit and think and relax without any intrusion except from nature.

Quiet footsteps approached the stables. The door creaked open. The soft sounds and the accompanying smell of apples roused the horses from their slumber. They knew the meaning of the dawn appearance. The only question was who would accompany their owner on an early morning outing.

In turn, each horse received its treat and a little attention. When all had been greeted, the owner retrieved a saddle and other tack from the tack room and led Zephyr from his stall. A short time later, rider and horse were winding their way up the mountain trail behind the cabin. The rider allowed Zephyr to set his own pace for a while, and he meandered through the trees and undergrowth, picking his way along a well-known if obscure path. When they reached an open meadow, horse and rider agreed it was time for a little more speed. A Friesian-Thoroughbred cross, Zephyr was born to run, and he sprinted for nearly half a mile across the lush green field until he came to a brook which led down to the Wolf River below them. Here, he was given the opportunity to quench the thirst he developed after his climb and sprint. Once satiated, they crossed the stream and entered more woodland not far on the other side.

After another climb, they reached the summit where another clearing gave a stunning view of the mountains to the north, west, and south. The foothills and the town of Elkford to the east lay hidden behind the tree line. His owner dismounted and allowed Zephyr to graze. The horse knew the routine well and would remain close by without the need to restrain him. His owner walked to the shed, which made up one side of the small cabin in the middle of the clearing, and checked the water trough before entering the room on the opposite side of the cabin to wait. The sound of a motorcycle approaching ensured the wait would be a short one.

The owner scanned the perimeter of the clearing from first one window then the other as the sound of the bike grew louder. It was unlikely anyone would observe a meeting here at any time, much less at only an hour past dawn, but it was not a time to take chances.

By the time the security check was complete, the motorcycle cleared the trees which obscured the narrow driveway. The bike slowed, and the biker eased it to a halt under the shed side of the cabin. As soon as he switched off the ignition, he stood and removed his helmet, revealing a shock of blond hair. He grinned at his compatriot standing in the doorway of the cabin and took a step in that direction for a warm greeting.

Instead, a thick, manila envelope was thrust toward him along with terse instructions. "Deliver this, but make sure nobody sees you do it. Use the private entrance so security won't see you on camera."

The biker took the envelope and tucked it inside his jacket. "I know the drill. I'll be careful." His grin returned. "Now may I have my hug?" The wry smile he received was all the reply he needed. "Promise when this is over, you'll come home officially instead of slipping in and out of town occasionally."

"We'll see. There are some pretty nice advantages to living this way." A sharp whistle brought Zephyr trotting to his owner's side. "You need to get out of here before traffic picks up down on the main road and somebody recognizes you on your bike and wonders why you're out this way so early."

The young man nodded and climbed back onto his motorcycle. Before he restarted it, he looked up at Zephyr and his owner now sitting astride the horse. "You need to come home to stay. You've been gone long enough," he reiterated.

The rider looked down at him a moment before giving the slightest of nods. "I know. Soon." A small kick sent Zephyr off across the clearing back toward the path he ascended earlier. Once horse and rider disappeared into the tree line, the young man cranked his bike and roared back down the driveway to deliver his message.

# Chapter 8

*Monday, May 21, 1979*

Matt heard the light knock on the rear door of his office. "Come on in, Vicky." He dropped his pencil onto the spreadsheet on which he was working, glad to take a break from the eye strain following all the numbers caused. "What's up?"

Vicky entered and walked around to the front of Matt's desk to sit down. "You'd have saved me the walk over if you would answer your phone," she said with a smile. "Have you found any errors in the spreadsheet so far?"

Matt frowned at the offending telephone and stretched his arms to work out a kink in his back. "No, not yet. Everything looks good. We should have a lucrative summer based on the reservations already on the books and the usual ones we get a couple of weeks or less out. Is that why you walked all the way over here?"

"Nope, I could have waited on you to tell me that. I walked over to tell you I wasn't the first one to call you this morning only to be ignored."

"Oh? Who's looking for me that I don't want to find me?"

Matt flashed a devilish smile, and Vicky rolled her eyes in response. "Laura Maddox. She called about half an hour ago."

Matt leaned forward on his desk in anticipation. "And? She accepted the job?"

"Yep, she wanted to know what she needed to do to accept. She's working every day this week, so I told her I'd take a letter to her at Fred's Diner for her to sign acknowledging the details of the offer and a start date. I plan to leave from here to drive over there. After what you told me about it, I thought I'd have lunch and see for myself how bad the food is. You know I can't pass up a greasy hamburger. I talked to Geraldine about the personnel particulars and typed the letter based on what you told me about the offer you made her. I need you to sign it." She handed him the folder she was holding.

Matt took it and signed both copies of the letter–one for Laura to keep and one for her to countersign accepting the job–and handed the folder back across to Vicky. "She's good starting in two weeks?"

"Yes, we talked about what was proper. She doesn't have any other job experience except summers when she was in high school, so she wasn't sure about working out notices. She doesn't know how her boss will react. He might not care about her giving a two-week notice, but we both thought it would be best for her to offer to do so. I told her if he didn't want her to work out a notice or got mad and sent her packing to call and we'd get her started here earlier."

"Good. If she can start sooner, that will be fine. Otherwise, we'll be ready for her to start on June fourth. I think she will be a great asset. She's a hardworking, responsible, bright young lady. We'll need to work with her some to ensure she can take care of her grandmother when she needs to, but that shouldn't be a problem, at least not for the short term. Her grandmother was still pretty sharp when I visited with her Friday." Vicky stood to leave, and Matt picked up his pencil again. "Let me know when you get back with the signed acceptance. I don't want anything to go wrong with getting Laura into the fold at CCI."

"Will do. Are you sure you don't want me to bring you back a burger from Fred's?" Vicky laughed, already knowing Matt's answer.

Matt blanched at the thought. "No, definitely not. I don't have your cast iron stomach. I'll stick with whatever Fleur serves for our special today. Don't get any hamburger grease on those letters," Matt called to Vicky's retreating form.

~~~

John Stuart rarely lost his composure at all, much less in a business meeting, but his patience had been tried. He stalked through the door leading into his office from the boardroom, slammed his notepad and folders down on his desk, and stopped to stare out his office window at the mountains. They had provided him with peace and solace most of his life, and today he needed at least the peace. He heard his office door close behind him.

Sandra stopped beside him and slipped her arm around his waist. "Do you want some company to talk things out or do you need some time to settle down?"

John grunted and put his arm across her shoulders. "I'm afraid talking won't do me any good right now." He remained silent for a couple of minutes. When he continued, most of his anger dissipated. "I wish I could say I'm surprised, but I was warned. The man knows no bounds."

"Yet you still aren't ready to fire him," Sandra said, completing his unstated thought.

John sighed in frustration. "I don't know. I need to think about it. He ignored specific and clear direction not to include his staff in this matter. It seems he marched right out of the first meeting when we discussed this, went straight to his office, and called in his personal favorites to discuss it with them."

"We don't know if they leaked the material to anyone, John. We don't know for sure if anyone leaked anything to anyone. All we know so far is that an old warehouse CCI expressed interest in suddenly has other people looking at it and one of them might be a competitor. What we do know is Hoyt ignored a very specific directive from you about not sharing information concerning the property."

"Yes, he did, but I'm not sure I'm ready to fire him because of this particular breach. He's good at his job, Sandra, ignoring secrecy edicts he doesn't agree with notwithstanding." He rubbed his hands across his face and took a couple of deep breaths, trying to clear his mind. "I wish this whole mess was over. I'd love for us to get away from here for a couple of weeks, but that's impossible right now."

Sandra smiled up at him. "Impossible for another few weeks, but then we plan to do exactly that."

John grimaced. "I wish the girls were out of school already so we could move up our timetable. I'd love nothing more than to take the three of you away for a trip to visit your mother in Arizona for about half the summer."

"Well, your golf game would get some benefit from that, but the business might suffer from your neglect." Sandra laughed at John's expression.

"My golf game is fine as long as I can play without thinking about work. Unfortunately, I almost always play with somebody connected to the business when I play anywhere around here, so it's pretty hard to forget about it." He huffed in frustration.

"Of course, dear. You'll do fine playing in Arizona. Only a few more weeks until we leave." Sandra slid her arms around his neck and leaned up to kiss him.

~~~

When Matt left the staff meeting, he walked in the opposite direction from John and Sandra to the east end of the building's top floor. Unlike John's office, Matt's wasn't adjacent to the boardroom, so he couldn't make a quick exit directly into his own office. He waded through the morass of managers congregated in the center of the top floor after the staff meeting. The intensity of John's anger with Hoyt had stunned most of the managers in the meeting. One or two of them hoped the matter would die because they, too, had been careless with the same data or ignored John's admonition.

Matt caught Jonah's eye and inclined his head slightly toward the eastern end of the floor with the less-traveled office suite. Jonah just blinked in recognition of Matt's direction and continued to stand with the marketing and personnel managers waiting for the elevator. When the doors opened, Jonah realized he left his pen in the boardroom and retreated there to look for it.

Two minutes later, Jonah entered the anteroom for the pair of offices on the east end of the top floor of the headquarters building. That it happened to be the location of his daughter's desk was a bonus. "Hey, Vicky, I thought I'd drop in and see how you're doing today. Is Matt treating my baby girl the way he should?"

Vicky looked around from where she was digging through a file cabinet behind her desk. "Hi, Dad. I'm great today, and yes, Matt is treating me very well. I don't get bored in this job."

"If you aren't bored in it now, just you wait until both of these offices are in full-time use." Jonah nodded toward the closed door of the office on the southeast corner of the building.

Matt stuck his head out of his office on the northeast corner. He looked toward the main door of the suite to ensure Jonah had closed it after he entered. "Ready, Jonah?"

Jonah smiled at his daughter before responding. "Yeah, I'm ready. I hope this double duty stuff ends soon. This is wearing me out." He walked into Matt's office where both men sat down at a worktable.

"Oh, it's just getting fun, Jonah." Matt grinned at his friend and passed across a manila envelope. "Vicky made copies of these for you this morning. I looked them over last night, and I think you'll like them a lot better than the last one. Oh, and it might not be double duty. It might be triple."

Jonah's eyes widened as he absorbed that tidbit, and he moaned. "Oh man, I need another job," he said before chuckling.

Both men looked up when Matt's door opened, and Vicky entered. "Fleur is on the phone. She's on the warpath with one of the restaurant suppliers. You might need to intervene."

Matt groaned. "Why did I let Pam take today off? She can handle these things without me getting involved. Jared is on duty, and he's good at the routine things, but he seems to incite chaos when he needs to handle something out of the ordinary." He leaned over to grab the receiver of his phone off his desk and punched the blinking light which indicated the call from his head chef/restaurant manager.

"What do you think, Dad? Will this be a problem job?" Vicky asked her father as he perused the papers Matt had given him.

"Well, considering the source, I doubt it. It's more suited than the other site." He looked up at Vicky and grinned. "Hey, I'm not gonna get John mad at me because you know about this stuff, am I? Not that I'm the one who let you see the information, but I don't want to get the blame for it. He was sure hot at Hoyt in the staff meeting."

Vicky laughed. "No, I'm sure you're safe. You have a couple of people to hide behind if he gets mad that I know any of what's going on."

"At least one of whom he can't fire," Jonah said with another chuckle.

"Nope," Matt chimed in as he hung up the phone. "Makes life a whole lot better when you can hide behind the one person John can't fire, doesn't it?"

~~~

What had been a trying day for John became worse when his phone buzzed late in the afternoon. He laid down his pen and punched the button to respond to the summons. "Yes, Mrs. Pierce?"

"Your mother is calling on line one, Mr. Stuart," his secretary said.

John rubbed his eyes. "All right, thank you." He started to punch the button for line one but remembered the lateness of the hour. "I don't have anything else for you to do this afternoon, so why don't you call it a day?"

"All right, Mr. Stuart, as long as you're sure."

"Yes, I'm sure. Have a good evening." He punched the button for line one. "Hello, Mother. How are you?"

"I'm well, dear. You sound a bit tired. Are you working long hours?" Jeanette's tone was pleasant, a rarity.

"As long as I need to. It's necessary to work long hours sometimes to run my business. As a matter of fact, I have a meeting I need to prepare for. Is there something you need or are you just calling to visit?" John flipped through the stacks of papers on his desk, wondering which project he could claim his meeting concerned if pressed by his mother.

"Of course I have something specific to discuss. I wouldn't interrupt you at work otherwise. I want to know what plans have been made for Margaret's sixteenth birthday. If we are to properly commemorate such an auspicious event, plans should already be in place, yet I have been told nothing. I would hope Winston and I would be included in her celebration."

John let the folders he had been sorting drop back to the desktop, and he leaned back in his chair, pinching the bridge of his nose. "Sandra handles things like that, Mother. You should call her."

Jeanette let out a very unladylike snort, which caused John to choke back laughter he knew would offend his mother. "You are well aware your wife rarely condescends to inform me of such things, much less consult with me to utilize my extensive experience in throwing proper society parties."

"Mother, Maggie doesn't want a proper society party for her sixteenth birthday. She wants to hold her party in the back room at Dilly's. It's her birthday; she gets to choose what kind of event she wants and where she wants to hold it as long as her wishes remain reasonable."

"It most certainly is not reasonable to hold such a celebration at such a place." Ah, there was the shrill tone John knew well. "Winston and I will arrange for her party to be held at the country club. I realize you refused to continue your membership for some unfathomable reason, but that does not prevent her grandparents from hosting it there for her."

"Mother, Maggie wants her party at Dilly's. She can invite her friends, and her family will attend. It will not be held at the country club." Jeanette remained silent after his pronouncement, and John thought perhaps she hung up. "Mother?"

"Have you chosen her car yet?"

John struggled to shift gears along with his mother's train of thought. "For Maggie?"

"Certainly. Your wife's older children received a car when they turned sixteen. I would expect you to ensure Margaret receives one also, and one at least equivalent to the others."

"Mother, Maggie has not shown us she is responsible enough to have her own car yet. I'm not even sure she will pass her test. Besides, Sandra and I didn't buy either KD or Doug a car when they turned sixteen. You are aware of where their cars came from."

"That is irrelevant. As Margaret's father, you must provide her with a car appropriate to her station in life. How would it look if you didn't purchase one for her when your wife's older children received one regardless of the source?"

John let the first comment pass, but he wouldn't allow the second reference to "Sandra's children" go unchallenged. "Mother, please refrain from referring to KD and Doug as Sandra's children and implying that they are not mine also. Twenty-three years has been more than enough of such insinuations from you. All four of the children to whom Sandra has given birth are mine. Do not imply that any of them are not. Am I clear?"

Jeanette plowed onward as if she didn't hear John's reprimand. "If you will not purchase Margaret a car, then you should give her something else appropriate." Without hesitating a second, Jeanette charged forward. "It is time she experienced

Europe, John. She has expressed an interest in fashion, so a trip to Paris would inspire her. I know how busy you are, so you likely wouldn't be able to leave your business for a month, but Winston and I would be happy to escort her on such a trip."

While he listened to his mother, John reached into a drawer of his desk and extracted a bottle of aspirin. With practiced ease, he opened it one-handed as he half-listened to what he understood to be the real matter she called to discuss.

"Why, to give her an appropriate celebration for her birthday equivalent to a gathering at the country club," Jeanette continued, "we could depart a few days prior to her birthday and celebrate it in Paris." She imparted the full level of enthusiasm John expected into her sudden inspiration. He pulled his coffee cup closer before popping two aspirins into his mouth and took a couple of swallows of coffee while he waited for his mother to wind down. "You could hold a small celebration with her friends and other family members before we depart. We should take Giselle also. You know how close those two are. Margaret would appreciate having a friend her age with whom to experience Europe for the first time."

John sat up straight at last, determined to put a stop to the extravagant plan. "No, Mother, Maggie is not going to Europe this summer, and I am not paying to send you and Winston there either and certainly not Giselle. All of you will eat at our expense for Maggie's birthday if you choose to attend her party at Dilly's. There will be no car, and there will be no trip to Europe. If you and Winston would like to go to Europe, Winston gets paid enough to afford the trip if you cut back on other expenses. I know how much he makes since I pay him."

When Jeanette spoke again, John felt the chill in her voice. "I will attend Margaret's celebration regardless of its location because she is my granddaughter. I only wish I could make up for the intolerable difference in status between her and those older children. You have afforded both of those children an expensive university education, one of whom spends all her time gallivanting around the world wasting her life and her ill-gotten fortune. I still find it intolerable that your grandmother made such a distinction as to give one child so much and the others nothing."

John's patience reached its end for the day, and he replied as sharply as he ever did to his mother. "The other three didn't exist when Grandmother died. She left the rest of her estate to me and expected me to grow it into a sufficient inheritance for any additional children Sandra and I might have, something I believe we have done quite well." John saw movement in his doorway and waved Jonah inside. "Mother, I need to go. I have a meeting now. Sandra will call you with details of Maggie's party soon. Goodbye." Before Jeanette could reply, John hung up.

"I could have come back, John," Jonah said. "We didn't have a meeting, did we? I just dropped by to show you preliminary ideas for this new location if you were free, and Mrs. Pierce wasn't outside to ask."

John waved him inside again. "I told her to go home for the day when my mother called. No, we didn't have a meeting, but I'm glad you happened in. My mother was on a roll, and you gave me a perfect excuse to get off the phone. Pull up a chair and show me what you've come up with so far."

# Chapter 9

Boyd Temples, deputy head of security for CCI in Elkford, flipped another page in the hotel's surveillance system reference book. One of the cameras overlooking the front door went out the previous night, and Boyd's job included maintaining that system. First, he and Clete, head of maintenance, needed to determine if the problem lay with the camera or some part of the cables and connections carrying the video signal back to the security control room. Clete and one of his assistants were outside testing connections while Boyd checked the cable routing information in case they needed to trace it through the building.

The slightest of shadows alerted Boyd to someone passing the security office door. He looked up to see Matt in the doorway.

"You're a hard man to sneak up on, Boyd. Your reflexes are as sharp as ever." As one of a generation of CCI staff members Matt had known and trained since they were quite young, he delighted in testing them on occasion, including repeated attempts to sneak up on Boyd.

The younger man straightened and stated flatly, "Then you shouldn't have taught me to be so watchful. Don't sneak up on me too well and test whether I can take you again."

A grin spread across Matt's face. A master of a couple of martial arts styles, Matt had taught a handful of the younger generation what he knew from the time they were six or seven years old. Boyd was one of the only students to take down Matt, something neither forgot. "Just remember who you work for. If you make me look too bad, I might remember it when you're due for a raise."

Boyd tut-tutted Matt's threat. "Unlike a lot of people around here, I know exactly who I work for. Your threats don't worry me, old man." The solemn face Boyd maintained thus far broke, and he returned Matt's grin. "Did you come down here just to test my awareness this morning or did you want something in particular?"

Matt walked into the room at last and looked over the schematics on the open page of the surveillance system reference book. "I heard about the camera outage. One of the front ones?"

"Yep, nothing systemic. I'm almost positive it's a camera issue. I called the vendor in Woodbury first thing. They can get one for us at least by Thursday, maybe tomorrow if we're lucky. I should hear back from them within an hour. Clete is checking cables outside, and he'll take the camera down in a few minutes unless he finds a cable problem. We'll test to verify that's the problem before we pull the trigger on a new one. Matt, even if it's not the camera, I'd like to go ahead and order a new one to keep on hand. Assuming it is a camera failure, I hope to figure out why it failed and if it's something likely to happen again. Regardless, we could lose one again to something as simple as a kid getting lucky throwing a rock."

"I agree. Once you verify the cause, go ahead and get a replacement and a spare. Get two spares if you think that would be better. We have quite a number of them between the grounds and parking garage and a handful inside the hotel. It's possible somebody could maliciously damage several one day. At least we'd be prepared to replace a couple without waiting to get them in from Woodbury."

"All right, I'll take care of it." Boyd pulled his notepad closer and jotted down the information. "Anything else for me to handle today?"

Matt rubbed his chin while he thought about Boyd's question. "No, not today, but I want to set up a self-defense class again this summer for the staff and for any guests who might want to sit in on one like we've done the last few years. I expect to be tied up with some other projects this summer, so I won't have much time to devote to class. Would you be willing to take over and run it this time instead of acting as my assistant and filling in for me? I'd be available to help or fill in for you some, but I'd like for you to take the lead." Matt pursed his lips and added, "As you're so good at reminding me, you're one of the few people around here who can best me on rare occasion."

Boyd picked up his pen again and scribbled the date on a fresh piece of paper. "I want to remember this day," he mumbled before he looked up at Matt. "Sure, old man, I'll be happy to take the torch from you. Couple of evenings a week?"

Matt gave an exaggerated sigh. "Yes, I'll get with the event staff this week to work out activities for the next three months. We'll include the classes." He flashed a grin on the way to the door. "Just remember, you've gotten the better of me a couple of times, but I got you the last three."

"I'm ready for a rematch, old man," Boyd called after Matt. Then he picked up a thumbtack and stuck the sheet of paper with the date and Matt's admission of Boyd besting him on the corkboard above his desk.

~~~

*Wednesday, May 23, 1979*

Laura bent over a table in the now empty diner, scrubbing at a spot of some indeterminate goo while she kept a wary eye out for Herb. He had avoided talking to her as much as possible since she informed him about her job offer on Monday afternoon. Meredith hadn't heard the news until she came in Wednesday morning to fill in for Helen. Laura pulled her friend aside to inform her when both ended up in the back room for a couple of minutes. Ever since, Meredith took every opportunity to whisper her shock to Laura when Herb was busy and not paying attention. As soon as he disappeared into the back, Meredith started chattering about Laura's departure again.

"I still can't believe you're leaving Fred's," Meredith whispered.

Laura continued to wipe the table as she replied, one eye fixed on the door to the back room in case Herb reappeared. "It's still hard for me to believe, too. I'm nervous about it at times. Working there will be so different. I lie awake at night thinking about how it will work out with my grandmother and what happens if her car breaks down before I can save up enough money to get it fixed right or get a better one. I don't know what to wear either.

"I called Vicky, Mr. Hunter's assistant, yesterday to ask what to wear, and she offered to go shopping with me. I don't have much money to spend on new clothes, but I can't wear my waitress uniforms. Some of my wardrobe might be acceptable, but I'm not sure. Vicky is coming over Saturday to go through my closet with me to sort out what I can use at the hotel. Then we're going shopping to get a few more things for me to wear to start. Grandma insists I use the money we've been saving to fix the car to get new things, since I should make the money back in a month or two. Then we can repair the car. I hope it holds out that long."

Herb shuffled through the door with four packages of hamburger buns and another box of doughnuts. The girls separated before he spotted them talking, Laura moving down to wipe another table and Meredith refilling the condiment containers. Herb mumbled something unintelligible and returned to the back room.

As soon as he disappeared, Meredith turned back to Laura. "I'll stop by during the day to visit with your grandma sometimes, Laura. I love to hear her talk about how things used to be in Elkford when she first moved here."

"Thank you, Meredith, I appreciate that, but before you commit to too much, you need to go back there and talk to Herb. Tell him you'd like my spot as a full-time waitress. He knows you do a good job on the weekends and when you fill in for Helen or me. Make sure he knows you'd like to work more. Tell him you want my job." Laura offered her friend an encouraging smile and nudged her toward the door to the back.

Meredith didn't budge, digging in her heels. "I don't know. I'm not as good as you are. What if he already found somebody else to hire?"

"He just found out I'm quitting Monday afternoon. He hasn't had time to look for anybody else. He'll need to put an advertisement in the newspaper, which takes a little time and costs money." Laura dropped her voice further. "You'd save him the cost of an ad if you go tell him you want the job. He can just promote you and be done with hiring for now. He's already grumbled about not being able to afford three waitresses a couple of times. He might be happy for you and Helen to split all the work. You know there are times like right now when he doesn't need two of us working. He might like for the two of you to split the hours and both come in only during the times when he needs two waitresses."

Herb came back out again, and Laura gave Meredith another little shove. "Herb," she said, "Meredith would like to speak to you."

~~~

*Thursday, May 24, 1979*

The waiter set Hoyt's dinner plate in front of him, backed away a step, and asked, "Is there anything else I may bring you for now?" He looked from Jeanette to Winston to Hoyt.

"No," Hoyt said. "Nothing right now, but don't be slow about bringing me another one of those in a few minutes." Hoyt pointed to his glass of gin and tonic. The waiter acknowledged the expected request with a slight bow and left them to their meal. A regular for dinner at the country club since his wife left for an open-ended visit with her sister, all the waiters knew Hoyt's preferences.

The three friends chatted about various things for most of their main course before the subject of CCI arose. Hoyt wanted to discuss CCI as much as Winston and Jeanette. It had been a contentious week with John after the squabble in Monday's staff meeting, and Hoyt still refused to consider he had been in the wrong.

"Has anything happened at home to make John more edgy and tense than usual?" Hoyt directed the question at Winston but kept a close eye on Jeanette out of the corner of his eye.

"No, not that I am aware of. Do you know of anything, Jeanette?" Winston shoveled another bite of prime rib into his mouth as soon as he tossed the question to her.

She paused, finger to cheek to appear as if she needed to consider the point before answering. "Perhaps he realized what a mistake he made in marrying that woman at last. They could be having some sort of issue. However, John has yet to confide any details to me. Did something occur with the business to cause you concern about John's actions?"

Hoyt shifted in his chair to get comfortable and took another sip of his gin and tonic. "Well, he's acted a little tense this week. Actually, the last couple of weeks. In my opinion, he overreacted about a non-issue on Monday, and the whole idea underlying the matter had no basis in reason. I won't go into details since it's considered a confidential company matter, but it relates to something I discussed with Winston a couple of weeks ago. John had some ideas that didn't make any sense. I'm afraid he adheres too closely to the advice of the same people he's depended on for years, and you know who they are. One had no formal education at all above high school."

Hoyt stopped, leaned forward, and spoke again in a lower voice as if pronouncing a deep, dark secret. "And she finished under difficult circumstances, as you well know. The other received a college education, but not in anything applicable to running a hotel or any kind of business. Yet they are the only two people John listens to after all this time. You would think after his company has grown and grown for twenty years, he would bring in more professional people.

"As I've discussed with Winston before, John decided to split my department into two parts without consulting me, and he cut me out of the process to hire someone to run the half he took away from me. His wife and Matt helped select the man who got the job, and neither of them possesses any qualifications for making such a decision." Hoyt picked up his glass and polished off the last drops of liquid he could get out of it.

Jeanette saw the opening she wanted and didn't wait to find out if Winston would speak up. "Hoyt, do you not believe John and the hotel would benefit from more outside experience on the Board of Directors? I agree that a limited number of people exercise far too much influence over him and over his company. I feel they forget John owns the major share of it and should be permitted to run it as he sees fit."

"Exactly," Hoyt said with a vigorous nod, warming to the subject. "He needs to take the advice of people who know more about the business world, but he needs to choose carefully. He needs people who have his and the company's best interests at heart."

Jeanette allowed a smile to creep across her face. "Do you realize that even after all these years, John has never thought to put his own stepfather on the board of directors? Winston should be there at each board meeting to offer his stepson advice based on years of experience in the business world. Who could have John's best interests at heart more than Winston?"

"What an outstanding idea." Hoyt's voice echoed across the stately dining room. "It would be a fine thing to have my friend and Stannum Academy classmate on the CCI board. Instead of discussing hotel business with Winston here or at Winston's office like I had to with the new site John is in talks to buy right now, we could have discussed it openly at CCI. I cannot believe John never bothered to add Winston to the board."

Accepting that Winston had no intention of entering the conversation to encourage Hoyt to broach the subject with John, Jeanette plowed ahead. "Hoyt, Winston is too modest to approach John to suggest such a thing." She batted her eyes at Winston's longtime friend in encouragement. "However, if you were to make such a suggestion to John, perhaps he would consider its merit and give Winston his due."

"An excellent idea, Jeanette. Winston would be a voice of wisdom in the wilderness. He could provide John with proper guidance sadly lacking right now. I'll discuss it with John as soon as I can. Tomorrow if possible, but Tuesday after the staff meeting at the latest. Since Monday is Memorial Day, we won't meet until then. I'll speak to him no later than Tuesday." Their waiter returned to bring Hoyt a new gin and tonic, which the older man downed in three gulps.

Further discussion was delayed when Vaughn Michaelson and his current girlfriend stopped by the table. "Good evening, my friends. I hope you are well. Do all of you have your tickets for the summer ball yet? As head of the committee, I hope to see all members of the club in attendance, but especially my old Stannum Academy mates."

"Of course, Vaughn," Hoyt said. "I bought a pair of tickets last week."

Winston flushed, tugged at his collar, and swallowed hard before responding. "Uh, we're not sure of our plans for August yet, Vaughn. We'll surely buy tickets if we plan to be in town. Jeanette has her head set on Europe though, so we might be away."

A smile played around Vaughn's lips. "That would be a fine trip for the summer. I hope you can arrange it, but I know you wouldn't miss something as important as our own summer ball. I'll hold a pair of tickets for you. Let me know when you will come by my office to pick them up. I know I can count on my old Stannum friends. We've always been able to rely on one another, haven't we, Winston?"

Winston's mouth went so dry he could barely speak, but he knew he couldn't disappoint Vaughn. He nodded in agreement and reached for his wineglass. Realizing it was empty, he grabbed up his water goblet, sloshing a few drops onto his pants before it found his lips.

A pleased, catlike smile flashed across Vaughn's face, and his eyes sparkled in amusement. "Good. I'll expect you at my office sometime next week to purchase your tickets." He bowed to Jeanette and tugged at his girlfriend's hand. The young woman waved with her free hand and allowed Vaughn to lead her onward through the dining room.

While Winston gulped down half a glass of water, Hoyt began reminiscing about Stannum Academy. "Has Winston told you about some of our exploits at Stannum, Jeanette? Well, of course he has over the years. We sure got into some scrapes in our youth, didn't we, Winston? One thing about those days is we formed some tight bonds. Several of us keep in regular contact. I miss the days when we went back every fall to get together with the old team and celebrate. Coach dying put an end to a lot of that I guess, though they still hold reunions for each class for big anniversaries.

"Doesn't get the right group together though, does it, Winston? We were in the same class, but some of our other teammates we were close to were ahead or behind us. Vaughn was a year back? Maybe two? Landry was a year ahead of us. Bud Langford was in the same class as Vaughn. Course, we see him when he comes to town for meetings at the hotel. He was a good choice to run CCI Halesburg."

Hoyt leaned forward, elbows on the table, and ignored the waiter who brought new glasses of gin and tonic and wine for Hoyt and Winston, respectively. "You know what we need to do, Winston? We should plan something at the Halesburg hotel to get everyone from the old team together. It's just a few miles from Stannum. It's been far too long since we got the championship group together. Not since the year coach died. I believe that was in 1958, wasn't it? Same year those girls died. First, the girl they found in the woods, and then the girl who got run over. Strange coincidence the girl who got hit by the car in Halesburg knew John and his wife. Matt Hunter, too. For that matter, she was Matt's girlfriend, wasn't she? I've heard people speculate that's why Matt is such a confirmed bachelor; he never got over her death."

Hoyt stopped speaking while he sought to retrieve further memories of that time. A pale Winston reached for his wineglass and drained it. Both men were too lost in themselves to notice the sour look on Jeanette's face.

~~~

*Saturday, May 26, 1979*

The blue Lotus purred through Elkford, streetlights flickering off the chrome trim. When he reached the back entrance to the CCI garage, Matt slowed and drove up to the gate. He punched in the code to raise the barrier and pulled inside. After rolling to a stop in his appointed spot, he reached to turn off the radio and spotted a pair of sunglasses on the floor. He sighed and scooped them up before climbing from the car.

The afternoon had been pleasant enough, but by the end of dinner he knew he probably wouldn't ask the redhead for another date. Besides, this had been their fourth or fifth, and Matt usually limited himself to no more than a handful with any particular lady. He told this one as much, as he did all the women he dated, but some thought they would be the one to persuade him to commit to a long-term relationship. The trick of leaving something behind in his car wasn't new. Several had tried it over the years when they knew their time with him was about to end.

He tucked the glasses into his jacket pocket and made his way up the steps to the private entrance. After unlocking the door, he strolled down the hall to his office. Inside, he tossed the sunglasses on a table. Tomorrow they would appear in the lost and found box at the front desk, for Matt Hunter manipulated people; he did not get manipulated. Any thoughts of one more date with the redhead ended with her attempted ploy.

His eyes drifted up to the framed picture on a bookshelf in front of his desk. Unable to help himself, he walked across the room and reached up to touch it. While he had others of her, this was the final one taken of Elizabeth, his long-deceased love. Taken at a gathering at Chestnut Cove–the real one, the home of John's grandparents up in the mountains–on a Sunday afternoon in 1958, it was among Matt's dearest possessions.

Elizabeth had brought her camera to take photographs of the secluded mountain cove while she, Matt, John, Sandra, and KD dined with John's grandmother before the youngsters returned to Coughton Tech for the beginning of the fall term. Winston and Jeanette had been there, too. Kathryn McDougal Stuart had asked Matt's girlfriend to take a photograph of the matron with the boys, Sandra, and KD. One of the many things for which Matt loved his goddaughter was her insistence that "Wizzy" be included in a picture. Once the initial one had been taken, Winston was recruited to take another which included Elizabeth in order to satisfy the child.

Twenty years later, no one would know where to find a copy of the first picture. It was the second which became so dear weeks later when Matt lost his future bride and almost his goddaughter.

He picked up the frame and brought it close to gaze at the face he still saw in his dreams. The long brown hair pulled back with a band; the dark, inquisitive eyes which still pierced his soul; the soft lips he longed to kiss once more; the silver locket he gave her on her last birthday hung around her neck.

When he could make himself return the picture to its place, he whispered, "We're working on it, Lizzy. I've waited until she could protect herself because I know that's what you'd want, but we haven't forgotten. We'll never forget."

# Chapter 10

"Mom, can I go over to Woodbury to the mall after dinner?" Maggie asked.

"Don't you need to finish a book report today and study for finals?" Sandra answered question with question.

"I can finish the book report when I get home. A new store opened at the mall yesterday, and everybody is going to see it except me if you don't let me go." Maggie's lower lip poked out a fraction with the beginning of a pout.

John interrupted to ask the question to which he expected he already knew the answer. "Since you can't drive yet, how do you plan to get there?"

"Oh, Giselle's going. She said I can ride with her and a couple of other girls. They're leaving in about forty-five minutes, so I need to finish dinner and go change clothes." A fretting Maggie patted her hair. "I have to fix my hair and makeup, too."

"I have a better idea. How about if you don't go? You can stay home, change into some comfortable studying clothes, finish your book report, and study for finals. Your grades haven't been too good this year. You need to study hard so you can improve your final grades," John said.

"Mom," Maggie whined, turning to her mother. "This is important. If I don't go, I'll be the only one in my group to miss out on shopping there this weekend."

"It wouldn't hurt to have a little less in common with that group. I agree with your father. You need to stay here and do your schoolwork today. You, Chris, and I will go over to Woodbury right after school gets out for the summer, and each of you may choose something from the new store then," Sandra said. When Maggie opened her mouth to argue, Sandra cut her off. "No, Maggie. The subject is closed. Finish your dinner. Then you may go upstairs to change out of your Sunday dress and study."

Maggie huffed, but she returned her attention to her plate and said nothing more, aware there was no reversing her parents' edict and further argument would get her sent to her room for the duration of the day. In mute protest, she made as much noise as possible, scraping her fork around on her plate as she chased peas across it, stirring her iced tea again, and clattering her knife onto her plate after buttering her roll.

Chris decided to fill the ensuing silence to bring a little peace back to the table. "Where's Uncle Matt today? It isn't like him to miss Sunday dinner very often. Is he out of town?"

John graced his youngest child with a smile. "He's at the hotel. They're busy getting ready for the summer season. He had a big crowd in this weekend, too. I'm sure he'll be here for dinner next Sunday."

"Do you think I'll get to help at the hotel this summer? I'm twelve now. I want to start learning more about how things work there. If I can't work at the hotel, may I work at headquarters? I'll make copies and deliver interoffice mail and answer the phone and sharpen pencils—"

"OK, OK." John laughed and raised his hands in surrender. "I'll see what I can do, but only a few hours a week. I'll talk to Matt. If he has something you can do in the back office of the hotel, you can help there. If not, you can help Mrs. Pierce."

Chris wrinkled her nose. "May I help Vicky instead?"

John rolled his eyes at his daughter. "That would be up to Matt and KD. She works for them. Contrary to her reputation, Mrs. Pierce is a nice lady. As my executive secretary, it's her job to be the gatekeeper to my office." Chris looked unconvinced, so he added, "How about if we can work it out for you to work with Vicky part of the time and for Mrs. Pierce part of the time?"

"Exactly. With Vicky, it would be like working with her. With Mrs. Pierce, I'd be working for her," Chris explained.

"You'd be working for each of them. You just see Vicky differently because she's been almost another big sister to you all your life. She'd still be responsible for keeping you busy and out of trouble while you're assigned to her."

"Will Chris get paid? Can I work at the hotel and get paid?" Maggie chimed in, her irritation at being denied a trip to the mall forgotten for the moment.

Sandra looked from Maggie to John as she waited for him to process the idea of Maggie asking to work. "What kind of job would you be interested in, Maggie?"

"I don't know. What kinds of jobs are there?"

"We've been in the hotel business your whole life, but you don't know any of the jobs involved?" an incredulous John asked.

"I know there are maids and waitresses and bellhops, but I wouldn't want to do those jobs. We own the hotel. Think how it would look if I spent the summer making up beds for people." Maggie wrinkled her nose at the thought of such degradation.

Sandra waved John off to handle the response. "Maggie, who do you think made the beds, cleaned the bathrooms, and washed the sheets and towels when we started the original inn? There weren't a host of people working for us then. I did all those jobs myself. When KD was old enough, she did those jobs, too. Your dad and Matt and Jonah did the maintenance and some of the construction when we made the modifications to make the house more suitable as an inn. Matt cooked breakfast almost every day and provided the entertainment on the evenings we offered any. Your dad kept the books and handled the reservations.

"We did everything at first. So did KD once she was old enough. Doug will spend this summer helping your dad and learning more of the business side of the company. He's spent the last several summers working at the hotel being a bellhop, waiter, and lifeguard. We'd love for you to spend some time learning the business, but you'd have to do the jobs for which you're qualified like any other teenager we employee like your older siblings did."

Maggie pushed the last bite of roast around on her plate while she thought about her mother's words. "OK, maybe I could change sheets or wait tables or something for one summer, but I'd get paid, right?"

"Yes, you would get paid," John answered. "You'll be sixteen in less than three weeks. We'll get you set up along with the other summer help. Do you think you'd rather work in the hotel or in the headquarters? We'll find something for you, whichever place you think you'd like better. You must remember you'll be expected to pull your weight, and you'll receive extra scrutiny from some people because you're a Stuart. Take some time to think about what you'd like to do. If you want to know more about what you might do in the office instead of the hotel, we'll go over that with you, but for now, you need to go finish your book report and study so you can get the best grades you can."

Maggie nodded. "OK, Dad. I'll think about it."

~~~

*Tuesday, May 29, 1979*

What had become a tense relationship between Hoyt and John over the last few weeks boiled over in the staff meeting. Hoyt argued that they needed to up their bid on the old warehouse to ensure they beat out any competitors for it. He disputed Craig's latest numbers upon which John intended to base their best and final offer for the old warehouse. He only relented when John stood from his seat at the head of the table, announced that the final decision belonged to him, and ended the meeting without bothering to complete the remainder of the agenda for the day.

John disappeared through the door leading into his office, and Hoyt started to follow to continue their discussion, but Mrs. Pierce stepped in front of John's door and held up her hand. "You must allow him to cool off before you approach him. Give him some time and then return. He has no appointments until late this afternoon, so you will have time to speak to him further in private."

Hoyt considered her advice and accepted it. He turned and joined the small crowd of managers leaving the boardroom via the main door. With John out of reach for now, Hoyt decided to buttonhole Craig to further expound on the errors and false assumptions replete within the finance manager's cost estimates, which formed the basis of the bid for the warehouse. Hoyt scanned the crowd in front of the elevator but found no sign of Craig. A glance back into the boardroom proved it to be empty. Spoiling for a fight with someone, Hoyt looked for Matt as a surrogate for John, but Matt had likewise disappeared. Neither was Jonah anywhere to be seen.

Frustrated, Hoyt shoved his way into the elevator when the doors opened and stalked off one floor down. He stormed by the finance secretary's desk without asking if her boss was in, barged into Craig's office, and looked around for any sign of him. A disappointed Hoyt finally accepted that Craig was not cowering under the desk and retreated to his own office to wait for Mrs. Pierce to contact him.

~~~

Giselle twirled around so her new orange skirt flared out as she and Maggie walked toward the student parking lot. "Isn't it cute? I got one just like it in red, too. Jessica got a green one. I wish you could have gone with us so you could buy one. They had a pink one just the shade you like. Then we could all match in different colors Friday. It wasn't right for your mom and dad not to let you go with us." Giselle tried to look sad but failed.

"I'll be sure to get one when my mom takes Chris and me shopping there next weekend." Maggie failed at looking happy as miserably as Giselle failed to look sad.

"Maybe, but they were going fast. I doubt they'll have any left by then. Probably don't have any left now. I'm glad I got a couple while they had them. Oh, wait till you see my new bathing suits. I got four of them." Giselle opened the driver's door and slid behind the wheel of her car. Maggie juggled several books before she managed to open the passenger door. "Why are you bringing all those books home, Mag?"

Maggie, stuffing her burden on the floor under her feet, answered, "My mom's making me study as soon as I get home every afternoon and quizzing me after dinner every night on things that will be on my final exams. She and Dad aren't happy with my grades this year."

"Oh, sorry." Again, Giselle failed to look too sorry. She started the engine, shifted into reverse, and began backing out. A car horn sounded behind her, and she slammed on brakes. "Ugh, it's so hard to get out of here, and cars sneak up behind you. Hey, what kind of car are you getting for your birthday? Have you picked one out yet?"

"No, not yet. It will depend on whether I can get my grades up. Dad said we'd talk about getting me something to drive when school gets out. I have to pass my driver's test, too. Whatever kind I get, I hope it's pink." Maggie stopped talking while Giselle backed out into the traffic flow of the parking lot.

"Pink? Maggie, they don't make pink cars. I know you love pink, but really. Just make sure you get something hot like Doug's Corvette." Giselle revved the engine of her Nova for effect.

Maggie shuddered a little as the car jerked when Giselle's foot nearly slipped off the brake. "I just hope I can pass my test and get something decent to drive. Dad said I could work some this summer at the hotel, and I'd like to be able to drive there instead of riding with him or Doug."

"They're making you work this summer? How cruel. I'm glad Mom and Harold don't make me work. I plan to spend the whole summer by the pool wearing my new bathing suits. I think you should tell your parents you want to move in with Grandmother and Grandfather. They'd be cool parents and let you blow off homework and not make you get a job during the summer and not make you miss a new store opening and all those cool things your parents don't let you do." Giselle slammed on brakes, stopping an inch from the car in front of her as the line winding its way out of the parking lot came to a halt again.

"They're not exactly making me. I asked about doing it. It's kind of cool to be at the hotel. Even Chris will work some, but she'll help around Dad's office with Vicky and Mrs. Pierce making copies and–"

Giselle cut her off before she could continue. "They're making Chris work, too? I bet they're saving money making you and Doug and Chris work, so they don't have to pay somebody else. I bet they've got you brainwashed into thinking you want to work. You know it would be more fun to go to the pool and shopping. Why would you ever need to work anyway? Your mom and dad are so rich you've never got to work. I don't even know why they think you need to get decent grades in school. They're so ridiculous."

"I don't think they're that rich, but–"

Giselle cut her off again. "Oh, everybody knows they're awful rich. They own hotels all over the place and a big house and probably a bunch of other stuff. All you should have to do ever is shop and go to the beach or the pool and go dancing with cute boys. Look at KD. She's running around France or Italy or Australia or wherever she is in Europe having fun. She never works. She plays all the time and hardly ever comes home. You shouldn't have to work either."

"I guess," Maggie said in a soft voice. She tried to keep her attention on the trees they were passing as they drove toward the Stuart home outside of Elkford while she pondered Giselle's words.

"Do you think your parents will let you date the guys staying at the hotel? There might be some cute ones. That might make it worthwhile."

Maggie shook her head. "No, Dad and Uncle Matt are really picky about the hotel staff not dating guests. I'd get sent to my room for a month if I got caught going out with a guest."

"Oh, well, I guess if you have to obey their rules, that makes it harder." Giselle stopped speaking while she negotiated the turn onto the road leading to the Stuart's home. When she resumed, she asked another dubious question. "I wonder how hard it would be to sneak a key to one of the hotel rooms?"

"I don't know, but I know it would get anybody who got caught doing it in a world of trouble." Maggie remained silent for the duration of the drive while Giselle chattered on.

~~~

What Hoyt began in a calm, reasoned voice soon became anything but when John cut him off and repeated his earlier statement that the issue was not open to further debate. Hoyt leaned forward with his forearms on the desk. It was all he could do not to get up and stalk about John's office. "If we lose out on this hotel location, you will have no one but yourself to blame. We cannot allow a competitor to purchase this warehouse out from under us."

John leaned forward on his desk with his posture a match for Hoyt's except the tall, muscular, younger man towered over his older accounting manager. "Must I remind you my family owns the majority of this company and I am the president? All final decisions remain mine, including this one, and I have made it. We will up our offer as discussed earlier. We will not increase it beyond that price. If we fail to secure the warehouse, we will find other property to develop.

"Do I need to remind you I believe someone leaked information about our interest in the warehouse? There had been no interest in it for some time until we began looking at it. Suddenly some other company began pursuing it and to this point has offered more than CCI for it. Do not think I have forgotten you ignored my specific directive not to discuss the property with anyone outside the managers of this company, and yet you went right back to your department and did exactly that. Did you discuss it with anyone else? Are you the person responsible for someone discovering our interest in it? That is likely what put us in a position requiring us to increase our offer if we want the property enough."

"I would never betray this company. I know my job. My job is to provide you with the best information and advice I can. If you do not see the need for me to utilize my best people in order to do so, that is your problem." Hoyt continued in a more reasonable, conciliatory tone. "John, I know you do the best you can with the tools available to you running CCI. I hope you will take a suggestion from me in the spirit with which I offer it. You've done fairly well, but you would do much better with a wider network of advice from people with much more experience. You should consider adding people to the board of directors who can advise you on things without having any kind of stake in the matter. You've allowed people like your wife–and a fine woman she is, though inexperienced in business–and Matt to dominate decision making for the board. You even put your daughter on the board when she was eighteen. Thankfully, she never attends or seeks to make any kind of input around here."

John leaned back in his chair and watched Hoyt as if waiting for something. An oblivious Hoyt continued with his speech.

"What you need are people who can give you good, solid advice with no bias. That includes more people outside CCI with no stake in the company as well as people inside who have its best interests in mind. Take Winston for instance. He's your own stepfather, yet you do not seek his advice regarding your primary business. I realize he provides invaluable leadership to your smaller enterprise, but–" Hoyt stopped when John shot out of his chair.

If Hoyt thought John angry before, now the younger man was livid. "Is this your idea or my mother and Winston's? Are you aware I provide them with the house in which they live in addition to the position Winston holds at JSS? And it is a position, not a real job. He does minimal work there, much of it shoddy. My wife and I must constantly keep after him to get basic reports completed, and never are they done on a timely basis. Why would I consider placing Winston on the board of this hotel? So I could pay him for useless advice like I pay him for worthless work at JSS?" John pointed to the door. "Leave my office now or else you will leave this company, Hoyt."

The older man rose from his chair, turned away in silence, and walked out the door.

~~~

*Wednesday, May 30, 1979*

"I don't see why I couldn't get a ride with Giselle again instead of running around town with you and Chris after school today," Maggie complained.

"That's enough, Maggie," Sandra said. "If I thought you were so enthusiastic to get home to study, I'd be thrilled, but you and I both know you just want to watch that soap opera you like. It won't take long to stop to pick up some paperwork from the JSS office and take it to your dad at the hotel headquarters. Then we'll go home." Sandra had regretted letting Maggie get a ride home with Giselle the previous day every minute since. Maggie had complained about one thing after another from a repeat of the discussion about not being allowed to go to the mall on Sunday to the fancy sports car she wanted for her sixteenth birthday but wasn't about to get.

"Can I go across to Dilly's to get a milkshake while you take the papers to Dad?" Dilly's was Maggie's favorite place to eat out. Located across the street from the hotel, it offered a more casual atmosphere and fare than CCI's restaurant.

"No, you'll spoil your supper. You'll both go up with me. We won't be there but a few minutes." Sandra felt her temper rising at Maggie's ongoing recalcitrance. She slowed the car and turned into a parking space in front of JSS Holdings. "Come on, girls. You can speak to your grandfather for a minute if he's here."

The girls climbed out and followed along behind Sandra with Chris looking around the parking area in front of the building. "I don't see Grandfather's car. Do you think he's gone to meet a client?"

"I don't know, Chris. We'll see what Cynthia says when we get inside. Maybe he parked farther down the block." Sandra didn't put much conviction behind her reply. Like Chris, she knew Winston probably wasn't in his office at JSS this afternoon.

As soon as Sandra and the girls entered, Cynthia, the secretary-receptionist, rose to greet them. "Hi, Mrs. Stuart. Hello, girls. It's nice to see you."

"Hey, Cynthia," Sandra replied, and the girls added their greeting. "Is Winston here? He was supposed to get a revised package together for us to look over for the first quarter."

"No, he left before noon and told me he had a lunch meeting which would last a good part of the afternoon." She stood and walked around her desk. "I typed up the revised report yesterday. Let me see if he left it on his desk. He didn't give it back to me to make any corrections, so I assume he was satisfied with it."

Cynthia hurried into Winston's office to look for the report. Sandra followed her and stopped in the doorway. It was largely unchanged from the last time she visited. An open golf magazine lay on the desk alongside scattered parts of Elkford's morning newspaper and an unopened *Wall Street Journal*. A putter leaned against the credenza behind the desk. A couple of golf balls were visible under the desk's front edge.

"Here it is, Mrs. Stuart. I don't see anything marked for me to correct, so I assume he was satisfied with it." Cynthia held out the report to the co-owner of the company. "I'll let him know you picked it up when he returns."

"Thank you, Cynthia. I appreciate you making the corrections to it." Sandra tried to maintain a pleasant air for Cynthia's sake. The girl was in an untenable position, and she no doubt knew it. The errors in the original version of the first quarter report had not been her fault nor had the errors in the second version. Hopefully the third version would be correct, and they could put the first quarter to rest a month before Winston would be expected to deliver the second quarter report to John and Sandra. She had little doubt what kind of meeting Winston was having today which had lasted for more than three hours and counting. If only he worked half as hard at his job as he did on his other interests.

When they arrived at Chestnut Cove's headquarters a few minutes later, Maggie started to protest her mother's requirement for the girls to accompany her to their father's office but thought better of it. Instead, she climbed out of the car and dragged along behind her mother and sister into the building and across the lobby to the elevator. She stood to the side while several people passing through the lobby greeted Sandra and chatted with her for a moment, each greeting the two youngest Stuart children also. Aware of how severe both parents' wrath would be if she were rude to their employees, Maggie acknowledged each person in turn.

At last, they arrived at the executive offices on the top floor of the building. Mrs. Pierce ushered them into John's office and managed to almost hide her disapproval at Vicky's presence.

"Hi, Vicky, I haven't seen you in about a month. They aren't working you too hard, are they?" Sandra considered the girl to be almost her fourth daughter. Sandra and Vicky's mother had been friends for years, and their children had grown up close, also.

"Hi, Aunt Sandra. I don't get bored around here, but I enjoy it." Vicky hugged Sandra and then each of the girls while Sandra moved across to greet her husband and deliver the papers from JSS Holdings. "Chris, I heard you'll be working up here in the office during the summer. I can't wait for you to spend some time with us."

"I know. I can't wait either. I want to learn about all the different departments and who does what. I know some of it, but not a lot," Chris replied. She stopped, glanced around to see if the coast was clear, and added, "I hope I can mostly help you and not Mrs. Pierce. Do you think Uncle Matt will mind?"

"Chris," John chided, "we talked about that."

Vicky, seeking to change the subject away from the dreaded Mrs. Pierce, asked Maggie, "Have you decided what kind of job you want to do yet? Your dad said you want to work in the hotel this summer. Depending on what kind of job you choose, you might need a few new things to wear. Won't it be fun to go shopping for work clothes? I went shopping this weekend with a new friend who starts at the hotel next week. She wasn't sure what she needed to wear at the hotel's front desk, so we went Saturday to get her a few things. She's only nineteen, and she's really excited about working here. I think you'll like her when you meet her. Her name's Laura."

"I won't work unless they make me. I don't think I should have to work. None of my friends have to work," Maggie complained.

A shocked Vicky glanced up at John and Sandra, who looked equally surprised at Maggie's response. "Um, I need to get this file to Matt. It was good to see all of you."

As Vicky retreated, Sandra called after her, "Plan to come to dinner with us Sunday. I intend to call your mother about a welcome home dinner for Doug and Joseph to celebrate the end of their first year of college."

"That sounds great. I can't wait for my bratty baby brother to come home for the summer," Vicky answered. "Let me know what time and what I should bring."

When Vicky was gone, John beckoned to Chris to go sit outside and close the door. Then he turned to Maggie and glowered at her for a minute. "I'm confused, Margaret. A few days ago, you asked your mother and me if you could work at the hotel this summer. Now you're acting like it was our idea and we're forcing you to work. Do you want to explain to us how that can be? You had no reason to snap at Vicky. Whatever your problem is with me or your mother, Vicky did nothing to deserve any of your wrath."

Maggie turned away from her father, her emotions fighting between anger at her parents and sorrow at hurting Vicky's feelings. At last, she shook her head and whispered, "I'm sorry I snapped at Vicky." Then the floodgates opened, and tears streamed down her face as she sobbed.

# Chapter 11

John's phone buzzed, and he gathered up the small collection of notes and sketches on his desk and shoved them into their envelope. Punching his intercom button, he answered, "Yes, Mrs. Pierce?"

"Mr. Hodges is on the phone, sir. Line one."

"Thank you, Mrs. Pierce." John punched the button for line one. "Hello, Mr. Hodges. This is John Stuart."

"Hello, Mr. Stuart. I need to update you on the situation with the old warehouse in Pearl." Mr. Hodges stopped as if waiting for John to prompt further discussion.

"Since you aren't congratulating me on CCI's offer being accepted, I assume the owners rejected it or someone outbid us." John leaned back in his chair to await the official verdict.

Through the phone, John heard Mr. Hodges sigh, no doubt realizing his hopes for a bidding war and his commensurate higher commission would end with his call to John. "I'm afraid so, Mr. Stuart. The other interested party increased their offer for the warehouse again. It once more exceeds that of CCI. If you would like to take a few days to consider the possibility of upping the CCI bid again, the owners will give you time."

John blew out a breath before making the end official. "No, I'm afraid our last offer was our best and final, Mr. Hodges. I appreciate the chance to consider things further, but we're done. Please thank the owners for giving us the opportunity."

"I will do so. I'm sorry we couldn't reach an agreement for you. Goodbye, Mr. Stuart."

"Goodbye, Mr. Hodges." John leaned forward, punched the button for line two to disconnect Mr. Hodges, and dialed the number for Matt's office in the hotel.

"Matt Hunter," came Matt's voice over the phone.

"It's John. We're officially out of the running for the warehouse in Pearl. We've been outbid again, and I declined the chance to take a few days to consider making a third offer."

"Good." Matt chuckled. "I was a little worried you let the second offer get too high and we'd end up stuck with the place."

"Remind me not to let you talk me into such a charade again. We've spent over a hundred manhours working on this bogus potential hotel when we could have been working on the place we really want, or at least a couple of people want. I'm withholding my opinion until you decide to let me in on where it's located and provide more details about the site than the little I've seen so far." John dragged the few pieces of paper he had been looking at earlier back out of their envelope.

"Now, John, don't get upset about this charade. It worked out rather well, didn't it? We suspect someone leaked the site location, which we thought happened at the last place we lost out on. We know Hoyt told at least his staff. Others might have talked out of school also. Once we know who outbid us for the warehouse in Pearl, we can narrow the field and possibly find out if someone was careless or if they deliberately leaked information. Regardless, no one will find out the location of the place we really want to expand into next because right now the list of people who know where it is consists of two people, and neither of them would ever talk. We have the basic data we need, and from what Jonah and I have seen so far, it looks good. You've had it for over a week now. What do you think?"

John grumbled and tried to stay irritated with Matt, but as usual that didn't work. "From what little I can tell about it, it fits with what we've done before pretty well, but the location is important, Matt. You know that. I need to see it. We need to know what the area around it has to offer."

"How about we take a trip to see it? Doug and Joseph finish school tomorrow and start working for the summer next week, don't they? Why don't we plan a little road trip for the latter part of the week for you, me, Jonah, and the boys? Nobody needs to know where we're going in advance. We can even claim we're off playing golf somewhere for a few days. We'll sneak away from here and go visit this new site and scout the area around it, though I'm sure that's already been done."

"So you admit you know the location?"

"Nope, not a clue. Yet. I'll find out soon though."

"Matt," John growled.

"Not my game, John. I'm just an intermediary. What do you say? We'll pile into a couple of cars and take the golf clubs with us. You can take out your frustrations on a pile of little white balls."

John brightened at Matt's suggestion. "Fine. We'll sort out the details Sunday when we have everyone over for dinner to welcome the boys home. At least Sandra and Mary will need to be told what we're up to. That will be a good time to talk away from here."

"Good. We'll plan it all out then. Somebody's knocking on my door. It's probably Pam, Fleur, and Maurice. We're due to discuss what's coming up at the hotel in June. I'll see you Sunday." Matt hung up before John could object.

~~~

*Friday, June 1, 1979*

"*Pearl Pioneer*," Rachel answered when she picked up her phone. She had barely settled at her desk for the morning, so a call regarding a story of interest to the small newspaper landing on her desk surprised her. She listened as the voice on the phone spoke and grabbed her pen. "Yes, we'll look into it and put together an article for

Tuesday's paper. Thank you for the heads up." She hung up and made a couple of notes on a piece of paper before walking out of her office and across the newsroom to the desk of one of her staff members.

Rachel held out her notes to her young ace reporter. With a double major in journalism and business, he was the perfect person to investigate this story. "Pete, I got a call about the old warehouse on Main Street between second and third. It sold yesterday, and there's a rumor it's to become a hotel. Would you contact the real estate company who listed it and find out what you can? If somebody bought it and plans to do something like that, it will be big for Pearl."

"OK, Rachel, I'll run over there and see if anything is going on at the building and find out which real estate broker handled the sale. If no one's working at the building, I'll go to the realtor's office." Taking the notes from Rachel, Pete scanned them and began jotting down some questions to ask about the acquisition and details of the forthcoming use of the property. Five minutes later, he hustled out the storefront door of the *Pearl Pioneer*.

The *PP*, as the locals referred to it, had been in existence since near the turn of the century. It served the town of Pearl and the surrounding area as their local newspaper. It published twice weekly–Tuesdays and Fridays–and reached almost every household in Pearl and more than half of those in the surrounding county. While the *PP* changed hands a few times over the years, it maintained a reputation for integrity in its reporting and fairness in its editorials through most of those years. There had been some trepidation when Appalachian Publishing purchased the newspaper a couple of years earlier, but the new owner promised to maintain the same level of quality and integrity the *PP* enjoyed in the past.

Longtime editor Rachel Pittman had been retained to continue running the newspaper. She suffered no interference from the new owner other than some welcome technical upgrades and a request to consider Pete for a position as reporter when he graduated from Coughton Tech a year earlier. When she interviewed him, Rachel found the young man to be a first-rate, up-and-coming reporter she would be happy to hire. Over the course of the last year, he proved both his editor and publisher to be astute judges of talent. Rachel's only concern was that the talented writer wouldn't stay in Pearl long. He had far too much talent to remain employed at a small-town newspaper for more than a year or two. She expected he would ask her for a reference and try to move on to something bigger and better before long, but for now she would utilize his talents as much as she could.

~~~

Pete stood when Mr. Hodges walked out of his office. "Sir, I appreciate you taking a few minutes to talk to me."

"Of course. I'm happy to speak to a representative of the *PP*," Mr. Hodges said. "Come on into my office. How is Rachel?"

"Rachel is fine, sir. She's most appreciative of you taking the time to give us an interview." Pete stopped in front of Mr. Hodges' desk while the realtor poured himself a cup of coffee.

"Have a seat. Would you like some coffee?" Mr. Hodges pulled out his desk chair and sat down when the reporter declined the offer. After taking a sip, Mr. Hodges made a face. "Ugh. Good choice to skip this swill. It's pretty bad. I gave my secretary the day off and had to make it myself." He shoved the cup away. "Now, what would you like to know about the deal I helped finalize this week?"

"First, can you confirm for us the warehouse on Main Street between Second and Third Avenues sold?" Pete held his pen and notepad poised to write.

"Yes, indeed, the sale closed yesterday evening. It was quite late, so I doubt the papers have been filed at the courthouse yet, but we held the closing right here in my office. Everyone involved seemed most pleased." A most-pleased Mr. Hodges patted his jacket pocket where his commission check rested. A quick glance at the clock assured him the bank would not be crowded when he arrived to deposit his check if his interview with Pete didn't last long.

"This warehouse has been on the market for some time, has it not?"

"For about two years. The family closed the business when the economy went bad. They owned a grocery distribution business. They reached retirement age about that time, and their children had other jobs and no interest in trying to revive the company, so they chose to put it on the market. They received little interest for a couple of years. One company sent someone to investigate it not long after it closed but found it unsuited to their needs. Then we suddenly received a surge in interest this spring. We had three parties contact us about it. I took representatives of each through the building, and two of them made offers." Mr. Hodges stopped his narrative. "I'm sorry, Pete. I'm getting ahead of your questions."

The reporter shook his head and waved away the concern. "That's fine, Mr. Hodges. You're answering many of them without me asking. I can ask about anything you haven't mentioned when you finish. Please go on."

"Well, as I said, we suddenly had all kinds of interest in the old place. Two parties made offers a couple of weeks ago. We went back and forth several times with each increasing their bid. Yesterday morning, one of the parties bowed out, so I called the other company immediately and told them their offer had been accepted.

"The buyer had offered a cash deal and asked if they could close as soon as the paperwork could be put together. It was almost as if they were concerned the matter would be reopened. I called the sellers to ask if they would be available to close yesterday evening or this morning if the buyer got everything ready. The sellers were happy to cooperate. A cash deal with no worries about inspections or title searches or anything like that can go quite fast. The attorney representing the buyer arrived here after dinner, and I called the sellers. They came over with their attorney, and we closed the sale in half an hour." Mr. Hodges leaned back in his chair and patted his coat pocket again. It was his largest commission ever. Having it in his pocket near his heart gave him an amazing thrill.

Pete checked his list of questions. Most of what he wanted to know about the sale had been answered. "Can you tell me a little about the buyer and what their intentions are for the warehouse? Is the buyer local?"

"No, the buyer is someone from Elkford. If you're not familiar with it, Elkford is another town a little larger than Pearl and also located in the foothills. It's about one-hundred-thirty miles southwest of here."

Pete's senses perked up. He had heard of Elkford and knew a little about its most famous company. "What's the name of the company?"

"Michaelson Properties."

Pete had begun to write the name of a different company and stopped to look up at Mr. Hodges. "I don't believe I've heard of Michaelson Properties. Do you know anything about them?"

"Other than they bought the old warehouse yesterday, not much."

Pete scratched his chin while he thought about his next question. "Did the representative from Michaelson Properties tell you what they plan to do with the warehouse? Will they put in another distribution center or renovate it to become something else or tear it down to build a new structure?"

"They didn't come right out and say, but from the questions they asked, I believe they plan to renovate it and turn it into something else. I don't know for sure, but that's the feeling I got from talking to their representatives when they toured it."

"But they didn't tell you what their plans were?"

"No, they kept pretty tight-lipped about those. So did the other interested parties. That isn't unusual in commercial real estate." Mr. Hodges looked up at the clock. Almost time to get to the bank before the Friday line got long. He planned to take the afternoon off to celebrate his well-earned commission.

"One more question, Mr. Hodges." Pete could tell the man had become antsy and lost interest in discussing the sale. "Do you know if Michaelson Properties has any connection to a hotel company? Elkford is the location of the headquarters for Chestnut Cove Inns. Do you think Michaelson Properties is associated with Chestnut Cove and the warehouse destined to become a hotel? Chestnut Cove owns a number of them up and down the Appalachian foothills and mountains."

"Chestnut Cove? No, definitely not. Funny you should mention them." He stopped and leaned forward. "Now this is off the record because it's confidential information, but Chestnut Cove was the other bidder. They lost out on the warehouse to Michaelson."

~~~

"Yes, ma'am," Rachel said, "Pete wrote a nice article about it. I appreciate the heads up. I hope it works out, but Pete has some concerns about the property being used as a hotel. By the way, the agent couldn't confirm what use the buyer might have for the property. Pete was surprised the buyer you heard might put a hotel in the warehouse was a company from Elkford, but it wasn't Chestnut Cove Inns and had no connection to it as far as we can tell." She stopped to listen to her publisher for a minute. "Yes, that concerned Pete also. Well, if it comes to fruition, it will be good for Pearl. If not, at least it was good for the Milgen family to unload the property.

"On the other subject you mentioned, you said you had another one of those little side projects for Pete?" Rachel listened again and made a couple of notes. "Yes, I'll make sure he has time to translate it and prepare something suitable. We'll send it to the printer along with next Friday's issue. Will there be a photo this time?" She made another notation and looked up when she heard a knock on her door. She waved for

Pete to enter and take a seat. "We'll be on the lookout for it in Monday's mail. Yes, ma'am, Italian this time. I'll make sure Pete remembers, and thank you again for the heads up, ma'am."

Rachel hung up the phone, made one more notation on her pad, and looked up at Pete. "Brush up on your Italian. We're getting another article to translate and prep for the printer. We should receive the article in Monday's mail, and she wants it sent over to Coughton to the printer along with Friday's edition of the *PP*."

"OK, I'll get out my Italian textbooks this weekend. It isn't as fresh as my French, but it's still pretty good. I'll be ready to translate it Monday afternoon as soon as we get it. Anything more from her about the warehouse?"

"No, but I expect she knows more than she's telling us. I'm just happy we got the heads up about the sale. I suspect that will be something to watch for the next few months regardless of what really happens with it." Rachel looked up at the clock on her wall. "It's almost time for the stock market to close. Get ready to write your weekly report, and then we'll get out of here for the week."

"OK, Rachel." Pete hopped up and hustled out of her office, ready to tackle his next project.

# Chapter 12

"Laura, hurry up with the coffee," Herb bellowed. "You're still working for me until four o'clock today. I don't want you slacking off just because it's your last day at the diner. We'll probably have a big crowd in here any minute for lunch."

Before Herb finished yelling for the coffee, Laura set the fresh can on the counter next to him. "I'm sorry, Herb. Someone put it up on the top shelf. I had to get the stepstool to reach it."

"I rearranged the storage pantry to make things more efficient back there. You've got to learn where they are." Herb caught himself and stopped. "Well, maybe you don't since you're quitting, but if things don't work out and you come crawling back here for a job, you'll need to keep up with where I store supplies."

"Yes, Herb, that's true." Laura smiled to herself before adding, "I need to go check on my customers." She hurried over to the booth where two businessmen were eating a late lunch and conducting an animated but hushed discussion regarding some real estate transaction. After refilling their tea glasses, Laura checked with the next table where a woman sat flipping through a fashion magazine while she munched on a BLT. Assured her customers didn't need anything at the moment, Laura walked to the other side of the diner to help Meredith clean tables while she waited for a customer to come in and take a seat in her section.

Meredith looked up from wiping at a stubborn spot of dried ketchup. "I can't believe this is your last day. Promise you'll come by to see us when you can."

"Of course," Laura said. She gave Meredith a quick hug. "But you'll hardly have time to miss me working fulltime. Herb seems pretty determined to have just you and Helen for at least a few weeks. The two of you will be so busy you won't be able to think about me."

"Oh, but I will, Laura. I'll miss you being here every day. I hope you enjoy your new job, and I'm happy to have a fulltime one now, but I'll still miss you. You've been such a great friend since we've been working together." Meredith stopped to wipe away a tear.

"I promise I'll come by to see you when I can, and you and I will still visit when we're not working. You only live a couple of blocks from Grandma and me. I wish you'd consider taking a class with me. I think you'd get a lot out of taking one." She stole a quick glance toward Herb before whispering, "One day you'll want to do more than wait tables here at Fred's. Knowing a little about things like bookkeeping would help you get something better one day."

"I don't know. I'm not smart like you are. I need to do a good job for Herb first." To add emphasis to her assertion, Meredith began to scrub extra hard on the table she was cleaning.

"Yes, you need to do well here, but you already know the job. You're just going to do it more hours a week now. You'll do great." Laura gave Meredith another quick hug.

"Miss?" one of the men at the opposite end of the diner called.

Laura hurried toward the table. "Yes, sir?"

"We decided we want some of that apple pie for dessert. Would you bring us a couple of slices and some coffee?"

"Coming right up, sir." Laura hurried behind the counter. "Is the coffee ready yet, Herb? I need two cups."

"Oh, I forgot to make it. I'll have some fresh made in a few minutes." Herb set his magazine aside and stood from his stool to make the coffee.

Laura hustled back to the men. "We're just making a fresh pot. Would you like for me to hold your pie until the coffee is ready?"

"Sure, we're in no hurry. We heard your boss say something about you quitting. Did you get a new job or are you getting married?"

"I start a new job Monday," Laura answered. She couldn't keep the smile from her face.

"Congratulations. Where will you be working?" For the first time since they entered the diner, the older man gave Laura more than a cursory glance. His eyes swept down her figure, making her a little uncomfortable.

She shoved the feeling aside to respond with as cheery a smile as she could muster. "Chestnut Cove Inn."

His eyes narrowed, and she thought she detected a slight downturn of the left corner of his mouth. "Ah, the pride of Elkford. I hope you enjoy it there. I expect they pay their waitresses better than this place. We eat there every month or two, so we might see you from time to time." The man leaned toward her and continued in a lowered voice. "Beware of the Stuarts and Matt Hunter. They're not the paragons some people think. If you find yourself in need of another job, come by the Elkford Country Club." He winked at her, his eyes openly appraising her figure again. "They're always in need of pretty girls. Tell them Mr. Michaelson said to give you a try."

Before Laura could process his comments, Herb called her again. "Laura, I need you to show Meredith how to work this new toaster." For once, she was glad for Herb's bellicose summons.

"Um, thank you," Laura stammered. "Excuse me, I need to help my boss." She backed away from the table a step. "I'll bring your dessert as soon as the coffee is ready." She hurried around the counter, grabbing Meredith and dragging her along.

After the two men departed, Laura picked up the small pile of change they left behind for her tip. She had considered correcting their assumption she would be a waitress at CCI but decided against it. The older man made her feel uncomfortable, and she didn't think they were people she wanted anything to do with. Giving them any cause to remember her further was not something she thought would be in her best interest. The comment about the Stuarts and Matt she filed away for now. She would make up her own mind about them based on what she learned firsthand, not on the unsubstantiated remark of some leering stranger.

~~~

*Sunday, June 3, 1979*

The Stuart home was full of delectable aromas as Sandra and her friend, Mary Jones, bustled around the kitchen finishing their part of Sunday dinner while their husbands manned the grills out back. Their respective sons had returned home from their first year of college on the previous day, and the families were enjoying an afternoon of celebration and fellowship. When the doorbell rang, Chris raced to the door to answer it. "Hi, Uncle Matt," she exclaimed. She threw her arms around his neck and received a big hug from him in return.

"Hey, Chrissie, did you miss me?"

Chris released him from the hug but took his hand to lead him through the house. "Yes, you've missed Sunday dinner for two weeks straight. How am I supposed to keep up with what's going on at the hotel if you aren't here to update me on Sundays? Dad said you had to approve me helping Vicky in the office this summer. Is it OK? Did he remember to mention it to you?"

"Yes, he did, and of course it's fine with me. Did you ever doubt that?" Matt flashed a grin at the exuberant girl.

They walked out the back to where John, Doug, Joseph, and Jonah were handling the grills and visiting, Chris chattering along the way. "No, but Dad keeps reminding me that you have to respect things like that at work. It wouldn't be right for him to say something's OK without asking the people responsible. I need to ask KD, too, but I don't know when she's coming home." Matt glanced at John, who had the good graces to look chagrined. "Have you talked to her lately?"

Matt smiled at her. "No, but I'm sure it will be fine with her. We might let Maggie help, too, depending on what she and your dad work out for her to do this summer."

"It would be so fun to have all of us work together. Do you think KD will come home so she can work in the office while we're working there? She's always somewhere else. I hope she'll spend some time here this summer while Maggie and I are out of school and Doug's home from college. I miss having her around. Even when she's here, she isn't really home since she stays out at her cabin now. At least Doug and Joseph are home for the summer." She grinned at her brother as the young men walked up.

"Hey, Doug, Joseph," Matt greeted the young men. "How was school?" He extended his hand to each in turn, and they shook warmly.

"It was great, Uncle Matt, but I'm glad to be done for a little while. Dad said he wants to take us to check out the new hotel site this week," Doug said with a nod to Joseph. He checked over his shoulder to ensure his father and Jonah weren't listening. "Do you know where we're going yet? Dad's a little aggravated he still doesn't know the location."

Matt glanced toward John, who was busy checking the ribs and paying no attention to Matt or the boys. "No, but I'm sure we'll get word in the next day or two. Plenty of time before we leave Wednesday afternoon." Matt ended further discussion concerning the hotel and shifted to horses, a subject which soon captured the attention of John and Jonah also.

Sandra interrupted the conversation five minutes later when she called from the back door, "Chris, come help bring the food out. Here, take this first and sit it on the buffet table." She handed over a bowl of potato salad and watched Chris make her way across the patio, carefully keeping a firm grip on the large, heavy bowl. When Chris was done, she scurried to the kitchen behind her mother to retrieve the rest of the food, passing Maggie and Mary along the way carrying their own burdens.

"Which one of you men is responsible for not burning the meat?" Mary prompted after she set down her baked beans and noticed that the men were engrossed in conversation and not tending the grills.

"Jonah," she called to her husband, "are the hamburgers ready? Sandra and Chris are bringing out the last of the food from inside. You men need to take up the burgers and ribs if they're ready."

"Yes, dear, everything's ready." Jonah nudged his son to grab a platter for the burgers. "John, you better get the ribs onto the platters, too. We aren't going to hear the end of it if we don't get our part of the food served up." Jonah smiled at his wife. "See, all's ready out here, dear." Mary shook her head at him and went back to checking that everything had serving utensils.

The doorbell rang again, and Maggie heard her mother call for her to answer it. She ambled through the house and opened the front door. "Hi, Grandmother. Hi, Grandfather. You're just in time. We're taking the last of the food out now. Come on." She headed back down the hall toward the back door, leaving Jeanette and Winston to follow.

"I fail to understand why Sandra insists on holding such a primitive Sunday dinner," Jeanette carped as she and Winston trailed Maggie through the house.

Maggie opened the sliding door to the patio where the rest of the family had begun to file through in a line to fill their plates. "Grandmother and Grandfather are here," she announced.

John set his plate aside and greeted his mother with a kiss on the cheek. "Hello, Mother, it's nice of you to come today. Winston," he said with a nod toward his step-father before returning his attention to his mother. She was staring at the parade of people passing along the row of food, filling their plates and paying little attention to her. "Mother, would you like to sit and allow me to fix a plate for you?"

He wondered just why his mother had bothered to accept the invitation to this afternoon's festivities. They were far from the more formal gatherings she preferred. When John invited her and explained that they were going to have a cookout, his mother had proceeded to inform him of the unsuitability of such events and to berate Sandra for planning such a thing. That had caused John to cut her off midsentence to tell her the cookout had been his idea, and she was welcome to attend if she wished or stay away if she found it so unsuitable. It had been a mild surprise when she and Winston appeared.

"No, I had Tanya prepare something light before we departed. I shall sit and visit with my grandson for a short time. Then we shall depart before it becomes too warm out here." With that pronouncement, Jeanette moved off to command Doug's attention. Her relationship with him was cool at best, though not downright frigid like the one with her eldest grandchild.

Jeanette made an occasional effort to be civil to the sole male Stuart heir. Should something happen to John, maintaining a civil relationship with Doug would be vital. The younger girls might not control their inheritance for years, and neither Sandra nor her eldest spawn would lift a finger to support Jeanette and Winston in John's absence. Therefore, regardless of her real opinion of Doug, she needed to retain some semblance of congenial rapport with him.

As his mother moved off to sit near Doug, John turned to Winston. "I hope you're hungrier than Mother. Please, make yourself at home. I believe you know everyone here."

"Yes, I believe so. Thank you, John." Winston ambled to the end of the buffet line and allowed Jonah to engage him in conversation.

Everyone had just finished their first pass through the buffet line when the doorbell rang again. Chris set aside her plate and hurried through the house to answer the door. "Hi, Vicky, hi, Derrick." Chris hugged each in turn before taking the cake box Vicky held and leading the couple through the house. "You're just in time to eat. I was afraid something had come up, and you weren't going to make it this afternoon."

"We wouldn't miss it, Chris," Vicky said with a smile. "Are we the last ones here?"

"Yes, unless KD decides to surprise us and show up. Even Grandmother and Grandfather are here." Without taking a breath, Chris shifted to her current most favorite topic. "Uncle Matt said it's OK with him for me to work with you this summer, and I think Maggie is going to work up there, too. I wish KD would come home so we could all work together. Of course, Maggie might change her mind again about working, but then you already know that." Chris stopped, realizing she might be discussing something better left alone. Maggie's summer occupation had been a tense subject in the household for the last several days. Today was a time for the families to relax and enjoy being reunited. "How is law school, Derrick? Are you out for the summer, too?"

"It's fine, and yes, I go back to interning in the CCI legal department tomorrow. It's a great opportunity for me to learn firsthand about corporate law. Plus, I get to see a little more of Vicky to make up for being away at school so much." He took Vicky's hand and gave it a squeeze before they stepped out into the backyard to greet everyone and take their turn at the buffet.

Across the way, Jeanette had plowed through the typical questions about Doug's first year at college and shifted to querying him about his summer plans. "Will you begin working in the hotel again tomorrow as a bellhop?"

Doug shook his head as he wiped sauce from his face. "No, ma'am, Dad wants me to work with him this summer. I'll be following him around to learn what he does. I'll also spend time with each of the department heads talking to them about what their group does and how their work fits with others."

"That seems most sensible. You'll need to know all those things in order to take over from your father one day. I hope you will listen most attentively to Hoyt. He knows a great deal about financial issues and has been with the company since soon after it expanded. I cannot fathom why your father treated that man so poorly, splitting his department in half and giving part to someone with much less experience. I understand the new man isn't even from Elkford."

Doug refrained from allowing her to drag him into that discussion and stuck to a diplomatic answer. "I'm sure Hoyt will provide me with a good overview of accounting. I took my first course in it last quarter, so I'm looking forward to discussing some details with him."

Jeanette's pinched face turned toward the sun, which had cleared the roofline and begun to shine in full force onto her chair. "I cannot abide a patio. Sitting outside on cement with no cover overhead in this sun is intolerable." She issued a sigh before continuing. "A veranda is much more suitable. When I was married to your grandfather, we would have drinks on the veranda at Chestnut Cove on summer Sunday afternoons. Never a meal out there, but drinks are acceptable outdoors in a suitable location such as a veranda." She stopped and shook her head. "While I could not stand the thought of Chestnut Cove becoming an inn, I believe it is even worse now. Such a stately home, and it sits up there in the mountains empty with no one except a caretaker to see it."

Mary, seated nearby, began to cough, causing Doug to smile at her before he redirected the subject to something less controversial than the old mansion. "How is Aunt Claudine? Dad said he invited her and Harold, but they had other plans."

"She is quite well. They had committed to another event before your mother bothered to invite them to attend today. They leave for their annual trip to Florida on Wednesday. Giselle is excited to spend time at the beach. She enjoys lying in the sun. I had hoped your parents would allow Margaret to accompany them since Rainier won't be going this time, but they insisted she remain here and miss the opportunity."

Two weeks of Giselle's uncontrolled influence over Maggie wasn't something Doug could imagine his parents ever allowing. Seeking to shift the conversation again, Doug asked, "Why isn't Rainier going with them this year? He just graduated from State, didn't he? I thought he would want to spend a little time enjoying himself before he starts working. Has he found a job yet?"

Jeanette's face pruned. "Some unreasonable bureaucrat at the university decided Rainier lacked a course to finish his degree. He's to receive a dual degree, as you know. Quite a brilliant boy to study philosophy and psychology. They are requiring him to attend this summer to complete his coursework. He has yet to begin seeking employment, but I am quite sure he will receive a multitude of offers to choose from." She raised her hand to shield her eyes and looked around the patio until she located John sitting with Matt and Jonah.

Though he doubted his grandmother knew the whole story behind Claudine's elder child's extended time at college, Doug downplayed the matter. "I'm sorry Rainier will need to attend school another quarter to finish his degree, but he seems to enjoy that environment. Maybe he'll like being there a couple of extra months. It also gives him time to apply for jobs. I hope he can find something suitable." When she didn't offer any response, Doug noticed her eyes focused on his father. The young man cringed when he realized what would follow.

"John, have you given consideration to what position Rainier will fill at the headquarters of Chestnut Cove Inns once he graduates in August? It is time for him to begin preparing to take his place as a vice president and board member. After all, you made Kathryn a board member when she was only eighteen and vice chair before she finished college, though she never appears in Elkford to perform any duties with the company."

Before John could form a reply, Sandra leaned forward in her chair and glared at Jeanette. "What possible qualifications do you believe Rainier possesses to entitle him to any position at Chestnut Cove Inns? What skills does a degree in philosophy or psychology provide which would be of use to running a hotel chain or any other business? List just one useful qualification he has. He's no more qualified than the high school students we hire each summer.

"KD and Doug–particularly KD–have worked there since they were young and learned the hotel business from the ground up and inside out. Rainier hasn't been bothered to work a day in his life." Sandra shot her husband a look before she continued, warning him she intended to have her say. "For the record, Rainier will never be given a seat on the board or an executive position at Chestnut Cove Inns. Doug will be given one only when he has earned it; so will Maggie and Chris. Regardless of what you think you know of her contributions and abilities, I assure you KD earned her board seat and title through years of hard work from the time she was a pre-teen helping at the original inn.

"The same goes for Vicky, Joseph, and Derrick. Vicky has helped out since she was in high school and earned her place as KD and Matt's assistant. Joseph worked at the hotel like Doug and for his dad in the construction and maintenance division since he could pick up a hammer. Derrick has worked for us during the summer for years and is attending law school now. He'll be helping in the legal department this summer to get some pertinent experience for his career. We hope he'll come to work for CCI when he finishes law school and passes the bar. Again, I ask, name one qualification Rainier has other than the accident of John's mother being married to Rainier's grandfather that makes him a candidate for bellhop, much less a seat on the board or an executive position at the hotel?"

Jeanette stared at Sandra as if expecting a second or even third head to pop out from somewhere. "There is no call for you to be rude. I am a guest in your home and expect to be treated as such, and insulting Rainier when he isn't here to defend himself is inexcusable." Huffing in indignation, she rose and beckoned to Winston.

He set aside his plate and stood to follow her.

"We shall be departing immediately," Jeanette announced. "I will not sit here and listen to Winston's poor grandson disparaged." She waved vaguely in her husband's direction again. "Come, Winston. We are leaving." Jeanette glared at her son before she marched into the house and toward the front door with Winston trailing in her wake.

John shook his head and followed them, bringing up a distant rear to the little procession. He wanted to be at least a tiny bit annoyed with his wife for her part in the short drama, but he knew she was right. He reached the front door in time to bid his mother and stepfather goodbye but said nothing more.

When John returned to the silent patio, he stopped in the doorway and blew out a breath. With a shake of his head and a boyish grin, he walked over to his wife, bent down, and kissed her cheek. Straightening, he raised his right hand and spoke loud enough to ensure everyone on the patio could hear him. "I promise I will not let her talk me into hiring Rainier to work in the corporate office. If he wants a job at the hotel, he can talk to the two people in charge over there."

The group broke into laughter, and all eyes turned to Matt, who held up both hands in surrender. "Won't be me. If he wants to work there, he knows who he needs to talk to, and we all know how that would go." Further laughter ensued before the group returned to the comity which existed before Jeanette and Winston's arrival.

# Chapter 13

*Monday, June 4, 1979*

Vicky stood waiting in the lobby of the CCI headquarters building at a quarter to eight when Laura walked in the front entrance. Determined her new friend and CCI's newest employee would feel welcome on her first day, Vicky decided to escort Laura to the personnel office for Geraldine Malone to process her in.

"Hey, Laura," Vicky called to the girl when she stepped through the door. "Did you have any problem getting here?"

Laura hugged Vicky before answering, "No, the car behaved, and I found a good parking spot and walked right around to the front entrance. I hope you didn't wait long. Grandmother stopped me before I left the apartment and made me model for her. It feels so different being a little dressed up to go to work compared to wearing my waitress uniform at Fred's."

"I hope it will feel normal before too long, and if you ever experience car trouble, call me or call the front desk at the hotel. We'll send someone to get you. Come on. Let's walk down to personnel. I'll leave you with Geraldine Malone to get all your paperwork done." The two young women walked down the hall leading into the heart of the first floor of the building. "When you've finished with Geraldine, she'll buzz me in my office. I'll come back down and walk you over to the hotel and introduce you to a few people like Pam Grant, who's the assistant manager on duty today, and take you to see Matt. Depending on how busy they are, I'll either turn you over to Matt or to Pam or take you around the hotel myself to get you oriented."

"Thank you for meeting me this morning to make sure I got where I need to be, and thank you again for going shopping with me the other day to pick out a few things to wear at the hotel. As you could tell, I didn't own a lot suitable. I can't wait to see how the outfits I bought look with one of those navy blazers. They look so distinguished."

"Oh, I enjoyed shopping with you. My boyfriend, Derrick, hates to be dragged around the mall, and my mom and I have such different tastes. My best friend has been away for a good bit the last few years with college and so forth, so we don't get to spend much time shopping together anymore. I enjoyed going with somebody who shares my tastes again," Vicky enthused. She pointed to a door on the right. "This is the personnel department. Geraldine is the person you'll work with on most things. She handles all the paperwork for new employees being processed in and for your health insurance and vacation and that sort of thing. Griffin Krebs is the manager, but he doesn't usually have much contact with the hotel employees."

Vicky ushered Laura into the personnel office to where the longtime personnel clerk sat at her desk. "Good morning, Vicky. This must be Miss Maddox, our new hotel employee."

"Yes, it is. Laura, this is Geraldine Malone. She'll take care of you. Let me know when she's ready to walk over to the hotel, Geraldine. That will free you up for the intern crush you'll have soon." Turning back to Laura, Vicky explained, "Today is the day most of our summer interns start work, so there will be a line of them outside her door in another hour."

Laura nodded to the woman. "Hello, it's nice to meet you."

"Just buzz me in my office when you two are done. I'll see you again in a little while, Laura," Vicky said before exiting.

"If you'll have a seat right there," Geraldine said, pointing to the chair across from her, "I'll give you the forms you need to fill out. Give me your driver's license and Social Security card and your diploma if you have it with you today. I'll make a copy of each while you fill out these forms."

"OK," Laura said. She dug her driver's license and Social Security card out of her wallet. "My diploma is in here." She handed across a manila envelope she brought with her along with the other items and received a clipboard with several forms and a pen.

"My copier isn't working, so I'll run upstairs to marketing to use theirs. I'll drive them mad by the time I get done copying all the intern paperwork today. I'll be back in a few minutes." Geraldine hurried out of her office, leaving Laura to complete her forms.

Laura was halfway down the second page when she reached a section to list references. She hadn't thought about needing any since she was recruited and hired without applying for a job at the hotel, and neither Matt nor Vicky had mentioned a need to supply any. She looked around for the clerk, who had yet to return from copying Laura's identification and diploma.

An older man entered from the hall and passed Miss Malone's desk on his way to an inner office. Laura noted the sign on the door, which declared it to be the office of Griffin Krebs. When she saw him produce a key and unlock the door, she assumed he was Mr. Krebs, the personnel manager Vicky mentioned.

A minute later, the man returned with his coffee cup in hand. "You don't happen to know where my assistant is, do you?" he asked Laura.

She looked up from her forms. "Miss Malone is making copies of my identification and diploma. She went upstairs to another office because her copying machine isn't working. I don't think she'll be much longer."

"Oh, well, I suppose I can get my own coffee this morning. You must be one of our summer employees. I'm Mr. Krebs, head of personnel at Chestnut Cove Inns." He extended his hand to Laura, and they shook.

"Hi, I'm Laura Maddox, and yes, today's my first day, but I'm going to be a regular employee, not summer help."

"Oh, I see." He noted the paper she was filling out and took the clipboard from her. "This is an application. You said you're starting today. If that's the case, why are you only now filling out an application?"

"Oh, well, I'm not sure. That's part of what Miss Malone handed me." Laura was perplexed. Surely, she hadn't been given the wrong form to complete.

"I see you've skipped over the references section. Don't you have any for us to check? We need them for everyone we hire including high school students who work for us in the summer." Mr. Krebs frowned, and Laura began to worry something had gone wrong. Did she quit her job at Fred's Diner only for her position at Chestnut Cove to fall through this morning?

"Um, I can get a couple of personal references, but I'm not sure my former boss at the diner will be interested in giving me a work reference. He was pretty mad when I told him I was quitting to come to work here." Laura's heart began to pound as Mr. Krebs' frown deepened.

"Oh, good morning, Mr. Krebs," Geraldine said as she hurried into the office. "I see you've met Mr. Hunter's latest find. He's very impatient to get her over to the hotel this morning before his interns begin arriving."

Mr. Krebs shifted his gaze from the clipboard to his clerk. "Too impatient for her to fill out a job application and provide references before he hired her?"

The clerk stared coolly at her boss for a couple of seconds before she replied. "I don't question the Executive VP's hiring decisions. She was a special hire made at his direction. He told Vicky and me to prepare an offer letter for her a couple of weeks ago. As manager of the Elkford hotel, he holds complete hiring discretion, as I'm sure you remember. She's filling out the application now, so we'll have the information it requests on file.

"As for her references, Mr. Hunter, as CCI's Executive Vice President, vouched for Laura. I'm sure you remember Mr. Stuart's policy is that our new hires need no further references if a CCI corporate officer vouches for them." Miss Malone set the documents she copied on her desk, took the clipboard from Mr. Krebs, and returned it to Laura. "Is there anything else, sir? Shall I get your coffee?" She picked up his cup from where he had set it on the corner of her desk and walked over to the coffeepot. She poured the coffee, added the three spoonsful of sugar he used, and returned the cup to him. Without comment, he walked back to his office, closing the door behind him.

Unperturbed, Geraldine walked back to her desk, sat primly, and passed Laura's driver's license, Social Security card, and diploma back to her. "Just skip the reference section. You have all the references you need at CCI."

A relieved Laura returned her attention to the clipboard to finish the paperwork while Miss Malone filed away the copies she made. Fifteen minutes later, Laura was done filling out her forms, and she held a small pile of copies of everything she signed. Geraldine had also taken Laura's photo for her CCI ID and called Vicky to tell her the newly-minted clerk was ready to go over to the hotel.

"Why don't you take your papers and your diploma to your car, so you won't need to keep up with all of it today?" the woman suggested. "Vicky said she needed to take something to Matt that would take her a few minutes to finish getting together, so you have time before she gets downstairs."

"That would be great. I'll run out there and be back in a couple of minutes. Thank you, Miss Malone. It was nice to meet you." Laura waved as she hurried out of the office and back toward the front door of the CCI headquarters.

When Laura was gone, Geraldine flipped through her paperwork to find the page with the blank list of references. She picked up her pencil and wrote two sets of initials on the list. No contact information would be necessary for either.

~~~

Vicky trotted across the hotel lobby with Laura in tow and a folder tucked under her arm. When they reached the reception desk, Vicky said, "Hi, Del. This is Laura Maddox. This is her first day at Chestnut Cove, and I'm taking her around to get her familiar with the hotel for Matt. Is Pam busy? I want to introduce them while we're here."

"Hi, Laura, nice to meet you," Del replied. "It's slowed a bit for now. Pam should be free in the back. I think Matt's there, too. He was a few minutes ago." The desk phone rang, and he offered an apologetic look before he answered it.

Laura waved goodbye to him, but her mind was on her previous visit to the hotel lobby. Thankfully, people were much friendlier this morning than the young man at the desk was before. She wondered if she would run into him today and what she would say to him.

Vicky led Laura along the side of the desk to an opening which gave entry to the back offices of the hotel. She looked in the first door behind the front desk where she spotted Pam at a computer terminal. "Hey, Pam. Do you have a minute?"

"Sure, Vicky. Oh, you brought our new employee, didn't you?" Pam rose from the desk and extended her hand to Laura. "Hi, I'm Pam Grant, one of the assistant managers. Great to have you aboard. Matt and Vicky told us how much they're looking forward to having you at CCI. I know you'll be a great addition to the staff, and I hope you like working here. I sure do."

Laura blushed at the praise from people who had yet to see her do any work. "Thank you, Pam. I'm thrilled to be here. I hope I live up to expectations."

"Is Matt in his office?" Vicky asked.

"Yep, he snuck back there while we're in a lull. The ends of holiday weekends are so busy with people checking out, and there are a lot who checked in this weekend who will stay through the week to beat the post-school surge starting next week. Of course, we'll have interns arriving shortly, and we'll need to get them started with their leads in each department, so it's been a little hectic and will continue that way for the next couple of hours." Del stuck his head into her office from the reception desk and beckoned to her. "Uh oh, I'm needed out front. I'll see you later, Laura." Pam headed to the reception desk while Laura and Vicky exited through the other door to the rest of the offices.

As they wound their way through the building, Vicky kept up a running commentary regarding their surroundings. "The employee break room and lockers are back here. The bookkeepers, event planners, and department leads have offices on those hallways, though of course people like the bell captain usually stay out front. Security is down that hall." Vicky gestured at a door at the end of another side hall. "They have video surveillance around the hotel grounds and public areas as well as uniformed guards. I'll take you downstairs later. Maintenance and housekeeping are in the basement along with the laundry and most of the electrical and mechanical systems." After traversing a couple more halls and turns, Vicky stopped in front of a door and knocked.

"Come in," Matt called.

Vicky opened the door and entered with Laura trailing behind. "Hi, Matt. I brought your newest protégé."

Matt stood and walked around his desk to shake hands with Laura. "Hi, Laura. Welcome aboard. We're glad you're here."

"Thank you, Mr. Hunter. I'm thrilled to be here. Everyone's been so nice to me. Vicky even took me shopping to help find the right clothes to wear," Laura said in a gush of the enthusiasm she felt at the opportunity she had received.

"It's Matt, and yes, Vicky's a gem. I don't know what I'd do without her." Turning his attention to Vicky, he continued, "Has she been fitted for a blazer yet?"

"I took care of that when we went shopping. There's one waiting for her. We'll get it next. I've introduced her to Pam and a few other people as we came through the hotel, but I wanted to stop in here while you weren't tied up," Vicky answered. "I can take her around the rest of the hotel to show her where everything is and introduce her to more of the staff on duty today and then bring her back to you and Pam by late morning if that still works for you. I know you two will be pretty busy with several interns starting today." Remembering the papers she put together for him, she added, "Here are those printouts you wanted me to run." She placed the folder she carried on the corner of Matt's desk.

"That should be fine. We worked out a schedule for you to shadow some of the staff this week and spend some time learning the desk clerk duties. Once you've mastered the process for making reservations and handling check ins and outs and learned our phone etiquette, we'll put you on the front desk during some light times with an experienced clerk and let you get your feet wet." Matt's phone rang, and he sighed. "Duty calls again. You two have fun touring. I'll see both of you later."

Vicky laughed at Matt's ongoing aversion to the phone and escorted Laura out to complete their tour.

~~~

Conversation around the boardroom table ceased when the door from John's office opened. To the surprise of those who already heard the company lost out on the warehouse on which they made an offer, John's face displayed no hint of disappointment or irritation. He took his place at the head of the table and looked around to note any absences before he began.

"Matt will be late joining us, but it looks like everyone else is present, so let's get started. I don't have much to discuss today, so this should be a short meeting. As most of you probably heard, we were outbid on the property in Pearl. I declined to increase our offer further on Thursday when the real estate agent called to inform me someone offered a higher amount. I appreciate the work everyone put into the warehouse. We'll continue to look for suitable locations for expansion, and when we find something else that fits our needs, we'll come back to you to try again. The next item on the agenda–"

"Hold up a minute, John," Hoyt interjected. "We need to discuss this warehouse in Pearl further. I warned you our offer might be too low. We should contact the agent this afternoon to tell him we've reconsidered and increase our offer by two percent."

John took a moment to check his rising temper. "No, Hoyt, the decision has been made. We'll locate another property and pursue it." He stared at Hoyt until the other man looked away. Taking a breath, John returned to his agenda. "As I was saying, the next item I want to discuss is a marketing suggestion Andrew made. Andrew, would you fill everyone in on what you and Matt and I discussed?"

"Yes, sir." Andrew Stein stood and passed out a small stack of papers detailing his suggestion as Matt slipped into the room and took his usual seat near the far end of the table.

Half an hour later, the discussion of the last agenda item concluded. "That's all I have for today except for a couple of small housekeeping issues. First, Matt, Jonah, and I will be away from the office on Thursday and Friday doing a little business and a little golfing. If you need to contact any of us, let Mrs. Pierce or Vicky know. Mrs. Pierce will be away on Friday, so if you need me, you'll need to go through Vicky that day. Since we don't have anything significant going on right now, I don't expect any issues for those two days.

"Also, my son, Doug, whom most of you have met, starts his internship here Wednesday. I've already spoken to some of you about taking time to talk to him about what your department does and how it interacts with other departments in the headquarters as well as in the hotels. He and Jonah's son, Joseph, who is also interning with us this summer, will be traveling with us Thursday and Friday, so you won't see much of them this week. However, you'll see them around a good bit after that. Both boys spent the last several summers working in the hotel. This will be their introduction to what happens over here, and I'd appreciate your patience with them while they learn this part of the business.

"Both my younger daughters will also work here part-time this summer. They'll help Mrs. Pierce and Vicky, and you might see them around the rest of the building delivering and picking up things." He looked around the table before adding, "If nobody has anything else, we're adjourned. Matt, Jonah, I need to see you in my office for a couple of minutes while you're both up here."

The rest of the managers moved out of the boardroom while John disappeared into his office. Matt and Jonah followed him, and Jonah closed and locked the door behind them.

# Chapter 14

*Wednesday, June 6, 1979*

John and Doug arrived at CCI headquarters well before most of the employees. Today would be a busy day for the elder Stuart and a big day for the younger. During previous summers and holidays, Doug worked in the hotel as a bellhop and lifeguard and spent a short stint as a waiter, but he had never worked in the headquarters. This summer, shadowing his father and various department heads would provide a far different experience.

Today would be even more exciting than most because John and Doug, along with Matt, Jonah, and Joseph, who would be shadowing his own father for the summer, would leave on a business trip late in the afternoon. His father had checked Doug's suitcase and given him a couple of pointers on how to best pack for such a trip the previous evening. Doug had worn dress slacks and a nice shirt and jacket to work per his father's direction, though he had been spared a tie.

At just before eight o'clock, Doug went downstairs to personnel to sign the required paperwork. However, he found the door closed. He knocked and waited for Geraldine to call for him to enter, but he heard no response after a couple of minutes. He knocked again lightly, concerned he might be disturbing a private conference with an employee.

Still hearing nothing, he turned to go back upstairs to his father's office and wait until later to fill out his paperwork. As Doug started to walk away, Mr. Krebs turned the corner up the hall, briefcase in hand as he arrived at work. While Krebs would know few if any of the interns at the hotel or in the headquarters, he had made it a point to recall what Doug Stuart looked like so he would be prepared to greet him should he happen upon him in the building.

"Good morning, Doug," Krebs said. "Did you and Miss Malone get your paperwork squared away?"

"Good morning, Mr. Krebs. No, she didn't answer when I knocked." Doug reached out and shook hands with Mr. Krebs. "I expect she's doing something which can't be interrupted right now. I'll come back down later this morning to take care of it."

"Nonsense," Krebs insisted. "She can stop doing whatever she's working on right now for the short time it will take to process you in." He tried the door but found it locked. "How odd. She always arrives first and opens the office." He pulled out his keys and flipped through them twice in search of the correct one before finally unlocking the door. Doug followed him inside and found the light switch as Krebs made his way across the room to his personal office. The personnel manager disappeared for a few seconds, long enough to set down his briefcase and return with his coffee cup. "My apologies that Miss Malone is not yet here to handle your paperwork." He stopped at her desk and shuffled the few papers on top of it. "I don't see anything here that looks as if she prepared a set of forms for your arrival."

"That's all right, Mr. Krebs. I'll come back down later this morning. My sisters will be here about ten o'clock to start their internships. I can do my paperwork when they do theirs." Doug started toward the door. "It's no problem."

Krebs continued to look around the empty office. "My apologies. I will have Miss Malone call Mrs. Pierce as soon as she arrives." He looked down at his empty coffee cup and over at the cold, empty coffeepot and retreated to his office.

~~~

John and Doug chatted about a few points regarding the relationships among the headquarters departments while they waited downstairs in the lobby for Maggie and Chris to arrive. Sandra wanted to stay clear of the building on their first day to allow them to enjoy a small amount of independence, though John would ensure they reached personnel and Vicky's office. Vicky had been tasked with teaching them how to operate the telephones and proper phone etiquette, where each department was located should they be asked to deliver, and how to operate the copying machine.

John saw Sandra's car pass the door on the way to the parking garage and pushed open the front door of the building to walk out to meet the girls, but he stopped when Griffin Krebs hailed him. John gestured for Doug to go ahead to meet his sisters and turned back to speak to the personnel manager.

"Good morning, Griffin. We're about to bring one of my girls to your office for Geraldine to take care of her paperwork and to get Doug's done," John said.

Krebs' color darkened, and he closed the distance to a couple of feet before he spoke. "I'm afraid we have a problem in personnel, and I'm most sorry about it. Miss Malone hasn't arrived for work yet. It seems she arranged some sort of class for herself this morning. I had no idea she scheduled such a thing at a time when she would be needed to take care of your children."

"It isn't a problem. The paperwork for my children can be taken care of whenever she returns. Don't let it concern you, Griffin."

"I appreciate that, John, but this is hardly the first irregularity." He moved half a step closer and lowered his voice. "I believe there was something off about how we received and processed Craig Fielder's application. Then there was Matt's newest young woman this week. I caught her filling out an application the morning she started work. That is most irregular. Miss Malone prepared an offer letter for her without an application or references to check. Those are just the recent issues."

"Griffin, you know Matt can hire at his discretion in the hotel. He decides whom he needs to run it and has his own budget to do so. Don't let it worry you and don't worry about Craig. He's highly qualified and a great find for us." John hoped his reassurance would be enough to settle Griffin's concerns. He wanted his attention to be on his girls this morning, not on an antsy personnel manager.

The front door opened, and Chris bounded in, followed by Maggie at a more sedate pace with Doug bringing up the rear. The security guard/greeter at the lobby desk welcomed the girls before they went to their father. Griffin excused himself and slipped away to his office.

"Hi, Dad," Chris said as she hugged John. He returned the hug and then greeted Maggie with a warm pat on her shoulder.

"I can tell Chris is excited to be here. What about you, Maggie? Are you ready to learn a little about this place?" John gave her an encouraging smile. It had been a contentious couple of weeks sorting out whether and where she would work for the summer.

"I guess. I think I'll like it better than working in the hotel, but I'll get to go over there some, right?" Maggie asked.

"You'll deliver papers to Matt or go over to pick up something from him to bring back over here a few times. Mostly you'll be in this building. Vicky will show you some basic things you'll need to know today. Geraldine is out at some kind of training this morning, so we'll take you upstairs for now and let Vicky bring you back down later today when Geraldine gets here. Maggie, you'll need to fill out a little paperwork. Chris, you're just here as my daughter. You're a little young to work officially, so your mother and I will give you a bigger allowance for the time you're here. Geraldine will make you a nametag though so people you haven't met will know you're supposed to be in the building."

A glowing Chris gushed, "I don't have to get paid, Dad. Just learning about what goes on in the headquarters will be great. I can't wait."

Maggie rolled her eyes, and Doug nudged her. "Just wait, Mag. You might find out you love it here as much as Chris before the summer is over."

John put his arms around his daughters' shoulders and urged them forward. "OK, kids, we need to get upstairs. I'll hand you two over to Vicky, and Doug and I will get back to what we're doing to get ready for our trip."

~~~

"Hi, Uncle Matt," Chris exclaimed from her perch at the unused secretary's desk across from Vicky's in the outer office at the east end of the CCI headquarters executive floor.

Matt grinned at the youngest Stuart child. "Hey, Chrissie, how has your first day of work gone?" He set his briefcase on the floor and perched on the edge of the desk.

"It's been great. I've learned the names of all the people in finance and accounting today, and I got my own nametag with my picture on it. See?" She pointed to the ID clipped to her blouse. "Maggie did, too. Maggie and Vicky went down to marketing for a few minutes, and Vicky left me in charge of answering the phone. That's something else I learned. I know how to tell which line is ringing and answer the right one and put somebody on hold. I can even buzz you in your office if you're in there to let you know when you have a phone call."

"Have you been allowed to touch the copier yet? Vicky is a wiz at that thing.

Even the copier service technician says so. It still intimidates most people around here."

Chris tried to suppress a smile. "No, not yet. Mrs. Pierce warned Vicky not to allow Maggie and me to tear it up. Vicky said she'll show us how to work it when Mrs. Pierce isn't around. She's taking Friday off since Dad will be gone, so I hope Mom will let me come in even though that's Maggie's day to work. I don't mind being here extra, especially if I can learn something like how to make copies. I wish Mrs. Pierce would take tomorrow off, too, since Dad won't be here then either, but she'll be at work. Dad said I have to help some over there, too, but I hope I can spend most of my time helping Vicky."

Matt leaned close and whispered, "I hope you can, too. Vicky is a lot nicer to work with than Mrs. Pierce, but don't tell your dad I said so."

Chris giggled. "I won't. He says she's good at her job, but she never smiles."

Vicky's voice could be heard approaching, and Matt put his finger to his lips to quiet his co-conspirator. Vicky and Maggie entered the outer office a moment later. "Hey, Matt," Vicky said. "I have the information you requested from marketing. Do you want extra copies of it to take with you or just the one?"

"Just the one right now. I want to go over it in my hotel room and talk to John and Jonah about how we might adapt what we've done in the past for this potential hotel site. Once we've debated it a little, I'll make some more notes and talk to marketing about putting together something for it if we go forward with this place." Matt noticed Maggie listening and asked, "Did you know marketing our hotels was so involved, Maggie?"

Maggie remembered she had yet to greet Matt and walked over to hug him. "Hi, Uncle Matt. No, I didn't know we did different things for each hotel. One of the people downstairs in marketing told me he designs all the little flyers for each hotel and one that sort of covers all of them, too. He picks out pictures and colors to show the hotels looking their best. It's sort of like designing clothes and having them modeled."

Matt considered the idea. "Yes, I suppose it is. Maybe we can arrange for you to spend a little time down in marketing this summer, so you can learn more about what they do. Designing the brochures is only a part of their job, but it's an important one. Something we'll do early on if we decide we like the hotel location your dad and Jonah and I are visiting is choose a color scheme for it. That's one of the things your mom still gets involved in. Maybe you can talk to her about how we decide on colors and designs for the lobby and the guest rooms and the exterior of each hotel."

Maggie brightened even more. "That would be so cool to do. I'll ask her tonight. I would really love to learn more about those brochures, too. Do you think Dad would mind if I spent some time in marketing?"

"No, I don't think he would mind at all. Why don't you go ask him to make sure?"

"Oh, thank you, Uncle Matt!" Maggie hugged him again and with a nod from Vicky hurried out the door in search of her father.

~~~

A grinning Matt walked into John's office where Doug, Jonah, and Joseph had already congregated. "Who wants to ride with me? Since I'm leading this little parade, I might need a navigator to make sure I don't get lost."

John glanced at the door and wondered if Matt had ensured no one was within earshot. "I wish you would just tell us where we're going, Matt," he said low enough no one outside his office could hear him. At least Mrs. Pierce had left half an hour earlier.

"Where's the fun in that?" When John still didn't smile, Matt added, "I'll tell you what. We'll stop to eat dinner in about an hour, and I'll let you know then."

"Do I have a choice?"

"Nope. You'll know soon enough." Beckoning to Joseph and Doug, he added, "I might even let one of you drive part of the way if you navigate when I need help finding the tricky turn we need to watch for."

Joseph jumped up from his seat after a quick glance at his father. "I'll go with you. Let's get on with this parade."

"OK, come on, guys. When we get to the cars, I'll tell you where we're eating dinner. That might give you a good hint to chew on about where we're going. Come on, Joseph." Matt, briefcase in hand, did an about face and headed toward the elevator, Joseph right behind him. Doug followed close on Joseph's heels, leaving John and Jonah to bring up the rear.

Shaking his head, Jonah mumbled to John, "Did you ever notice Matt's resemblance to the Pied Piper? Those kids follow him around just like in the fable."

At last, John smiled and then laughed. "Yes, he's nothing but a big kid himself."

When they reached the otherwise empty garage, Matt whispered the name of a well-known restaurant about forty miles from Elkford. He grinned at the surprised look on John's face. "Matt, we don't own anything in that direction. We've always stayed on this side of the mountains."

Matt shrugged. "We will soon. It's a done deal, John. Already bought and paid for."

"What? You're kidding!"

"Nope. You won't believe where the site is. It's a fantastic location. Of course, you can decline to franchise it, but if you do it will still go forward as a hotel, and you do not want to miss out on this place."

"Come on, Matt, tell me the location," John demanded.

Matt slid into the driver's seat of his Lotus. "Tuseeca," he called right before his engine roared to life.

Doug nudged his father. "Come on, Dad. Let's go. Are you really surprised she bought it outright after the information leak before? I expect she always intended to buy it herself before anyone knew where she was looking."

"No, I suppose it shouldn't surprise me. Nothing those two cook up should." John waved for Jonah to get into the car, and ten minutes later the two cars passed the entrance to the Stuart home on their way into and over the mountains.

# Chapter 15

*Thursday, June 7, 1979 - morning*

An apprehensive Laura tucked her purse into her locker in the staff area of Chestnut Cove Inn. She enjoyed the first three days of her new job, and she liked all the people she worked with so far. The previous day she met Martha, who helped show her the ropes at the front desk during a quiet period there. Martha started working for CCI about eight months earlier and had nothing but good things to say about her time with the hotel. The two young women found they had several things in common, and Laura hoped they would become good friends. So far, she had already gained a new friend in Vicky. She had so much more in common with the people she was working with now than her former co-workers at Fred's Diner.

However, today she would come face to face with the young man who had been on the desk when she came to see Matt a month earlier. The previous afternoon, Matt called her back to his office and talked to her about working with Jared as her shift supervisor. He told her he spoke to Jared at length on the issue and asked Laura to give the young AM a chance to prove himself more civil and professional than at their first meeting. She assured him she was willing to begin anew with Jared, and she intended to do just that, but still she was apprehensive about getting past their initial interactions. Unfortunately, Matt would be gone today and tomorrow. He apologized for the timing, and she was sure he regretted he wouldn't be at the hotel the first day she and Jared worked together, but he and John Stuart needed to attend to some business out of town.

Martha entered the staff area and greeted Laura. The two young women would be working as the front desk clerks together again today, and they chatted while Martha put her things in her locker. Then the girls walked to the office where they and the leads for the various departments would meet with the assistant manager for the day shift before taking over from the night crew.

Jared stood at the assistant manager's desk speaking to a young man Laura assumed to be the AM who had been on duty during the night. Jared's back was to the door, so he didn't see her come in. When he and Donald, as the night manager's nametag proclaimed him to be, finished their discussion, Donald walked out of the room, and Jared took a seat at the desk. A few other people had entered the room in the meantime, including Janelle, the head housekeeper, and Maurice, the concierge. Laura met them earlier in the week and spent a little time with each learning how their jobs fit with hers at the front desk.

Janelle was a treasure-trove of information about the hotel because she had worked for the Stuart family and Matt at the original inn. She shared a little history about CCI Laura felt was more accurate than anything she had heard from others who had only worked for there for a year or two. One thing Janelle's intelligence had done was confirm Laura's own assessment of Matt Hunter as someone who was not only friendly but fair and trustworthy, two characteristics she thought essential for a good boss.

Right at seven o'clock, Jared looked up from the nightshift report he was reviewing to go over the things the staff needed to be aware of that day. He opened his mouth to speak but stopped when he saw Laura. He had almost forgotten she would be working at the desk today. His complexion darkened a fraction, and he swallowed hard before beginning to go over his list.

When he finished, Jared cleared his throat and finally looked at the new clerk. "In case any of you haven't met her, this is Laura Maddox. She started Monday as a desk clerk. Um, welcome to CCI-Elkford, Laura."

She offered him a smile and said, "Thank you, Jared."

He cleared his throat again and hurried on, anxious to put their initial interaction behind him. "That's all I have this morning. Unless anybody has questions, let's get to work. We have a nearly full hotel today." The crowd began to disperse. Jared set his notes on the desk in front of him and watched from the corner of his eye until everyone left except Martha and Laura. They stood in the doorway leading to the front desk talking to the clerk who had been on duty overnight. "Um, Laura?" Jared called. "Would you wait a minute?"

Laura looked back at the assistant manager. "Of course." She excused herself from the conversation with the other two clerks, who walked out to the front desk while Laura approached Jared. She stopped across from him and waited.

He cleared his throat again and tugged at his collar. "Um, I wanted to apologize for being a...a little abrupt with you before. I mean, back when you came in here the first time. I should have taken you at your word and made an appointment for you to come back when Matt was here." He stopped, struggling to determine how much he needed to say to pacify Matt.

"Thank you, Jared. I'm sure it was unusual for someone to bring a note in here written on a napkin, and I wasn't dressed to meet with someone like the hotel manager of a place this nice. I'm afraid I was in over my head even walking in the hotel's front door that day."

"Well, uh, I still should have been more professional. I hope there are no hard feelings."

"No, it all worked out for me in the end, and I hope we can put that day behind us. I'm looking forward to learning all I can from you and the other assistant managers and the more experienced people here." Laura saw the night clerk hovering near the door, waiting for the coast to be clear so he could leave but not wanting to interrupt a conversation between the assistant manager and the new clerk. "If there's nothing else, I need to go out to the desk to help Martha."

A relieved Jared nodded. "Of course. It will get busy out there soon."

~~~

The morning passed busily but with no problems for Laura and Martha. Martha took her lunch break before the desk became busy again, leaving Laura alone to handle the light time. Jared had been apprehensive about having a brand-new clerk alone at the reception desk, especially one with whom he had clashed a few weeks earlier, but Martha needed a lunch break. He hovered nearby in the back office, listening with one ear to everything that happened at the front desk while Laura worked there alone.

The peaceful interlude ended when Janelle hurried into Jared's office. "Jared, I tried to call Geraldine Malone to ask her a question about sick leave and health insurance requirements for one of my girls who needs surgery next week. Geraldine's gone. Whoever answered her phone said she doesn't work at CCI anymore. Have you heard anything about her leaving? Mr. Krebs has had someone from the secretarial pool assigned to answer the phone, but she doesn't know anything about personnel issues. I called Vicky to see if she knew anything, but she didn't answer either."

Jared scowled up at Janelle. "No, I haven't heard anything about it, but you shouldn't have called Mr. Hunter's secretary without coming to me first. I'm in charge today in his absence."

Janelle took a deep breath before she replied. "I'm sorry, Jared. I wasn't trying to circumvent your authority, but Vicky is Matt's assistant in the headquarters building, and as you know our personnel work is handled there instead of here in the hotel since we're all right together in Elkford. I'll be happy for you to handle the matter, but I need this sorted out as soon as possible. Ginger needs surgery, and her doctor wants to do it next week. We need to make sure our insurance is prepared to pay for it like they should, and we need to work out sick leave for her. She's been absent quite a bit with this problem and might not have enough leave to cover the days she'll miss work. Geraldine always helps us with working out extra sick leave when it's a serious health issue." Janelle set the clipboard with several forms and a sheet of notations she had made on Jared's desk. "Here you are. We need to get this sorted out by the end of today so they can schedule the surgery next week." Janelle turned and marched toward the door, not waiting for Jared to reply.

Annoyed by Janelle circumventing him to call Matt's assistant and dumping a perplexing problem on his desk, Jared stewed for a couple of minutes considering how to handle the issue. He decided the solution lay in discussing the matter with Mr. Krebs himself. Unused to dealing with the department heads in the headquarters, Jared decided to read through all of Janelle's notes first to familiarize himself with the matter.

Meanwhile, Martha returned from her lunch break, and Laura left for hers with a cursory wave from Jared, who remained immersed in the papers Janelle dumped on his desk. Laura went to her locker and retrieved her sandwich and entered the break room to buy a soft drink and sit and eat. She just sat down in the otherwise deserted room when Janelle and Gabe, who was also on his lunch break, walked in. The two were deep in whispered conversation, which ended when Janelle noticed Laura in the room.

Janelle looked around to ensure no one else was present. "May we join you, Laura?"

"Of course," Laura answered. The others sat down, Gabe with his lunch in hand. Gabe had become one of Laura's favorites at CCI. The doorman greeted her warmly on her first day when Vicky took her around to meet the staff and show her all the public areas and back hallways and rooms of the hotel. Neither Gabe nor Laura acknowledged their brief encounter the day she came to the hotel the first time, but both knew the other remembered the distressing day, and Gabe made sure to make her feel welcome.

As soon as Janelle sat down, she checked the door for anyone passing by and then began. "Did you hear me tell Jared Geraldine Malone isn't working in the personnel office anymore? She was there Monday when you filled out your paperwork to start working here, right?"

Laura gave a nod. "Yes, I heard part of what you told Jared. She was there Monday, and she was so nice and helpful. Mr. Krebs didn't say why she wasn't there anymore?"

"No, I couldn't even talk to him. The girl who answered the phone told me he was out, and she had no idea when he would be back. That's when I called Vicky's office. Vicky can find out what happened and how we're supposed to manage without Geraldine. She's the one who knows everything about insurance, and she tracks sick leave and knows all the ins and outs and works with us when we have a problem. If this was any of the other CCI hotels, we'd have our own personnel representative in the hotel, but because we're right next to the headquarters, they put it all together there."

Janelle let out a loud huff before continuing. "I hope Jared has called over there by now and can get some answers. If Pam were on duty today, she'd have either found Vicky and gotten some help from her in finding answers or gone over to talk to Mr. Krebs herself to get some, but Jared's not like Pam. For one thing, he's too new as an AM. Pam's been here longer than most of the corporate managers. She would walk into Mr. Stuart's office if she needed to do so to handle a problem, but of course he's gone today and tomorrow like Matt."

~~~

Vicky pulled a key ring from the bottom of her purse and selected one of the color-coded keys on it. She checked behind her again before inserting it into the door lock. As soon as it clicked, she opened the door and slipped inside the darkened foyer. She closed and locked the door behind her without a sound and stood listening for a minute before she turned on the lights to illuminate the stairwell ahead of her. After assuring herself all remained quiet on the other side of the door, she slipped off her high-heel shoes and ascended the steps. At the top, she used another color-coded key to unlock the steel door barring entrance to the upper floor.

When the door opened, Vicky made her way across the outer office in the semi-darkness. The blinds were closed, and in broad daylight there was little chance anyone would notice the lights on over Dilly's, but she wouldn't chance anyone knowing she was here. She hated that she couldn't make this phone call from her office in the CCI headquarters, but she wouldn't risk someone overhearing the forthcoming conversation.

She set her purse and shoes on a most familiar desk–one which had been hers for several years before she began working at CCI headquarters–and took a seat in the chair. This suite above the teen hangout and casual restaurant on the first floor had been a private meeting place for the most exclusive inner circle in Elkford for several years, so exclusive that few people even suspected it for what it was. Today, Vicky was grateful for its location right across from CCI.

She dialed a well-known number and held her breath, hoping she would be able to reach the person she needed. With Matt and John out of town and even Sandra off in Woodbury with Vicky's mother shopping today, only one person might remain available to deal with the Geraldine situation.

When the phone clicked on the other end, Vicky let out an audible breath. "Hello," the voice on the other end answered.

Vicky began speaking immediately. "I know I'm breaking protocol, but I had to try to reach you. I snuck over to Dilly's to call you to ensure no one could overhear anything I said. Mr. Krebs fired Geraldine this morning. With Matt and Uncle John both out of town today and tomorrow, it can't be a coincidence."

The voice on the other end of the line remained calm but firm. "You did the right thing. I'm glad you caught me here. I agree Krebs' timing wasn't coincidental. That man doesn't think ahead. He has no idea about the day-to-day details of his own office. Who does he think will do all her work now?"

Vicky arranged a notepad and pen on the desk in front of her, ready to take notes when required. "He had Mrs. Pierce assign someone from the pool to his office, but of course she knows nothing about anything to do with personnel. She can do nothing but answer the phone and type what he tells her. I assumed you and Matt would want to pick up Geraldine and her job at the hotel, but I needed confirmation from one of you. I didn't think you would want me to sit on this until I could reach Matt since that might not be until tomorrow evening."

"Absolutely. Have Pam find a spot for her to sit somewhere in the hotel until they can shuffle offices as needed. If nothing else, she can use Matty's until he gets back. He'll be fine with that. And Vicky, make a spectacle of this. Have Boyd get a couple of his guys, parade them into the personnel office as soon as Geraldine can get to the hotel, and seize all the hotel's personnel files and anything else she needs. Tell Craig to move the budget for her job from headquarters to the hotel. Make it effective today or even retroactive to the first of the month if possible. If he expresses any concerns, tell him to get the franchise agreement from legal and read it. Matty put it in there we can pull our personnel budget and function back from headquarters at our discretion. Get Derrick to pull a copy for him if he wants to read it. If Craig has any concerns and wants to wait until Monday, tell him that's fine. The main thing is to get those files out of headquarters along with anything else Geraldine needs to do her job for the next couple of days. And I mean a spectacle, Vic. I don't want anyone to forget it for a long time."

Vicky grinned at the thought of Mr. Krebs' face as he watched Geraldine supervising the removal of hotel records from his office. "Boyd will love it; so will Geraldine. Oh, but Pam isn't on duty. Jared is assistant manager today. He might be a little bit of an issue."

"Don't let him. Tell him you're carrying out Matty's orders. He doesn't need to know the details of what you tell Boyd and Geraldine. Do whatever you need to do to take care of this. Matty and I will back you."

"I will. I'll call Geraldine from here as soon as I hang up with you. For that matter, I'll call Boyd from here, too. Hopefully he's in the security office right now. I know he's working today." Vicky began jotting down a list of tasks she needed to perform to execute their plan.

"Good. Anything else? I'll be here until about midmorning tomorrow. Then I won't be reachable for a couple of weeks at least, but Matty will be back tomorrow evening, right?"

"Yes, they're due back late tomorrow. They took Doug and Joseph with them."

"Good, that will make for a nice learning experience for them."

"Oh, I need to run back by my office to check on my summer helper before I go to the hotel. Want to guess who's covering the phones for me over there right now?"

"Chris or Maggie?"

"Yes, Chris," Vicky said with a laugh. "Maggie is working Mondays, Wednesdays and Fridays, and Chris is working Tuesdays and Thursdays. They're helping both me and Mrs. Pierce, which means I'll have them most of the time. I found out about this mess because of Chris. I sent her downstairs to take something to Geraldine, and Chris came running back upstairs to tell me Geraldine didn't work there anymore according to some secretary sitting at her desk. A few minutes later Janelle called my office and said she had tried to get me earlier to find out what happened to Geraldine. Jared kicked up a fuss about her calling me, so she officially washed her hands of it, but she called again when she got a chance to make sure I heard about it."

"I see," the young woman replied. "I knew Chris was working up there a little this summer, but I didn't know how they resolved the Maggie situation. I'm glad she's working up there, too. It will be good for her. Good for both of them. Keep them in line, Vic."

"I will. I know you need to get back to other work since you're leaving CasCav again tomorrow, and I need to handle this issue with Geraldine." Vicky hesitated before adding, "I hope this will be over soon. It's dragged on too long."

"Not much longer, Vic. Just a few more pieces to put into place."

"Good. We have lots of catching up to do. Bye," Vicky said before she hung up. She checked down the list of calls she needed to make and added a couple of other notes before she picked up the phone again. First, she needed to call Geraldine at home.

Geraldine answered on the first ring. "Hello?"

"It's Vicky. Get your things and head to the hotel. I need to make two more calls first to deal with the controversy this will cause. Then I need to check on Chris before I can go over there to tell Jared. You're to set up wherever we can find you a place until Matt gets back–even if it's in his office. As soon as he can gather the troops, Boyd and his guys are to escort you to headquarters, and you are to collect all hotel personnel files and anything else you need. Boyd and his men will take them to the hotel. We'll put them anywhere we can for now. I have a master key and have been authorized to act for management. We'll find somewhere safe to put them."

"Thank you, Vicky. I wasn't worried, but I knew it would get messier the longer it took for them to get me transferred and set up next door."

"No, there was no way Mr. Krebs firing you would stand. The first thing you need to do is take care of your transfer paperwork. Matt can sign it when he gets back. Also, Janelle needs help for Ginger, who needs surgery next week, as soon as you can get set up enough to help."

"OK, I'll find Janelle as soon as I get to the hotel to get the details. I might be able to make a call or two from Janelle's office without anyone else's knowledge to take care of Ginger's needs. What about the poor people who work in the headquarters? Something will need to be done there, too. Mr. Krebs has no idea about any of the details of my job. I bet he hasn't done any of the day-to-day personnel paperwork in thirty years."

"I know, but she didn't mention that. I imagine she intends to let Mr. Stuart deal with it when he gets back. I bet he'll have heard from all quarters by the time he returns on Monday."

Geraldine laughed. "Yes, he will. I'll stay out of it though."

"I need to call Craig about budgeting and try to contact Boyd before I walk to the hotel to tell Jared he's landed in a hornet's nest not of his making. I'll see you shortly."

Next, Vicky called Craig to pass along the instructions regarding budget changes and franchise agreements. As soon as she completed that task, she called the security office in the hotel.

"CCI security. Boyd speaking."

"Hey, Boyd, it's Vicky. Have you heard about Geraldine?"

"Just heard it a few minutes ago. Janelle's on the warpath, and Jared got nowhere with Krebs. Has Matt intervened? Or Mr. Stuart? I heard they were both out of town."

"No, they're unreachable right now, but I...acquired a directive for us to follow to take care of the problem. To quote as best I can, as soon as Geraldine gets to the hotel, you and a couple of your men are to escort her to the headquarters personnel office." She stopped to giggle. "The exact words were to 'parade them into the personnel office' to take the hotel's personnel files and anything else Geraldine needs. I was told for us to make a spectacle, so keep that in mind."

Boyd howled in laughter. "I don't need to ask who issued that directive. I'll borrow Gabe to help us. He'll fully appreciate that order. Where are we to put the files? We don't have a space for personnel over here right now."

"I have Matt's master key. We can put them in Matt's office or anywhere else we need to put them. We can even use her office. I'll take responsibility for that. Jared will need to be distracted, and you, Gabe, Geraldine, and I will have to do the moving if we need to use a couple of those private areas, but hopefully we won't need to."

"All right, I'll ask maintenance for their dollies. They'll wonder why security is moving file cabinets instead of them, but I'll make up something."

"Great. Thanks, Boyd. I'll be over there in about fifteen minutes. I need to inform Jared of this decision. He'll squawk that he hasn't heard it from Matt, but Matt will back us up when he returns tomorrow evening. I'll try to contact him and Uncle John when I get a chance, but I might not be able to let them know directly. If all else fails, I'll tell Aunt Sandra what happened when I can. She and Mom are off shopping right now, but she'll be by to pick up Chris later. Chris is working in the office and answering my phones there right now. I didn't want to handle this from inside CCI."

"You're above Dilly's?"

"Yes, it seemed best to make my calls from here."

"You're probably right. OK, I'll see you soon. I'll be ready by the time Geraldine gets here and you've informed Jared."

# Chapter 16

A smirking Matt tossed the empty wrapping from his sandwich into the trashcan in the former mill office. "You've seen all of it now, John. What's your first impression? Remind you of the Elkford building before we converted it into a hotel?"

John tried to maintain a stoic expression just to annoy his gloating cousin. However, he couldn't manage to do so and smiled. "Yes, it's a little smaller, but it has the same potential we saw in the Elkford mill. This place is in decent shape, too." He turned to Jonah, seated to his left. "Based on the engineering data we received and what we've seen this morning, I think we might open in a year. Do you agree, Jonah?"

Still munching on his second sandwich, Jonah took his time to consider a couple of details before answering. Once he swallowed his food, he replied, "The information we started with a couple of weeks ago gave us a good head start. If we don't find any surprises and we can agree on the layout details and décor and get everything ordered, I think we can open by sometime next summer. Maybe not the beginning of summer. I still need to finish digesting the fuller set of engineering data Elliott turned over to us this morning, but he seems sure there are no surprises to cause any delays." As the most conservative of the three men, Jonah's assessment pleased Matt and John.

"Any reason we can't use the same décor as in Elkford?" Doug asked. He and Joseph were there to listen and learn, and they had been encouraged to ask questions.

John shrugged. "We haven't repeated exact colors and patterns and so forth between hotels so far, but that doesn't mean we can't. We could use similar but slightly different schemes. Your mother will need to see this place and give her opinion soon. I doubt that will happen before our vacation to Arizona, but right after we return, we'll make another trip out here for her to look it over and start making decisions on those things." He remembered his short conversation with his middle daughter the previous day and added, "Might even bring the girls. Maggie's sudden realization that Sandra selects the décor for all our hotels and what she learned about how we market them sparked some interest yesterday. Sandra and I would like to encourage her where we can."

John stood and walked over to the window to look out at the mountains behind the mill. "We can take this afternoon and part of tomorrow to walk through at a slower pace, look closer at the little details, and take some measurements while we discuss placement of facilities."

Jonah tossed his sandwich wrapper into the trashcan and pulled out his sketchpad. "If we're all done eating, let's walk the main floor again to see if we're in agreement on the major things to start with. Then I can sit here and sketch a little of it and the basement while the rest of you walk around the upper floors again. The main issue with upstairs will be how to divide between rooms and suites once you allow for hallway size based on the fire code and space we need for housekeeping and storage on each floor."

Matt sat forward and pushed across a sheet of paper with handwritten notes. "The new owner sent a few ideas to consider before we get too far into this."

John rolled his eyes but remained silent, and Jonah picked up the paper and scanned down the list of bullet points on it.

"Looks like we're on the same page." Jonah stuck the sheet into his sketchpad. "Are we ready to do a more detailed ground floor walkthrough now?"

John nodded. "Yes, let's get on with it. Doug, Joseph, you have the cameras and plenty of rolls of film. Take photos of everything from every angle and make notes of what you photograph."

"Yes, sir," they said in unison. Both young men grabbed their camera bags and bounded out into the main floor of the old mill to perform their task.

~~~

"I must speak to Matt myself," Jared repeated for the third time. "If Mr. Krebs fired Miss Malone, I cannot simply make her a place to sit in the hotel three hours later like nothing happened."

Vicky used every bit of both her natural height and the extra three inches her heels gave her along with the lessons she learned from her best friend about standing her ground in the office. She took half a step forward and leaned slightly toward Jared, invading his personal space. "I'm sorry, but Matt won't be available for the rest of the day. Do you want to take responsibility for defying management by ignoring the directive relayed through me? I am executive assistant to the Executive Vice President for Hotel Operations. I assure you Matt expects instructions relayed through me to be treated as if he made them directly to you. If you refuse to act on this, you will leave me no choice but to call Pam at home and ask her to come into work. As you know, she is the senior AM and Matt's deputy in the hotel. I can't imagine either Matt or Pam will be happy if she gets called in on her day off because you refused to implement an order relayed through me."

Jared blinked and looked down, aware a small crowd hovered right outside around the front desk where they awaited his official word to proceed. Geraldine stood out there chatting with Laura and Martha while waiting for the discussion between Vicky and Jared to end.

Boyd had informed the bell captain he needed to borrow Gabe from the front door and brought him along with one of the junior security guards he could spare from duty for an hour. Boyd wanted Gabe because the longtime doorman would understand where this directive came from and because the older man served twenty years in the Marine Corps before he began work at CCI. He knew how to intimidate someone like Krebs into submission if needed. It was also why he was so effective on the front door. He could be the friendliest of men when greeting guests, but he shifted into Marine-mode in a hurry if someone looked like they wanted to cause trouble near the front of the hotel or in the lobby.

Indeed, Gabe laughed out loud when Boyd told him about their mission. Gabe especially liked the term "spectacle" and wanted to do his best to fulfill that part of their instructions. He had handed over door duty to one of the bellhops and shed his gold-braided jacket to help facilitate Geraldine's move.

When Vicky and Jared emerged from the back office, Jared cleared his throat and repeated the directive all expected. Boyd, Gabe, and the junior security guard each grabbed their dolly and fell into line behind Geraldine and Vicky and began their parade across the lobby toward the headquarters building.

~~~

Sandra pressed the phone to her ear and shushed Chris, who was chattering to Maggie about the events of the day. "Fortunately, Geraldine was set up at a temporary desk in the AM's office by the time I learned about any of this. Jared decided she should sit in there with him for now, and he asked maintenance to find a desk in storage and bring it upstairs and rearrange things enough to fit it in. I went over to the hotel after I went to pick up Chris, and Vicky told me what happened. They put the hotel personnel files in the two private offices for now. They'll need to work out something else later, but Geraldine can manage until Matt gets back and figures out where he wants her located."

John sat on the bed in his hotel room rubbing the back of his neck. "I'll let Matt know. I agree Griffin timed this for when we were both gone. He apologized yesterday afternoon for the delay in processing the kids, and I told him it wasn't an issue. Chris and Maggie were fine upstairs learning where things were and how to work the phones with Vicky, and Doug was shadowing me. There was no hurry getting our kids' paperwork through personnel like the other interns. The same goes for Joseph. Geraldine processed all of them yesterday afternoon as soon as she got back.

"I'll talk to him Monday and find out what caused him to dismiss her today and if he still thinks it was a problem our children weren't processed in until midafternoon yesterday. Maybe something happened we don't know about with Geraldine, but regardless I wouldn't have any control over the hotel hiring her and taking the budget back for her position. That's their prerogative, and nothing I could say would impact them hiring her."

"No, there was no doubt they would grab her when they found out Griffin fired her. Geraldine has worked for us for too long. They know her quality of work; her diligence and attention to detail over the years speak for themselves. It was just a matter of how fast they picked her up at the hotel. You'll have the problem at headquarters. Griffin Krebs is decent with big picture things, but he knows little about the day-to-day tasks involved with hiring and terminating employees, processing insurance, tracking vacation, and all the other things Geraldine does. He'll need to hire somebody new to do that for the headquarters staff, but he won't have the budget to do so because almost everything allocated for the headquarters personnel office came from the hotel. The only other budget is for his own salary."

John lay back on his bed and rubbed his temple with his free hand. "Somehow I suspect he'll be gone before long. I'm sure the parade to remove all the hotel personnel files was the first volley in another internal war. He's almost old enough to retire. I expect he could be encouraged to do so by the end of the summer with a little extra incentive. Does he even know the budget for Geraldine's job has been moved to the hotel?"

"I don't know. I looked for him before I walked over to the hotel to try to soothe a few ruffled feathers, but the personnel office was locked up and dark. I know Vicky didn't tell him. It wasn't her place. Besides, she had enough to do relaying and overseeing other directives today. Craig might have told him though. Wouldn't he normally document something like that with an internal memo? Though he might wait until you get back to sign something official directing the budget change."

"Me or Matt. Matt can pull that budget without my authorization based on the franchise agreement. Regardless, I'll sign something Monday authorizing it. Maybe Matt and I will co-sign a memo to Craig and to Griffin making the move official. We'll need to decide what date to use."

"Craig was instructed to use June first if possible. I think she didn't want there to be any chance Geraldine's firing looked real. If Geraldine shifted to the hotel under Matt retroactively before Griffin fired her today, the firing didn't happen."

John chuckled. "Ever efficient, especially when angry and exacting revenge on somebody, isn't she?"

"Yes, just like her namesake. On the other hand, it was lucky Vicky found her since you and Matt were out of reach. Even if Mary and I hadn't been off shopping and out of touch for a few hours, I'm not sure I would have wanted to intervene. I'm glad you called last night to tell me where you were since Matt had been so mysterious. All in all, it worked out for the best that Vicky reached her to get official direction about what to do."

"Yes, it did, but it will be yet another point of contention for us."

"I expect so, but we'll sort it out. Matt will help on that as usual."

"Speaking of Matt, I'll tell him in a few minutes. I'm overdue downstairs to meet him and Jonah and the boys for dinner. I'm surprised Doug hasn't come back up here looking for me." On cue, John heard a tapping on his door. "There he is now." He sat up and walked as close to the door as the phone cord would allow and stretched to reach the doorknob. "Come on in. Your mother caught me before I left my room."

"Hi, Mom," Doug called as he walked into his father's hotel room.

"Tell him hello and the rest of the guys, too. I'll let you get to dinner. Call me if you think of any more questions and tell Matt to call if he has any, too. I'll see you tomorrow evening."

"All right, honey. We'll see you then. Love you. Bye." John hung up the phone and picked up his wallet from the dresser. "Come on, let's go eat. I have a tale to tell you and the rest of the group about a spectacle at the headquarters and hotel today."

Doug grinned and followed his father out of the room. "Can't wait."

~~~

"I've never been so humiliated, Hoyt." Griffin Krebs' expression would have tugged at the heartstrings of almost anyone. Sadly for both men, Hoyt was not almost anyone.

"Don't worry about it, Griffin. We'll talk to John Monday and get this straightened out. Hunter can't storm in and undo your decision about your department. I'll make John see sense. He lets Hunter run rampant. The man is unchecked running our flagship hotel right under John's nose. That's why we need stronger oversight on the Board of Directors. We need some people both inside the company added to it and from outside to provide an unbiased view. I tried to get John to put his own stepfather on the board a couple of weeks back. He wouldn't hear of it." Hoyt slammed his fist down on the table hard enough to spatter a few drops out of his glass.

"John is the majority owner of the company, Hoyt. He can do as he pleases, Board or no Board. Besides, Winston doesn't have any experience with running a hotel or a major company. He wouldn't bring any real value to the Board." Griffin looked at his watch and noted they had been in the bar a few blocks from the CCI headquarters for at least two hours. "I need to get home. Mary Nell will be wondering where I've gotten to."

"Nonsense, Griffin. Don't let a woman have so much control over your comings and goings. Have another drink." Hoyt signaled to the waitress to bring another round to the two men.

"I'm sorry, Hoyt, but I promised her I'd be home. It's bad enough I left work early after the horrible afternoon I had. I need to get home to her in time for dinner. Tomorrow I'll have to figure out how to fix this with John." Griffin stood slowly, aware he imbibed a little more than usual. Once sure of his balance, he started off toward the door without further comment.

When Griffin had disappeared out of the bar, Hoyt leaned back in his chair to consider how to maneuver things to his advantage. He had encouraged Griffin to dismiss Geraldine Malone. Griffin had mentioned several instances over the last couple of years when some small irregularity occurred in hiring. None had been more egregious than the hiring of Craig Fielder.

Hoyt had objected to John's decision to split accounting and finance into two departments. When he realized John would not be swayed on his decision, he set about identifying the best person to become the finance department head. To his mind, that meant someone who would defer to his opinions and judgements. Griffin allowed his friend to screen the applicants before John saw their applications and to winnow the field to suit himself. However, Craig Fielder somehow bypassed the personnel office to get his application to John despite Hoyt's interference, and John hired Craig without consultation with the accounting manager. From his first day at CCI, Craig refused to solicit, much less accept, any advice or suggestions his predecessor put forth.

That more than anything drove Hoyt to seize the opportunity to push Griffin to dismiss Geraldine. Two fortuitous events just prior to John's absence gave him his opportunity. First, yet another odd hiring occurred on Monday, though it involved only a lowly clerk at the hotel. Two days later, Geraldine attended a training session with CCI's health insurance carrier the very morning John Stuart's children started work at the headquarters. It hadn't taken much to push Griffin to dismiss the woman in John's absence the next morning.

Now Matt somehow thwarted that plan. Hoyt could not imagine how the man managed to rehire Geraldine through the hotel within three hours of Griffin firing her when Matt, like John, was out of town at a location not even Mrs. Pierce knew. He wondered if Griffin realized Matt could and probably would take the budget for Geraldine's position. That meant Griffin would be left to do all the personnel work himself until John relented and moved budget around to hire a new personnel clerk for headquarters.

An uneasy thought struck Hoyt. What if John didn't relent? What if he told Griffin to either do the job himself or leave? After all, Geraldine Malone had worked for the Stuarts before they opened the new hotel and headquarters. She was one of a handful of people at CCI who had worked at the old inn in John's grandmother's mansion. John and Matt were extremely loyal to the people who had remained with them through thick and thin from the early days. Hoyt mused that perhaps he should have thought things through further before urging Griffin to fire the woman. If the plan backfired, Griffin could be out at CCI, costing him one of his most useful lackeys.

# Chapter 17

*Friday, June 8, 1979*

The hotel lobby buzzed late Friday afternoon. The arrival of summer meant a full or nearly full house for most weekends and no shortage of guests during the week. Martha and Del staffed the front desk since they were more proficient at checking in new arrivals while Laura handled the phone calls from guests making requests and passed those along to the appropriate department. Jared even spent some time out at the desk to help clear the backlog of people checking into the hotel.

Matt walked through the front entrance, greeting Gabe who remained late to allow the evening doorman to help the bellhops with the glut of luggage accompanying the crowd of incoming guests. "It looks a little chaotic this evening, Gabe. Any problems today?"

"Hey, Matt. I didn't think we'd see you back this early. No, no problems. It's been busy since the check-ins began, but nothing more than any normal summer Friday afternoon. You know about yesterday's excitement?" Gabe grinned.

"Yep, gave up golf with John and Jonah and the boys this afternoon to come back and check on things here. I heard you got pressed into fetch and carry work like you were a bellhop again, though this time with file cabinets instead of luggage." Matt tried but failed to maintain a straight face.

Gabe's grin widened. "I'm glad I got included. I would have hated to miss the parade out of the personnel office right in front of Krebs. I can't figure what the man was thinking, Matt."

Matt shook his head. "Not thinking. I'm sorry John's left to clean up the mess over there, but he'll figure out something, and Geraldine might help them out later." Matt looked toward the front desk where Jared and the three clerks had begun to thin the crowd for now. "Do you know if Geraldine is still here?"

"As far as I know. Jared put her desk in with the AM's, but I expect you know that." Another car pulled up to the front door, and a valet and bellhop hurried out to assist the new arrivals. Gabe stepped to the door to open it as the young couple and their small son approached.

"I'll see you later, Gabe. I need to check on Geraldine and see what she needs that Jared hasn't managed to get her yet." Matt patted Gabe on the shoulder and walked behind the crowd at the desk, circling around to the doorway into the back offices.

When he reached the entrance to the main office, Matt saw Geraldine sitting at the AM's desk with an extra desk now squeezed into a corner where a small table had been located. She noticed movement and looked up to see Matt and smiled at him without interrupting her phone call. Matt could tell from Geraldine's side of the conversation she was speaking to CCI's insurance carrier, so he gestured for her to come back to his office when she got a chance.

Five minutes later, Geraldine walked through Matt's open door. "Hi, Matt. I didn't expect to see you this afternoon. Jared said you wouldn't get in until late."

Matt gestured for her to close the door and sit down in one of the chairs across from him. "I came back early and left John and Jonah and the boys to finish up. Under the circumstances, John and I both thought it would be best if I came back earlier. When you have a chance, make me a list of what you need. For starters, a more private place to work and a telephone."

"Those are the most important things, but Jared did the best he could on short notice. He's been good about swapping places with me or going out to the front desk when I needed to use the phone. Do you think we can get my phone number in the headquarters moved over here? It would be helpful not to need to call all my contacts with the insurance companies and others I coordinate with to give them a new number. I can manage if I have to though."

"I'll make it happen, and between John and me, maybe we can get it handled Monday. First, we need to figure out where to put you for at least the next few weeks and get the telephone moved there. I can put you in the office next door temporarily. The inactive files are in there, right?"

"Yes, that would be great if it's OK."

"It will be fine, and that will give us a little time to shuffle things around to open up a permanent space somewhere else. I'll get Jonah over here Monday to look at our options and give us some input on where we can carve out a new office in some empty space." Matt leaned forward, elbows on his desk, while he considered his next question. "Geraldine, will you be all right helping out the headquarters staff with insurance issues in a pinch? Griffin needs to suffer with his mess, but none of us wants this conflict to cause problems for our other employees."

"Of course, Matt. Those people–most of them–are my friends. They don't need to suffer because of this. I'll go over there to handle those things if I need to as long as I can sit somewhere other than in the personnel office."

"I thought you would be OK with it, but I wanted to ask. You can use my office on the top floor, and Vicky can act as your liaison when you need one. She'll be happy to help out."

"That will work well, and I'm so grateful for her assistance in sorting this out in a hurry yesterday. With Ginger needing help setting up for surgery on short notice, it was a terrible time for me not to be available. Vicky stuck her neck out to get things resolved and help me get set up over here as fast as she could, and it made a difference. I'm thankful things worked out for you to pick her up as your assistant when the dreadful woman Mrs. Pierce pushed on you left." Geraldine laughed at the face Matt made.

"Vicky is a gem. I'm glad I get to share her instead of fighting John's guard dog for someone I can put up with. Mrs. Pierce still resents her presence on the executive level. However, Vicky's neck is about the safest around here regardless of Mrs. Pierce's dislike of having a twenty-two-year-old guarding the opposite end of the executive level. It also makes her the best choice to act as your intermediary until things get sorted out in their personnel office. She can be impervious to anything anyone throws at her. Everybody knows her and would trust her to get anything critical over to you in a hurry."

A knock at Matt's office door ended further conversation. "Come in," Matt called.

The door opened, and Jared leaned in. "I didn't realize you had returned, or I'd have come back here earlier to give you a report on how things went while you were away."

"I've only been here a few minutes, and you and the clerks had your hands full when I came in. I didn't want to interrupt you then. Geraldine filled me in on some of what happened the last two days. You can fill in the rest when you have time. Is the evening shift in place now?"

"Yes, sir," he replied. Geraldine excused herself to allow the men to speak in private.

"Since you're working tomorrow, why don't you go on home? We'll talk in the morning. You've already had a long day."

"Yes, sir, but I don't mind staying if you need me."

"No, everything looks to be going along fine now. You did a good job getting Geraldine settled over here on short notice. We'll get Jonah to help figure out where we can build out a permanent office in some free space Monday so she can have her files handy. If you have any ideas, let me know."

Jared relaxed a little and nodded. "I will, and thank you, sir. I'll see you in the morning."

Matt stood and gestured for Jared to precede him out the door. "Now that the crowd has died down out front, it should be a good time for me to wander out to greet a few people."

At the end of the back hall, the men separated with Jared heading for the exit and Matt continuing farther into the back area of the hotel. He stuck his head into the security office but found it empty. When he reached the staff break room, he saw Janelle and Laura chatting while they gathered their things from their lockers.

"Hello, ladies. I hope you two had a good week." Both turned toward the voice and found Matt leaning against the doorframe smiling at them. "I understand you had some excitement around here yesterday. Next time there's a parade through my hotel, I hope I'm not out of town."

Laura just smiled, but Janelle burst out laughing. "You'd have been leading it if you had been here. I wish I could have been in the personnel office for the start of it."

Matt laughed, too. "I imagine it was pretty shocking for Griffin." His face shifted to a more serious expression. "Everything is set now for Ginger's surgery next week?"

Janelle sighed. "Yes, Geraldine sorted out everything as soon as she got over here yesterday. She'll miss about two weeks of work. She's already missed some as you're aware, but Geraldine and Jared worked out how to deal with her leave. He was a big help on that."

"Good. I'm glad they've determined what's wrong with Ginger at last and can do something to help her and our end got taken care of for her. Jared's pretty good with those things." He glanced at Laura, who stood listening, and added, "He needs to learn more in other areas, but he's coming along as an assistant manager. He's just been one for a few months. It takes time to learn the ropes, and our system and philosophy are different from where he worked before he came to us. Speaking of new things, how do you like it here after your first week, Laura?"

Laura beamed. "It's amazing. There is so much going on and so much to learn. I couldn't believe how busy we were this afternoon. Jared let me handle the desk on my own for half an hour while Martha took her lunch break yesterday, and I'm not sure who was more nervous. Jared stayed right there in the office the whole time in case I needed help or messed up something, but it stayed quiet while Martha was gone. I couldn't have handled it by myself today with so much happening."

"Nobody could. We had quite a crush at the desk when I got here. I saw you helping Del and Martha during that time. Jared wouldn't have let you work out there with them if he hadn't been satisfied you could handle it."

"I hope I did all right today. I did my best. Answering the phone while Martha and Del and even Jared handled the crowd was the easier job."

"None of it is easy when there's so much going on. We'll have busy weekends most of the summer, so brace yourself," Matt said. "Now both of you get out of here. You've had a busy week and deserve some time off. Who knows? Maybe next week we'll try to follow up the parade with a circus."

Laura and Janelle laughed at the thought. Janelle said, "I expect the circus will arrive here before too long. Things have begun to bubble quite a lot. I hope I get a front row seat." She chuckled again as she waved and slipped out the door.

Matt took the opportunity to check that no one else was nearby and asked, "How were things with Jared? Did you two have any conflicts while I was away?"

"No, sir. We talked for a minute after the staff meeting Thursday and agreed to put the past behind us and start fresh. He showed me a few new things when we had some slack time at the desk. He said I did OK when I covered it on my own yesterday. Like I said, it was only for half an hour and nothing much happened during that time except for a couple of phone calls and one guest stopping by to verify checkout time."

"That's a good way to get your feet wet. We'll make sure to get you more and more time on your own when things are quiet. You're bright and a quick learner. You'll be ready to staff the desk without anyone hovering nearby in no time. Maybe next Friday we'll have you handle the crush with Martha or Del and one of them can handle the phones." Matt grinned at the startled look on Laura's face.

"I'm not sure I'll be ready for that big a crowd so soon, but I'll do my best."

"That's why we hired you, Laura. You always do your best, and you do it with a smile and a kind word to the customers. You are also very bright and a quick study.

That combination is hard to find in people. We're glad you're here." He waved her toward the doorway. "Now I need to get out front and take credit with our guests for how well our hotel runs, and you need to go home to tell your grandmother how great we treated you today and how much you love working here. We'll see you Monday."

Laura grinned at Matt. "Yes, sir. I'll do my best to fill her in on all the details. She'll be waiting to hear about what went on today, especially after she heard all about yesterday's excitement."

~~~

Bud Langford, manager of the Chestnut Cove Inn in Halesburg, sat at the rear of the lounge of the hotel watching and waiting. A sparse crowd murmured while the pianist played in the background. The singer Bud employed for the last few months left several weeks ago, and he had tried out different acts to take over since then. None impressed his guests so far, neither the hotel guests who visited the lounge during their stay nor the locals who came by for an evening. Tonight, he had a new singer for whom he held out some hope. They had agreed to a weeklong booking, but Bud had no one lined up to follow her the next week. He hoped she would be an improvement over the recent uninspiring talent and would agree to stay on longer if she performed as well before a crowd as she did in her audition a couple of weeks earlier.

When the pianist shifted from playing his own selections to the intro for her first song, the young blonde sauntered out onto the stage. A few patrons noticed though most kept their attention on their dinner and conversation. When the young woman began a sensuous ballad, a few more people paid attention. She moved around the stage as far as her microphone cord would allow, crooning to first one corner of the room and then another. The first song ended, and the second, a more upbeat number, began. When the girl sashayed across the stage during her third number, dancing to her own song and sending her curls bouncing in all directions, the attention of the room belonged to her.

Bud leaned back in his seat. His mind ran through the numbers, adding up how much he could make off her with some well-planned advertisements and a few words in the right ears. The sixty-year-old man also wondered how long it would take him to make Eve Dunkel, his new twenty-something singer, his next girlfriend. He would promise to help her make all the right contacts in the recording industry. After all, one of his former classmates from nearby Stannum Academy worked at a recording studio in Nashville. Bud could even act as her agent and sign on for a cut of her earnings. When the girl broke into a rousing Broadway show tune, the crowd all but got up and danced around their tables. Bud couldn't stop counting the money he could make with Eve.

# Chapter 18

*Monday, June 11, 1979*

The elderly man pocketed the receipt Del passed across to him, reached for his wife's hand, and followed the bellhop toward the front door where the valet already parked their car. Laura took advantage of the brief, early-morning lull to whisper to Del, "Isn't it unusual for the assistant manager not to hold a shift meeting before we start? I thought Pam said they always hold a short gathering like we did each day last week to tell us about anything to pay special attention to and so forth."

"Yes, it's very unusual. I haven't seen Geraldine this morning. I hope nothing else happened with her. At least Pam is on duty, and Matt is supposed to be here, too, so one of them will tell us if something has happened once they come out here."

A quick glance into the back office confirmed to Laura that neither Pam nor Geraldine had slipped in unnoticed. Before she could ask anything further, another couple approached the desk to check out. The phone rang, and Laura moved over to her post to answer it while Del helped the departing guests.

When things quieted again, Laura heard voices approaching from the back hall. She heard the already familiar sound of Matt's laugh just before he appeared around the corner with Geraldine and a tall, fortyish man. Then Pam walked through from the back office, and Laura shifted her attention to the assistant manager.

"Sorry I'm late getting out here this morning," Pam said. "Any issues I need to know about?"

Dell shook his head. "No, we've had two rooms check out so far." He looked over at Laura. "Any issues from guests calling downstairs?"

"Just a request to have 328 cleaned after lunch, which I relayed to Janelle, and a question about breakfast hours," Laura replied.

"Good. I'll just pass the word individually to the shift leads today instead of trying to gather everyone for a five-minute meeting." She checked the notepad in her hand. "We should have seven more checkouts this morning, and five check-ins this afternoon. That leaves us with four rooms available once housekeeping cleans them and two already empty."

Through the door behind Pam, Laura saw Geraldine walk to the small desk crammed in for her last Thursday. Pam heard her and looked back before returning her attention to Del and Laura. "Jonah will be over here later this morning to look at places to put Geraldine long term, so I'll be tied up for an hour or so with that."

Remembering Laura didn't know most of the corporate staff yet, Pam added, "Jonah Jones is head of construction, maintenance, and anything related to those areas for CCI. Clete supervises regular maintenance in the hotel, but for larger things like moving or adding walls, Jonah gets involved."

"Jones? Is he related to Vicky?" Jones wasn't an uncommon name, but Laura remembered Vicky mentioning her father worked at CCI.

"Yes, he's her father. He and Vicky's mother have a long history with both the hotel and the Stuart family. They're very close friends. Oh," Pam said, stopping to wave to Matt. He stood nearby still talking to the man Laura had seen him with earlier.

Matt touched his companion on the arm and pointed toward the front desk. They walked across to stop opposite the clerks, and the unknown man reached across to shake hands with Del. "Good morning, Del. How are you today?"

"Good morning, Mr. Stuart. I'm well."

Matt waved Laura forward and said, "John, this is Laura Maddox. Laura, this is John Stuart, president of CCI. He likes to think he's in charge, so don't let him know otherwise."

Laura managed to giggle and blush at the same time when John scowled at Matt. Then he extended his hand and said, "It's nice to meet you, Laura. Matt has told me how pleased he is to have stolen you away from your previous employer."

She shook hands with him, her blush deepening. "Thank you, Mr. Stuart. I'm happy to be here. You have a beautiful hotel, and I love working here already."

"Good, we want to keep it that way. I understand you and your grandmother live in an apartment building Sandra and I own. Please let me know if you ever have any issues with it."

"We're quite comfortable there, Mr. Stuart. It suits my grandmother's needs well."

"Good, good." He nodded to her before turning to Matt. "I need to get over to my office. Let me know if there's anything else I can do to help Geraldine get situated over here. I'll see you at the staff meeting." He patted Matt's shoulder and strode across the lobby.

~~~

Jonah, Matt, Pam, and Geraldine wandered back into Matt's office after their ramble through the hotel in search of the best long-term solution for a new personnel office in the building. Before the four settled in to continue discussing their options, Laura tapped on the open door.

"Excuse me, Matt, but a young man came to the front desk looking for you. I told him you were in a meeting and asked him to sit in the lobby for a moment while I checked with you. He handed me this." Laura stepped inside at Matt's beckoning and passed him a plain white envelope. She allowed herself a tiny smile when Matt grinned up at her; she would never make the mistake Jared made regarding her a month earlier.

Matt tore open the envelope and extracted the two sheets of paper within. A quick perusal of the first sheet caused his grin to widen. "We'll finish here in a few minutes. Tell him Geraldine will take care of him then." He passed the second, still folded, sheet across to Geraldine. "We're adding some temporary help with IO experience to assist with the next update to it."

Laura excused herself to return to the reception desk and pass along Matt's reply to the young man. A few minutes later, Geraldine appeared at the front desk, and Laura pointed him out.

"Dan Fielder?" He looked up from the book he was reading. "I'm Geraldine Malone from hotel personnel. Mr. Hunter asked me to take care of your paperwork. Then I'll take you back to meet him and get you set up to assist us with our IO update implementation."

The young man stood and extended his hand to shake Geraldine's. "It's nice to meet you, Miss Malone. I'm looking forward to spending a couple of months here helping out," Dan said before he followed her toward the back offices of the hotel.

~~~

Matt took his traditional seat near the far end of the boardroom table just before John entered via the door from his office to take his own place at the opposite end. Griffin followed from John's office. Matt suspected Griffin had prostrated himself and apologized for the mess he caused when he fired Geraldine the week before. Matt and John discussed the issue over the weekend and agreed on how to ensure no one on the headquarters staff would go without Geraldine's assistance on insurance matters should they need it. However, Griffin would need to try to handle the remaining headquarters personnel work himself before Geraldine would be allowed to step in.

John called the meeting to order with a rap of his knuckles on the table. "I don't have a lot today, but there's one important thing I need to tell you about. We identified a new property we're considering. After our recent potential acquisition site leaks, we won't discuss any details in this meeting; we'll discuss it with each of you individually if and when we need to do so."

Neither John nor Matt showed surprise when Hoyt objected. "Really, John, you cannot treat us like children. You must trust your management team with all available material and allow us to give you our best advice."

A frustrated John had hoped rather than expected Hoyt to back down after their heated exchanges over the last couple of weeks. "I can and will do what I think is in the best interest of this company. I trusted you and others in this room with confidential information regarding acquisitions twice in the last year. Twice I learned my trust was misplaced. I won't make the same mistake again. The subject is not open for discussion." John let his gaze linger on Hoyt for several seconds before returning his attention to the room in general. "As I was saying, we'll bring each of you in individually if we need your input. Now let's continue with the regular weekly reports. Jonah, update us on any facility issues we have."

Half an hour later, the managers filed out of the boardroom. John signaled for Craig to join him in his office. Matt and Jonah already knew John wanted to meet with them right after the staff meeting, and they followed Craig through the door to John's office. Doug and Joseph, seated along the windows away from the table during the staff meeting, trailed the group. Joseph reached back to close the door behind him, but Hoyt pushed by him into John's office.

Before Hoyt could speak, Matt took three steps back and tugged on Hoyt's arm. In a low voice, Matt said, "You've already pushed your luck too far, Hoyt. Leave it alone, whatever it is you want to complain about now."

One look in John's direction convinced Hoyt of the wisdom of Matt's advice. When Hoyt disappeared back through the door to the boardroom, Joseph closed the door and, at a gesture from Matt, locked it.

Hoyt paced in front of the elevator, impatient for the car to arrive to take him back down to his office. When the doors slid open, he almost collided with Sandra as she stepped out.

"Hello, Hoyt. How are you today?" she asked pleasantly. A participant in the conversation Matt and John held over the weekend involving both the new property and Geraldine's firing, she wondered what part Hoyt played in the latter.

"Hello, Sandra. I'm well but late for my own staff meeting if you'll excuse me." Hoyt hurried onto the elevator and stabbed at the button for his floor.

Sandra continued to the west end of the building, simply waving at Mrs. Pierce before opening the main door into John's office. "Am I late?" She closed the door behind herself and set her bag on the coffee table around which the men were arrayed.

"No, we just finished the staff meeting and came in here. You're right on time. Did you get the photographs?" John received his answer in the form of a package Sandra extracted from her bag.

"I haven't had a chance to look at them yet." She handed John the package containing a dozen packets of prints of the photographs taken by Doug and Joseph the previous week.

John handed the packets to Joseph and Doug. "Sort these into the different areas of the building and exterior shots. We'll go through the areas of primary interest today as we go over Jonah's preliminary sketches." The boys took the photos and moved over to John's desk to spread out and perform their assigned task.

Jonah rolled out his sketch of the overall site, and the five adults began to discuss it. The boys found the general site and exterior photos, and Joseph brought them over to add to his father's presentation of his work.

~~~

When the meeting broke up about an hour later, Sandra went in search of Maggie to take her home for the day, and Jonah and Joseph went downstairs to Jonah's office to update their preliminary plans based on the afternoon's discussions.

As Matt and Craig walked out the door of John's office, Matt remembered his newest staff addition. "I saw your brother this morning, Craig. I assume you know he'll be working with us for a time this summer."

Craig smiled. "Dan called and told me a few days ago. He's staying with me while he's in Elkford. I guess I owe him since he's the one responsible for me getting involved with IO. Hard to believe my little brother worked on developing it as a student at Tech."

Doug had walked out behind them and caught a little of their conversation as they reached the elevator. "Dan Fielder is your brother? I should have made the connection earlier. I met him a few times when I interned at CasCav during the school year. He's working here now?"

Matt stopped and turned to include Doug in the conversation. "Just for the summer. He'll be an IO assistant. There's an update to IO he's to teach us. He'll work with the desk clerks and bookkeepers to get them trained, and he'll also learn a little more about what they do to take the information back to the IO team. The arrangement helps both us, as the user, as well as the IO developers. They can do a better job of meeting our needs if they understand how we work."

Doug smirked at the idea. "CasCav's IO development team hardly needs to bring in somebody to learn how CCI hotels work," he said. At a rare scowl from Matt, Doug spoke in a softer voice. "That makes sense though. Maybe this fall Joseph and I will help incorporate some ideas Dan brings back to the IO development team at CasCav."

"It sounds like you're getting a pretty well-rounded exposure to the business world," Craig said. "You're working here for your father during the summer and sitting down with me and the other managers to learn what role our departments serve and working part-time at CasCav when you're at Tech. That will help you a lot when you finish school and start here fulltime. You should have a good understanding of the business by then."

"I hope so." Doug glanced at Matt. "I've already had a number of people discussing what job I'll take on when I graduate, and that's still three years away."

"I'm sure to have assistant manager slots I can put you in," Matt reminded him. "You can always opt to spend a little time at one of our hotels to learn more of the business from the inside once you graduate. You've spent time working as a lifeguard and bellhop but not as a clerk or one of the back-office staff. I still think you'd be well-served to spend a little time doing some hands-on operational and managerial work in one of our hotels."

"I think you're right, Uncle Matt. Maybe I'll work in one of the hotels as a desk clerk next summer if you have a spot for me. I think Dad would be OK with me doing that. Of course, Mom will want it to be here in Elkford," he added with a warm smile.

Matt chuckled. "She isn't the only one. I'm sure we can accommodate you in the Elkford hotel if that's what you decide to do next summer." The elevator doors slid open. "I need to go see what Pam has Dan and the rest of the team doing this afternoon. I'll see you later, Doug." Matt and Craig stepped into the elevator, and Doug continued across the lobby toward Vicky's office.

# Chapter 19

*Wednesday, June 13, 1979*

The birthday girl sat quietly alongside her younger sister in the backseat of their mother's Town Car. Maggie had been told in advance she would not be receiving a car for her birthday, so it hadn't been a surprise when she didn't get one from her parents. She was pleased with the clothes they gave her and the gift certificate for her favorite store in the Woodbury mall from her grandparents. Chris gave her a book, which was typical Chris, but it was about the major fashion houses in Paris, so Maggie was happy with it also. Doug gave her a sweater for Coughton Tech, though she wasn't sure she even wanted to go to college, much less the challenging and well-respected university her older siblings attended.

She received several nice gifts from her other friends and family members now tucked away in the trunk of the car, but no collection of presents made up for the two notable absences from her birthday dinner at Dilly's. While she hadn't been surprised KD didn't turn up tonight, her Uncle Matt's absence had been both surprising and hurtful. Matt never missed a birthday for any of the Stuart children. Why did he miss her sixteenth birthday party tonight?

John slowed the car as he wound down the driveway toward their home. Neither he nor Sandra was too surprised when they came within sight of the house that Matt's Lotus sat out front. They were only mildly surprised there was a second car parked behind Matt's, partially hidden from view and covered with a tarp. Sandra sighed and rolled her eyes as she turned to look at John.

"Did you know?"

His look answered the question before he spoke. "No, but I'm no more surprised than you are." He turned toward the backseat where Maggie sat behind her mother. "Maggie?" She looked up at her father, who nodded ahead of them. "It seems you have at least one more present."

She looked ahead out the front windshield toward the house. First, she saw Matt's Lotus. "Oh, I wonder what happened that Uncle Matt couldn't be at dinner, but he got here ahead of us?" Then she realized something else was tucked in behind Matt's car. She stared at the canvas tarp covering an object about the same size as the Lotus. After a few seconds to process the scene, she shrieked, "I got a car? Uncle Matt got me a car?"

The Town Car pulled up behind the other two vehicles and stopped, and all four occupants piled out. The front door of the house opened to reveal Matt, Doug, Vicky, Joseph, and Derrick. When the two groups met at the tarp-covered car, Maggie threw her arms around Matt. "Is this why you missed my birthday dinner? You were sneaking my car to the house?"

Matt returned her hug with a chuckle. "Yes, and I'm sorry I missed your dinner, but I hope you'll forgive me." When she released him, Matt reached into his inner coat pocket and withdrew a small oblong package. "This is from me. I wanted to get you something to go with your car."

Maggie looked confused for a minute before realization hit her. "KD bought the car for me?"

Doug laughed at his sister's shocked question. "Of course. She got me one for my sixteenth birthday, too. Remember?"

"Oh, but...oh." She returned her attention to the package Matt handed her and ripped away the paper to reveal a glasses case. "These are the sunglasses you and KD and Doug wear I love so much!" She removed the aviators from the case and put them on. "Awesome! Thank you, Uncle Matt." She hugged him again and then turned to the car. "How do I get this cover off?"

Doug motioned to Joseph and Derrick. "We'll get it off for you if that's OK, Mag. Why don't you stand back so you can get a good look at it when we pull the tarp off?"

"Oh, OK." Maggie backed away, and Matt directed her to stand a few feet from the left front fender. The three young men went to the opposite side and began to pull up the tarp, trying to keep the car hidden for as long as possible. At last, they tossed the cover forward and let it settle to the ground across the front of a pink hatchback. "It's pink!" Maggie squealed. "Hot pink! KD got me a pink car. Giselle said they don't make pink cars!"

Matt, standing next to John and Sandra, mumbled, "They don't. It had to be repainted. She ordered one based on the interior color and sent it off to be repainted." To Maggie, he called, "There's a card inside. You're to read it carefully."

Maggie, who was dancing around the outside looking at the car, hurried to the driver's door and opened it. She slid inside and found the card on the passenger seat next to her. Ripping it open, she read it aloud. "Happy Birthday, Maggie. I'm sorry I couldn't be there today, but I hope you like your present. Take good care of it and remember that, like Doug's Corvette, this car is yours to drive but belongs to me until you are old enough to get and pay for your own insurance, tag, and gas. At that point, I will sign it over to you. Have fun learning to drive it."

Maggie looked up at Doug, who was leaning in the door looking at the interior. "That's what she did with your Corvette?"

"Yep, you can't own a car at sixteen. It would have been the same thing if Mom and Dad bought it except without the typical KD explanation to go with it." Standing at the open door, Doug noticed something he missed up until now and began to laugh.

Maggie put the card back on the seat and began to look around the interior of her new car, ignoring her brother's mirth. When she looked down at the floor, she blinked in confusion. "Hey, why are there two brakes?"

Doug's laughter intensified, and he looked over at Matt to see the anticipated grin. Realization dawned on John, and he walked over to the car door and peered inside, then closed his eyes and shook his head. "Maggie, the one on the left isn't another brake pedal. It's the clutch."

Maggie turned an innocent face up to her father. "What's a clutch? Mom's car doesn't have one of those."

John's gaze shifted from Maggie to Doug to Matt. "No, her car doesn't have a clutch pedal."

Matt shrugged. "Hey, it's the least you can do. It's a small car with an engine that's supposed to put out about seventy-five horsepower max, none of which is much use unless you're proficient at shifting. You just need to teach her how to shift so the transmission will last until at least her seventeenth birthday."

Chris wandered around the car to look at the exterior and then stopped next to Vicky, Derrick, and Joseph. "How long do you think it will take Maggie to realize she can't drive her car anywhere in Elkford without everybody noticing it, including the police if she drives too fast or runs a stoplight?"

~~~

Elsewhere in Elkford, Jeanette and Winston returned home from Maggie's birthday dinner in silence. As soon as they entered the house, Jeanette led Winston down the hall to their sitting room and called for Tanya to bring them their evening coffee.

When the maid entered with the coffee service, she set it on the table in front of Jeanette. "Shall I pour for you, ma'am?"

"Yes, please, Tanya." Jeanette settled back in her chair and waited for the maid to serve her.

As she poured, Tanya asked, "How was the birthday party, ma'am? Did you enjoy yourself? Did Miss Maggie?"

"Margaret had quite a nice turnout of her friends. While we would have preferred a more formal event befitting her station as the daughter of a pillar of the community, the gathering proved to be pleasant. Winston and I enjoyed ourselves well enough, didn't we, Winston?" Jeanette didn't add how much Matt Hunter's surprising absence added to her enjoyment.

Winston heard his name and nodded in agreement, not quite sure to what he might be agreeing. "Yes, of course, dear. Two sugars, please, Tanya."

Tanya handed Jeanette her cup and prepared Winston's. "Sixteen is a big milestone. I'm glad Miss Maggie had a nice gathering of friends and family to celebrate it. Did she take her driving test today?"

"Yes," Jeanette replied. "Naturally, she passed it with ease. John and Sandra allowed her to drive their car to Dilly's, but of course she wasn't alone. She is to drive to our house tomorrow for lunch on her own. Sandra will take Christina to work and then allow Margaret to use the car to come here to spend a couple of hours with me."

Jeanette sipped her coffee while she considered her plans for the next day. "We should have something special for lunch, Tanya. Perhaps a tray of finger sandwiches. I believe an assortment of chicken salad and pimento cheese would be nice. Do we have what you would need to prepare those?"

Tanya handed Winston his coffee and picked up the serving tray. "Yes, ma'am, that's no problem. I'll prepare the chicken salad and pimento cheese right after breakfast tomorrow."

~~~

*Thursday, June 14, 1979*

"Mom and Dad said I have to wait until I learn how to drive it, but as soon as I know how, I'll drive it over here for you and Grandfather to see it. It's so pretty. I can't believe I have a pink car. Doug tried to explain what a clutch pedal does, but I didn't understand. I just know you have to mash it before you change gears, and it has a whole bunch of those. You can tell because the shift thing, which is in the middle on the hump instead of on the steering wheel, has all these numbers on it. All the way up to five." Maggie paused to take a breath and a bite of her sandwich.

"That sounds like a lot of extra work for no reason. Why on earth couldn't she buy you one with an automatic transmission?" Jeanette knew her most detested grandchild deliberately purchased a car for Maggie which the child would never learn to drive.

"Doug promised to help teach me to shift it. His car has the same extra pedal in the floor, and he drives it all the time except when he rides his motorcycle. He said it's not hard, but it takes a little practice and you have to learn how to time moving your feet right to keep it from stalling or jerking. He rode me around in it last night out the driveway to the road and back." Maggie picked up another pimento cheese finger sandwich from the tray.

Tanya entered the dining room to check on her mistress and her lunch guest. "Are the sandwiches to suit you, Miss Maggie?"

"Oh, yes, I love both chicken salad and pimento cheese. They're wonderful, Tanya." Maggie took a bite of her sandwich to emphasize her appreciation.

As she busied herself tidying up the dining room, Tanya continued to chat with the young girl. "Did I hear you say you received a pink car for your birthday? How very unusual."

Maggie nodded while she finished chewing and swallowed. "Yes, but I love pink, and KD is great at managing things like finding pink cars when nobody even makes them. She's the one who gave me the car."

Tanya picked up the tea pitcher and began to refill Maggie's glass. "It's a shame she couldn't be at your party, but at least she was able to send your present to you."

"Yes, I wish she had been there. Giselle missed it because she's in Florida visiting Aunt Claudine's mother. Uncle Matt missed the party, too, but he was at our house when we got home. He's the one who brought my car there for KD. He did that while we were at Dilly's for my party. I was so surprised to get my car." Maggie beamed at the memory of finding out about her sister's gift the previous night.

After ensuring her mistress didn't need her glass refilled, Tanya set the pitcher back on the buffet. "Oh, it's too bad Mr. Hunter missed your party, too, but it sounds like you had a good turnout even with your elder sister and Miss Giselle and Mr. Hunter absent."

Jeanette had heard enough discussion involving her two least favorite people. "Tanya, please see to dessert. Margaret, we have strawberry shortcake. I know how much you like strawberries."

"Yum." Maggie turned her beaming face to the maid/cook. "Thank you for making it, Tanya."

"You're welcome, Miss Maggie. I'll whip the cream while you finish your sandwiches." Tanya slipped out of the dining room with Jeanette staring daggers at her.

"It was most thoughtless for Matt to be absent from your birthday dinner. Surely he should have arranged things differently to ensure he could attend." Jeanette stabbed her fork into the small serving of chicken salad on her plate. She had eschewed the sandwiches, preferring to eat the salad filling without bread for lunch today.

"I wish he could have been there, but since he missed dinner because he was bringing my new car to the house, it's OK. I wish I had more time to learn to drive it before we leave for our vacation. Dad and Doug will be busy with the new hotel project right up until we leave for Arizona, and Uncle Matt will be at the new hotel place a lot the next few weeks. That will make it hard for any of them to spend much time teaching me to drive it. I want to be able to drive it really good before school starts back."

Tanya had reentered with the strawberry shortcake during Maggie's monologue, and she set a serving before each of the ladies before rejoining the conversation. "Goodness, so much traveling. Mr. Hunter will be away working on another new hotel a great deal this summer?"

"Yes, Dad and Doug, too, though not as much as Uncle Matt and Uncle Jonah and Joseph. They won't even tell Chris and me the town it's in yet, but Doug and Joseph know because they went with Dad and Uncle Matt and Uncle Jonah last week. Uncle Matt and Uncle Jonah always spend a lot of time at new hotels when they start remodeling the old buildings they put them in. Uncle Matt said at least one of them will spend a couple of days there every week for the rest of the summer."

"It's a good thing Mr. Hunter has good help at the hotel. He must trust them to leave it so often. Not even your father and mother will be around to help deal with any problems that pop up when you go on your trip to see your other grandparents. I'd be a nervous wreck leaving such an important business alone for over a week." Tanya caught a look in her employer's eyes and stopped talking. After collecting the lunch plates, she left grandmother and granddaughter to their dessert.

The two women ate in silence for a couple of minutes, but Jeanette's mind churned all the while. Choosing her words with care, she said, "Tanya does have a point. Matt must trust his employees a great deal to leave at a time when your father is also away. At least last week when they were both away your mother remained in town. Do you believe Matt will work out of town for a time during your trip to

Arizona?"

"I think so. They're pretty picky about getting things started right when they buy an old building to turn into a hotel, and Uncle Matt goes out of town to check on the other hotels every so often to make sure they're running the way he wants them to and just leaves his assistants in charge. I'm sure that's what he'll do this time."

"I see." Jeanette forked up another bite of strawberry and chewed as the beginning of a plan formed.

~~~

Jeanette laid the newspaper on her lap. Nothing in it could distract her from the idea coursing through her mind. "Winston, it has been far too long since we dined at the hotel."

Winston looked up at his wife. Rarely did she surprise him anymore, but a suggestion of a visit to the hotel run by Matt Hunter stunned him. She steered clear of the man at all costs and that included the CCI flagship hotel he managed. While she could at times manipulate her son, she thought Matt saw right through her on every occasion and even looked at her like she had some ulterior motive even when she did not. Only for special occasions like Maggie's birthday party would she attend any event at which Matt would be present.

When Winston looked at her without comment, she continued, "As John's parents, it behooves us to support his business on occasion. While there would never be any call to stay at the hotel in Elkford as guests, we should take the opportunity to dine there. I believe we should do so soon. We could invite Claudine and Harold to join us. We don't dine out with your daughter and her family enough. Perhaps we should host a dinner party there and invite Hoyt and some other friends."

Winston stared at her a moment longer before he clarified, "At Matt Hunter's hotel?"

"That hotel does not belong to Matt Hunter, but yes, that hotel, Winston." Jeanette's harsh tone didn't surprise her husband.

"Thank you for the correction, Jeanette. You have not wanted to visit there in years unless John invited us for some special occasion. Why do you suddenly want to go of your own volition now?"

Tanya entered the sitting room with the coffee service and set it on the table in front of Jeanette. "Shall I pour the coffee, ma'am?"

"Yes, Tanya, please do," Jeanette said.

Winston remembered the conversation among Jonah and Mary Jones and John and Sandra, all of whom had been seated with Jeanette and Winston at one end of the private room for Maggie's birthday dinner while the younger family members and friends visited at other tables. "Ah, Matt will spend a good deal of time at this new hotel location over the next few weeks, including during the time John and Sandra are away. A perfect time to host a dinner at the hotel."

Jeanette almost sneered at her husband. "It is only right for us to spend a little time there when both John and the person paid to manage it will be away. After all, we are family, and we should step in to ensure no one is taking advantage of the complete absence of those in charge."

Tanya handed Jeanette her coffee, then passed Winston's cup to him. She walked across to the table at the end of the room to retrieve the mail and set it before her mistress per the latest instructions on handling their correspondence each day.

Winston didn't have any objection to dining at the hotel. After all, chef Fleur Girard ran the best restaurant in Elkford and the surrounding area. However, Jeanette's aversion to ever darkening the doorway of the hotel, much less the restaurant within, kept them from dining there more than the few times John had issued them an invitation. "If you wish to dine there in Matt Hunter's absence, I have no objection. You will need to determine when he will be away during John and Sandra's vacation if you wish to host such an event without their foreknowledge."

"It has nothing to do with John's presence or absence. I simply believe it would behoove us to assist him by keeping an eye on things while he is away."

Tanya laid the mail on the coffee table next to the serving tray. "Your mail is on the table, ma'am."

"Thank you, Tanya."

"Did I hear you say you plan to host a dinner party at Mr. Stuart's hotel, ma'am? That sounds most elegant."

"We're considering the idea. We need to entertain more than we do, and hosting some of our friends at the hotel's restaurant would be special." Jeanette set down her coffee cup as she ticked off a list of friends to invite to dinner at the hotel.

"Yes, ma'am, it sure would be special to eat dinner in such a high-class place. Of course, I expect elegant friends like yours dine there quite often." Tanya saw the frown on her employer's face and beat a hasty retreat from the sitting room.

~~~

The Hathaway house had settled for the night, or nearly so. The light in the bedroom of the maid switched back on after being off for over an hour. Tanya checked for any sounds of stirring from the Hathaway's bedroom before hurrying down the hall. She stopped when she reached the kitchen to listen again, but no sounds of human movement emanated from the house.

Picking up the phone, Tanya dialed the number of the answering service she had long memorized. When the call was answered, she reported, "This is Tanya. Mrs. Hathaway wants to host a dinner party at the hotel restaurant during the time Mr. and Mrs. Stuart are on their vacation and Mr. Hunter is away from Elkford on business. She doesn't know what days Mr. Hunter will be away yet. I'll report again when I know more." She listened while the answering service attendant repeated the message. "Yes, that's correct. That's all I have this week. I'll report again as soon as I learn more about her plans. Goodnight."

Tanya hung up the phone and switched off the kitchen light. She listened once more, heard nothing to indicate her employers had exited their bedroom, and hurried back to her own room. In less than a minute after hanging up the phone, she climbed back into bed and extinguished her bedside light.

# Chapter 20

*Monday, June 18, 1979*

Maggie bobbed down the hallway toward Matt's office, glad to be out of the stuffy headquarters building for a few minutes. Even more, she was happy her father wanted something delivered to Matt. With Vicky already at the hotel working on something with her boss, Maggie had been left to assist Mrs. Pierce for the morning. When her father needed a set of drawings taken to Matt, Mrs. Pierce couldn't send them to the hotel via the girl fast enough.

While Chris wasn't a fan of her father's secretary, she remained respectful and efficient when helping the older lady. On the other hand, Maggie could always find somebody to talk to, something to distract her from the task at hand, or a reason to gripe. Neither Mrs. Pierce nor Maggie enjoyed their time together. Sending her to Matt's office with the package of drawings made for a more pleasant morning for everyone.

The teenager reached Matt's closed door and knocked. When she heard him bid her enter, she did so. "Hi, Uncle Matt. Here are the drawings Dad wanted me to bring you."

He flashed a smile at her. "Thanks, honey." He stood and gave her a big hug. "How do you like working in the headquarters so far?" He took the plans from Maggie, resumed his seat, and gestured for her to sit down across from him while he unrolled the large sheets on his desk.

"It's OK most of the time, but it gets kind of boring sometimes, especially when I have to help Mrs. Pierce instead of Vicky. Where is Vicky? I thought she was over here with you this morning." Maggie glanced around the office devoid of her friend.

"She went down the hall a few minutes ago. We needed some information from Pam. She'll be back in a minute." He set his coffee cup on one corner of the drawing, which was determined to roll back up, and began searching for something to put on the other three corners. "Would you hand me a couple of those books?" He gestured at the bookcase behind Maggie.

She looked behind her at a shelf lined with tomes not only on real estate, finance, and investing, but also on horses, forestry, and myriad other things. "Which ones?"

"Any of them. I just need to hold down the corners to keep these plans from rolling up." He picked up the stapler and set it on another corner.

"Oh, OK." Maggie picked up two books and handed one to Matt and put the other on one of the still curling corners. "How's that?"

"Perfect. Thank you, Maggie. Have you seen these plans yet?" He directed her attention to the top sheet rolled out on his desk.

"No, is this for the new hotel everybody is so secretive about?" She moved closer and looked at the page, which showed a layout of the ground floor of the building.

"Yes, we're announcing details about it in the staff meeting this afternoon. These are the preliminary drawings Jonah drafted for it. He and Joseph will go back this week to do a more detailed survey based on these." He pointed to the layout and spent the next few minutes explaining to Maggie how to read the drawing.

The door to Matt's office opened, and Vicky entered. "Hey, Maggie," she greeted her young friend and assistant. "Pam is getting those figures for you, Matt. She'll send them back here as soon as she gets them together."

"Good. In the meantime, we can check over these plans a little more. Jonah will be happy for us to quit tweaking them for a few days," Matt chuckled. "He thinks we should at least be able to finalize where on the ground floor we want to locate the reception desk, staff offices, restaurant, and lounge."

"Dad grumbles about any changes because he's expected to, but he said everybody agreed on the big things last week. Has the building owner seen these?" Vicky laughed at the wicked grin that flashed across Matt's face.

"No, but she sent a sheet of 'suggestions' via Elliott along with the keys and engineering data. I don't expect any major disagreements on these layouts since she suggested a similar one herself."

"When do you pick wallpaper and paint colors and decorations for it?" Maggie remained intrigued by her visit with the marketing team more than a week earlier.

"We'll start talking about those soon. Probably right after you get back from Arizona. Your mom will visit the site with the rest of the team, and we'll talk about what works for the building and the area around it. She still takes the lead on the décor. We each have areas we know the most about, but we all sit down and discuss things and come to an agreement." Matt hoped Maggie would express an interest in accompanying her mother to see the building being converted into their newest hotel. Instead her mind went another direction.

"If everybody can't agree on where to put things like the front desk, who gets to decide?"

The innocent question lacked an easy answer. Matt and Vicky exchanged a glance before he responded. "Thankfully, we don't experience that problem too often. If we don't all agree about something, we sit down and try to hash it out and come to a compromise."

"Who would?" Maggie probed further.

Matt shrugged, realizing Maggie would settle for nothing less than a definitive answer. "Well, it would be your dad, me, Jonah, and KD. Your mom, too, if it involved something like the décor. The final resolution would hopefully be a consensus. If it were three or four to one, that would usually settle it."

"What if the one is Dad or KD? Like the computer thing they got so mad at each other about?"

Direct and to the point, just like KD, Matt thought. "You mean if your dad and KD were at loggerheads?" Maggie nodded, and Matt sighed in resignation. He wanted to encourage her interest in the business; right now, that meant answering her question. "If it was clear Jonah and I and maybe your mom couldn't help resolve things, we'd get out of the way and let your dad and KD have at it." Maggie and Chris were aware of the recurring squabbles between KD and John over the last couple of years. Older and more informed Doug already chose his side, ensconced as expected in his big sister's camp.

Maggie thought about Matt's answer and nodded. "That's pretty much what I thought. They're both real stubborn." Matt shot a look at Vicky, who backed away from the desk a couple of steps while she tried to stifle a laugh.

Matt's rescue from further questions came in the form of another knock on his door. Vicky stepped over and opened it. "Hey, Laura, come on in," Vicky said as she waved the girl inside.

Laura held out a set of papers to Matt. "Pam asked me to bring you these. She said this is the information you asked for."

Matt took the papers from Laura and tucked them into a folder on his desk. "Thank you, Laura. Tell Pam thanks for getting it together so quickly."

"I will."

Laura turned to leave, but Vicky stopped her. "Laura, have you met Maggie?"

Laura shook her head. "I don't think so, but you look familiar." She extended her hand to shake Maggie's. "It's nice to meet you."

"She's one of Mr. Stuart's daughters who is helping out over in the headquarters building this summer."

"It's nice to meet you, too," Maggie said.

Another inspiration struck Matt. "Hey, why don't you three girls go to lunch in the hotel today? Laura and Maggie can swap stories about their first weeks working at CCI. I need to go through these plans a little more before I get back to the figures Vicky and I were working on this morning."

Laura shook her head. "I don't think Pam can spare me right now. We're a little shorthanded at the front desk until Dan gets back from the headquarters. He went over to help with an IO problem in finance."

"Craig called about fifteen minutes ago. Dan finished and just needed to write up a few notes for them. He should be back anytime now. As soon as he returns, you girls go eat lunch in the restaurant on me. While you're waiting for him, Laura can show Maggie what goes on at the reception desk." He waved the young women out his office door.

"Well, OK, if you're sure. Thank you, Matt," Laura said before exiting.

Maggie stopped right outside the door and turned back. "What about Mrs. Pierce? She's expecting me back."

Matt gestured to Vicky. "We'll take care of her. Now scoot." Maggie hurried back out the door and down the hall behind Laura, and Vicky reached for the phone to call the dreaded Mrs. Pierce to tell her Matt had commandeered Maggie for the next hour.

~~~

"Do you like working at the hotel?" Maggie prompted as the waiter set their plates in front of them. Laura had given the girl a brief overview of a desk clerk's day at CCI.

"I love it," Laura answered. "I'm just starting my third week, so I have a lot more to learn about my job and how the hotel operates, but I like the people, and Matt is a great boss. Pam is, too."

She stopped, regretting how it might sound to single out one of the assistant managers but not another. While she and Jared had managed well enough so far, things remained a little strained between them. She shifted the conversation to another tack. "This week, I move to my regular schedule. I'll be here Mondays, Tuesdays, and Thursdays through Saturdays. It helps me to have a day off during the week to take my grandmother to the doctor and to study. I take a bookkeeping class at the business school on Tuesday and Thursday nights. I expect Saturdays at the hotel will be different. Fridays are busy, but Martha says weekends can be even busier. I won't ever get bored at the front desk."

Maggie began to regret ending up in the headquarters for the summer instead of the hotel. "I bet working for Uncle Matt is fun. I almost worked over here, but Mom and Dad and I talked about it and decided it would be better for me to be in the headquarters building in his office and in KD and Uncle Matt's other office with Vicky." Her cheeks pinked at the slight fib. After her outburst in her father's office three weeks earlier, any chance of working in the more public setting of the hotel got nixed. "Chris, my little sister, is there two days a week and I'm there three–Monday, Wednesday, and Friday–except last week we swapped so I could be off on Wednesday for my birthday. I turned sixteen and got my driver's license.

"KD, my big sister, bought me a car. It's pink because I love pink, but I can't drive it yet. It's got something called a clutch that I don't know how to use. Doug, my brother, tried to teach me how to use it on the driveway at home, but he said it takes practice to get used to it. Mom let me drive her car a little over the weekend as long as I stayed near our house, and I drove to my grandmother's house Thursday. We live a little bit outside of town, so there's not much traffic out there to watch for. I'll get to drive myself to the headquarters soon though when Mom doesn't need her car. I hope I can go shopping by myself before long to spend some of the money I'm making here and the money I got for my birthday." At last, she stopped to take a sip of her tea and a bite of her lunch.

A sympathetic Laura said, "I'm sure you won't have any problem learning to drive your new car. I drive my grandmother's with a clutch pedal. It just takes a little practice. I'm sure you'll get the hang of it in no time."

"I think so, too," Vicky concurred. "You'll have more time to practice when you get home from your trip. You'll be the envy of Elkford High School when you roll into the parking lot for the first day of your junior year."

"You think so?" Maggie smiled at the thought. "The boys might not like it because none of them would want a pink car, and it isn't fast like Doug and KD's cars, but the girls might be jealous. Especially Giselle. Oh, I can't wait for Giselle to see it," she squealed. "She'll be so surprised." She grabbed a quick breath in order to continue and caught Vicky's subtle hand motion; they were dining in an upscale restaurant, and Maggie needed to remember to control her enthusiasm.

The girl took another breath and charged ahead, though in a more subdued tone. "Giselle is my cousin; step cousin really. Her grandfather married my grandmother after my real grandfather died. I didn't know him because he died before I was born. Way before. Dad was still in school. Giselle is one of my best friends most of the time. She's in Florida visiting her real grandmother, my grandfather's first wife, Aunt Claudine's mother. She's the one who told me they don't make pink cars, but I get to show her she was wrong when she gets back.

"Grandmother said Giselle is staying longer than Aunt Claudine and Uncle Harold. He's Aunt Claudine's husband right now; I think he's the third one. I wish we weren't staying in Arizona so long. I'd have time to learn to drive my car before she gets back. Doug is going to one of our other hotels Wednesday and Thursday, so he won't be here most of this week to teach me, and Dad's real busy right now. How long did it take you to learn to drive your grandmother's car?" Maggie shoveled in another bite of her chicken to fuel her next burst of conversation.

Laura took a quick swallow of tea to wash down her last bite of salad before answering. "Oh, just a couple of days of practice. A little longer to get good at it, but I could manage OK as long as nobody got right on my bumper when I stopped on a hill. That was the trickiest part for me. I had to learn how to time the clutch and brake and accelerator together. I'm sure you'll pick it up in no time."

"I hope so. I want to drive my car to Grandmother and Grandfather's soon, so they can see it." She stopped to consider something she hadn't thought about before. "I might not should take it over there though. Grandmother already complained about it not being a regular car like Mom's. She said KD bought me a car I can't drive on purpose to be mean." Maggie cut her eyes at Vicky. "KD and Grandmother don't like each other. I think they pretty much hate each other. I don't know why, but it's always been that way." Maggie winced, stopped speaking, and pressed her lips together before she reached down to rub her shin and look over at Vicky again.

"You need to finish your lunch, Maggie," Vicky prompted. "We need to get back to work soon." Turning her attention to Laura, she continued, "How is your grandmother? Is she OK with you not working close enough to run home to check on her at lunch?"

"Yes, she and Mrs. Obert check on each other every day now. One day last week, they even walked down the street to a new sandwich shop, Mac's Snacks. It opened a couple of weeks ago at the opposite end of the block from our building on the same side, so they don't even need to cross the road. Both enjoyed it, and they're talking about making it a weekly outing as long as the weather is good."

"That's great. Have you tried it yet?"

"No, but I want to soon. I'm concerned it will put Fred's out of business. It's close by and..." Laura stopped to look around her and spoke softly when she continued. "Well, everybody I know who's eaten there says Mac's food is better than Fred's. A lot better. I'd hate for Herb and Helen to be out of a job, but they could both retire if they wanted. Poor Meredith, though, she just got hired as a full-time waitress when I left. She'd be out of work if Fred's closed." A wave of sadness and concern for her friend caused Laura's voice to quiver. "It took so long for her to get a full-time job, and here I am with a great new one and talking about dining at a place that might cause her to lose hers."

Vicky reached across and patted her friend's hand. "It wouldn't be your fault if Fred's closed, Laura, even if you ate lunch at the new place. You've been to Herb's to eat since you left there, haven't you?"

Laura nodded and wiped at her eyes where tears threatened to pool. "Yes, but just once so far. Herb wasn't too happy to see me."

Maggie had remained silent through the latest turn of the conversation, munching on her lunch, but she felt compelled to suggest the obvious. "Why don't you tell Uncle Matt to hire your friend here? Then she could have a better job like you."

Laura smiled at the suggestion. "I'd love for her to work here, but I can't ask Matt to hire her. He met her at Fred's. If he wants to hire her, he can, but I'm not sure he would think her the right fit for CCI."

"What about Dilly's? They always need waitresses. If I was a waitress, I think I'd rather work at Dilly's anyway." Maggie realized her shin might be in danger again and shifted out of range of Vicky's toe.

"She might be a better fit at Dilly's, but I doubt she's got the experience to get hired there. I was lucky somebody suggested to Matt I would be a good person for CCI." Laura fiddled with the fine cloth napkin in her lap, remembering the damaged paper one with the note scribbled on it tucked into a drawer in her bedroom.

Maggie shrugged. "You could ask Uncle Matt about it. He can tell Trent to hire her if he thinks she'd be a good waitress."

Laura looked from Maggie to Vicky in confusion. "At Dilly's?"

Vicky gave up trying to stop Maggie from babbling about further details of the Stuart family and sought to slow the torrent of information by filling a gap herself. "Yes, Dilly's is a Stuart property. Trent is the manager, but Matt sort of provides over-watch on it. He could and probably would get Meredith a job over there if she needed one."

Laura let out a breath, a weight lifted from her. "That would be so great. I hope it doesn't come to that, and I wouldn't want Matt to feel obligated to hire her if he didn't feel she would do a good job, but at least it could be an option for her. She's sweet and fun, but she's always chatty, and when she gets nervous, she gets extra chatty. I don't think she would leave the best impression with a potential employer who didn't know anything else about her."

Maggie beamed, taking credit for solving Laura's friend's employment conundrum. "When I get back from vacation, we could all go eat lunch at Fred's one day and at Mac's another day. When I learn to drive my car, I can drive us over there." At the thought of her new car, Maggie once again began to fret about the clutch. "I wish Doug didn't need to go to Halesburg tomorrow. He's a lot better to drive with than Mom or Dad. I hate he's got to go there at all. The place gives me the creeps, and I've never even been there. It's where Aunt Elizabeth got killed."

Laura's eyes went wide. "Your aunt was killed? Oh my, what happened? How long ago was it?"

Maggie studied the last of the food on her plate, poking at it with her fork before looking up at Laura. "A long time ago. It was before I was born, so I didn't even get to know her, but there's a picture of her up high on a shelf in Uncle Matt's office. She was his fiancée. She wasn't really my aunt, but she would have practically been my aunt like Uncle Matt is practically my uncle but not technically. He and Dad are cousins, but they're like brothers, and Dad doesn't have a real brother or sister. Aunt Elizabeth was one of my mom's best friends, too.

"Aunt Elizabeth was working for the Coughton Tech newspaper. She was in school there. She went to Halesburg to research something for an article. Mom and Dad and Uncle Matt were all at Coughton, too. Dad and Uncle Matt went to college, and Mom stayed home and took care of KD. She was a baby or toddler then. Oh, and Uncle Matt and Aunt Elizabeth were KD's godparents, too. That's one reason KD and Uncle Matt are so close. KD was with Aunt Elizabeth that day. Mom needed a sitter on short notice, and Aunt Elizabeth offered to take care of KD as long as it was OK to take her to Halesburg. Mom said it was, so Aunt Elizabeth took KD and drove over there. While Aunt Elizabeth was pushing KD across the street in her stroller, a car came zooming down the road and hit her."

Laura gasped. "How horrible. Did your sister get hurt?"

Maggie continued in almost a whisper. "No, but she could have gotten killed, too, if the car went a little bit farther over. I can't even imagine not knowing my big sister, but it could have happened. I'm glad she didn't get killed."

The table's occupants remained silent while each processed their thoughts. Both Vicky and Maggie, familiar with the details of the rarely-spoken story, knew how that day affected Matt and the Stuart family. For Laura's part, she was shocked to learn the effervescent Matt Hunter suffered such a traumatic loss.

Slowly, conversation turned to cheerier subjects until Vicky checked her watch. "I better get back to work. Matt might have something I need to prepare before staff meeting, and Mrs. Pierce will have things for you to do by now, Maggie." Vicky rose, and Laura and Maggie followed suit.

"This was fun. I hope Uncle Matt will buy us lunch again soon," Maggie gushed. Vicky rolled her eyes at Laura, who smiled at the young girl's effusions.

"It was nice to meet you, Maggie. I'll see you around the hotel again soon when you're delivering things to Matt," Laura said. "I need to get back to the desk to relieve Del so he can go to lunch. Bye, Vicky. I'll see you later."

"It was nice to meet you, too, Laura." Maggie waved at her new friend before following Vicky across the lobby toward the rear of the hotel.

Later during a lull at the desk, Laura's mind wandered back over her lunch with Vicky and Maggie. Something tickled the back of her mind, and she tried to remember the thought that struck her earlier only to get lost amidst the babble of lunch conversation. Something Maggie said? Then Laura's eyes went wide as she realized why Maggie looked so familiar. She also understood at last why Matt took her mysterious napkin note so seriously.

~~~

Vicky looked up from her typewriter when she heard a tap on her door. Her face lit up when she saw Derrick standing in the doorway. "Hey, what are you doing up here?"

Derrick walked closer to Vicky's desk but remained a professional distance from his longtime girlfriend. "Mr. Lawrence asked me to sit in on the staff meeting with him this afternoon. We've been putting together some details about a project Mr. Stuart wants to discuss at the meeting." His voice dropped as he looked behind him to ensure the coast remained clear. "I'm sure you know all about it. We need to set up the legal paperwork between the companies involved. Standard stuff, but Mr. Lawrence said there are always details to sort out for each one."

Vicky giggled. "I'll be glad when it's announced. All this sneaking around has been exhausting."

Derrick smirked at her. "I knew you had one of those secrets you can't divulge. I can understand why though. Losing out on that property last year because of a leak from inside CCI didn't sit well."

The door to Matt's office opened, and he walked out with a folder in hand. "Hey, Derrick. How are things down in legal? Are you learning anything useful this summer?"

"They're great, Matt, and yes, I've learned a lot. Every summer I've worked for Mr. Lawrence, I've learned a little more about the practical side of corporate law. I can't wait to finish up law school and pass the bar and begin doing this for real. I just hope Mr. Lawrence and Mr. Stuart think I've done a good enough job over the years and my grades are good enough to hire me when the time comes."

Matt patted the younger man on the back. "I'm sure you'll continue to do well in school, and I know they're happy with your work. They need to worry about keeping you here instead of letting some other company steal you." The corner of Matt's mouth twitched upward. When she saw it, Vicky tried to stifle a giggle.

Derrick looked shocked at the suggestion. "No, I can't imagine wanting to work for another company in Elkford. The Stuart family has been too good to me over the years."

Vicky won her battle with the giggles and clarified Matt's comment. "I think he's referring back to a conversation in his office this morning. There very well could be a bidding war for your services in Elkford within the Stuart family."

Derrick's eyes widened. "Oh, I guess that's possible. Do you think they'll be feuding again–still–a year or more from now? I don't know what I'd do if it came to that."

Matt indicated the doorway through which a trickle of management could be seen milling around outside the boardroom including Derrick's boss, Sam Lawrence, CCI's corporate attorney. "Let's hope it doesn't. I have some hope the war will officially end soon. I think they're both ready. For now, we need to get to the boardroom for the fireworks. John doesn't cause those too often, but today's revelation will cause a few."

"Yes, sir, I expect you're right." Derrick made sure the coast was clear and leaned down for a quick kiss from Vicky before he followed Matt out into the foyer to take up position near Mr. Lawrence.

The crowd eased into the boardroom, and Derrick took a seat along the wall behind his boss. Doug and Joseph came in behind their fathers and took seats beside Derrick to watch the show. A minute later, Vicky slipped in followed by Maggie. John and Matt had discussed her budding interest in the new hotel and in marketing and agreed she could sit at the back with her brother and Joseph if she promised to remain quiet and professional. Matt recruited Vicky both to keep an eye on Maggie as well as to watch reactions from some of the managers for him.

John took his place and made a quick count of his management team. Assured everyone was in attendance, he sat down and rapped his knuckles on the table.

"We need to discuss a significant topic this afternoon, but first I want to get the regular agenda items out of the way. If everyone will give a quick report, we'll be able to move onto the main topic of the day. Jonah?"

Jonah gave a short report on changes in work to provide a location for Geraldine in the Elkford hotel and a few other small items his office was working on. When he was done, Matt gave a quick list of activities of note at each of the hotels.

Reports continued around the table until it was Hoyt's turn to speak. When he completed his regular update, he drove onward into his current favorite subject. "John, I'd like us to discuss how we handled the bid for the warehouse in Pearl. We don't need to repeat such a big mistake again." Hoyt's gaze shifted from John to Craig, at whom he stared with narrowed eyes.

"We're about to discuss acquisitions, Hoyt. We have some news on that front. If you're done with your report, I have an announcement to make regarding the property we discussed last week."

"It's hard for the rest of us to discuss a site we know nothing about, John. I hope you give us enough information today for us to make some decisions regarding it and come up with a decent offer this time."

John pressed his lips together, his displeasure with Hoyt written on his face. "That won't be necessary." Turning his attention to the rest of the senior staff, John continued. "CasCav has purchased a property in Tuseeca for the purpose of converting it into a CCI hotel similar to, though a little smaller than, the Elkford hotel. The sale closed a short time ago, and Jonah, Matt, and I toured the property last week. We've done some preliminary work on layouts, which Jonah has brought with him to discuss. We're still working out details, so keep in mind these are preliminary drawings. I expect we'll tweak things several times, and we might even make a major move or two before we finalize the design."

Hoyt half rose from his seat. "John, we can't decide to put a hotel somewhere on a whim without studying the financial aspects of it. I realize you have some divided loyalties regarding CasCav, but–"

John slammed his hand on the table. "Hoyt, it is not open for debate, and I'll thank you not to question my loyalties. I've been running this company in one form or another for almost twenty years. I know a thing or two about what it takes to make a successful hotel on our model." He tore his attention from Hoyt and forced himself to relax the tightening muscles in his neck and shoulders. "I discussed some details of this property with a handful of managers on a need-to-know basis. Craig made some calculations based on input from Matt and me. Also, Sam pulled the standard franchise agreement and started going through things we need to tweak in it for the Tuseeca hotel. We hope to work out everything with CasCav and sign off with them in two or three weeks. In the meantime, we're cleared to go ahead and do preliminary work in the building. Jonah, let's show them what we have."

Jonah stood and walked to the end of the room where the overhead projector awaited. When Matt winked at him, Jonah did his best to ignore his friend.

# Chapter 21

*Wednesday, June 20, 1979*

The sleek, silver Corvette turned into the parking lot adjacent to the Chestnut Cove Inn in Halesburg and pulled into a spot near the outside entrance to the lounge. Doug opened the door and slid out, unfolding his lanky frame from the small, low cockpit of his car. He opened the trunk to retrieve his suitcase before walking across to the main entrance of the hotel.

He took three steps inside before a pudgy, disheveled man hurried forward to greet him. "Doug, it's nice to see you. Welcome to Chestnut Cove's Halesburg hotel. I'm Bud Langford, the manager here." Bud extended his hand and shook Doug's, pumping it an unnecessary number of times. Putting his hand on Doug's shoulder, he guided him toward the front desk. "Matt called to let me know they wanted you to see how other CCI hotels differ from the Elkford flagship. I'm pleased he and your father chose mine as the example for you to study."

"Thank you, Mr. Langford. I'm excited they let me drive over to Halesburg to spend a little time learning more about this hotel. I also appreciate you taking time to show me around today. I'm sure you have more important things to do."

"Nonsense." He waved away the desk clerk who approached to handle Doug's room registration. "Young Mr. Stuart here will be in suite 307. Just pass me the key to his room." The clerk retrieved the key and handed it across to Bud. "Suite 307 is one of our best. Of course, I don't have as many suites or even as many rooms as the Elkford hotel, but I have a great little place here if I do say so myself. In addition to tourists, we do a lot of business at certain times of the year associated with Stannum Academy, the exclusive boarding school located outside Halesburg. Course, you've heard of Stannum. It's where I first met your grandfather, Winston. He was a couple of years ahead of me in school."

Doug nodded. "I believe I've heard him mention it." Seeking to change the subject away from his step-grandfather, Doug added, "I'll go up to my room and drop my suitcase there. Then I'll look around if that's all right with you, Mr. Langford."

"We can't have you hauling your own luggage up to your suite," Bud said with a laugh. He signaled a nearby bellhop, who hurried over. "Take Mr. Stuart's bag up to his suite. He's in 307."

"That's not necessary," Doug tried to argue, but Bud would have none of it.

"Nonsense, I can't have you carrying bags around my hotel, even if it's your own.

The boy will put it in your room for you." Bud gestured for the bellhop to take Doug's suitcase and tossed him the room key. Doug relented. He handed over his bag with a nod of thanks to the young man and dug out a quarter for a tip. "He'll drop the key at the desk for you to pick up later. Meantime, we can take a walk around the hotel before we grab lunch in the restaurant. Tonight, I've got a real treat for you. I've got a sweet little thing singing in the lounge by the name of Eve Dunkel. She's first rate. I've arranged for us to eat dinner in there to watch her show."

Doug began to cough, covering his mouth with his hand and taking a step away from the overbearing manager. He recovered after a few seconds and forced a smile. "Sounds great, Mr. Langford."

"Call me Bud, son." Bud slapped Doug on the back again and escorted him toward the hotel office.

~~~

Sandra opened the door to the study and slipped inside. John sat behind the desk, leaning back with one hand covering his eyes while the other held the telephone receiver. His hand moved away from his eyes, and he saw her and smiled. At a wave from him, she seated herself in one of the plush leather chairs across the desk and waited for the call to end. She knew Jonah was calling from Tuseeca to pass along some information, and she waited to learn of any problems identified today.

As soon as John hung up the phone, he gave her a brief overview of Jonah's latest assessment of the new property. Sandra leaned forward to look at the sketches spread across John's desk as he spoke. Tracing her finger across the ground floor layout, she followed along as he told her about a minor change Jonah suggested.

"Nothing he wants to do will cause significant expense or extend the preliminary schedule? You do remember this is CasCav's property, right?" She raised one eyebrow. "We've reached a rapprochement on the IO issue and the location CasCav lost out on last time because of a CCI leak. I don't want to spend another tense holiday season like last year, much less Thanksgiving and Christmas without one of my children at home like we did the year before."

John sighed and rubbed his eyes. "Neither do I, and no, this shouldn't have a negative impact. Elliott is supposed to meet Jonah and Joseph tomorrow. He'll relay any changes we want to consider for CasCav approval."

Sandra relaxed and sat back. "Good. I hope this will be the beginning of a new, peaceful, working relationship which won't create perturbations within the family." Her lips curled into a mischievous smile. "There are still a couple of issues to look forward to. This little escapade with the Pearl warehouse has confirmed we have a leak, and we all know the most likely path it took. You know something will happen at some point to exact retribution above saddling Vaughn with that old relic."

John shifted in his chair with a groan. "I'm afraid you're right, and Matt will be right in the middle of the action. I wish they would let it go now that they've sold him the old place."

"So do I, but we know both of them better than that. However, further action against Vaughn will be the lesser issue. If they prove Winston or your mother had any involvement in the warehouse information leak, it will get personal." Unwilling to think of where such a path might lead, Sandra shifted the subject. "Speaking of your mother, have you talked to her since Maggie's party?"

With a shake of his head, John said, "I know I should call her before we leave for Arizona, and I will. I've just been too busy to set aside fifteen or twenty minutes to listen to her next pitch for a trip to Europe, a bigger house, or whatever she thinks she needs next that Winston can't afford." He stood and walked around his desk to take a seat next to his wife. "She will never accept that we are not a bottomless pit of money just waiting for her to tell us what she wants us to spend it on next."

"If she had ever worked a day in her life, she might have a modicum of understanding of what hard work goes into making money to spend on such things."

"To be fair, not many women born in 1914 were raised to work outside their home. She never expected to need to work, and to be honest, what would she have done? Can you see her doing what your mom did and learning to be a secretary? A very good secretary," John emphasized. "Grandma Kate relied on her and thought the world of her. On top of that, I might never have met you if your mom hadn't worked for Grandma."

Shaking her head in resignation, Sandra said, "Yes, and look how much less complicated my life would have been if we hadn't met. I might have married a plumber instead. Maybe even a plumber whose mother ran off with the circus when he was a baby."

John snorted out a laugh. "Unfortunately, that's probably true, but you're stuck with me, so you'll have to continue to suffer through her delusions, too."

Sandra gave an exaggerated sigh. "I suppose I must. I'd hate to dump you and leave you to deal with your mother, Winston, Claudine, and both of her children on your own because I'm sure most of our children would follow me out the door."

"Doug and Chris would go running right behind you. I'm not sure about Maggie. I worry about her being too influenced by Giselle. It was bad enough when they were little, but both girls have their driver's license now." He paused to consider a thought. "Is it wrong to be sorry Maggie passed her test?"

"Yes, you know it is. I share your concern about Giselle's influence, but Maggie not having her license wouldn't help anything. It would give her a reason to ride with Giselle, and we suffered with that several times over the last year. Your sentiment is correct though. We need to find a way to minimize Giselle's influence, and no, we cannot lock her in her room until she's thirty," she said, referring to a suggestion John had made a couple of times over the last year regarding Maggie.

"Are you sure? That's still my favorite idea for dealing with Maggie. How did we end up with a child so irresponsible, impractical, unrealistic..."

As his voice trailed off, Sandra added, "So like your mother?" The mischievous grin returned. "We should be happy we only have one like her. Other than a few facial features and other physical characteristics, I don't think the other three inherited a thing from your mother."

"No, thank goodness. Doug and Chris seem to be a good mix of you and me, and KD, well, I'd swear she's Grandma reincarnated and modernized except that she was born before Grandma died. We sure named her well when we named her after

Grandma."

"Yes, we did." Sandra squeezed his hand before returning to their original topic. "You need to remember to ensure information she needs gets forwarded to her. She is as good as your grandmother at finding out things. Leaving her to find out hotel business which concerns her by other means won't end well."

John raised her hand to his lips and pressed a kiss to it. "I know, and I've promised not to repeat that mistake. I hope it will cease to be a concern before long. Doug hinted he thinks she's almost ready to shift her base back to Elkford. Regardless of which side of the street she chooses to work from, everything will work better if she's here much of the time."

"I hope he's right, and if she wants to rattle Winston or your mother as payment for leaking company information to Vaughn, all she needs to do is show up in Elkford. I can't imagine anything worse for your mother. We're likely to be looking for another live-in maid for them soon. Tanya has lasted far longer than any of the others, but KD's presence in Elkford might stress Jeanette enough that Tanya won't put up with her anymore."

John moaned. "I don't even want to think about replacing Tanya. Matt did us a huge favor when he found her. I'd offer her a supplement if it would help encourage her to–" He burst into laughter, leaving Sandra to wonder what suddenly amused him so much.

"John, will you please let me in on what's so funny?"

He wiped a hand across his eyes and managed to bring his mirth under control long enough to get out a few words. "Matt recommended Tanya, Sandra." He began to chuckle again. "You can bet she's already being paid a supplement. Probably one considerably higher than her official pay. It's the only explanation for why she's lasted so much longer than anyone else working for my mother and Winston."

Sandra's eyes went wide when she made the same leap John had a moment earlier. "They're paying Tanya to spy on Jeanette and Winston," she gasped out before joining John's laughter. "Your mother once accused me of having someone spy on them. KD knew about the accusation and never let on she was doing exactly what Jeanette accused me of. John, how long do you think they've been paying people to report to her about what goes on in your mother's house? Tanya can't be the first."

He closed his eyes and shuddered. "I bet it's been years." He sat up suddenly. "I bet Matt began it even before KD was old enough to be involved. For that matter, Grandma might have begun it. There's no telling what they know about my mother and Winston, not to mention Claudine, Rainier, and Giselle from when they've lived there off and on when Claudine was between husbands. Why didn't we pay someone on Mother's staff to spy for us all these years?" Then his eyes widened, and he stared at his wife. "Do you think KD's paying anyone to spy on us?"

Sandra broke into peals of laughter again. When she recovered enough to speak, she said, "Of course not. There wouldn't be any need. Chris and Doug would rat us out to her in a heartbeat if we had anything to hide, which we don't. Matt and Vicky would tell her anything concerning the hotel." She wiped at the tears rolling down her cheeks. "I wonder if it's too late to pay Tanya to spy for us. Do you think she would spy for us and them at the same time? I cannot believe that child has been paying people to keep tabs on your mother's household. I can't wait to ask her how long she and Matt have been paying them, and you're right, it's got to be more than just Tanya. I bet it's been a number of people who worked there, and I bet it's been going on for years." Sandra stood and reached for a box of tissues on a nearby table to dry her face, still chuckling at KD and Matt's audacity.

~~~

Doug leaned back in his seat, enjoying the show in the hotel lounge. Bud, seated next to the young man, eyed first the girl on the stage singing and then the scion of the Stuart family seated next to him. He could see that the younger man showed an interest in the vivacious singer. Bud wanted to facilitate Doug's enjoyment of his short visit to CCI's Halesburg hotel in any way possible. Ensuring John Stuart's son enjoyed himself could only benefit Bud. If he managed to find other ways to profit from Doug's stay, so much the better.

The young woman had performed in the lounge for almost two weeks, so Bud was familiar with her sets. He knew she was nearing the end of her last set of the night, and he needed to finalize his plan for ensuring the elusive girl would be willing to meet and entertain Doug for a few hours tonight. Bud had seated himself and Doug at the front of the room. He simply needed to ensure she didn't leave the stage without noticing the handsome and wealthy young man.

To Bud's surprise, during her next to last song his singer stepped down off the stage. She walked among the front tables as far as the longer microphone cable she had requested would allow. One by one, she fawned attention on several of the men seated near the front, singing to each as she stroked their face or arm with her fingertips.

When she reached the table occupied by Doug and Bud, she ignored Bud, but to his delight she paid particular attention to Doug. By the time she finished her song, she was seated on his lap and crooning in his ear. Doug, clearly enjoying himself, only released her to return to the stage for her final song after she whispered something in his ear Bud was sure had been her room number. Sure enough, as soon as the set ended and the girl left the stage, Doug thanked Bud for his hospitality, feigned exhaustion, and excused himself for the evening.

~~~

Fifteen minutes later, Doug had stopped by his room to refresh himself and walked one floor down to search for the room number the girl gave him. When he found it, he tapped on the door and checked the hall for anyone who might take note of his actions. When the door opened, the young woman smiled up at him and crooked a finger in his direction. He grinned and entered, closing and locking her door behind him.

She wandered across the room, and he followed. "Hey, don't I get a kiss?"

The young woman flashed a seductive smile and sauntered back to him. When she reached him, she slipped her arms around his neck, leaned up, and brushed her lips against his cheek.

"How's that?" Her voice came out as a soft purr.

"Under the circumstances it will have to do, Sis," Doug said with a chuckle. He hugged her tightly, lifting her off her feet, before they moved across the room to sit at the small table. "You still sing great, but I almost blew the whole gig when Bud told me he had a new singer we were going to see tonight named Eve Dunkel. I hadn't heard that name since you used it on a fake ID in high school. When Matt asked me to relay information to you in Halesburg, I expected to find you lurking in the shadows somewhere, not in full disguise singing in the lounge under one of your aliases. How long have you been here spying on Bud?"

"Almost two weeks. It's been interesting. I can't keep tabs on Bud all the time, but I had a few chances to get into the computer system to run reports, and I even got to check the register after recognizing a couple of interesting guests. As I expected, neither registered under their real name. I know who was working the desk to allow that to happen, too. We'll do some housecleaning above and beyond Bud when this is over."

"Who will take over this hotel? Is there someone who can step in right away?"

The young woman shook her head. When she did, a curl flipped around, and she pushed it back in irritation. "That will be grounds for discussion. Or argument. We'll need to bring in someone new, but in the short term I expect it will mean Matty and me alternating with one of the current assistant managers from Elkford brought in to learn the ropes and cover when one of us can't be here. We need to figure out if any of the Halesburg AM's can be retained or if we'll need to replace them all. I haven't seen any sign one is capable of stepping into Bud's place long term, and I wouldn't trust any of them to do so without significant vetting." When another curl fell into her face, the young woman gave up on fighting the flaxen wig she had worn in public for the last two weeks. She snatched out a couple of hairpins and with a vigorous tug pulled the wig from her head and tossed it onto her bed. "I hate that thing."

"Now you look a lot more like yourself without the blonde hair. What about the colored contact lenses? Aren't those irritating to wear?"

"No, I'm used to them. I've used them enough off and on over the last few years; I don't think too much about them anymore. Just another bit of the costume to turn myself into whomever I need to be when I go snooping around the hotels." She sighed and rubbed at her eyes. After Doug mentioned the contacts, they started bothering her. "I think I will take them out. I want to take off all this makeup, too. Make yourself comfortable. I'll be back in a couple of minutes."

She stood and walked into the small bathroom. When she returned, her auburn hair was brushed out, her makeup removed, and the colored contacts which turned her hazel eyes blue were absent.

"Much better," Doug said.

"Much," she agreed with a laugh. She took a seat across from him at the small table again. "Now tell me what's been going on in Coughton and Elkford I need to know about."

Doug sat up, ready to fulfill one of his tasks in Halesburg to the best of his ability.

"Before I do that, I need to tell you someone went through my suitcase this afternoon. Bud insisted the bellhop take it up to my suite for me. When I got upstairs before dinner to change clothes, I checked it like Uncle Matt told me, and sure enough someone had searched it. They were very careful to put things back close to how I packed them, but I was prepared like Uncle Matt told me and knew what to look for."

The young woman shrugged then smiled at Doug's surprised expression. "Now you know why Matty didn't give you anything in writing to bring here. We'd have been surprised if Bud or one of his people didn't check to see if you had a list telling you things to look for. Bud thinks you're here to spy on the Halesburg hotel operations and report back to Matty."

Doug chuckled. "While the spy has been here for two weeks right under his nose."

~~~

*Thursday, June 21, 1979*

Doug stood with one hand on the doorknob of his sister's room. "Are you sure about this? I know how you feel, but..." His voice trailed off. Arguing with her always proved fruitless.

"No, Doug, I won't change my mind. It's all worked out. I just need you to deliver my envelope to Matty. He'll take care of the details for me. I want you on an airplane to Arizona Saturday. Now go." The young woman pointed toward the door of her hotel room. "Be sure to note the name of the bellhop who took your bag to your room yesterday. Bud could have sent someone else to rifle through your things while he kept you as a captive audience, but most likely it was the bellhop. He could check for anything of interest in your bag as soon as he got it into your room. Sending someone else to check it later would risk another guest seeing a staff member enter your room for no reason or you escaping Bud's presence and not giving him another chance for someone to get to your things.

"We'll deal with the bellhop once we've dealt with Bud. Even if he was following orders, all the staff should know better than to go through a guest's belongings no matter what. Such violations of policy, not to mention the law, need to be reported to Matty's office in Elkford. They're supposed to be told to report such orders as part of their training. Now you need to leave and get back to Elkford." With a sly smile, she added, "Don't forget to stop by to thank Bud for his hospitality before you go."

Doug grinned in return. "Yes, boss." He reached up and ruffled his hair a little more for effect. "How's that? Does it look like I had an entertaining night?"

The young woman laughed and stood on her toes to rearrange his hair. "There, much better. Let's don't overdo it. Subtle, Doug, nothing too blatant. Bud won't need to be hit in the head with a two-by-four to believe he has something to use against you if he needs it. After all, we led him right down the path where we want him. If he tries to use something against you, so much the better. We don't need it, but I won't complain about having anything extra to use against him."

"All right, but my reputation might never recover from this." The smile faded from Doug's face. "You're leaving here soon, aren't you? Of all the places CCI could choose to own hotels, why did you put one in Halesburg? It's got to be hard on Uncle Matt to come here even after all these years, and I know he's never happy when you're here. It hits too close to home for him as well as for Mom and Dad."

"My gig here ends Sunday. Bud keeps pushing to extend my stay, but of course that can't happen; I have other things to do. I'll leave first thing Monday morning if not Sunday night." Seeing he remained unappeased, she added, "Doug, I'm not Elizabeth. I know I need to watch my back, and I do so here in Halesburg more than anywhere except in Elkford. It's partly because of Elizabeth that I need to do this, and in a way it's because of her that I can do what I need to do. Matty saw to that."

Doug reached out and encircled her with his arms and pulled her close to him. "Just be careful. As much as it would hurt the rest of us if anything happened to you, it would devastate Uncle Matt, and if it happened here where Aunt Elizabeth died, it would kill him."

"I know, Doug, and I have no plans to depart this life anytime soon. I plan to be a thorn in a lot of people's sides for a long time to come." She pushed back and grinned up at him. Then she stood on her toes, kissed his cheek, and stepped back. "Now go before Bud sends somebody up here to stir things along and catches me out of costume."

He sighed and smiled at her before reaching for the doorknob again. "All right, I'm going, but remember your promise. We're throwing a big party at the old house like we used to on Independence Day. I'm holding you to that."

In a more serious tone than before, she said, "I always keep my promises to you, don't I?"

"Yes, so far. I want you to keep it that way. Remember, you promised me you'll stay safe here until you leave."

"I remember. I'm here to gather information, not act on it, Doug. Now go, and take good care of my envelope."

He nodded, feeling for the papers tucked inside his jacket, and opened the door at last. Peeking out, he saw a maid's cart a few doors down but no one in the hall. He turned back inside, gave her a quick smile, and slipped out of the room.

With Doug gone, she put the chain back on the door and walked across to the table where her wig sat on its stand. She picked it up and began repairing a couple of loose curls.

# Chapter 22

*Friday, June 22, 1979*

"John, I need to pick up Chris from her riding group at three o'clock. Do I need to do any last-minute errands for you on the way there? I don't want to come back into Elkford this evening. We still need to finish packing." Sandra stood in the interconnecting doorway between her rarely-used office and John's, a small packet of documents in hand.

"No, I plan to stop off at JSS on the way home to pick up a couple of things, but I want to stop in myself and talk to Winston should he happen to be there. I want to discuss those increased expenses with the apartments and get the actual invoices to review. I also intend to press him to investigate the issue and provide us with a better explanation by the time we return from vacation. That's the only outstanding matter I know of, so if you have what you want from here, I think you should head home." John stepped aside for the maintenance men who were moving furniture away from the walls in his office. "I know this place needs painting, but it might take me days to find things when I get back."

"It will be worth it though. It hasn't been repainted since we first renovated this building to turn it into our headquarters. With all the traffic in and out of here, it needs updating. I wish you would consider getting new furniture, too." Sandra poked at a worn spot on the sofa.

"Let me survive the repainting first. Of course, I could move into your office. It's almost exactly like mine only reversed." John grinned as he waited for her reaction.

"You can have it, but on the condition that I remove myself from the company now instead of waiting until Doug finishes college and moves in here. I believe that was our agreement." She smiled sweetly at John, and he laughed.

"Yes, it was, but I'm not ready for you to cut back any further. You only come in a day or two a month as it is. I'll have to suffer with the pain of this paint job. As for Doug, I think he would do well starting off downstairs in one of the departments learning things in more detail instead of moving into an office up here right out of college. Finance would be a good place for him to start his career. Craig already has a thorough understanding of CCI after just a couple of months working for us; he would make a first-rate mentor. That's where Doug is this afternoon; I asked Craig to go over some basics of forecasting our finances."

"No doubt that's why he was put forward as a candidate for finance manager."

Sandra looked up at the portraits still hanging on the wall of John's office. "Those need to be put somewhere safe, so they won't get paint on them. Why don't we ask maintenance to hang them in the boardroom? That's where we discussed putting them when we decided we wanted all the children to sit for portraits when they graduated. KD's started out here temporarily and stayed; then Doug's joined hers last summer. Now is a good time to move them."

John looked up at the paintings of his eldest children. "I know, but I like them hanging in here with me." He sighed in resignation. "Before you leave, why don't you grab Clete and ask him to get someone to move them? Show him where you want them hung."

"All right. I think we should put those two at the far end on either side of the door. When Maggie and Chris get theirs done, we can hang them at this end flanking the door into your office."

John smiled at the idea. "I like that. I can look at the two children I see least when I'm suffering through a dull staff meeting."

"Yes, that's one benefit, isn't it?" Sandra laughed at the idea. "I'll go find Clete." She poked at the worn sofa again. "This goes soon, John."

~~~

"Don't worry about a thing, John. I promise to keep the ship on course while you're gone." Matt, perched on the corner of John's desk, pasted on a smile reminiscent of the Cheshire Cat.

"Your reassurance gives me about as much comfort as always when I leave you in charge. Like the proverbial fox guarding the henhouse." John's deadpan delivery of his standard line before leaving Elkford for more than a couple of days caused Matt to burst out laughing.

"I promise not to do anything rash. I won't sell the company out from under you or buy beachfront property in Kansas. I won't even hire strippers to take over the secretarial pool." Matt picked up a can of paint and read the label. "Eggshell. Going out on a limb with the color, aren't you?" He glanced around at the bare walls and drop cloth covered furniture. "I won't promise not to decree a change in color for your office though."

"No, Matt, don't even think about it. I'd rather you replace the secretarial pool with strippers than paint my office pink or orange or lime, and I know those are among the lesser evils you would select. Sandra already lost that battle." John stuffed yet another folder into his briefcase and began rummaging around his desk for more paperwork to take with him.

"You remember you're going on vacation, not a business trip, right? Why are you taking all those files? Leave me something to do." Matt reached toward the briefcase to snatch a folder or two out of it, but John slammed it closed before Matt could complete his mission.

"Fine, I'll leave it at that, but I need to do a little work while I'm gone. I won't do much. Sandra won't let me," he mumbled.

"Good. She knows you need a break. I plan to call out there and ask her mom if she and Sandra need reinforcements to keep you from working too much on vacation."

John locked the briefcase and set it on the floor next to his desk. "Are you going to Tuseeca with Jonah part of next week?"

"I hope so, but I might go later in the week than Jonah. Maybe leave Thursday afternoon or Friday morning. Between filling in for you and having a hotel full of guests, this isn't the best time to be gone. Jonah doesn't need me looking over his shoulder. He already made a good start sorting out what we want to do with the place. I just need to walk through and look for any issues with the preliminary layout we've established." Matt glanced over at the briefcase peeking out from the corner of John's desk. Those drawings would be among the papers headed to Arizona.

"Speaking of your busy hotel, don't you need to be over there tending to the influx of guests on a summer Friday afternoon instead of bothering me?" At last, John flashed the boyish grin so familiar from their childhood together.

Matt stood and stretched before responding. "Yeah, I suppose I need to get back to my other job. I'll give you a call in Arizona if I change my mind and decide to sell the place before you get back."

John shook his head as he walked around his desk, and the cousins embraced before Matt ambled out of the office to return to the adjacent hotel.

~~~

After shuffling through the folders on his desk once more, John accepted the fact he had all the work Sandra would allow him to do during their vacation already crammed into his briefcase. Thus, one more significant task remained. With a stifled groan, he picked up the phone and dialed his mother's house. He owed her a call before he left Elkford for ten days; better to get it over with from his office than tonight from home.

Tanya answered the phone on the second ring. "Hathaway residence."

"Hello, Tanya, it's John Stuart. Is my mother available?" Once again, John remembered his debt to Matt for finding someone who would tolerate working for Jeanette and Winston, even if the suspicions regarding dual paychecks and spying were correct. They had run off a score of live-in maid/cooks over the years before Matt suggested Tanya to John. She had stuck with the Hathaways for several years now, relieving John of what had become at least an annual crisis when previous help quit on short notice.

"Oh, good afternoon, Mr. Stuart," answered a cheerful Tanya. "Yes, she's in. Let me get her to the phone." John heard a bump as she set the receiver down. She came back within less than a minute. "She'll pick up in the sitting room momentarily, Mr. Stuart."

"Thank you, Tanya." Before he could say more, he heard another extension pick up.

"I have it now, Tanya. You may hang up in the kitchen." Jeanette's voice sounded sharp compared to the pleasant voice of her hired help. When a click signaled the kitchen phone had disconnected, Jeanette addressed her son. "I wondered if I would hear from you before you left town for an extended time."

John settled back into his chair. He could tell it would be one of those conversations. "I'm sorry I didn't call earlier in the day, but things have been hectic at work. How are you, Mother?"

"I am well enough, I suppose. I have accepted the fact Winston and I will be forced to remain in Elkford for the duration of the summer months though everyone else of our acquaintance has travel plans. Have you seen Claudine since she and Harold returned from Florida? She is quite tan, and she spoke of their wonderful time at the beach. Giselle was having such a good time they allowed her to remain with Claudine's mother for another two weeks." John noted that as usual his mother avoided calling Winston's first wife, Hortense, by name. She also didn't mention that Claudine and Harold afforded to spend two weeks in Florida because they stayed with her mother.

"Perhaps you and Winston can take a short trip somewhere later, Mother." John knew where such a comment would lead, and he braced himself for the tirade to come.

"I had hoped to spend time in France this summer, but as you know such a trip will not occur. Unlike many of my friends, I am unimpressed with Florida. While I am happy for Claudine and Giselle to enjoy their time there, I have no desire to subject myself to such heat and humidity." She issued an exaggerated sigh. "No, if I cannot spend time in Europe, I have no wish to leave my comfortable little home. I will make myself be satisfied that you and your family will have a pleasant time in Arizona." She hesitated a second before broaching another taboo subject. "I assume most of the children will travel with you tomorrow?"

"Yes, all three of the younger children are going. KD goes to Arizona to visit her grandmother and grandfather on her own schedule since she's grown and out of our house."

As expected, reference to the eldest Stuart child drew Jeanette's ire. "She does everything to suit herself. She always has. She gives no thought to anyone else. I hope you notice how little you see of her since she came into her inheritance."

John wondered if his mother realized the warm bond all his children maintained with Sandra's family in comparison to their mostly-strained one with his. While Jeanette maintained an intimate connection with Maggie and a cordial if not close one with Chris, she and Doug only tolerated one another. Worst by far, Jeanette and KD shifted between grudging dislike and open hostility. So it had been almost from KD's birth.

For years, it bothered John how his firstborn refused to refer to his mother as grandmother, but he gave up trying to get her to use that sobriquet long ago. Upon his last attempt, she had told him she would be happy to call his mother something other than by her given name and proceeded to rattle off an extensive list of options from which he could choose. Needless to say, neither grandmother nor any similar affectionate appellation appeared on her list, and he dropped the subject forever.

John chose to bring his conversation with his mother to a close rather than get into a protracted discussion with her about KD or anything else contentious. "We all like to do as we please when we can, Mother. She's no different than anyone else in that regard. I need to finish a couple of things before I leave, so I'll let you go. I want to stop by to speak to Winston on the way home. I'll give him his paycheck for June or leave it with Cynthia if he happens to be out. Goodbye, Mother. I'll see you in a couple of weeks." He hung up before she could reply.

~~~

"Whoa, your office looks different with everything moved around and covered with drop cloths, Dad. Did Mom convince you to paint it some color other than off-white?"

"No, I like it the way it is. Did you learn anything from Craig today?" John leaned back in his chair which, along with his desk, was the only thing not covered to prepare the room for painting.

Doug sat down on the sofa, drop cloth and all. "A lot. He explained all about budgeting and forecasting expenses. Fall quarter I'll take an entry-level finance class. I understand more about why we need to predict spending now, and I think that will help me in class." He leaned back on the sofa and noticed the off-color rectangle where his sister's portrait had hung for the last five years. "Hey, where did you put KD and me? In Mom's office?"

"No, you two moved into the boardroom. Your mother reminded me that we originally planned to hang them there, and this seemed like a good time to move them. Clete did that a few minutes ago." Doug saw the frown on John's face.

"Not ready to give us up, Dad?"

"I'll never be ready to give up any of my children, but you all grow up regardless of how much a part of me would like for you to remain kids living at home forever. I'm glad you're here for the summer and want to go to Arizona with your old fogey parents and your bratty younger sisters to visit your ancient grandparents. I miss having my whole family together. At least I'll have most of it for over a week."

"Don't worry, Dad. Everybody will be together again before long. I have faith it will happen soon."

John took a deep breath and tried to shake off the sudden melancholy that gripped him. "I hope so, Doug. I hope so." He pushed back from his desk and stood. "Come on, let's get out of here. You head on home and finish packing. I'll be along as soon as I stop to talk to Winston for a few minutes. I need this vacation and a break from the business."

"OK." Doug popped up off the sofa and followed his father out the door. "I promised Maggie I'd give her another shifting lesson this evening. I expect she's pacing around her car waiting for me, so I better get there before she wears a trench in the driveway."

While John locked up the office, Doug punched the elevator call button and wandered across to the open boardroom door to look inside. When he spotted the portraits of himself and his elder sister staring down the length of the room toward his father's chair at the opposite end, he grinned. "Might scare a couple of people," he told John when the older man joined his son in the doorway.

"Yep, but not as much as the real thing will," John said with his second real smile all day. The elevator doors slid open behind them, and father and son turned and crossed the lobby to begin a well-deserved vacation.

~~~

Sandra put her hand on the telephone but snatched it back. She had promised to adhere to the rules set forth a few months earlier, but tonight it proved difficult. She went back to the stand where her suitcase rested and poked through the clothes folded neatly inside. John's already sat on the floor ready to go except for the last-minute addition of his shaving kit in the morning.

Forcing herself to find some distraction, she walked down the hall to check on Maggie's packing. She knew Chris finished the night before. Maggie, on the other hand, could never decide which outfits she would want and would try to stuff in enough clothes for a month instead of the ten days necessary.

After a stern word to the girl about not taking a second suitcase, Sandra went in search of John. She found him at his desk in the study sifting through the papers in his briefcase. She asked if she could help with anything and then continued through the house when he declined. She found Doug in the yard doing some last-minute cleanup before they left for their trip. She wanted to ask for more details about his short stay in Halesburg, but what she already knew weighed on her. The few details he admitted the previous evening kept forcing its way back into her thoughts.

A glance at her watch told her she needed to act or lose her window of opportunity. It might already be too late. She turned and marched back to her bedroom, stealing a peek at John still engrossed in the study as she passed.

She closed the bedroom door and sat on the chair next to the phone. A quick check of the note card she pulled from the drawer earlier told her the number she needed to dial.

The phone on the other end rang six times before someone answered. "Chestnut Cove Inn Halesburg. How may I assist you?"

"Room 212, please."

"Just a moment." Sandra heard the click which signified she had been placed on hold while the clerk connected her with the room.

The phone rang three, four, five times. Sandra almost gave up. Then someone answered, "Hello."

"I'm breaking our agreement, but I needed to know you're OK. I hate you're in that place. I hardly slept at all knowing two of my children were in Halesburg this week. You're really leaving there Sunday?"

"Yes, and don't worry, I'm fine. No one knows who I am, and even if they knew I don't believe I'd be in any danger. It's not like this is my first trip to Halesburg in twenty years."

"I know, but I don't usually find out about your trips there until after the fact, and you never stay long. I still hate that we have a hotel there."

"Duly noted."

"Have you been downtown?" She already knew the answer, but she asked anyway.

"Yes, two or three times, and before you ask, yes, I've been to that spot. I go there almost every trip to Halesburg. It's something I need to do."

Sandra shivered at the memory. She only went there once. Matt needed to go;

John wanted to support him; she went along to support both. For days afterward, Sandra had awakened from horrible dreams of Elizabeth and KD caught in the middle of the street, the brown sedan bearing down on them. Sometimes the stroller made it across to safety; sometimes she lost both her friend and her child to the terrible act of a never-identified perpetrator.

More correctly, though unofficially, they suspected multiple perpetrators, some of whom were very well known. Bits and pieces filtered out in the aftermath which led Matt, John, and Sandra to the certainty that people lied about some details related to Elizabeth's death. Those people held strong associations with Halesburg, Stannum Academy, and Elkford. They were also well-connected. One of those connected people, the sheriff's lead investigator, declared it the act of a transient criminal who probably left Halesburg immediately after Elizabeth was hit. His pronouncement, along with tacit support from the sheriff and district attorney, left Elizabeth's family and friends with no recourse and no formal evidence to pursue the matter. No way to prove a conspiracy to murder Elizabeth...or KD.

That was the detail which kept Sandra awake so many nights. If Elizabeth died in a deliberate act, what possible motive could exist? She knew no one in Halesburg except the man she went to interview for the newspaper. Did someone kill her because of something she learned during her few hours in the town? That always seemed unlikely.

However, the child was an heiress. Her death could have had consequences even at such an early age. But no one knew Elizabeth would take KD with her that day. Only the evening before, KD's regular babysitter cancelled a commitment to keep her the next morning. John and Matt both had exams, so neither could skip class to keep her. Elizabeth was scheduled to drive to Halesburg to conduct an interview with someone connected to Stannum Academy. However, she volunteered to take the child with her, insisting she could manage KD during the meeting, which would allow Sandra to keep her appointment. KD loved spending time with Elizabeth, so Sandra agreed.

But no one knew except Sandra, John, Matt, and Elizabeth. In the unlikely event someone wanted to eliminate the young child to prevent her inheriting part of the Stuart estate, they could not have planned to do so in Halesburg in advance. Moreover, if KD was the target, why Halesburg? She lived in Elkford and Coughton. Surely someone would have tried to get to her in those places instead of taking a random chance in Halesburg on the spur of the moment.

Thus went the discussion among Matt, John, and Sandra for twenty years. KD became a part of the debate as she grew older, for the chance she had been targeted overrode all else. She had to know; she had to be forewarned and trained to defend herself.

Sandra reminded herself of that now. Matt, in particular, made it his business to ensure his goddaughter could protect herself.

"Mom? Are you still there?"

Sandra drew a breath. "Yes, I'm here. I worry about you. You know that. Promise you'll stay safe the next two days and leave Halesburg as soon as you can."

"I will. I plan to leave here after my last set Sunday night."

"All right. You know we'll be at Gran's by then. Would you call when you get to Coughton? I've given you all the space you've asked for, KD, except this."

"Yes, I promise to call, but it might be late even in Arizona."

Sandra breathed a sigh of relief. "Thank you. You promised we'll see you sometime later in the summer. I'm holding you to that."

"Yes, I remember."

~~~

The computer terminal keys clicked as Matt typed. He checked his notes to verify he entered the information correctly, made one last entry, and logged off the IO system. He stood from the small desk in his private suite and picked up the sheet of paper containing the notes. Walking across to an end table, he tore the sheet into several small pieces and dropped them into an ashtray. It seemed obsessively careful even to him at times, but he developed the habit more than twenty years ago and would continue it throughout his life. He picked up a small CCI book of matches, tore one out, and struck it. After lighting one of the bits of paper, he dropped it onto the pile in the ashtray and watched until nothing remained except ash.

~~~

*Saturday, June 23, 1979*

The black limousine pulled to a stop in front of the hotel door. A bellhop hustled out with a luggage cart, but he pulled up short when the driver stepped out and held up two fingers. The doorman on duty, Ben, signaled for another bellhop to attend the limousine. To the surprise of both Ben and the bellhops, no one exited the car except the chauffeur.

The black-clad man dismissed the valet, stating that he would only remain at CCI long enough to ensure his employer's luggage and that of her staff were attended to. The doorman opened the door for the chauffeur, who led the bellhops across the lobby to the desk.

"My name is Starnes. I am to deliver the luggage of my employer and her entourage. Is Mr. Hunter present? He has the particulars for her reservations."

Martha smiled up at the man. "I'll check for the reservation information. Under what name are they listed?"

The impeccably-dressed man looked apologetic when he responded. "I'm sorry, but Mr. Hunter must handle this matter himself."

"Oh, well, let me check to see if he's in his office." Her bafflement at the unusual request written on her face, Martha picked up the phone and dialed Matt's extension. "Matt, it's Martha. You're needed at the desk to handle a private check-in? A Mr. Starnes says you're aware of his employer's reservations."

"Yes, I am. Tell Mr. Starnes I'll be right out." Matt appeared from the back in less than a minute. "Hello, Mr. Starnes. I have everything ready for your employer. I take it she and her entourage aren't with you today?"

The man gave the slightest of bows to Matt. "No, sir. They'll be along soon. I was instructed to bring their luggage and handle their check-in."

"Of course. Suites 500 and 502 have been prepared. Janelle is here today to assist in organizing your employer's things in her suite, 502, as requested. We'll have the bellhops deliver the luggage to 500. Janelle will handle distributing it between the two suites."

"Thank you, Mr. Hunter. Miss Janelle will be the sole member of staff permitted in my employer's suites for the duration of her stay unless she requests otherwise?"

"Yes, I already made arrangements with Janelle, but I'll ensure the assistant managers are aware of that requirement also. Your employer and her staff will have complete privacy as long as they desire it."

"Excellent. Allow me to pass along her thanks in advance." Almost as an afterthought, he added, "The reservation is listed under her group name?"

"Yes, it's listed as Castanea Cavas. No personal names given to protect her privacy. I'll hold the keys until they arrive." Matt signaled to Martha, who handed him the keys for the two suites, and he put them into his jacket pocket.

"Excellent. She will be most pleased." For the first time, the chauffeur couldn't prevent a smile tugging at his lips. "If you'll excuse me, the car is blocking your entrance, so I should be on my way. Thank you for your excellent work, Mr. Hunter."

"My pleasure." Matt allowed his own smile and bowed to the chauffeur.

Once Janelle arrived at the desk and led the bellhops to the fifth floor, Matt walked into the back office to find the assistant manager on duty.

"Jared, a special guest and her staff will be staying with us for a week. They're in 500 and 502. Due to the lady's wish for privacy, the suites are booked under a travel group's name. We've also agreed to limit staff access to those suites to only Janelle unless otherwise requested. Janelle is aware of this and will come in on her days off for an hour each morning and afternoon to check on our special guests."

A surprised Jared picked up a pen and jotted down the suite numbers. "Has that ever happened before, Matt?"

"Oh, it happens on occasion. Sometimes tabloids or sycophants or whomever harass certain people overmuch. It's nice for them to be able to take a break somewhere like this and maintain their privacy for a short time. The least we can do is agree to such an easy request. Be sure to let the staff on duty today know. I'll inform Donald when he comes on duty tonight and Pam when she comes in tomorrow morning." He smiled and walked on down the hall.

When he returned to his office, Matt walked through it and out the rear door into the hall behind. He passed a couple of other doors until he reached a third. He pulled a key ring from his pocket and selected a rarely-used key to admit himself to the suite adjacent to his own. Stepping inside, he placed the keys for suites 500 and 502 on the table in the small foyer. Then he pulled a gum wrapper from his pocket, scribbled a three-word note on it, and tucked it under one of the keys. His laughter echoed off the walls of the deserted hall as he walked back to his office. "Welcome home, kid."

~~~

"You should have seen the pile of luggage, Laura. It took two carts. They weren't both full, but there sure was a lot of it. No wonder the lady and her staff didn't arrive with their things. They couldn't have fit in the limo with so many bags," Martha whispered when the girls had a quiet moment after Laura returned to the desk. Laura had missed the event by minutes because she went to lunch right before the limousine arrived.

She looked at an empty luggage cart in a nearby corner, imagining how many suitcases it would take to fill one. "I wonder if we'll even see the lady or her staff? Will they remain in their rooms? If they order room service, will the waiters leave the cart in the hall or take the food into the rooms? I suppose that would be a request from the guest and would be OK. I hope Janelle receives a nice tip for coming in extra to take care of their rooms on her days off."

"I hope we get to see her," Martha exclaimed. "I can't imagine someone owning so much. I couldn't fill up half a luggage cart with all the clothes I own. I expect she's an elderly widow. Maybe from Europe even. I tried not to pry while Matt talked to the chauffeur, but I heard something that sounded foreign when he mentioned the company name she checked in under. Maybe she's some duchess or even a princess."

"I don't know, but since the lady went to the trouble to keep her identity hidden, we shouldn't speculate and spread any rumors about a duchess or princess staying here." Both girls held a straight face for a couple of seconds before they burst into a fit of giggles.

~~~

*Sunday, June 24, 1979*

It was nearing midnight in Elkford. The new Moon and the sun had set more than two hours earlier. A few tourists wandered the downtown district and the waterfront enjoying a late evening stroll in the cool air. Out in the darkness, the Wolf River crept northward under the highway bridge that brought tourists into Elkford each day before bending back to the east beyond the town. Unnoticed, a navy-blue Dino crossed the bridge into Elkford. It turned left to follow the highway, passing some of the most well-known landmarks of the small town including the Chestnut Cove Inn and its corporate headquarters.

The small sports car continued through Elkford without slowing until it turned right with the highway on the south side of downtown and exited Elkford to the west. Ten minutes later, the Dino sped past the entrance to John and Sandra Stuart's home, driving deeper into the mountains.

Another fifteen minutes went by before the car slowed at last and took a darkened driveway past a small brass sign. After winding along the wide path for three-quarters of a mile, the Dino came to a stop at a pair of imposing, wrought iron gates. Leaving the headlights on, the driver stepped out of the car and walked up to the barrier. She stopped and stared through the elaborate bars into the darkness beyond, her mind aware of what lay on the other side without the need to see it. Her thoughts wandered back to the last time she had been here and then further back, mentally flipping through a series of memories, both good and bad, associated with the old mansion.

After several minutes, she took a deep breath and let it out. Then she pulled a key from her pocket, inserted it into the lock, and swung open the gates. Returning to her car, she drove toward the house another half mile away, leaving the gates open behind her.

When she reached the mansion, she pulled around to the left side and through the open portcullis into the courtyard on the west side of the building. She parked the Dino next to the kitchen where a single light shone over the door. After walking back to the portcullis, she pushed the button to activate the electric motor which lowered the gate. She watched as it eased down, stopping with a soft thud when it reached the ground. She retreated to the car, reached inside, and removed a small suitcase. Two steps led up to the kitchen entrance where she inserted a key into the lock and allowed the door to swing wide. This time she stepped forward without hesitation, closing and locking the door behind her. By instinct borne of countless repetition, she reached for and flipped the light switch.

As expected, the room was spotless, maintained by a former CCI maid who came regularly to clean the old inn whether anyone else set foot inside it or not. The young woman set her suitcase on the floor and took a glass from the cabinet. When she opened the refrigerator, she found fresh-squeezed orange juice inside and poured some into her glass.

Grabbing her suitcase in one hand, juice glass in the other, the young woman walked through the house to the main staircase and took the steps two at a time up to the third floor. Not slowing, she walked down the hall to the bedroom at the far west end. She set the suitcase on a chair and her glass on the small desk in the corner.

She kicked off her shoes and went into the adjacent bathroom to remove her makeup. When she returned to the bedroom, she changed into a well-worn t-shirt and jeans, picked up the juice glass, and walked downstairs.

On the first floor, the young woman unlocked the study and walked around behind the antique desk and sat down. She looked up at the portrait of the older woman over the mantle and raised her glass in silent salute. Despite her long history with the old building, this was one of the few rooms in which she felt at home, for indeed home it was to her though she had rarely used it as such. The small cabin deep in the woods remained the place that felt like home, and it would always remain a private retreat for her. However, life moved forward, and for her that meant home would be here in the old mansion. In days past, this had been a seat of power for the area around Elkford and often in the state. As her great-grandmother intended, Kathryn Duncan Stuart had been raised to sit behind this desk and wield that power again one day. Twenty years after the elder Kathryn's death, that day had come.

# Chapter 23

Voices in the hall caused Janelle to stop her work and listen to discern who and what outside the suite might interfere with her morning tasks. Two people spoke as they passed suite 500 near the end of the hall. The sound of a nearby door opening confirmed what Janelle suspected; the guests in 501 had finished an early breakfast in the restaurant and returned to their suite.

Satisfied all was well, she fluffed the pillow she was holding, laid it in place, and continued making the bed. Then she went into the bathroom and picked up the toothbrush and toothpaste and moved them to the opposite side of the sink. She dampened a washcloth and towel and tossed them into her cart before retrieving a new set to replace those she soiled.

She returned to the suite's main room and shuffled a couple of chairs at the small table and moved the open typewriter over a couple of inches. Satisfied with her efforts, she went to the closet to perform her last task. She retrieved a suitcase and carried it to her cart. Pushing aside the curtain meant to hide the sheets, towels, and other supplies, she tucked the suitcase into the nearly empty cart and pulled the curtain back down to hide her bit of thievery.

Twenty minutes later, Janelle had repeated the process in suite 502. As she pushed her cart out the door, the guests in 501 exited their room. Janelle acknowledged them, asked if they needed anything from housekeeping, and bid them a good day. They walked down the hall toward the guest elevators while Janelle took the service elevator downstairs. Instead of going to the basement to deposit the soiled sheets and towels from the two suites she serviced, she stopped on the ground floor and took a back hall.

When she reached her destination, she tapped on the door of a private suite and waited for a response from within. She had no idea if the owner would be present, but this was one of two doors in the hotel Janelle would never enter without explicit permission. In this instance, she had been instructed to continue with her assigned task should the suite's owner not respond. She pulled at the chain around her neck and drew out a key tucked into her uniform, leaned down, and unlocked the door. After ensuring no one happened to wander into the rarely used hall, she pulled out the two suitcases hidden in her cart and carried them into the suite. She placed them in the same corner as those from the previous day before hurrying back outside.

After ensuring the door locked behind her, Janelle headed to the basement laundry with her cart.

~~~

Dew still dampened tips of green in the meadow behind the old mansion, though the sun had broken over the trees more than two hours earlier. Light danced across the surface of the pond when a gentle breeze stirred the air of the isolated mountain cove. A hawk drifted overhead looking for breakfast.

A lone figure, immobile as a statue, stood on the veranda as memories flooded her mind. One of her earliest occurred here, a family gathering before her parents and Matt returned to Coughton Tech for the fall term in 1958. Great-grandmother's cocker spaniels prancing around their tiny, two-legged playmate, eager to chase the balls she held. The aroma of Lila's cooking wafting from the kitchen. The bright sun shining on a clear Sunday afternoon.

Jeanette and Winston had been there, too. Even at two-and-a-half, the child sensed the tension her grandmother's presence created. It was as if a chill fell over the house from the moment the pair clomped down the half-flight of steps from the foyer that afternoon.

Great-grandmother Kathryn, impervious rock of the family, took little notice other than a curt greeting, wise enough not to let anything mar her day with her grandson and his small family and Matt and his girlfriend, Elizabeth.

Closing her eyes, she could still see Elizabeth standing before them fiddling with her camera–carefully adjusting focus, readying the flash–to get the family photo Kathryn requested. The older woman had taken to Elizabeth as quickly as Matt, John, Sandra, and little KD. She had been destined to become an integral part of the family as Matt's wife after they graduated from Coughton Tech if not–

Matt had told KD more than once over the last twenty years how grateful he was that she had insisted "Wizzy" be included in a photograph. At Kathryn's request, Elizabeth had taken a photo of the matriarch surrounded by John, Sandra, Matt, and KD. Per the child's request, as soon as Elizabeth snapped the first photo, Winston had been recruited to snap a similar one with Elizabeth included. It would be the last photo taken of her excluding those made by the Hale County sheriff and coroner weeks later. Even now, copies of it set high on a shelf in Matt's office and on a table in the great room of the old mansion.

After a time, more pleasant memories forced their way to the surface. Matt strumming his guitar to accompany himself as he sang to a group of guests. Her father mixing drinks at the small bar. Her mother smiling as she moved among the guests with a tray of some savory snack in one hand and Doug perched on her opposite hip.

Flashing forward, she remembered a day not long before the new inn opened in downtown Elkford. It would be the last spring before the old inn ceased regular use. Occasionally, it would open for a month or two to supplement the newer hotel or be rented for a week to some special guest. However, it had remained frozen in time until the previous year when its owner directed a few modifications to make it more accommodating as a private residence again.

On the day in question ten years earlier, Claudine's son, Rainier, and his sister, Giselle, accompanied their mother who wanted to visit friends staying at the old inn. Seven-year-old Giselle had been taken up to play with Maggie, but twelve-year-old Rainier slipped away to do as he pleased. When he decided to torment one of the dogs and then Chris, he found himself facing off against Matt's best martial arts pupil. It took her seconds to send him into the pond. She smiled at the memory. It fell to Gabe to pull the shivering boy out. Already chilly relations between KD and Rainier turned frigid, though his insulting bluster about her quieted for a time. Like his step-grandmother, he continued to disparage KD in her absence but avoided her at all costs.

Turning away from the meadow, she crossed the veranda to enter the house. She carried her juice glass into the kitchen, rinsed it, and placed it in the sink. Backtracking, she walked through the great room to a corner table and picked up the framed eight-by-ten photograph. She studied it for a couple of minutes, forcing her mind to scrutinize the analytical details instead of the emotions it brought into focus. Those must wait.

~~~

The photograph stared back at her from the study desk. She had what she needed in her inventory, thanks to her time participating in theater at Coughton Tech. While a natural on stage, she declined most offers to act in the student productions in favor of learning the art of costume and makeup. She participated just enough onstage to hone her ability to transform herself to suit her personal quests. In the interim, she gathered a collection of clothes, jewelry, makeup, and wigs. All she needed now was to learn the details of Jeanette's plans. Her spy in the Hathaway household should supply those in the next day or two. With a little luck and guile, the last pieces of the plan would fall into place.

The sound of a car pulling up to the house focused her mind on one of those pieces. She picked up the photo and placed it in a drawer of her desk while she waited. Soon, footsteps approached; then a face peeked around the open door of the study.

"As I live and breathe, child. I wondered if I'd ever set eyes on you again."

"Hello, Mary, it's good to see you."

Mary Jones put her hands on her hips and glared. "You better get up from behind that desk and give me a hug. I changed your diapers. The least you can do is greet me properly." She clung to her stern expression as long as she could, determined to outlast the girl's own. As usual, the girl won, though only by a second.

Both women broke into broad smiles, and KD stood and walked around the desk. Encircling the older woman with her arms, she managed to reclaim a frown. "Are you ever going to quit using that line?"

"Of course not. I'll use whatever advantage I can manage over you. Heaven knows those are hard to come by." Releasing the girl, Mary continued, "I see you left me the breakfast dishes to clean up. What else do I need to do around here today?"

"I did not leave them for you," KD countered. "I just haven't taken time to wash them yet. Nothing needs doing but the usual weekly routine as far as the house goes, but I'll handle that. I need to burn off some energy today. However, there's something else I need you to do for me." She waved toward the pair of leather chairs in one corner, and the women sat down.

"Before you get started," Mary said with a wag of her finger, "you know better than to drag me into one of your schemes."

KD held up her hands in surrender. "To the contrary, I want you to help me clear the field to keep Vicky out of one. She needs to be far away from this, so if there's any blowback no one can try to drag her into it. For that matter, I want all of you away from here. Jonah and Joseph are already going to Tuseeca this week. I want you and Vicky to go with them."

Mary didn't respond at first, instead holding KD's gaze as if she could look deep enough into the girl's mind to discern whatever plans lurked there this time. "Is this something your mama is going to hate me for if I do as you ask?"

Shaking her head, KD said, "No, she'll never know the details, and if she learns of the results, she will understand and even approve...sort of. I'm not going to do anything rash, Mary. I just want my friends clear in case something goes wrong."

Mary tilted her head to one side, trying to detect any untruths in KD's statement. "It's no coincidence you're doing this while Sandra and John and your brother and sisters are in Arizona."

KD sighed. "No, but it's more a matter of the stars aligning, not a specific plot on my part."

While Mary couldn't spot the least twitch, she knew KD's plans tended toward the elaborate. Coincidence rarely invaded them. Giving up on one line of questions, she resorted to the most pertinent. "Any guns involved? Knives? Blunt instruments?"

KD laughed and held up her right hand. "I solemnly swear to use none of those in the execution of my plan. I won't even throw anyone into the pond...or the pool or the river..."

Mary blew out a breath. "All right, I'll call Jonah and tell him I want to go with him Wednesday. I haven't seen Vicky much since Derrick came home for the summer. I can complain about that and maybe convince her to go with us to Tuseeca. Matt would support her going to see the new hotel site, wouldn't he?"

"Yes, he would. I can even get him a message to ensure he pushes her to go. He knows I'm scouting the Elkford hotel this week, but Vic doesn't. Having her elsewhere so I don't accidentally run into her would be good. I can fool a lot of people in disguise, but fooling Vicky, Doug, or Joseph would be almost impossible." She stood and walked to her desk to make a note to leave a message for Matt at his answering service.

Mary knew the girl well enough to know their visit was at an end. KD would need to dress to go to the hotel to test–or possibly terrorize–the staff who didn't know her. Standing, Mary crossed the study to claim one more hug from the girl she had known from birth. "Do not get into too much trouble. Don't cause too much either. Oh, and leave me a list of what you want me to do here before Independence Day. I won't have long to do any work if I'm going to Tuseeca this week."

KD reached into a folder on the desk and extracted a sheet of paper which she passed to Mary. "Very little. We'll handle most of it. Doug has a list and started on it before he left for Arizona. You and Jonah mostly need to come enjoy yourself that day."

"Will I be allowed to tell your mama I've been getting this place ready for your return behind her back by next Wednesday?"

KD laughed, a rarity for the last few years. "Are you brave enough to tell her that? I'll get enough heat from her and from Dad for a host of things. If you want to tell her what you've been doing and take some of that heat, you're welcome to do so."

Mary narrowed her eyes at KD. "I'll need to think about that." She shifted her attention to the sheet of paper in her hand as she walked toward the door.

"I thought so," KD said, resuming her seat behind the desk. "I'll see you next Wednesday, Mary, and thank you."

~~~

*Tuesday, June 26, 1979*

Vicky heard voices in the foyer and looked up from her desk in time to see her father and brother walk into her office. "Hey, Dad. Matt called a few minutes ago from the hotel to tell me he's running late, but he was about to walk out the door on his way over here. You can go ahead into his office and spread out your drawings and notes if you want."

Jonah leaned down and kissed his daughter on the cheek. "We will, but first I'm supposed to relay a message to you. Your mother said she hasn't seen you in two weeks. Joseph's been home from school three weeks during which time she's seen both her children at the same time twice. Since you got your own place, she doesn't see you enough. At least I get to see you at work."

Matt walked into the office suite in time to hear Jonah's admonishment. "Uh oh. You better do something to make your mom happy, Vicky," Matt said with more seriousness than normal. "Why don't you take a couple of days off while things are quiet up here? You could spend some time with her while Jonah and Joseph are in Tuseeca."

"One problem with your plan, Matt," Jonah said. "Mary's decided to go with us to Tuseeca. She wants to see the new site we're developing. She misses working around here at times, and Sandra is in Arizona this week, so she doesn't have her best friend around to do anything with right now. She told me last night she's going with us. She's also decided we're staying over the weekend to check out the area. You remember she used to do that with Sandra when we looked at places where we were interested in developing a new hotel, so she's got an eye for businesses we can contact about working together once we open."

Matt's face brightened. "Why don't you join them, Vicky? It would be sort of a mini Jones family vacation with a little work thrown in. You can go as my assistant, and we'll get another set of eyes on things. I'll be there by late Thursday afternoon or Friday morning for a day or two, so you can assist me officially part of the time."

Vicky chewed on her lower lip while she considered the idea. "It would be good timing. Derrick's friends want to leave Thursday evening for a long weekend of deep-sea fishing, but he was hesitant to go since we only have so much time together this summer. If I plan to go to Tuseeca, he'll be free to go with his friends without feeling guilty."

Matt's grin appeared in a flash. "Perfect. As soon as you're done gathering those figures for me, go home and pack. Don't forget to tell Mrs. Pierce you won't be here. She'll love being alone up here for a day or two." He stole a glance out the door toward her office. "I'll need to make a special effort to spend a little time up here Wednesday and Thursday needling her." He turned back to Jonah. "Any more problems I need to solve today?"

Jonah laughed as he followed Matt into his office, Joseph trailing behind them. "Well, maybe one or two small ones, but Joseph and I have brought a couple of solutions of our own. We've figured out how to fit everything we want into the second floor. We drafted some things for you to look at."

"Great. I knew you'd figure out how to make it work. You always do." Matt took a seat at the worktable, and Jonah and Joseph joined him there.

They spread out the latest Tuseeca hotel drawings and began to go through the changes. When they completed their discussion of those plans, they shifted to the issue of creating an office suitable for Geraldine in the hotel.

Before they got far into those discussions, Joseph asked, "Wouldn't it be easier if Geraldine moved back over here into the personnel office? Mr. Krebs acts like he's so far in over his head just keeping track of vacation time for everybody I think he'd welcome her back even if she still reported to Matt and handled just the hotel staff."

Matt leaned back in his chair and considered the best way to answer Joseph's question. "Maybe in some ways, but you know as well as I do, he'll pay a price for his actions. He humiliated Geraldine by firing her even though she expected she'd get put right onto CasCav's payroll and not miss a paycheck. Firing her was unjustified and vindictive. We're not about to ask her to sit in the same place with him even if they would be equals working for the two companies out of a common office."

"What happens when Mr. Krebs retires or if Uncle John gets fed up and fires him? Would Geraldine come back here then?" Joseph couldn't hide the twitch at the corner of his mouth. He had been around the Stuart family all his life. He was also well-versed in the disputes of the last few years between the president of CCI and the owner of CasCav. No doubt any attempt to poach Geraldine back to CCI would erupt into another dispute.

Matt and Jonah exchanged looks before both burst out laughing at Joseph's question. "That will be a good day for all of us to be in Tuseeca or wherever we can find to hide. With a little luck, the warring factions will work out a solution that works for both sides without bloodshed. They both think a lot of her." He waited a beat before adding, "I still want to be out of town though. I don't want any part of that fight."

~~~

The country club dining room lacked bustle at lunch today for some reason, which suited Hoyt and his companions. Hoyt intended to take a long lunch to enjoy both the food and company. His relief at John's absence had lasted only until the staff meeting Monday afternoon. The outwardly easygoing Matt Hunter proved himself as difficult as John had been in recent months. Hoyt's rant about the staff meeting began as soon as Winston and Jeanette arrived and seated themselves.

"I cannot comprehend John's loyalty to Matt Hunter. I realize they are cousins, but only second cousins or some such. Matt wasted no time taking control of things yesterday. When we attempted to bring up for discussion this sudden announcement of a new hotel in a location none of us knew anything about last week, he shut down the subject. He said the deal was done, agreed to by the people who hold authority to do so, and we needed to move on to something new. We hardly discussed the matter at all except for Jonah's report about the preliminary design status, which Matt didn't let him get into with any detail.

"Legal reported the standard franchise agreement changes have already been agreed to by both companies though details need to be finalized. No doubt Matt will sign the final agreement for both companies while John is away if he can get away with it since I assume he still holds a corporate title at CasCav."

The subject gave Hoyt his second wind, and he plowed onward in a rant. "I cannot understand why John continues to allow such a conflict. How can Matt give unbiased advice about interactions between CCI and CasCav when he sits as a corporate officer on the boards of both companies? Or what passes for a board at CasCav. I suppose it is still wholly owned and its owner can do as she pleases, or her representatives can. I assume she remains in Europe?" Hoyt stopped and waited for Jeanette to take the bait.

As usual, she seethed at the allusion to her two least-favorite people. "I haven't the faintest idea where she is, though to the best of my knowledge she continues to run wild in Europe. Her father and I do not discuss her at all." She took a sip of tea while she brought her voice under control. "I do agree with you Matt Hunter wields too much power. I'm sure he remains in control at her company in addition to acting as second in command to John at the hotel chain. No doubt he looks out for her interests first."

"Exactly." Hoyt's head nodded like a bobblehead doll. He looked to Winston for concurrence from him also, though Winston maintained his focus on his plate of Kobe beef. "Why should he be allowed such sway in the company when his loyalties are divided? But John will not see it."

Further derogation of Matt Hunter ended when Hoyt noticed Vaughn nearby. Winston, who had begun to push away from the table, stopped when Vaughn approached.

"Hello, Hoyt." Vaughn extended his hand to Hoyt first before turning to the other two occupants of the table to do the same. "Winston, Jeanette, I'm especially pleased to see you two." A catlike smile creased his face. "Since I've heard nothing of any plans for you to make a tour of Europe this summer, I assume you will attend our ball in August." Vaughn pulled a packet from the inside pocket of his coat. "I have the tickets for you right here." He made a deliberate show of pulling two from the set and placing them on the table. "If you don't happen to have sufficient cash for them with you today, I'll be happy to accept a personal check from my old Stannum Academy comrade." He stood staring down at Winston in expectation.

Winston shifted in his seat, trying to find a way out of spending hundreds of dollars he didn't have on the tickets. The brusque conversation with John the previous Friday stuck in his mind. John had supported Jeanette and Winston for years. His stepson expected little in return from Winston and got less, a fact he made plain the afternoon before leaving town the previous week. Spending hundreds to buy tickets to a ball for which Jeanette would then insist required a new and expensive gown would anger John, but Vaughn Michaelson stood before him waiting with his hand out, and Winston owed Vaughn.

Winston's shaky hand drew out his checkbook, and he wrote out a check for the two tickets. He even managed something resembling a smile when he passed it across to Vaughn. "We're looking forward to it, aren't we Jeanette?"

"Of course, we are," she agreed. "I had no idea you had yet to purchase our tickets. I must go to Woodbury soon to select a new ball gown, and you might need a new tuxedo. I'll have Tanya bring your old one out this week to check it." She beamed up at Vaughn. "Thank you for reminding Winston. We are so looking forward to such an elegant event."

"As am I, Jeanette. You must save me a dance. I insist." Vaughn looked across the room to where his eldest son, Roger, beckoned. "I see Roger has someone he would like to introduce to me. I will see all of you again soon I hope." He took one last look at Winston, who had drained his glass of wine, before he strolled toward his son.

The discussion of elegant parties brought Jeanette's mind back to her primary purpose in arranging today's lunch with Hoyt. Within a couple of minutes, she managed to work the conversation around to her goal. "Hoyt, doesn't Matt Hunter have responsibilities which require him to spend time at the other hotels? Even the one being built in Tuseeca?"

"Yes, he and Jonah both spend quite a bit of time at new properties when they're being converted from old mills and warehouses and factories into a hotel."

Before Hoyt got on another roll about Matt, Jeanette interrupted him with another question. "With John out of town this week and part of next week, will Matt continue that practice, or will he remain in Elkford for the duration of John's absence?"

"He'll be here most of the time, but I believe he plans to follow Jonah to Tuseeca at the end of the week. Some details they need to work out seem to require Matt's presence. I'm quite sure Jonah could handle it without Matt running off. I've a good mind to find him this afternoon and tell him he needs to stay put while John's away."

The horrified look on Jeanette's face failed to give Hoyt a hint his idea didn't fit with her plans. "No," she said a bit louder than intended. In a lower voice, she continued, "He would tell John, and John would blame you for interfering again. Why don't you let Matt do as he pleases? If a problem occurs in his absence, you'll have something substantive to discuss with John."

Hoyt sipped his drink as he considered her suggestion. "Yes, there's something to what you say. If we had an issue while Matt is in charge that he isn't there to handle, it would reflect badly on him."

Jeanette almost purred at the idea her coveted window of opportunity at the hotel might exist. "So, Matt will be away Friday? Will he return Friday evening or on Saturday or...?"

"Um, I believe he'll be away until at least Saturday, maybe Sunday. I should find out."

"Yes, yes, you should." Jeanette thought through her plans and how best to enlist Hoyt with or without his knowledge. "Hoyt, if you discover he'll be away until Sunday, perhaps it would be helpful if we spent some time at the hotel in his absence." Hoyt's attention shifted to Jeanette in full. "It has been some time since I hosted a dinner at the restaurant in the hotel. Perhaps Saturday evening I could– rather Winston and I could–host a dinner there. Everyone knows Matt employs spies to keep an eye on the other hotels. We should do the same at his own." Jeanette caught herself too late referring to the CCI flagship hotel as Matt's.

"I believe you're onto something. It would be a good test of how well they can put on a proper dinner, and you could discuss any shortcomings with John yourself. Surely he would listen to his own mother."

Jeanette had her doubts about that, but she let the matter go. "We must know if Matt will be away until at least late Saturday night. Can you find out, Hoyt?" She batted her eyes at her husband's old friend. "If I knew that bit of information, I could plan a dinner for Saturday evening. We three and Claudine and Harold would attend. I'll select a few more friends who will appreciate attending a sophisticated dinner, and we will test the hotel's ability to put on such an event."

"An excellent plan." Hoyt slapped the table with his hand. "I'll make it my business to learn Matt's schedule for the rest of the week and the weekend. Mrs. Pierce should be aware when he'll be away. I'll find out and call Winston this afternoon." Hoyt raised his empty glass to signal their waiter to bring him another.

~~~

*Wednesday, June 27, 1979*

Late in the afternoon, an efficient-looking young woman in a navy skirt and white blouse entered the busy hotel lobby carrying a small bag from the stationery store a couple of blocks away. Upon entering, she donned a cream-colored sweater to fend off the cooler temperature inside before turning left toward the restaurant in search of the hostess.

When Ellen returned from seating a couple for an early dinner, she noticed the young woman. "May I help you? One for dinner?"

"Oh, no, not tonight. My employer plans for us to dine upstairs. I'd like to take care of our orders if I may and arrange for dinner to be delivered a little later. In an hour?" The young woman pulled a small notepad from her purse and flipped it open to a page full of neat printing. She dove into her bag again, this time extracting the key to suite 500, which she held up for Ellen to see.

"Of course. Let me take down what you and your employer would like to eat, and I'll make sure the kitchen knows you want it in an hour." Ellen pulled out an order pad and pencil from her stand and jotted 500 in the top right corner of the page.

"Three orders. There's her maid also. You may have all three meals delivered to suite 502. My employer wishes us to dine in there with her this evening." She passed her notepad to Ellen, who began transferring the order information to her own pad. "Oh, ask the waiter to knock and leave the cart outside the door. I'll take care of bringing it into the suite and arranging things to suit my employer."

Ellen stopped and made a note at the top of the ticket regarding the delivery instructions. "I think that's everything," she said once she checked the two lists together. "Is there anything else we can do for you today?"

"No, not today. I hope my employer will come down later in our stay to dine in the restaurant once she's more rested."

"If she chooses to do so, we'll be happy to host her here, but if she prefers to dine in her suite, we're happy to provide room service."

"Thank you, she's most appreciative of the hotel's consideration of her needs and wishes." The woman held up her package from the stationery store. "I need to speak with the reception desk and then go up to take care of some typing for her before dinner. Thank you again for your assistance."

"Certainly. If you or anyone in your party needs anything, feel free to stop here or call down to the restaurant and let us know. We can handle almost any request."

On her way back through the lobby, the young woman stopped at the desk where Martha stood with Dan discussing the changes to IO she needed to learn. When the woman approached the desk, Martha broke off the conversation to attend the guest. "May I help you?"

The young woman stepped up to the desk and spoke in a crisp, soft voice. "Hello. My employer, who is in suite 502, asked me to find out if you have information on theater tickets in Woodbury. If not, would your concierge check into what might be available for her should she wish to attend a play while she is in residence here?"

"Of course. Maurice will have those details. Let me call him and ask if there's a play or musical running in Woodbury. I'm sure he can acquire tickets should she desire them. If you'll wait a moment, I'll call him." Martha called the concierge desk and explained the request. In less than a minute, she completed the call and handed the young woman a piece of paper with the information jotted on it. "If your employer would like us to arrange tickets, just let us know."

"Thank you. I'll give her this and let you or Maurice know should she decide she would like to attend." After a quick glance at her watch, she bid Martha good evening and hurried to the elevator bank to go up to her suite.

When she reached the fifth floor, she pulled the key for 502 from her skirt pocket. Once inside, she placed the stationery bag on the coffee table. She would take care of the contents later. She walked to the writing desk in the living room of the suite, called the number for her answering service, and waited for the operator.

When the operator answered, she said, "Good afternoon. This is Yekaterina. Do I have any messages?"

"Yes, ma'am, you have a message from Tanya. Mrs. Hathaway is planning to hold her dinner at the Elkford hotel on Saturday evening. She learned Mr. Hunter will be away all day on Friday and until late in the evening on Saturday. She plans to come to the hotel Friday to handle the arrangements in person. Tanya will relay further details when she knows them."

"Excellent. Thank her for the intelligence. I'll check in with you Friday evening if not before to get any details she relays to you. Thank you." She hung up and sat drumming her fingers on the desk while she thought about her own plans. All was coming together, and Saturday night suited her quite well.

# Chapter 24

*Thursday, June 28, 1979*

Pam jotted another entry on her list. "Anything else we need to take care of while you're away, Matt?"

Matt paused from sorting through papers related to the new Tuseeca hotel to consider Pam's question. "Not that I can think of. You know the drill and so do the other AMs. The newest ones have come a long way in the last couple of months. I don't expect any issues while I'm gone. If something comes up, you have the phone number of the motel where we're staying. Leave a message there or with the answering service, and I'll call you as soon as I can." He picked up the drawings and placed them into his briefcase and closed it.

"Do you want me to come by to check on things at the hotel Saturday since you won't be in until late in the evening? Or I can rearrange the work schedule and take the Saturday evening shift from Jared." Like Matt, Pam knew Jared had improved, but he remained their greenest AM.

Matt stopped and looked up at her to ensure she paid attention to his answer. "No, I want you to go to Woodbury for the whole day to watch Bobby play ball. Jared will do fine. He's got a couple of good clerks out front Saturday evening to run the desk. Everything will be fine. I want a full report on how many homeruns Bobby hit when I get back." When Pam still looked unconvinced, Matt added, "That's an order. Do not show your face around here Saturday unless you find out the hotel is on fire."

A look of horror crossed Pam's face. "Don't even joke about such a thing. Let's stick to rhetorical fires at worst."

Matt laughed at the thought. "Much better. Let's keep those to a minimum, too. Well, at least when I'm not here. I missed the last one with Geraldine a few weeks ago. We don't enjoy that kind of fun around here too often. I want to be present for the next rhetorical fire."

After Pam left his office, Matt checked around for anything else he needed to take with him. His suitcase waited next to the rear door of his office, and he set his briefcase by it. Assured everything was in order, he closed his front office door and locked it from the inside. Then he picked up his desk phone and dialed the number for his answering service. When informed he had no messages, he thanked the operator and hung up. While he didn't expect anything in particular, something tickled the back of his mind. Pam's reference to a rhetorical fire left him thinking;

things had been too quiet this week. He expected some sign of life from the secretive guest in suite 502 by now, though her timing was her own. He considered prodding her with a message to her answering service but thought better of it. She wouldn't take even his prompting well. With luck, she would end her assessment of the Elkford hotel by the time he returned. She committed to Doug for Independence Day, so she needed to finish by then.

Not known for dwelling on things beyond his control, Matt picked up his suitcase and briefcase and exited the rear door of his office. A short walk down the private hallway to the parking garage took him to his marked spot where his Lotus waited. He dropped the bags into the passenger seat and drove out of Elkford for Tuseeca.

~~~

*Friday, June 29, 1979*

The slight lull of the early afternoon between checkouts and check-ins broke when Gabe recognized the sixtyish woman who exited a gray Cadillac at the hotel door. He waved off the bellhop who started out to collect her luggage but allowed the valet to continue forward to park her car. When she reached the door, Gabe opened it and bowed to her. "Good day, Mrs. Hathaway. How are you?"

Jeanette sniffed before answering. She considered Gabe one of Matt Hunter's people. "I am quite well, Mr. Wilson. I see you haven't progressed beyond opening the door for people since you worked at the..." Jeanette allowed her voice to trail off rather than continue. She hated referring to the old Stuart mansion as an inn. After all, it had been her home for sixteen years before the old dragon kicked her out when Jeanette and Winston married, and she still resented its disposition at the old woman's death.

"Well, all of us must earn our way as best we can, Mrs. Hathaway." Gabe managed not to smirk when Jeanette worked through his real meaning.

She started to stalk off but remembered her purpose. "To whom do I speak about hosting a dinner at the restaurant tomorrow since I understand Mr. Hunter has yet again abandoned his post to go gallivanting off to who knows where?"

"You may speak to Ellen in the restaurant. You should catch her in a bit of a lull right now, or you might want to speak to Misty. She's the event coordinator on duty today." Gabe hoped Misty would forgive him for directing Mrs. Hathaway toward her. Involvement in a mere dinner in the restaurant hardly rated for use of the event staff, but Mrs. Hathaway would not consider her dinner beneath the top planning talents of the hotel. Either way, Matt would enjoy the tales sure to greet him when he returned.

Jeanette gave a curt nod and walked off without further comment to Gabe. She started toward the restaurant but thought better of the idea. Instead she turned in the direction of the front desk. One young woman stood post, and Jeanette walked up to stand opposite the girl.

Laura was making notes with one hand while she held the phone with the other listening to a guest's list of requests. She smiled at the older lady and held up a finger to signify she would take care of her momentarily. The call completed, Laura hung up and made one last quick notation before turning her attention to the new arrival.

"Good afternoon, ma'am. How may I assist you?" Laura tried to place the woman but couldn't. Not a guest she had assisted, though possibly one who arrived the previous evening when Laura was off duty.

"I am Mrs. Hathaway. I will be hosting a dinner party in the restaurant tomorrow evening, and I want to make arrangements with the event coordinator. I believe her name is Misty."

"Yes, ma'am. Just a moment while I call her office. Is she expecting you?" an innocent Laura asked.

"If she were, would I stop here to ask for her?" Jeanette snapped.

Laura's face reddened, and she hastened to calm the woman. "Oh, I'm sorry, ma'am. Let me call her to find out if she's available."

"Find out if she's available? Certainly, she is available to me. My son owns this hotel chain. She will make herself available."

Before Laura could respond, Pam appeared at her side. "Hello, Mrs. Hathaway. If you'll come around to the door on the side, I'll escort you to the event office." Pam patted Laura on the arm when Jeanette turned and stalked around to the entrance to the hotel offices. "Don't let her bother you," she whispered. "She has quite the reputation, but she rarely shows up here. Matt scares her to death. I think they've been feuding for more than twenty years. She'll try to throw her weight around in his absence and threaten to talk to Mr. Stuart about whatever displeases her, but it's all talk. Neither Matt nor Mr. Stuart will pay any attention to her complaints." Pam hurried through the back office to meet Mrs. Hathaway and escort her to Misty.

Laura turned her attention to an efficient-looking young woman in a cream sweater who had stopped behind the older woman during her brief rant. "May I help you?"

A smile tugged at the corners of the young woman's lips as she stepped up to the desk. "Yes, thank you. My employer asked me to find out if it would be possible to extend our stay beyond Sunday. She is enjoying her time here and is considering changing her plans to remain beyond this weekend if you have space for us. She knows it's unlikely, but we agreed I should ask."

Laura didn't need to check the computer reservation system to know the answer. "No, I'm afraid we're booked for the next two weeks. I'm so sorry. If someone cancels, I'll make a note to let you know."

"That's all right. Next time we'll plan to stay longer. Thank you, Laura," the young woman said before hurrying to the elevator.

An hour later with Jeanette Hathaway clear of the hotel premises, Pam gave Laura a brief sketch of the planned dinner since Laura would be one of the clerks on duty Saturday evening and could get dragged into any imbroglio. Then she wrote a note for Jared, who would be the assistant manager on duty Saturday evening when the dinner party occurred. Pam considered swapping shifts with Jared to handle any damage control herself. However, Matt had been firm; she should not miss her son's baseball tournament in Woodbury this weekend. Jared had improved as an AM and should be capable of handling the situation. Pam added another couple of lines to the note and located a photo of Jeanette and Winston so Jared could recognize them if necessary.

<p style="text-align:center">~~~</p>

"What do you think, Mary? You've spent a couple of days rambling around the place. Does it remind you of the old mill in Elkford before we converted it into the hotel?" Once again, Matt sat in the old mill office in Tuseeca with Jonah and Joseph going over plans. This time Mary and Vicky replaced John and Doug in discussing development of a new hotel in the building.

"Yes, it does, Matt," Mary answered. "The river below us is wider and the town behind us is smaller, but otherwise the setting appears about the same, too. I remember the first time I walked through it with you two and John and Sandra and the kids so well. The more we talked, the more we could envision it as a hotel." She turned to Vicky, who sat next to her. "Do you remember?"

Vicky's mind drifted back a dozen years to a day she and KD spent galloping around the ancient mill investigating every nook and cranny, KD with a measuring tape and small notebook in which she scribbled copious tidbits of information about every facet of the behemoth. "Yes, I remember. I couldn't believe any of you were serious about turning such an old building into a fancy hotel. Of course, I had no memory of the Chestnut Cove mansion before it became the original inn, so I didn't grasp the concept at first."

A broad grin spread across Joseph's features. "I remember Doug and me getting into trouble for climbing up those rickety stairs. When they shimmied with us halfway up, probably ten feet off the ground, Aunt Sandra nearly gave birth to Chris a month or two early."

Mary cringed at the memory. "For a pair of seven-year-old boys, you two could get into a heap of trouble in a hurry. I hope you've outgrown such habits. If you haven't, I don't want to know about it."

"We've learned a little since then, Mom. For one thing," he tapped on the hardhat on his lap, "I've learned to wear this thing anytime I'm in a building under renovation or construction."

"That's good, but I hope you're more careful at other times." Her attention shifted to her daughter. "You, too." Vicky's eyes widened at the sudden shift of her mother's focus. "You think I don't know some of the things you and KD got into? Speaking of the chief instigator of trouble, are we adults invited to the party next week?"

Vicky pressed her lips together and shot a quick look at Joseph and then Matt. "I have not been informed of any party...officially. Have either of you?"

Joseph shook his head, but the grin on his face belied his answer. "I haven't talked to her since before school ended for the summer, and I didn't see much of her for the last few months in Coughton."

His mother held his gaze, refusing to allow him to wiggle off the hook. "But?"

Joseph squirmed in his seat, feeling nine instead of nineteen. "But Doug ordered a passel of stuff for a cookout before he left: hamburgers and hotdogs, cases of soft drinks, bags of chips and cookies. We took a pile of paper plates, cups, and napkins to the old inn–the big house–Thursday after he got back from Halesburg. Even Doug isn't allowed to go there without permission."

Mary looked from Joseph to Jonah to Matt. "Anything to add? Is there a chance she's cooled off enough to come home to stay?"

Matt shrugged. "I don't know. I hope so. I haven't spoken to her as recently as Joseph and Doug and Vicky. I know the Independence Day party is an important tradition to her and cancelling it the last couple of years isn't something she did lightly. As to whether she plans to allow Doug and you two to handle it in her absence or to show up herself to host it? I don't know. I hope she'll be there."

"Did you know about Doug buying food and taking the paper goods out there?"

"Yes, he told me when he reported in about his time at Halesburg." Matt's gaze turned inward at another mention of the small town where his life changed forever, and the room became quiet.

Seeking to change the subject to something less painful, Joseph asked, "How does Dan like helping at the hotel? Do you think working there for the summer will help him get a better handle on what to include in the next IO update?"

"I hope so, but this isn't his first time working at one of the hotels." Matt smiled at Joseph's surprised expression. "You know he was one of the first two people KD hired when she decided to create IO, don't you?" Joseph nodded. "Well, since she didn't want to let anybody know she was working on it until she knew they could make it work as she envisioned, she arranged for Dan to get a job at our new Halesburg inn. She could tell the programmers she hired what she wanted, but she saw the value in at least one of them learning firsthand what the clerks and bookkeepers and others did. If Dan knew the details of the job, he would be better positioned to write the code to help make their job more efficient."

"Oh," Joseph murmured. "Why does she want him in Elkford this summer? She sent one of her head programmers to play intern and teach the clerks the updates to IO when Doug and I could teach them. She made us learn to use the new updated version of the system when we worked at CasCav during the school year."

Matt had wondered the same thing when he received the letter directing him to put Dan on the payroll for the summer. He also knew not to question her. While he founded CasCav on KD's behalf soon after John's grandmother died and ran it for years, Matt relinquished all control to her when she turned twenty-one. Three years before that, she began managing it with Matt providing advice, acting as a sounding board, and holding veto power though he never needed to exercise it. John and Sandra hadn't liked his decision to give KD so much control so early, but Matt held the reins of her trust. The choice had been his, based on the terms of the trust, to begin turning over control to her when he believed her capable of managing her assets.

In hindsight, he knew he made the right choice. While Matt's performance as its manager turned a large amount of land and a scattering of commercial property into a valuable portfolio, KD watched, learned, and superseded even his golden touch when she assumed control. IO succeeded to a degree no one except KD expected. It alone doubled her net worth. Matt looked around the office of the old mill. She would net an impressive amount from the Tuseeca project, too.

CasCav owned about half of the CCI hotels under franchise agreements like the one Matt negotiated with John for the old mill in downtown Elkford. Matt's refusal to sell the property to John almost caused a rift between the cousins a dozen years earlier. However, cooler heads prevailed, and John agreed to Matt's terms; CasCav would own the hotel and run it as a franchise under CCI. Both companies made good money from the deal, and decisions to purchase other properties for development into hotels often came down to which side identified a new property first or saw the greater potential in it.

Their plan worked well until a property KD wanted to buy and develop became a topic for discussion within CCI management one month and left the market the next courtesy of Vaughn Michaelson. Along with an earlier dispute over CCI not considering just-unveiled IO along with Limmer and other computer systems, warm relations between father and daughter turned icy. A two-year conflict wore down John until he admitted his errors.

First, Matt proved IO the superior computer system and Limmer, advocated by Hoyt, an abysmal failure. Then KD found and forwarded to Matt proof Vaughn received information from within CCI on the property he poached. Matt hoped the final thaw came with Tuseeca. John went along with the false trail laid out to the management team while KD pursued the property she wanted. He swallowed any issues with the location as soon as he saw it. He took his medicine upon learning she bought it outright without any consultation with CCI management with nothing more than initial shock. Perhaps John accepted at last that his eldest child was not only an adult but the master at a game for which she trained since childhood.

Matt shook off the reverie he had slipped into for a minute. "I hope to ask her that question before long." He flashed a grin at last. "Hopefully no later than Wednesday at the party."

<center>~~~</center>

Late that evening, Matt set aside his notepad to turn in. He, Jonah, Mary, Vicky, and Joseph planned to spend the next morning at the old mill before scouting the area for restaurants and other businesses the hotel might want to work with in the future to the advantage of both. He suspected they would be following in his prize protégé's footsteps. No doubt she performed such a survey before she bought the mill. For that matter, he wondered what else she already bought in or near Tuseeca. It wouldn't surprise him if she planned to invest in restaurants, riding stables, boat rentals, and other businesses like they had done in Elkford and other cities home to CCI hotels. It would be a challenge to see if he could identify something she missed.

Almost as an afterthought, he picked up the phone in his motel room to call his answering service. The operator informed him he had two messages. The first from Pam surprised him; Jeanette planned to host a dinner at the hotel's restaurant Saturday evening. Before he could consider if he should return to Elkford in time to greet her at the hotel door Saturday night, the second message ended such a thought. It informed him a package would arrive at his motel near Tuseeca on Saturday evening. In it he would find documentation necessary to fire Bud Langford. The instructions were explicit; once he received the package, proceed to Halesburg and dismiss Bud for cause on Sunday. There would be no surprise for Jeanette Saturday night.

In a heartbeat, Matt realized the error of his thought. In fact, Jeanette would receive a terrible surprise Saturday night, one even worse than seeing Matt. He was being kept from Elkford because that honor belonged to another.

# Chapter 25

*Saturday, June 30, 1979 - early evening*

The promenade began promptly at seven o'clock. Winston pulled up to the front of the hotel in Jeanette's Cadillac and eased out before handing the keys to the valet. He tugged on the hem of his linen suit coat to straighten it. Satisfied with his appearance, he looked around for his wife before realizing she remained ensconced in the passenger seat waiting for her door to be opened. Winston finally took a step in that direction, but another valet beat him to her door and opened it. The young man took her extended hand and helped her out. Once escorted around the front of the car to where Winston waited for her, she slipped her hand through the crook of his arm and urged him toward the entrance.

Winston's daughter and son-in-law followed in Harold's Buick and caught up to Winston and Jeanette just inside the restaurant entrance. Hoyt ambled across the lobby from the lounge to join them right before Ellen, the hostess, led the initial arrivals to the rear of the restaurant to Jeanette's expressed preference of a somewhat secluded area. Another couple arrived and trailed the group through the bustling room.

Jeanette took the seat at the head of the table with Winston to her left. Once the others were seated, Jeanette took a headcount. Seven so far, another four yet to arrive. Their waiter greeted them and took their drink orders. Winston and Hoyt each ordered a glass of their preferred liquor while the rest ordered summery cocktails.

Two hours later, the stragglers had arrived, dinner had been ordered and consumed, and Winston and Hoyt felt no pain. A giddy and tipsy Jeanette looked smugly down the length of the table at her triumph.

~~~

The light of the near-quarter Moon streaming in from the southwest lit the boardroom just enough for anyone inside to move about without bumping into the furniture. A lone figure stood at the window looking across at the hotel to the south. She checked her watch again before walking back through the open door at the east end of the room. She retrieved a cream-colored sweater laying over the back of a chair in Vicky's office and wandered out into the foyer, lit by a lone safety light, and across to the suite at the west end of the floor. Slipping a key ring from her pocket, she used her master key to open the outer door and entered Mrs. Pierce's office. She crossed to the door on the right and unlocked it with the same key. Walking inside the neatly-maintained office, she folded the sweater and placed it on the corner of the desk.

After retreating along the same path and relocking doors behind her, she returned at last to the boardroom where she stopped in front of the windows to gaze once more at the hotel. The restaurant and lounge would be bustling with activity on a summer Saturday evening with tables of people enjoying an evening of good food and conversation. However, only one table in the restaurant interested her; one guest at that table dominated her thoughts.

After a final reflection on the plan she had put into place and its probable consequences, the young woman pulled a two-way radio from her pocket, keyed the talk button, and uttered one word: "Execute."

~~~

The front desk phone rang yet again. It had been a busy night. Del looked over at Laura, who was checking in a young couple. He stepped away from the computer terminal and grabbed the phone. "Front desk, this is Del. How may I assist you tonight?" He listened for a moment before grabbing a pencil and jotting down a note. "Yes, ma'am, we'll send someone up to take care of it right away, ma'am." He hung up and called the maintenance desk number. "Hank? There's a leak under the sink in 208. Would you see to it? Thank you."

When he hung up, Laura had finished with the guests she had been checking in and held the other desk phone listening and making notes. As soon as she hung up, she dialed housekeeping and requested extra towels for 319. When she hung up again, she looked around for the next person waiting for assistance at the front desk. When she saw no one, she looked over at Del. "Is it always this hectic on Saturday night?"

Del chuckled. "Not always, but it isn't unusual for us to be busy. Holiday weekends in the summer and fall tend to be the worst. That's why Matt likes to keep an extra hand around. If we didn't have Dan helping us tonight, we might not have time to eat dinner all shift."

"Speaking of Dan, where is he? Shouldn't he be back from his break by now?" Laura looked around for any sign of their intern.

Del glanced at his watch. "I think he's working on something in the back. Let me check with Jared. I've had my dinner, but you haven't had a break since you came on shift." Del disappeared into the back room, and Laura turned her attention to a couple of teenagers walking toward the desk.

~~~

Jared hurried into the restaurant and stopped at the hostess stand. "Ellen, I need to know where Mr. and Mrs. Hathaway are seated. I must deliver a message to Mrs. Hathaway."

Ellen looked up from the reservation list and table map in front of her to see a flushed Jared glaring at her. "I can take the message and deliver it for you. Don't you have enough to do with the hotel so busy this evening?"

Jared pulled himself up straight. "Mrs. Hathaway is the mother of the President of Chestnut Cove Inns. I doubt many tasks are more important than delivering an urgent message to her. If you'll direct me to her table, I'll handle this myself."

Ellen bit her lip before the response she wanted to make could pop out. "The Hathaway party is at table twenty-eight. It's almost to the back of the restaurant," she added. She knew he had never bothered to learn anything about their table numbering.

Jared took three steps into the restaurant before he turned back and said, "Thank you, Ellen." Then he hurried away in search of Mr. Stuart's mother.

After a short search of the farthest part of the dining room, Jared spotted the table of eleven with Mr. and Mrs. Hathaway seated toward the far end. He stopped, took several deep breaths to try to slow his heart rate, and licked his lips. The last thing he wanted was to appear tongue-tied or buffoonish when he spoke to Mr. Stuart's mother.

Slipping the photo of the Hathaways from his pocket, he verified his objective before taking the last dozen steps to their table where he stopped next to Mrs. Hathaway. He cleared his throat and touched her on the shoulder. "Mrs. Hathaway?"

The older lady looked up at him and recognized from his blue blazer that he was a hotel employee, though not from the restaurant. "Yes?"

"Mrs. Hathaway, my name is Jared Everett. I am the assistant manager on duty tonight for Mr. Hunter." The older lady cringed, and he wondered if he had done something to offend her. "Um, I'm sorry to interrupt your dinner, but I have a message for you. We received a call asking you to go upstairs to speak to a guest while you're here at the hotel tonight."

Jeanette's face lit up. "Ah, some old friend who happens to be staying here perhaps? Who is it?"

Jared flushed. "I'm afraid we weren't given that information. I believe the person wishes to surprise you."

"Oh, how sweet. I'm to meet this old friend in the hotel?"

"Yes, ma'am. Suite 502."

Jeanette made to push her chair away from the table, and Jared assisted her by pulling it back. Both were startled by a voice from down the table. "You're the assistant manager, but you don't know who is registered in 502? What kind of fools does Matt employ in this hotel?"

Jared's head snapped up, and he searched the table for the man who spoke. "Oh, Mr. Dalton, I'm sorry I didn't see you earlier. Yes, normally we know the names of our guests, but right now we have two rooms registered and paid for under a corporate name, not under individual names of guests. Suite 502 is one of those." He looked around and lowered his voice so no one other than the group at the Hathaway table could hear him. "We're not supposed to say, but the rooms are for the small entourage of some wealthy older lady, a foreign dignitary who wished to remain incognito, so Mr. Hunter registered them as a corporate group. No one except our head housekeeper may attend those rooms for the duration of their stay." Hoyt looked surprised but said nothing more.

Jeanette took a step toward Jared and said, "Thank you for bringing me the message, Mr. Evers." Turning back to the table, she continued, "If you will excuse me for a few minutes while you continue to visit, I will pop upstairs to see who wants to speak to me so mysteriously. No doubt one of my old friends from Paris or London is in town." She swept along the length of the table toward the front of the restaurant, Jared trailing in her wake.

Unsure of his responsibilities once he delivered the message to Mrs. Hathaway, Jared followed her through the restaurant and across the lobby to the elevators. He waited next to her in silence for a moment before he felt the urge to explain himself. "Mrs. Hathaway, allow me to apologize for not knowing the name of the person staying in suite 502. Mr. Dalton is correct that it is an unusual situation, and I can assure you I would have ascertained the information for you in advance if it were available to me."

"Oh, do not worry yourself, Mr. Evers," Jeanette said.

"Everett." Jared blushed at correcting Mr. Stuart's mother.

"Pardon me?"

"Everett, my name is Jared Everett, not Evers," he croaked out. He wondered why he attempted to correct her.

"Oh, of course." She waved a hand in dismissal. "I expect one of my old friends wishes to surprise me, which is why she has concealed her name. No doubt it will be quite a nice surprise." She turned to note the floors where the elevators were located. Neither was moving. "Are they broken? They seem to be stopped."

"No, ma'am, it's a very busy night with people coming and going. I apologize that I can't override one and call it to the ground floor for you."

~~~

The steel door leading from the lowest level of the parking deck into the bowels of the hotel opened and closed with a soft bump. A lone figure took a deserted basement hall past the electrical systems rooms and the laundry before ascending the stairs and working her way to a private hallway on the ground floor. She inserted a key into a door lock and slipped into the private suite near Matt's reserved for her. On the way into the suite's master bedroom, she shed her blue blazer and dropped it over the back of a chair.

~~~

Dan scurried down the hall, into the office behind the front desk, and through the other door where he stopped between Del and Laura. "Sorry I've been gone so long. Jared wanted me to take care of something. I can help at the desk now, Laura, if you want to go eat dinner."

Laura held up a finger while she finished making a notation on the wakeup call log. When she was done, she looked up and smiled at Dan. "OK, thank you. It's a little quieter now. Maybe you and Del won't be too busy while I'm gone. I brought a sandwich from home, so I'll be in the back if it gets hectic again and you need me."

"We'll try to manage without disturbing you. You're long overdue for your dinner break, Laura. Take your time."

"OK, I will. I'll see you in half an hour." She waved at Del who was on the phone again as she headed to the back, and Dan moved over next to the other phone where Laura had been standing. Five minutes later, she found a quiet corner table in the deserted break room and laid out her sandwich and apple on a napkin in front of her.

~~~

Jeanette stood outside suite 502 tapping her foot. No one came to the door when she knocked on it. She waited and waited, but no one answered, even when she banged on it the third time. Jared became more and more nervous as he waited with her. Then he wondered why he had thought it helpful to accompany her up to meet her mysterious friend. Surely there had been no real call for him to attend her up to the fifth floor. Standing next to her when her impatience turned to wrath became most unpleasant. After accusing him of bungling the message or room number or both, she dismissed him to find the correct information. He had cringed when forced to admit that an intern helping the desk clerks took the message.

Jared hurried down to the concierge's station on the fourth floor to call Dan and pry the correct room number out of him. "Del, it's Jared. Is Dan there? I need to speak to him right now."

When Dan picked up the other desk extension, an irate Jared demanded, "Are you sure the person who called to ask Mrs. Hathaway to visit her upstairs said 502? No one answered the door when she knocked. We waited several minutes."

"Yes, sir, her secretary made the call for her and said 502." Dan picked up a pen and scribbled on the notepad in front of him as he listened.

"OK, thank you." Jared hung up and took a series of deep breaths, wondering what he could do to pacify Mrs. Hathaway.

~~~

Del looked over at Dan when he hung up the phone. "Is everything OK? Does Jared have a problem we need to help with?"

Holding up the note he scribbled while speaking to Jared, Dan said, "No, but he asked me to relay a message from Mrs. Hathaway to Mr. Hathaway. It will only take me a couple of minutes to run over to give it to Ellen. I'll be right back to help you." The phone rang again, and Del reached for it with one hand and waved for Dan to go on his errand with the other.

A minute later, Dan hurried into the restaurant in search of Ellen. She was busy seating a late-dining couple, so he waited at her station for her to return.

When she came back to the front of the restaurant, she saw him waiting at her stand. "Hey, Dan, what's up?"

"Hi, Ellen. I was told to ask Mr. Hathaway to join Mrs. Hathaway and her friend for a few minutes so Mrs. Hathaway can introduce them. They're using the empty office where Geraldine's old files are stored. Would you pass that request along to him? I need to get back to the desk. Laura's on her break, so Del is covering it alone while I'm away, and it's busy right now."

"Sure, I'll tell him. Go on back to the desk to help Del."

"Thanks, Ellen," Dan said, and he hurried away.

Ellen hailed the waitress covering the tables nearest the door and arranged for her to watch the hostess station for a couple of minutes before walking to the rear of the restaurant. Winston Hathaway held court at their table in his wife's absence, although the size of the court had diminished a few minutes earlier with the departure of several guests including Hoyt.

"Mr. Hathaway?" Ellen prompted when she reached his side.

Winston offered the pretty hostess a charming but sloppy smile. "Yes?"

"Mrs. Hathaway would like for you to join her for a few minutes so she can introduce you to her old friend. They've come downstairs to one of the empty offices to chat. If you'll take the hallway leading to Mr. Hunter's office, you'll find them in the fourth office down the hall. Do you know where that is?"

"I'm sure I can find it." Winston excused himself from his remaining guests and stood up. He swayed just a bit before gathering himself to trail Ellen to the front of the restaurant. "Just across and to the right and around the corner, is it not?" he confirmed with Ellen.

"Yes, that's correct, sir." Ellen watched Winston wobble toward the lobby before turning her attention to the nearby waitress to thank her for covering the hostess stand.

~~~

When he returned to the fifth floor, Jared found Jeanette indiscriminately knocking on doors in search of the person who left her the message.

"Mrs. Hathaway, I spoke to Dan. He took the message from your friend's secretary. He says she told him suite 502." He considered whether he should have told Dan to come up to the fifth floor to verify the information to Mrs. Hathaway in person. "Please, you cannot knock on all these doors. Our guests will complain at being disturbed for no reason."

"No reason? There is every reason. I have been asked up here to see an old friend, and because of the incompetence of you and the staff and Matt Hunter's terrible management, I have not been able to locate my friend." Jeanette glared at Jared until his face turned beet red.

"I'm so sorry, Mrs. Hathaway. Look, I have a passkey. We were told only Janelle, the head of housekeeping, is allowed to use a passkey to enter these suites while these special guests are here, but under the circumstances I'm sure Mr. Hunter will understand. I'll just take a quick peek inside 502 and see if I can find out anything for you." Jared stepped around Jeanette and inserted the key into the lock.

As soon as he turned the doorknob and opened the door, Jeanette stunned him by pushing by him into the room. She marched ahead a full ten steps, Jared gaping behind her, before she stopped in shock. Whatever she expected to find, this was not it. The room was devoid of anything other than the standard furniture, fixtures, and so forth of any unoccupied suite on the floor. There was no sign of anyone, any luggage, any anything except for a set of newspaper clippings arrayed across the coffee table, each featuring a photo that included a particular young woman.

Jeanette rounded on Jared. Her eyes flashed in a seething rage, and her voice came out in a shrill screech. "I shall have you fired for your part in this mockery, Mr. Evers. My son shall hear of this, and you shall never work for any hotel or any other place for as long as you live."

Jared's mouth flapped wordlessly. He couldn't fathom what happened and had no idea of the meaning of the clippings. When he managed to squeak out, "I'm sorry,"

Jeanette's eyes narrowed, and a bony finger lifted to point at him in accusation.

"So you admit you had a hand in this travesty?" She took a step toward him, and he backed toward the door.

"What? No, I just delivered the message. I assure you, Mrs. Hathaway, I have no idea who is behind this, but I will report it to Mr. Hunter as soon as he returns. I have no doubt he will be upset and will get to the bottom of it."

With the mention of Matt Hunter, Jeanette's attention shifted back to her two chief tormenters, and she stormed around Jared and stalked to the door. "I have no doubt that man played a major role in this charade. I shall insist my son deal with this abomination personally."

Jared breathed a sigh of relief when she left the room, until it dawned on him that she was loose once again in the hallway knocking on doors in search of whomever she held responsible for the trick played on her. Whatever she might or might not be able to do regarding his future employment with CCI or anywhere else, he was in charge this evening. If he couldn't rein her in somehow, he knew Matt Hunter and John Stuart would be angry with him.

He scurried out the door and down the hall toward her to attempt to limit any damage to the hotel's reputation. He saw her raise her arm to bang on another door and realized she had picked up an ashtray somewhere along the way and intended to use it to bang on the doors this time. Then he grasped that not only might the hotel's tranquility be at stake, but its physical wellbeing also.

~~~

Costume donned and new wig in place, she peered into the mirror and then scrutinized the photograph on her dresser. Details must be adhered to tonight. Satisfied with her hair and clothing, she checked her makeup once more before walking out of the bedroom, doing her best to mimic the movements and mannerisms captured on home movies years earlier.

She moved aside a painting on the living room wall to reveal her small safe and dialed its combination. The door swung open, and she removed a microcassette recorder and a cylindrical object about fifteen inches long. She slipped the latter into the special pocket hidden in the folds of her calf-length skirt, careful not to let the sharp tips poke through the fabric. Near the hall door, a stroller–the stroller–waited for her with a doll made to her specifications already seated within. She walked to the door and dropped the recorder onto the top of the stroller next to her two-way radio. All that remained was to await the signal and begin the performance of a lifetime.

# Chapter 26

Winston ambled across the lobby and turned into the hall leading to the back offices of the hotel. While he knew in general the path led somehow to Matt's office, he refused to admit to anyone he had never been beyond the hotel's lobby and restaurant. It required John's intervention ten years earlier to score Jeanette and Winston an invitation to the grand opening. Since then, they had only been as far as the hotel's restaurant three or four times and those only at John's invitation.

He forged ahead down a hallway he hoped would prove to be the correct one. Winston saw light coming from an opening ahead and decided perhaps Jeanette and her friend were there. He stuck his head inside, but the sole occupant was a young woman eating a sandwich and reading a book at one of the tables in the room. Engrossed in her tome, she didn't look up to notice him. He continued down the hall, checking for unlocked doors and listening for Jeanette.

"Hello, Mr. Hathaway," a voice behind him called. Winston turned a bit too fast and grabbed at a doorframe to steady himself. "You've taken a wrong turn. You're looking for Mrs. Hathaway?"

Winston tried to focus on the young man's face, sure they crossed paths at some point in the past. "Urm, yes. A veritable maze in the staff area, isn't it?"

Boyd smiled. "Yes, it's easy to get lost in these halls. Let me show you a shortcut to get to those offices." He took the older man by the elbow and guided him along until they reached a rarely-used cross hall. "If you'll go this way to the end, you'll see a steel door on the left. Go through it. The room you want will be about two-thirds of the way down the hall on the left."

"Thanks much," Winston slurred before he stumbled along the route indicated.

Boyd stepped back around the corner and stopped to watch Winston. Satisfied his quarry would follow directions, Boyd reached into his pocket and clicked the button on his two-way radio twice. When Winston opened the door at the end of the hall and disappeared through it, Boyd followed in his wake. As soon as it bumped shut, he slipped his master key into the lock and secured it to prevent anyone from entering or exiting the private hallway on the other side. Then he waited. When the radio in his pocket clicked three times, he flipped the switch to extinguish the lights in the hall on the opposite side of the door and returned to his previous post to ensure no one ventured near until he received his next signal.

"Hey," Winston called out. "What happened to the lights?" He stumbled around to look back in the direction from which he had come. At least he thought he turned back. He couldn't be sure considering the darkness and the amount of alcohol he consumed during the evening. He took three steps forward in an attempt to find the door and open it to let in more light. Instead, he crashed headlong into the wall. Stars flashed before his eyes from the impact.

When his head cleared enough for him to regain his senses, a bump and a bit of light from behind him registered in his brain. He managed to turn without toppling over and saw someone farther down the hallway pushing something. At first, he thought a maid must be pushing her cart, but he determined the object wasn't large enough to be a maid's cart. A baby buggy? He stared hard at it through bleary eyes. Yes, definitely a baby buggy.

His attention shifted to the woman pushing it. He couldn't distinguish her features because the tiny bit of illumination in the hall came through a door standing ajar behind her, capturing her silhouette but revealing nothing more.

As she approached, Winston said, "Pardon me, but do you know where to turn on the lights? I need to find my wife somewhere around here, and I can't see a blasted thing."

A soft, surreal voice responded, "Your wife is elsewhere. You've come to see me. Don't you know me, Winston? You sent me into darkness forever more than twenty years ago. It's time for you to get a taste of it."

Winston gasped, his eyes wide with recognition as the young woman stopped in front of him and turned enough for the dim light to show her shoulder-length brown hair pulled back with a band. The style of her clothes screamed late 1950s, a style even Winston remembered. The white of her saddle Oxfords flashed when she stepped to the side of the stroller to lean down and fuss with a blanket. A child of two or three seemed to doze there. When she straightened and turned to face him again, a ray of light reflected from the silver locket around her neck.

"Who are you? Why are you here?" Winston stammered. He took a step backwards and jumped when his heel found the wall.

"You know the answer, Winston. It's my turn to ask the questions. I want to know why, and I want to know who. You're far too much the coward to do something so rash yourself. I want you to tell me who helped you. I want to know who drove the car. I want you to admit who paid off those involved. You certainly didn't, at least not monetarily." She took a step toward him when he maintained a frightened silence. "You will tell me, Winston. Why did you do it?"

Winston slid along the wall to maintain his balance while he tried to elude the woman. "I don't know what you're talking about. I did nothing."

The woman followed Winston step for step, pulling the stroller along behind her with one hand, the other pointing at Winston in accusation. "You were there in Halesburg along with your friends that day. You know it as well as I. We spoke in the alley beside your hotel. Is that when you decided to get your friends to do it? Was the child a target, too? Did you try to kill your own step-granddaughter?"

The accusation sobered Winston somewhat, and he gathered himself as best he could. "I don't know what you're talking about. I never–"

"Do not lie to me," she growled. "It was the girl you were with, wasn't it? You wanted to hide your involvement with her. Did you think no one would find out? She disappeared that very night, didn't she? Did you assume your friends dealt with her like they dealt with me? You're wrong. She took off and hid until she thought it was safe. She was lucky. She had friends you didn't know about who helped her." The young woman stopped and allowed the first smile to cross her lips. "Something else you don't know; you have another child out in the world. Wouldn't Jeanette be excited to know she has another stepchild? Oh, wait, perhaps not one conceived years after the two of you married. I suspect you're lucky if there aren't others."

Winston, caught short with such shocking news, stopped retreating. "No, she couldn't. They must have handled her. I told her to get rid of it, but she refused."

The girl stepped directly in front of him this time. "So you admit you knew she was pregnant and you thought your friends dealt with her the way they dealt with me. Tell me who, Winston. We both know their names. I just want to hear you say them." She slid her hand into the secret pocket of her skirt and felt for the switch on the cylinder, her finger toying with it.

"I can't," Winston gasped. "They'd kill me."

She pulled the cylinder from her pocket and took a step back from her target. "They aren't here, Winston. I am." She flipped the switch and tagged his left calf with the two prongs on the end of the device. Winston jerked at the shock, screamed, and fell to the floor. "I won't ask nicely next time. Tell me who was involved. Landry Peters? He arranged the driver and identified the car to steal for the hit and run, didn't he?"

Winston whimpered and tried to slither away, but the tip of the cylinder struck his forearm, and he screamed again. The girl allowed him to lie blubbering on the floor for a few seconds before she began again. "Just admit it was Landry who arranged the driver and stolen car, Winston. That's all you have to do." She reached out and tagged him again before he could even think about answering. In the near darkness, she saw him nod his head. "Tell me, Winston. Just say yes. Say Landry Peters did it."

Before she could strike again, Winston wrenched out the words she wanted to hear. "Landry did it. I didn't know the man who drove the car, but Landry did. He arranged it."

"Now that wasn't so hard, was it?" She stepped close again. "It was Vaughn Michaelson's money which paid off the driver, wasn't it? Of course, they killed him afterward so he couldn't talk, didn't they? You've paid Vaughn back ever since by passing along information on CCI, JSS Holdings, and the Stuart family finances when you came across any tidbit of interest to him, haven't you?"

Even in minimal light, she saw the look of terror cross Winston's face. His eyes widened, and his mouth twisted. She reached out and tapped him with the cylinder before he could deny it and let him scream and writhe at her feet while he considered his answer. When he recovered enough to open his eyes, he saw the dreaded object less than an inch from his nose.

"I tire of this game, Winston. The next touch will be somewhere more sensitive than your forearms or calves. Tell me whether or not Vaughn Michaelson financed the hit and run." She flipped the switch off and tapped his nose.

Winston screamed without realizing the prod wasn't powered. "Yes! Vaughn said he'd make the problem go away. I didn't know the details. I just knew Vaughn and Landry could make any problem go away if they wanted to."

The girl allowed herself a grim smile, her goal at hand. "You knew Elizabeth wouldn't live to return to Coughton or Elkford to tell Matt or anyone in the family she saw you with a young woman–your pregnant mistress–in Halesburg because Vaughn and Landry would take care of the matter, didn't you?"

Before he could answer, she flipped the switch on, shifted the prod down his body, and tapped his inner thigh. "Yes," he screeched. "They had her killed."

She held the prod close again and asked her last question. "And the child? Were they to kill KD and missed or was she to be spared or did no one care one way or another?"

Winston flinched away as best he could. "We never talked about her. I wish they'd killed her, too. If she had died, John would have gotten everything from his grandmother. Jeanette would have gotten much more out of him then."

KD Stuart switched off her modified cattle prod and slipped it into the hidden pocket of her skirt. Leaving Winston sniveling on the floor for the moment, she retreated to the stroller and switched off the recorder before pocketing it also. Then she picked up her radio and keyed the talk button. "It's done."

The door at the far end of the hall opened and closed, admitting Boyd, who locked it once more. KD pushed the stroller into her suite and retrieved a glass into which she poured the contents of a small vial and a generous amount of Scotch. Boyd followed her and retrieved a wheelchair from the suite. He took the drink from her and pushed the wheelchair into the hall.

"Mr. Hathaway? You look like you could use a drink." Boyd helped the older man sit up and held the tumbler to his lips. Winston drained the contents and tried to stand, and Boyd slid his hands under the older man's arms. "Let me help you, sir. You've had an accident. I've brought a wheelchair to help get you to the car." Boyd lifted Winston and deposited him in the chair. His passenger slumped to the side, already fading from the effects of his latest drink and his stressful night. Boyd strapped him in and rolled him toward the private entrance.

KD emerged from her suite with a mop to clean up any sign of the night's festivities. "Don't dawdle. I should be able to hold Jeanette at bay long enough without any problem, but you and Tanya need to get him inside and into bed as fast as you can. He'll sleep until morning after the evening he's had."

"We'll be fine. You go enjoy visiting with your grandma." Boyd shoved open the door to the parking deck and rolled his burden through before KD could throw something at him.

"Do not call her that," she yelled toward the closing door.

~~~

Silence reigned in the elevator. Jared and Jeanette stood in opposite corners like prizefighters waiting for the next bell. Jared sported a bump on his shin significant enough to cause a limp; Jeanette cradled her right wrist in her left hand, determined Jared caused serious damage when he wrested the glass ashtray from her. The ashtray suffered the night's lone irreparable damage, shattered into pieces on the fifth-floor hall.

As soon as the door slid open to reveal a peaceful lobby, the factions stalked out one after the other. Jared deferred to Jeanette as older, a lady, and a hotel guest to exit first. However, once they cleared the elevator doors, he surged around her, limping across the lobby toward the door leading to the back offices. Jeanette stormed after him, glued to his heels.

To Jared's chagrin, Jeanette continued down the hall when he turned into the office behind the front desk. He spun around and hustled to catch up with her, terrified she might cause further damage to the hotel or a staff member in the back offices.

When she found a door open, Jeanette walked in to confront whoever happened to be inside. It took a few seconds to place the girl seated at a table eating an apple.

"You! Are you involved in this charade, too?"

Laura looked up from her book. Wrinkling her brow, she said, "Hello, Mrs. Hathaway. I'm sorry, but I'm not sure what you're asking about."

Jared caught up to Jeanette and stopped behind her while he caught his breath.

~~~

Her wig shed to reveal her natural auburn hair and the longer skirt exchanged for a more modern look, KD scooped up her navy blazer and donned it once more. She picked up the microcassette recorder and popped in a fresh tape before hitting record and dropping it into the blazer's pocket. She exited her suite, walked the few steps to the rear door of her hotel office, and cut through to the front hall. She hadn't gone far when she heard a familiar voice screeching. She smiled and followed the noise.

~~~

"Please, Mrs. Hathaway, you must lower your voice," Jared pled. "I promise to look into the records to find what I can about the mystery guest in 502."

The older woman spun on him, a move which would have surprised him less than half an hour earlier. "And I told you I do not need you to investigate any records to know the identity of your so-called special guest. I know exactly who she is. What I want to know is where Matt Hunter is and who else is involved in this charade."

Laura set aside the remnants of her apple and joined Jared. If she could sort out what happened upstairs, perhaps she could assist in diffusing the situation. "Mrs. Hathaway, why don't we go into the assistant manager's office so Jared can look into the matter for you? I'm sure there's been some kind of mistake."

Jeanette took a step toward Laura. "The mistake is your participation in this plot. My son will hear of this, and I will insist he fire both of you and anyone else involved in this attempt to humiliate me." She turned and stormed out of the break room and charged back down the hall toward the lobby, muttering to herself as she went. Jared and Laura hurried after her, though Jared lagged as he limped along with his bruised shin.

Almost blind in her rage, Jeanette would have plowed into the person who stepped out in front of her just short of the lobby had the younger woman not spoken.

"Hello, Jeanette. Miss me?" The despised granddaughter flashed a brilliant smile at the reviled grandmother.

Jeanette froze in her tracks, her eyes locked on KD's. "What are you doing here?" she spat.

KD's eyes sparkled in merriment. "What? No warm greeting, Jeanette?"

"Go back where you belong. You have no place here." Jeanette realized the falsity of her words even as she spoke them. After all, KD owned the hotel in which they stood.

"Funny, I keep being told I should come home to stay, though I'm not surprised you don't share such a sentiment," KD snapped.

Laura caught up to the pair and stopped. In an instant, her mind jumped from thankfulness that another CCI employee halted Jeanette's tirade to confusion at the unknown staffer's identity. Then recognition dawned. She tipped her head toward the woman she last saw walking out of Fred's Diner weeks earlier. "Hello, ma'am."

Before KD could respond, Jared caught up to the small group. "Who are you?" he raged at the unknown woman. "Where did you get that blazer?" A hand touched his arm, and he jumped before he realized the hand belonged to Laura, not the insane woman he had dealt with for half an hour.

The clerk spoke softly, a voice of calm amid the turmoil. "She's the lady who wrote the note on the napkin. She's Kathryn Stuart." Returning her attention to her benefactor, Laura continued, "I'd like to thank you, Miss Stuart. I'm sorry I didn't know how to get in touch with you to do so earlier."

Ignoring a snort of disgust from Jeanette, KD smiled at her most recent find. "You're welcome, Laura. I've heard good things about your performance here. I'm glad to have you onboard as a hotel employee. I hope you remain with CCI for a long time."

"Thank you. I hope to be here a long time."

Jared paled once he realized how much worse his evening might get. "I'm sorry, ma'am. I didn't mean to..."

KD waved her hand in dismissal of his concern. "Considering you apparently spent significant time tonight trying to make Jeanette see reason, I understand, Jared. I noticed you limping." Her eyes darted to Jeanette, then back to Jared. "She's got a wicked right toe, doesn't she? Why don't you take the rest of the evening off? It's almost time for the night staff to start their shift. I'm sure Laura and the rest of the team can manage for an hour or so without you. I'll take care of things with Matty when he returns. He's well-versed in Jeanette's fits of pique. He'll understand."

A pained Jared slumped in relief. "Thank you, Miss Stuart."

"You're welcome." The three women watched Jared limp toward the office before any of them spoke again.

When Jeanette started to circumvent KD also, the younger woman shifted into her path, bringing the older one to a halt once again, an even deeper scowl ravaging her face.

KD ignored her, returning her attention to her clerk. "Laura, would you check to see if any of Jeanette's party remains in the restaurant? I expect most of them departed once Winston left. Also, you can clear 500 and 502 for use. Janelle cleaned them earlier except for a few pieces of paper which need to be collected from 502." KD turned back to Jeanette with a wicked grin. "Unless you did significant damage to the room." To Laura she added, "Better check it to be sure before you let any late arrivals have it tonight."

Laura nodded and slipped away as Jeanette's next tirade began. She ignored references to the ruse on the fifth floor. "What do you mean Winston left? He would not abandon me here."

"He became a bit of a problem wandering around the hotel after you–" KD stopped to chuckle, "–left the restaurant to visit with your friend. I ordered security to remove him. They drove him home in a CCI van, so your car is still here. The valet will retrieve it for you."

"How dare you remove my husband from this hotel," Jeanette seethed. "I'll–"

The smile left KD's face, and the venom in her voice matched that of her grandmother's. "You'll what? Tell my father? You keep forgetting, Jeanette. My father doesn't own this hotel. He may own controlling interest in the hotel chain, but this is part of CasCav's franchise. It belongs to me. I can and will throw out anyone I choose. Only thing is, with Winston I ordered security to do it and had him taken out through the back. I'll see to it personally with you if you raise your voice once more and it won't be via a back entrance. I can't think of too many things that would give me more pleasure than to drag you across the lobby and toss you out the front door of my hotel."

Jeanette took a step away from her granddaughter, her anger turned to mortification. She would never live down the humiliation of such an event, and she had no doubt KD could and would follow through on her threat. In silence, she took a wide berth around her granddaughter and walked out into the lobby.

KD followed close behind, stopping in front of the reception desk to watch. Jeanette went straight to the entrance of the restaurant where she met Laura. When the clerk told the vanquished woman that her entire dinner group had departed, Jeanette stalked out the front door of the hotel without another word.

KD took a couple of deep breaths to allow the tension to slip away. Tonight had been the culmination of a game she had played for a long time. She wanted to enjoy the moment, so she looked around and absorbed the atmosphere of the hotel she had avoided for most of the last five years. Guests strolled through the lobby, chatting about their day exploring the mountains, boating or fishing on the river, riding horses, playing golf, or shopping. Surrounded by smiling guests enjoying their stay at her hotel, she hoped for a small amount of pleasure for herself before she began her next game. That would start Monday. For tonight and tomorrow, she would relish her homecoming.

# Chapter 27

*Monday, July 2, 1979*

Mrs. Pierce hung up her phone and pulled out the notecard with the extensions of all the corporate managers and their secretaries. The instructions she received lay outside the normal order of things at CCI, but with Mr. Stuart still away on his vacation, and Mr. Hunter and Mr. Jones also absent today, Hoyt was the senior manager in the headquarters. If he directed her to call a special staff meeting for nine o'clock, she would do so as long as his request did not violate some defined policy set by Mr. Stuart.

Half an hour later, Hoyt swaggered into Mrs. Pierce's office. "Did you have any problem with anyone about attending the meeting this morning?"

She looked up from her filing. "No, Mr. Dalton. Everyone is available. I expect they will all be up here in a few minutes. May I get you some coffee?"

"No, I still have half a cup, but I need some copies made of these pages. One set for each of the managers." Hoyt handed over three sheets of handwritten scribbles.

John's secretary cringed at the reference to the copying machine. Twenty minutes earlier, she lost a battle with it only for Vicky to walk into the copier room and in less than a minute take care of the paper jam causing the problem. Remembering Vicky told her she had little to do this morning, Mrs. Pierce found a solution to dealing with the confounding contraption again. "Of course, sir. I'm quite busy at the moment, but I will assign the task to Miss Jones. It will take her less than five minutes to make the copies and collate and staple them into sets. She will bring them into the boardroom as soon as she gets them ready. Will there be anything else?" She reached for the phone to buzz Vicky.

"No, that's all." He turned and walked out to the lobby area and across to the boardroom. Hoyt extracted his key and unlocked the door. He took a quick glance behind him to ensure no one was nearby. Confident the coast would be clear for at least a couple of minutes, he entered, switched on the lights, and closed the door behind him. He strode to the head of the table and set his notebook and coffee cup there. He pulled back John's leather chair and sat down. Rolling forward, he leaned on the table and stared down the length of it to the other end before allowing his gaze to wander up one side and back down the other.

His gaze landed on the door at the opposite end. Like the one behind him leading into John's office, the door at the far end led into the office that shared a secretarial suite with Matt's on the opposite corner. Hoyt once lobbied for it as one of the most senior managers at CCI beyond the family, but John nixed the suggestion without comment other than to state the space was reserved for the Vice Chair of the company.

Hoyt bristled at the memory and leaned back in John's seat to consider any arguments he could make which would be sufficient to bring up the subject again. Before he could do so, he heard voices approaching and stood up to refill his cup from the coffeepot nearby. He had just reached the pot and realized no one had made coffee in it this morning when the door to the lobby opened to admit Andrew and Griffin.

"Good morning. I hope this little meeting didn't disrupt your schedule too much, but I thought it imperative we meet to discuss a few things," Hoyt said. He shook hands with each of his fellow managers. Craig and a couple of others entered, and Hoyt greeted them before pulling Griffin aside.

"Griffin," Hoyt said just above a whisper, "I plan to discuss some of the issues you and I have expressed concern over while I have the opportunity. It's high time we managers take the bull by the horns and come to a consensus to make John see reason."

When a young woman entered the room, ponytail bouncing, Hoyt stopped speaking until he realized she carried the stack of copies he requested. An intern, maybe even one of John's young daughters, though he thought they should be absent today like their father. Hoyt resumed his conversation with Griffin, and when they finished speaking, he noted that everyone appeared to have assembled at last. A clink nearby alerted him to the continued presence of the young woman, who had stopped at the coffeepot to set it up.

"Let's take our seats and begin. We need to discuss some important issues this morning. I'm sorry for the short notice, but I felt it necessary to discuss some problems CCI dealt with over the last few months, and today seemed to be a good time to do so. You have each received a copy of some concerns I jotted down." Movement along the opposite end of the room distracted him, and he stopped speaking. To his surprise, the young woman took a seat in the never-used chair at the foot of the table. "Miss, we don't need you to take minutes for Mrs. Pierce. This is a private managerial discussion. Please excuse yourself and close the door behind you."

The young woman smiled. Not the pleasing, supplicating smile of an ingénue eager to ingratiate herself with a highly-placed, older man who could assist her career or advance her in some other way or the smile of a vacuous teenager enthralled with a new adventure. It was the smile of someone who knew more than he did, who held the upper hand over him, who wielded power of which he could only dream.

Hoyt swallowed hard. "Did you hear me? You need to leave." His commanding voice came out strained. He realized he was missing something, but he didn't know what.

"Oh, I don't think so. I'm eager to hear what you intend to say this morning." She leaned back in her chair, perfectly at ease. It was then Hoyt noticed the portraits behind her which had hung in John's office until about ten days ago. Hoyt was familiar with the young man depicted on the right. Doug had been in and out of CCI with his parents as long as Hoyt could remember and had worked as an intern in the hotel. However, the other was of a young woman Hoyt hadn't seen in several years. Not since about the time her portrait had been painted before she left for college. Until now, when he recognized the girl seated beneath her own image.

"You're supposed to be in Europe burning through your money. You have no place here." This time, Hoyt's voice came out as little more than a gasp.

The girl's smile broadened. "For someone so consumed with titles and positions, you are most forgetful, Hoyt. Unlike you, I have a corporate title. Vice Chair has a nice ring to it, doesn't it? It also makes me the ranking corporate officer present. That qualifies as a place for me here in CCI's boardroom." She sat forward. Her eyes left Hoyt at last and moved from one face to another around the table. She held each person's gaze until either the other's eyes dropped to the table or they smiled in acknowledgement. "For anyone who doesn't know, I am Kathryn Stuart, Vice Chair of CCI and owner of Castanea Cavas, which most of you know as CasCav." She stopped to smile again at Hoyt. "And no, I am not in Europe burning through my money despite whatever Jeanette might claim. One should be careful of their source of information."

She picked up a copy of the sheets Hoyt had prepared and scanned down the first page. "I see you're still harping on the division of accounting and finance into two departments." She looked up with a wicked smile. "I suggest you let that go or else you will find them recombined quite soon." She looked from Hoyt to Craig. "Hello, Craig. Are you enjoying your new job here at CCI so far?"

"Yes, Miss Stuart, I like it very well. Thank you for recommending me to your father." Craig failed at last to hold back the smile which had tugged at his lips since he recognized KD earlier.

"You're quite welcome. I understand he is delighted with your work so far." KD returned her gaze to Hoyt. "Come to think of it, you might have a good argument for recombining the departments, Hoyt. Too bad it would result in one of the two managers involved losing his position." The wicked grin on her face widened.

Glancing back at Hoyt's list, she continued, "Griffin, are you still concerned about hiring at the hotel next door?" She stopped and looked up at the personnel manager. "One of CasCav's franchised hotels, not one CCI owns directly," she reminded him. "I see you mention the Laura Maddox hiring. Are you aware Matty hired her at my explicit direction? Do you have any question as to my authority to dictate hiring at CasCav or its subsidiaries since I own it wholly?" Griffin shook his head in silence, unwilling to become a prime target for the girl's wrath like Hoyt.

"I didn't think so," KD said. "As for issues regarding Craig's hiring, I believe I have clarified that matter somewhat already, but let me be perfectly clear. I personally asked Craig to apply for the finance manager opening at CCI. When I learned his exemplary resume did not get forwarded to my father for consideration, I remedied the oversight by sending a copy to him myself. In order not to delve into personnel matters in this forum, we will discuss how his resume failed to make the cut of those forwarded for consideration in a smaller setting." Her gaze shifted from Griffin to Hoyt before returning to the sheets in front of her. "As for my siblings and Joseph's personnel paperwork, which was delayed for all of perhaps six hours at most, we dealt with that issue already by the agreement which moved Geraldine to CasCav and by Griffin assuming all personnel duties in the headquarters. I fail to see a further issue.

"Ah, speaking of personnel issues, though as a CasCav-owned hotel it falls entirely under Geraldine and Matt's concern, we will begin an immediate search for a new manager for our Halesburg hotel." She watched Hoyt for his reaction. "Matty dismissed Bud Langford yesterday at my direction. That's why Matty isn't here this morning." Hoyt, defeated already, allowed his shoulders to slump further and held his head in one hand.

KD's voice dropped to a low monotone, dripping with sarcasm. "Shall I continue down your list, Hoyt? I see you're still concerned your advice to increase CCI's bid for the warehouse in Pearl was ignored." She looked up from reading Hoyt's list to stare the length of the table at him again. "Since I believe you bear partial guilt for the existence of a bidding war over that particular piece of property, I find it most ironic you are the one who continued to push for us to raise our offer on it. Did you forget you got caught dispensing information to your team about that property minutes after you left the staff meeting in which you were told not to discuss it with anyone outside CCI management?"

She stopped to scan the other faces around the table and note anyone else who felt the need to tug at their collar and avoid her gaze. "But then I suspect the actual leak outside of CCI came not from your employees but from you yourself. You discussed the warehouse in Pearl with Winston, who passed the intelligence along to your mutual friend, Vaughn Michaelson. Are you even aware Vaughn is the one who outbid CCI for the Pearl warehouse property?"

Hoyt's head snapped up, his eyes wide. Clearly, he had no knowledge of Vaughn's plans. Hoyt managed to mumble a reply this time. "I assure you I didn't discuss anything about it with Vaughn. I can't believe Winston did either."

KD shrugged in dismissal. "What you believe Winston did or did not do is irrelevant. I have proof he told Vaughn, and I know why he did so." She set aside Hoyt's list, ignoring the slight disruption caused when the door from the foyer opened to admit a grinning Matt Hunter. "The good news is the warehouse was always a ruse. It kept everybody's attention focused on one place while I finalized purchase of the site announced two weeks ago in Tuseeca." Turning her attention to Matt, KD continued. "Did you find someone to run Halesburg already?"

Matt pulled out his usual chair adjacent to the seat reserved for the Vice Chair and plopped down in it. "I called Jared to Halesburg yesterday evening, showed him around, and left him in charge temporarily first thing this morning. I had checked in at the hotel here after I dropped Vicky at home yesterday and found out Jared left a little early Saturday night because of some vague dustup and minor injury. I called him at home to get a few details about what happened. The traumatized guy needed a break from here and earned a chance to prove himself. I'll go back there first thing in the morning." He looked around the table at a mix of amused and shell-shocked faces. "Apparently, Jared isn't the only person you've traumatized with your return."

KD shrugged. "The list has piled up the last few days." Standing, she waved her hand in the general direction of the people seated around the table. "Unless anyone has something more they wish to bring up, we're done here." As an afterthought, she added, "No, I haven't forgotten the issue of Craig's resume and no doubt others getting weeded out by someone who had no authority to do so. We'll get back to that once I've put out another fire or two." She turned on her heel and disappeared through the door behind her seat into the Vice Chair's office.

Matt laughed and spoke loud enough to ensure she heard him. "Starting fires is more likely." He hopped up and waved at the crowd of departing managers before heading into KD's office.

She had already seated herself behind her desk, and Vicky sat across from her with notepad in hand, ready to take down any directions from her best friend and other boss. Matt took a seat in a chair next to Vicky.

"Do you want something, Matty?" KD asked coolly. "If you aren't careful, the next fire I start might be under you."

Matt laughed. "Wouldn't be the first. You've already got me busy between working with Jonah on plans for the Tuseeca hotel and replacing Bud at the Halesburg hotel. You realize there is only one person available to help me manage both the Elkford and Halesburg hotels at once, not to mention working on the operational planning for Tuseeca?"

KD let out a long sigh. "Yes, I realize I'll have to remain handy until you find someone to run Halesburg. Don't dawdle or I'll leave you to deal with all of it on your own."

"Since you announced your presence to the hotel Saturday night and to the headquarters management team this morning, can't we dispense with the fiction that you and John are still feuding? There's no reason for you to remain away from Elkford anymore." The corner of Matt's mouth twitched. "I hope you intend to appear at the CCI Board meeting in two weeks. The external directors will have plenty of time to hear from their spies on the management team. They'll be bracing for what you might do at the third-quarter meeting."

Chuckling, KD answered, "Hey, technically I am an external director. I may have an office here, but only because you and Mom and Dad insisted on it and slapped vice chair on my door. Regardless, my presence at the Board of Directors meeting will depend on what else I need to do. I'm more concerned with Tuseeca and Halesburg than the Board. Dad can handle them without me. He's been doing it for years.

"And don't get carried away dismissing my issues with Dad and CCI. He conceded and reversed course on IO, and he agreed to the deception with the Pearl warehouse. However, he needs to convince me we won't repeat those scenarios in the future, and those weren't our only issues, just the most egregious. I expect we'll continue to clash at times."

Matt held up his hands in conciliation. "You're both strong-willed. I expect you'll continue to disagree on some details, but hopefully neither of you will let anything get to the point it reached for the last few years." Matt decided to let the matter drop for now. He didn't want to get bogged down in the history of KD and John's business disagreements when another issue needed resolution. He glanced over at Vicky and wondered how much she knew of KD's actions on Saturday. For that matter, how much did he know? Jared told him some, but Matt knew there had to be more to the evening than what the young AM saw. "Are you going to tell me what happened Saturday night? I should have realized sooner I'd been gotten out of the way." He allowed himself to grin. "I know you too well to fall for your ploy. Heck, I taught you such tactics."

Vicky giggled beside him. "You weren't alone, Matt. She got all of us out of here, and none of us realized it until it was too late. She's admitted that she prompted my own mother to help get me to go to Tuseeca, so I wouldn't be here when Mrs. Hathaway held her dinner at the hotel. I cannot believe my mother participated in your con. She even asked about the Independence Day party and probed Joseph and me for information about you coming home when she knew more than we did. I can't believe she's been taking care of the old house for you without me knowing it."

KD leaned back in her chair with a dispassionate expression on her face to listen and wait while the banter between her godfather and her best friend played out.

"Yeah, she's been more devious than even I gave her credit for," Matt whined. "She carefully timed the package she sent me about Bud along with her direction to handle that immediately. I expected some sort of fireworks while I was away and you were at the hotel incognito, but not the confrontation with Jeanette until I got the message from Pam and your Halesburg directive." To reiterate his earlier point, he stabbed at the top of her desk with one finger as he protested. "I taught you such tricks. You aren't supposed to use them on me."

Vicky's giggles turned into peals of laughter when KD rolled her eyes. "Your absence in conjunction with Mom and Dad's trip to see Gran and Gramps gave Jeanette her window of opportunity. I couldn't have arranged that," KD pointed out. "I just took advantage of it when I found out she wanted to utilize her chance. I admit I tried to ensure nothing happened to interfere with it. Now are you two done? I have other things to do than sit here while you discuss Saturday evening's events. I'm sure you need to be in either Halesburg or Tuseeca or over at the hotel, Matty, not here in my office."

Matt looked to Vicky and tipped his head toward the door. "Would you give us a minute, Vicky?"

Vicky looked from one of her bosses to the other. KD gave the slightest of nods, and Vicky rose and left KD's office, careful to close the door behind her.

Matt leaned forward and put his arms on the desk while he selected his words. Unlike her father at times, Matt did not forget KD was an adult now and very capable of running her life and her businesses. He had played a large role in training her to handle everything the world would throw at her, and she had been a stellar pupil. He did not want to imply she required his guidance any longer or that he had some right to scold her for any of her actions.

"Why do I think something more happened Saturday night than just getting your entertainment from surprising and needling Jeanette? What were you really up to, kid?"

KD shrugged and answered in a low, flat tone. "I had a little chat with Winston. A long overdue chat for my part and a painful one for his."

Matt's eyes widened at her response, and his breath caught. It was the answer he hoped for and feared. He swallowed twice, trying to get some moisture into his dry mouth. "I wish you had told me what you were up to with Winston. This blitz attack Saturday night wasn't some spur of the moment thing, was it? We agreed we would work out a plan to get to him once you returned to Elkford to stay, KD. We would find out the truth about what happened to Lizzy together." Even after almost twenty-one years, he still had to stop and gather himself at the mention of her name. He raked his hands through his hair. "I should have been there."

KD saw the pain in Matt's face he had become adept at hiding under most circumstances. "You couldn't be there and be a part of it, Matty. You couldn't have stood it. I knew what I needed to do; I had to shock Winston so severely that I could force him to tell me what I wanted to know. I knew how, but I needed the right opening. I got my opportunity and arranged the details for Saturday night." She leaned forward and reiterated her earlier words, emphasizing each one. "You could not be there."

Matt felt his throat constrict at the thought something might have gone wrong and the young woman who was the closest he would ever have to his own child could have been hurt. However, he was also proud of her for a couple of reasons. She pulled off a masterful plan involving the manipulation of a host of people to attain her goal utilizing skills he instilled in her from childhood. Even more important to Matt, she used her talents not for some selfish goal but in an effort to avenge the loss of someone close to her at the hands of people whom the law would never bring to justice. Their close connection to the very people who should have enforced justice ensured that.

Finally, Matt asked the questions to which he most needed answers. "Did Winston admit complicity in Lizzy's death? Did he tell you who killed her? Who arranged her murder?"

KD leaned forward on her elbows and spoke in a soft voice. "He doesn't know the name of the person who drove the car, but he confirmed what we suspected. Vaughn pulled the strings and supplied the payoff money; Chief Deputy Landry Peters arranged the driver. I'm also pretty sure I know who the driver was based on what I found in the Halesburg newspaper files." She saw the surprised look on Matt's face and allowed herself to smile. He tried for years to gain access to the paper's morgue. "It came up for sale almost a year ago. I had someone watching it, and as soon as it went on the block, Appalachian Publishing bought it. The very night after the sale closed, I began raiding their files looking for unpublished photos and notes. As you always suspected, they contained a treasure trove of information, both published and unpublished.

"One item I found of particular interest concerned a ne'er-do-well who got released the day Aunt Elizabeth died. He disappeared afterward and turned up dead days later. No doubt Landry silenced him to tie up a loose end."

She waited while Matt processed the knowledge she imparted before adding one last detail. "Matty, I know why. Winston was with a girl in Halesburg that day. I found several unpublished photos of them in the morgue. They were across a range of dates, so he saw her for several months. The last photo of them was dated the day before Aunt Elizabeth died. It was from some birthday party at the old hotel in downtown Halesburg."

KD's voice dropped lower as she continued. "The girl was a local. I managed to identify her from other photos in which she appeared." Matt's eyes locked onto KD's. He realized what her next words would be before she whispered, "I found her, Matty. I talked to her. Aunt Elizabeth saw Winston with the girl in Halesburg and confronted them. His reaction frightened this girl. When she learned that the young woman who confronted Winston was the same one hit by a car about two hours later, she fled Halesburg fearing she might be next. She's never returned there."

Matt sat quietly while his mind churned. Confirmation Winston's friends from Stannum arranged Elizabeth's murder came not as a shock but as almost a relief after twenty years. Matt suspected something of the sort almost from the beginning once the shock and initial grief wore off. The only questions had been why and what proof could be found to bring them to justice. Now they knew why and had a confession from Winston's own lips. Elizabeth died at the hands of Winston's friends to prevent news of his infidelity reaching Jeanette and her family.

One other question always remained for Matt. For twenty years it drove him to do everything in his power to protect KD and to hone her ability to defend herself. "Were you a target, too, or would killing you that day have been a bonus?"

"It doesn't appear I factored into the matter for Winston at the time. Of course, he realized later how the dominoes fell as a result of Aunt Elizabeth's murder. I think he knows it played into the final version of great-grandmother Kathryn's will with the resultant division of her estate and establishment of my trust with you as trustee." A tight smile spread across her lips. "Ultimately, his actions also led to him sprawled on the floor in a back hall in the hotel with an electric cattle prod encouraging him to spill his secrets. I believe he understood that quite well before we completed our little chat."

A smile crept across Matt's face. "I assume Jeanette doesn't know anything about your conversation with Winston."

"No, and I'm not sure what he remembers. He started out well lit, got stung several times with my new favorite toy, and then drugged to knock him out so it wouldn't be a problem getting him home. As far as Jeanette knows, I sent him home via CCI security because he got drunk and became disorderly in the hotel. She might suspect something more happened, but even if he pieces everything together, Winston won't talk. I intend to pay him a visit with a recording of his admission. I think he'll do anything I want to keep Vaughn and Landry from finding out there's a tape of him blubbering details about that day."

Matt bolted from his chair. "Where is the tape? I want to hear it."

"No, I've told you what I learned. We know the truth. We also know the tape isn't admissible in court. We've always known the law wouldn't punish Aunt Elizabeth's killers, especially since Landry Peters became the sheriff with jurisdiction in Halesburg. We've already begun to deal with Vaughn. We'll make them pay every way we can. Every way, Matty."

Matt paced around the room running both hands through his hair. "KD, I need to hear it. I want to hear him admit it."

"No, you're emotional enough with what I've told you. You do not need to hear the tape. Maybe one day I'll let you listen to it, but not anytime soon." She had considered leaving out one last detail she uncovered, but Matt deserved to know it all, and it might divert his focus from the tape for a time. "Matty, there's something else, somebody else, we must consider. The girl was pregnant. She gave birth to a daughter, who happens to live here in Elkford now. The child was put up for adoption at birth and knows nothing of her real parents. We can't do anything to risk endangering her or her birth mother."

The pacing slowed, and Matt wiped his hands down his face. "No, I won't do anything to risk putting another innocent person in harm's way. Have you seen her? Is the girl safe? Does she need anything we can do for her without letting anyone know why we would get involved in her life?"

"Yes, I've seen her, talked to her even, though of course I didn't admit I knew anything about her. She's safe where she is, and we'll keep her that way." She waved for Matt to retake his seat. "Since you've cleared your plate for today, why don't we start planning our next game?" The wicked grin returned to grace her features. "Time to make Vaughn Michaelson and Landry Peters pay."


The End

B. A. Howell is a native of east Alabama. She attended Auburn University followed by a career in engineering in Huntsville and Auburn, Alabama, and Columbus, Georgia, before embarking on the adventure of writing. *Chestnut Cove: Poseurs and Portraits* is her first published novel.